IZZY

This is an IndieMosh book

brought to you by MoshPit Publishing
an imprint of Mosher's Business Support Pty Ltd

PO Box 4363
Penrith NSW 2750

indiemosh.com.au

 A catalogue record for this work is available from the National Library of Australia

https://www.nla.gov.au/collections

Title: Izzy

Author: McAlister, Moira

ISBNs: 9781922703347 (paperback)
            9781922703354 (ebook – epub)
            9781922703361 (ebook – Kindle)

Subjects: FICTION: World Literature, Australia; Historical, General; Women; Romance, Historical, Victorian

Cover concept by Moira McAlister.

Cover design and layout by Ally Mosher at allymosher.com.

Cover images used under licence from Adobe Stock.

IZZY

Moira McAlister

For Inez

Prologue

Cadiz 1859

Sometimes, when the night is black and silent, you can hear the earth breathe. It is soft, almost imperceptible and you need to concentrate all your efforts to catch it, but it is there; a slow, quiet in and out, the rustle of a leaf, the sudden stifled cry of a night thing. Here in Cadiz the seabirds laugh in the blackness, sharing their old familiar jokes. They can see in the dark, you know, and maybe their jest is the false bravado of men. Or rather, and more probably, the passion of women, and perhaps in the end, it is just the foolishness of me that sparks their humour.

And there has been much foolishness, not all of my own making. Wisdom is the prize of experience, if we claim it. This is the story of how I came to wisdom.

Part 1
Miss Marchbank

Chapter 1

Dublin 1829

Blackrock House was bathed in moonlight when twelve-year-old Izzy awoke to the sound of the carriage wheels on the gravel. She stumbled to the window and looked down on the front courtyard, saw her father emerge from the carriage, heard his voice and the clipped Scottish accent of Colonel Peabody, saw the lamplights swinging as the grooms led the horses away to the stables. She watched until the courtyard was empty and silent. She pulled her night shawl around her and waited.

In the past Father would have bounded upstairs to see her as soon as he arrived, to give her a small present or just a kiss goodnight. But in the last few months he seemed to have grown more distant, preoccupied with his own thoughts, and Izzy could not be sure that he loved her as much as he used to. Or perhaps he simply thought she was asleep at this late hour. Yes, that was it, he thought she was asleep.

She snuggled down in her bed and tried to sleep but the thought would not leave her and her mind returned to the day when she began to doubt her father's love. It was at

Winton, just a few weeks ago, when she and Mrs Betts were on their yearly holiday – Winton, set in the beautiful rolling hills of Yorkshire. Winton, with its towers and gardens and its famous ballroom, large enough to host the grandest ball, a rival it was said, to any of the royal palaces.

It was at Winton that Father had announced his engagement to Miss Paul and there had been parties and picnics, the house full of people and laughter, the staff talking of nothing else. Mrs Betts said it was a great match for Father and we would have to see what comes of it, whatever that meant. Was it Miss Paul? Was Miss Paul angry? Izzy squirmed with embarrassment as she recalled the day that she offered Miss Paul a posy.

'I picked them for you, Miss Paul,' Izzy said, holding the flowers up to her.

Miss Paul raised her chin and averted her eyes and moved away towards the window and with her back to Izzy said, 'Who is in charge of this child and why is she here in the drawing room?'

'I'll take her now, Miss,' said Mrs Betts, coming forward and moving Izzy gently towards the door.

'And see that she does not come into these rooms again while I am here. I do not wish to see her again.'

Izzy had stamped her feet and thrown the posy at Miss Paul's back. She stomped from the room but that had only earned her a rousing from Mrs Betts, and she had to miss her supper to remind her of how to behave. But worse was a lecture from Father, who said he was very disappointed in her.

But it was Wesley Peabody, that last holiday, who really started the doubt rising in Izzy. The Peabody family were regular visitors each summer at Winton, and Izzy was glad of five children to play with, but Wesley, being the eldest and now fourteen years old, was too big to play and usually entertained himself by taunting her. It was at Winton on a wet Sunday afternoon, when all the children were in the nursery, that Wesley Peabody spoke.

'Now you're in for it,' he sneered and, sensing Izzy's fear, he aimed his words to wound her. 'You don't think Miss Paul will want you around after she marries your father, do you?' Izzy looked blank and he drove the words in further. 'You're a natural daughter.' Her teeth tightened together. The book on her lap slid to the floor as he continued, 'Born out of wedlock.' Her heart raced and she could feel the blush flaming up her neck. 'Where's your mother?' he said in a singsong voice as Izzy stumbled to the door. 'An embarrassment you are. Miss Paul will send you packing!'

She ran along the hall to her room and threw herself on her bed, choking on the sobs, hearing the words over and over inside her head. It seemed a long time before Mrs Betts found her. She encircled Izzy with her big, soft arms and listened as Izzy repeated the words to her. 'There, there,' she cooed, 'you don't want to go listening to young Wesley Peabody, my dear. He's a mean and nasty boy and he doesn't know what he's talking about.'

'But what does it mean, Mrs Betts, a natural daughter? Why did he say that about my mother? My mother died when I was a baby and Father brought me here to live because Spain was so far away. Father said she was beautiful but she died and there was no-one to look after me and the war in Spain was over and his regiment had to come home.'

'Ssh, ssh, my dear, don't upset yourself. Yes, it's true, all of it is true; your father brought you home. So pretty and such a good baby you were. But look at you! You are almost grown now and my job is nearly done. When I was your age I had already left home and was working in the scullery here at Winton. Master Peabody should have had more breeding than to talk like that. I hope his father finds out what was said.'

They had returned to Ireland and Mrs Betts would say no more on the matter and slowly the sting went out of Wesley's words and Izzy could examine them more calmly. Yes, that was it. Her mother was not married to Father and that was the shame of her birth. Mrs Betts explained how babies come to be and it all began to make sense to Izzy. Father was fond of her, she knew that. He was always kind to her and made sure she had everything, but it was true that in the last few months since his engagement to Miss Paul he wasn't as attentive to her. He was often away in London or Dublin and when he did visit Blackrock House, it was never for very long. She felt an overwhelming tiredness and closed her eyes. I'll see him in the morning when we go for our ride. God bless you, Father.

~ ~ ~

The sun was barely above the horizon as Izzy made her way to the stables at the back of the house. The grooms were opening the horses' stalls and she could see Honey looking her way, waiting for the carrots, the treat that Izzy brought every morning. Izzy reached up and rubbed Honey's muzzle, talking to her as Honey greedily ate the carrots. Ajax, her father's big, black stallion, snorted and stamped the ground as Jock, the head groom, lead him to the exercise yard. 'Mornin' Missy,' he called as he passed.

'Good morning, Jock. I heard my father arrive late last night.'

'Yes, Missy, I expect he'll be wantin' to take Ajax up t' th' hills this mornin'.' Izzy unlatched Honey's stall, slipped the halter over her head and led her along the path behind Jock and Ajax. Jock walked Ajax around the exercise ring and then gradually increased his speed to a canter.

Honey stood patiently as Izzy watched, mesmerised by the smooth, sleek movements of the big horse. It was eight years ago that Jock had lifted her high on top of Ajax into her father's arms and they had ridden into Dublin. She felt she was on top of a mountain, so high was Ajax, so strong and secure were her father's arms, so excited was she because it was her fourth birthday. All around Izzy was the warmth of her father's body and the smell of the soft Irish rain on his woollen coat. 'A surprise,' Father had said, her pleas for him to tell met with his headshakes and laughter. 'Just wait and see,' he kept saying. And see she did. Honey was very young, small and light brown; the colour of her name. As they returned home Izzy couldn't stop turning to watch as Honey pranced behind Ajax, her lead rope slack, then tight, then slack again, her legs spindly and thin.

Now she was shaken out of her reverie by the arrival of one of the junior grooms, who tipped his cap to her but addressed Jock. 'Master says he won't ride today; too busy.' Jock acknowledged the message and the groom turned to Izzy. 'I'll take Honey for you, Miss. We'll give her a run at the straight with the others.'

The disappointment was like a weight, but as she returned to the house, she realised it was more than disappointment; it was agitation, worry. Her father loved to ride, couldn't wait to break free of the house, to rush up the mountainside in the early morning light. Izzy would follow with one of the grooms and wait for him to come back down and they would ride sedately back to the house. It was their time together.

Suddenly Mrs Betts interrupted her thoughts, calling to her from the back of the house and clapping her hands. 'Quickly, Izzy, your father wants to see you. You will need to bathe and dress beforehand. Come now.'

~ ~ ~

The gloom was all around Izzy as she stood in her father's study, alone inside the heavy curtains and the dark wood. The portraits of her grandparents, Lady Pamela and Lord Edward Marchbank, looked down on her through the half-light. A *romantic*, Father had called his father, nearly costing the family its heritage, whatever that meant. Their eyes seemed to be watching her fingers twitching, watching her best white dress too fine to warm her against the chill in the room, watching her as she strained to think of what she had done wrong.

'Why didn't he just come upstairs to see me? Why do I have to go to the study?' she had asked but Mrs Betts had given no clue. 'Your father wants to see you is all I know,' she said as she gently plaited Izzy's long, dark hair. Izzy noticed how Mrs Betts ducked her head so their eyes wouldn't meet in the mirror as she lied. Mrs Betts knew everything that went on in the house and Izzy swallowed hard to keep the panic down.

Suddenly the study door opened and Father entered with Colonel Peabody.

'For God's sake, Izzy, you could have opened the curtains. It's like a tomb in here.'

So saying he jerked the drapes aside and light flooded the room, making Izzy cower and squint as the brightness stabbed her eyes. Her father was facing her but with the brightness behind him she could not see his expression. Was he angry? Colonel Peabody stood stiffly beside the door as her father approached and took hold of both her hands, his voice suddenly tender.

'I'm sorry I frightened you, Izzy. Come and sit over here with me. There. Are you all right now? Say good morning to Colonel Peabody.'

Izzy stood and greeted the Colonel uncertainly and he returned her curtsy with a stiff bow and remained standing by the door. This is different to the way Father normally is. I can see the Colonel is the reason we are in the study, but why is he here?

'Sit down here with me now. Have you done all your lessons? Have you been a good girl for Mrs Betts?'

'Yes, Father. She says I am an excellent reader and I know my numbers very well and that I nearly know everything there is to know about growing vegetables now.'

'Do you like to grow vegetables, Izzy? Is that your favourite thing?'

'Yes, I do like it but my favourite thing is sewing. I love to make dresses for Alice.'

'Alice? Who's Alice?' Her father's face was blank.

'My doll; don't you remember Alice? You gave her to me ages ago. She has fourteen dresses that I've made her. I love to make up new styles and match colours together; her last one has three shades of blue.' Izzy knew she was babbling but she wanted this conversation to last; the pleasant small words comforted her, and her father seemed pleased with her. 'Mrs Betts says my needlework is exquisite. Isn't that a lovely word, exquisite?'

'I'm glad you have learned so much, Izzy.' His smile faded and he looked into her eyes steadily, his grip tightening on her hands. 'When you were born, I promised your mother I would care for you and I have fulfilled that promise. Look at you now. Now you are grown and you know so much.' He smiled again but his voice faltered as though he was looking for words. He paused and she looked at her fingers entwined with his as he found the words and said them slowly. 'Would you, would you like to go on a big ship?' he said. 'And sail across the sea? And see strange new lands?'

His fingernails were perfectly clipped, rounded and smooth and Izzy stroked each one, the little pale moon at the base of each in its own pink sky.

'Colonel Peabody and his family are going to New South Wales and they want you to go with them. You will be well cared for and you can help Mrs Peabody with the younger children.'

She felt the warmth of his hand as the words tumbled around in her head mixed up with the questions she wanted to ask. Go where? How far is it? Go for how long? She looked up into her father's eyes and saw in the clear blue of them that the decision had already been made. She smiled at him, not at what he said, but he didn't see the difference.

'Excellent! Good girl!'

'You'll come too, Father, won't you?'

Edward paused and leaned towards her. 'No, Izzy, I'm not coming with you. You're a big girl now. You'll be quite safe with the Colonel.' His voice was soft but Izzy could see that he meant what he said. She threw her arms around his neck and held him tight.

'But I don't want to go without you.'

Edward held her at arm's-length. 'I'm sorry Izzy, I cannot—'

'But when will I see you? Will you come soon? How long will I be away?'

'There are things I must do here; important things and you must be grown up about this. You'll have great adventures and see wonderful places.'

'But I will miss you. Will Mrs Betts come?'

'No, Mrs Betts has other work to do.' His grip tightened slightly. 'Izzy, you have had your twelfth birthday and you are big enough to do this.'

'Have I've done something wrong?' Her eyes were filling with tears.

'No, Izzy, no; it's just that my life will change now that I am to marry Miss Paul. You are fully grown and this is a great opportunity for you.'

'Am I never to come home again?' she whispered.

'One day, Izzy.' Edward held her close and she hoped he was telling the truth.

'Will you write to me?'

'Of course I will.' He held her at arm's-length. His eyes were rimmed with red and his shoulders hunched as he turned away from her. 'Now, say thank you to the Colonel and go and help Mrs Betts to pack your things.' She looked back as she left the room and saw he had slumped forward, his head in his hands, his shoulders heaving. The Colonel bowed as he held the door open for her. His eyes were soft though she could barely see him through her tears. 'Thank you, Colonel Peabody.'

He followed her through the door and shut it behind him, leaving Edward alone in the study. 'It is hard for you, lassie, I know, but it is best in the long run.'

She stared at him, not comprehending his words, and then ran to find Mrs Betts.

Mrs Betts wiped her own eyes and called it a great adventure.

'But where is it, Mrs Betts? New South Wales? Where is it?'

'In heaven's name child, how would I know? It's ... it's somewhere across the sea. A hot place, they say, with interesting animals. No need for you to worry. The Colonel and Mrs Peabody are good, Christian people and I'm sure no harm will come to you.' She blew her nose and turned away. 'Now we need to turn out your wardrobe and see what we can fit in this sea chest.'

'Can Alice come?'

'Of course, Izzy, and her fourteen dresses.'

Izzy hugged the doll as she watched Mrs Betts lifting the clothes out and placing them on the bed. Yes, she thought to herself, Miss Paul is the reason I'm being sent away. Miss Paul hates me. And I hate her. Her warm winter cape was on top of the pile and Mrs Betts had turned away again, almost hidden in the wardrobe. Suddenly Izzy put down the doll, snatched up the cloak and silently ran from the room, her heart racing as she fought to keep down the tears.

At the back door she saw her outdoor boots and quickly pulled them on over her best stockings. She buttoned the boots and threw the cape over her shoulders, her thin white dress hidden beneath. Her face was red with anger and tears but all she could do was run, run to the stables, to Honey, run to escape the house, to make this nightmare go away. Honey was in the yard, still saddled after her exercise at the straight, and Izzy saw Jock and the young groom emerging from the stable with the brushes. 'It's all right, Jock, I won't be long,' she called as she leapt onto Honey's back, turned her head towards the driveway and spurred her, galloping wildly, heading for the hills.

She galloped through the pastures, scattering the sheep and towards the hills, not thinking of where she was going or what she was doing. Honey seemed to sense her urgency and responded strongly, travelling at a rate Izzy had never experienced before. When they came to the lower hills Honey slowed, but Izzy urged her on, beyond the point she usually waited for her father. Up, up the steep mountainside they climbed, Izzy's mind blank, the wind in her face, her hands cramped on the reins. She could smell the salty wind coming off the ocean, the bare hills surrounding her. But on she went, down into shaded valleys and up the other side, on and on without reference to where she was, distancing herself from home.

Finally, she pulled Honey to a stop. They had reached the crown of a hill and ahead lay a soft green valley, warm in the midday sunshine, a small stream winding its way through the lush, spring grasses. Izzy realised that Honey was panting, her mouth open, her sides glistening. 'I'm sorry, Honey, I'm sorry I made you gallop so hard.' She lay forward on Honey's neck, stroking her mane and crying. 'You are my one true friend. How can I leave you? How can I leave Mrs Betts? What will become of me, alone in the world, with no father, with no-one to love me? How can he send me away? Why is it that he doesn't love me anymore?'

It seemed they stood still for a long time before Izzy straightened up, clicked her tongue and moved Honey down the side of the valley towards the stream. She was exhausted, her face streaked with dust and tears, her eyes swollen and red. She got off and led Honey to the stream and let her drink her fill, then tied her to a low branch so she could graze easily. Izzy stretched out beside the stream and wrapped her cape around her. 'I'll just rest awhile,' she said out loud to the sky, to the light clouds moving slowly. But the grass was soft and sweet smelling and with the sun warm and comforting, her exhaustion soon turned to sleep. Had she looked up one more time she would have seen a lone horseman watching her from the crown of the hill.

~ ~ ~

It was Jock. He had sent the young groom in search of Sir Edward and then followed Izzy at a distance. He held his breath as she cleared logs and raced at breakneck speed up the mountains, confident in the skills he had taught her, but fearful lest she should miscalculate. He was not surprised with her action and knew, along with all the staff, its cause.

The whole household had been tense, waiting for this visit from the Master. Ever since Mrs Betts had returned to Ireland three months ago with the news that Sir Edward was to marry, they all knew that little Miss Izzy would be sent away. No room in a new marriage for an accidental daughter, a reminder of his past soldiering life, the freedom of his youth. But New South Wales was too far, too fearful, too hard for a little princess who had grown up loved by everyone around her; even if they were only servants and she with no rights.

Jock dismounted and led his horse to the cover of some nearby trees then sat on a boulder and resumed his vigil. He hoped Sir Edward would come, would be concerned enough to want to comfort his daughter, but he may not, may have other, more pressing matters to attend to. No matter. He would let her sleep for an hour or so, sleep was a healer in itself, and then he would take her home. Meanwhile he would see that no harm came to her.

~ ~ ~

'Izzy, Izzy, wake up, Izzy.' The voice seemed to be coming from far away as she emerged from the fog of her sleep. She

13

blinked in the bright sunlight and saw her father's face, close to hers, his breath on her cheeks. He gathered her into his arms and they sat together in silence for several minutes.

'I'm sorry Father, that I ran off as I did, that you had to come and find me.'

'No, it's me that should be sorry. I should have given you more time to get used to the idea. I know that it is hard for you to understand, but there are some things in the grown-up world that we must accept and this is one of them.' Izzy could see the determination in his jawline and rather than argue she chose a different tack; the sun was warm and they were alone, perhaps for the last time. She wanted to prolong the comfort of this moment.

'Tell me about my mother.'

He was silent but she could sense his mind working, travelling back in time to the story which was at once familiar and foreign, comfort and discord together.

'She was beautiful,' he began as always, 'her long black hair, just like yours, her eyes, alive and sparkling, always up to mischief, and dance! She could twist and turn to the music, clapping her hands, stamping her feet, swishing her skirt, she could dance until the stars left the sky.'

'And you fell in love with her.'

'Yes, I fell in love with her. My regiment had been in Cadiz since the end of the Siege as peacekeepers. Colonel Peabody was my commanding officer and he and Mrs Peabody always invited the officers to dine with them on special occasions. Rosita was one of their serving girls and it was on the King's Birthday that I first saw her, serving the dishes, following Mrs Peabody's directions.' His voice slowed. 'I could not take my eyes off her, so beautiful she was.' He was silent, but Izzy knew the prompts to use to keep him talking.

'And her family?'

'They were a poor family who lived in the back lanes of Cadiz, near the Cathedral. After she died, I would visit you there. It was there you learnt to walk, tottering along the path towards your grandmother, Isabel, whom you are named for. I remember you used to laugh when I would swing you up high in the air, so high you could grab the grape vines that grew over the veranda.'

'Why did she die?'

He paused and Izzy wondered if she perhaps should not have asked this question. But he smiled sadly and simply said, 'Sometimes it happens, Izzy, and there is nothing that can be done about it. She died in childbirth.' Izzy waited for the next part, the part she loved most. 'But she left me the beautiful gift that is you.' She laid her head on his arm and felt she could stay like this forever.

'Then what happened?'

'You were baptised Isabel Rosita Marchbank, daughter of Rosita Ortega and Edward Marchbank. I brought you back to England when the war was over and my family arranged for you to be educated and cared for here at Blackrock House.'

'I used to think that Mrs Betts was my mother.'

'No, Mrs Betts was chosen to care for you because she could educate you in domestic skills. My family insisted that you should learn skills which support you in life – cooking, gardening, sewing – so that you can look after yourself.'

'I see,' Izzy said, and for the first time she did see. That was it. She had been heading towards this separation for her whole life. She was always going to be sent away, it's just that no-one ever told her before.

'I see,' she repeated, 'so, I was always going to be sent away?'

'You have to start your own life sometime, Izzy. Colonel Peabody will be your guardian and you will be part of their family. It's not as if you are on your own. You know the Peabody children and Mrs Peabody is very kind and you can help her with the younger ones. Although your life will be different, I know you will be happy, as part of a large family and with new places to see.'

Yes, it was a large family. Izzy thought of the eldest – Wesley Peabody, his scowling face and taunting words – she would have to avoid him, but the others, Will, John and Charles, although boys, were about her age and always included her. Mary and Thomas were the younger ones that she would be 'helping with'. She had never been part of a family. What would it be like?

'Will I know how to behave in a family?'

'Yes, of course Izzy, just as you know how to behave normally. Mrs Betts has taught you well and I am very proud of you. Mrs Peabody will be very glad of your help.'

'Will I be a servant?'

'No, Izzy, not a servant, but a helper, a companion.'

She only knew Mrs Peabody from holidays at Winton and immediately saw her sharp features, her angular body, her efficient way of doing things. She couldn't imagine being comforted by Mrs Peabody, but then again, she had six children so she must have a soft and gentle side, somewhere. Mrs Betts was all gentleness, round, soft, smiling, her hair always escaping her cap, her eyes softening whenever she looked at Izzy.

'I will miss Mrs Betts.'

'Yes, I know you will. You must write to her and tell her of your adventures.'

She held her tongue, though her mind was racing; adventures! I don't want adventures. I want to stay where I am. Why hadn't they warned me of what was to come? No-one, not even Mrs Betts, had hinted that the end was coming, and coming fast. Instead of speaking she sighed a long and sad sigh. There was no use arguing. It had been decided long ago and she had no power to change anything. She smiled because she wanted to stay where she was, here in this beautiful valley with its sweet grass and clear water, wrapped in her father's arms for as long as she possibly could.

'And you, will you miss me?'

'Of course, I will miss you, but Izzy, you need to understand that I too am compelled to act in certain ways. I'm expected to marry and produce an heir, a male child, to secure the future for my family. I have little choice in this matter. The time has come for me to do this and it is fixed. I must put aside my preferences and do what is best for my family. And you must do the same.'

And so it was that Izzy understood the reasons for her separation from her former life. She could understand that her father was a cog in the wheel of his family and that their lives were always meant to travel on different paths. She could understand it in her head, with logic and reason. But in her heart, she could not.

~ ~ ~

Two days later Izzy stood in the stable dressed in her travelling clothes. Honey's breath was warm and comforting but Izzy knew that she would never see her again. She held Honey's neck and cried until she could cry no more. It was Jock who put his hand on her shoulder and said, 'Don't worry Missy, we'll look after her.'

Mrs Betts took her hand and led her to Colonel Peabody and the waiting carriage and she knew, as Blackrock House faded from view, that her childhood was fading with it.

Chapter 2

Sydney 1829–1834

The voyage was nearing its end. Izzy longed to see trees and hills and fields instead of the endless swirling, heaving water. The barque, *George Canning*, was a sturdy vessel but she looked forward to the day when she would never again have to feel the sway of the ship or fear what was beneath.

She was dressing three-year-old Thomas Peabody, and at the same time watching his sister Mary, who at age five was mastering the buttons on her boots. Both children were clean, Izzy having washed them thoroughly using a bucket and a cloth. At the beginning of the voyage she had known nothing about children, having grown up alone at Blackrock House, but now she was confident in her care of them and found that they responded lovingly to her. The children played with her doll, Alice, in the cabin, but Izzy never risked taking her on deck for fear she would lose her only precious object from home. Izzy slept with the children, ate with them, played with them, sang to them, fed them and then slept with them again, and so one hundred days of this voyage had passed, with only another thirty or so to go. They would arrive in Sydney before year's end.

The Peabody family was so large that they had to have two cabins. The Colonel and the older boys, Wesley, William, John and Charles, slept in one while Mrs Peabody, Izzy, Mary and Thomas slept in the other. It was cramped and hot and Mrs Peabody was often sick. Izzy could see that there was another baby on the way and Mrs Peabody spent several hours of the day lying on her bunk. At those times Izzy would take the children out on deck and the Colonel would tend his wife, emptying buckets and arranging the bedding for her. The Colonel supervised the boys' lessons every morning but on days when his wife was ill, they were left to look after themselves.

This morning Izzy walked the children around the deck several times, greeting other passengers and avoiding the busy sailors. She held the children's hands tightly even though they had all become expert in rolling with the movement of the ship. Izzy leaned against the cutter, the brave little boat that she prayed they'd never have to use. She closed her eyes and breathed in the air, cool and fresh after the cabin, the salty wind licking her face. It was in the peace of this moment that she heard the familiar words, this time coming from behind the stowed cutter.

'Here comes the dirty girl, dirty girl. Look out, Will, here's the dirty girl.'

She turned and saw Wesley's face twisted with hate, spitting the words at her. William was behind him, his head bent so she couldn't see his face. It didn't happen every day, but Izzy had lost count of Wesley's insults. She never replied to him, never showed how he wounded her. As she stumbled away from the cutter, dragging the children after her, she caught the last of his rant.

'She's baseborn and dirty, dirty girl.'

Izzy pushed her chin forward and thought again of what Mrs Betts had said. 'Young Master Peabody should have more breeding than to talk like that.' It always comforted her.

'Are you crying?' asked Mary, when they finally stopped on the other side of the deck.

'No, I am not.' Izzy's eyes were flashing. 'It's the wind; it's making my eyes water.'

'Why did we have to run so fast?' Thomas complained.

'Did you hear any voices near the cutter?' asked Izzy, suddenly realising that the children may have witnessed the incident. Did she want them to? Certainly, if the children told their parents how Wesley taunted her, they would see that it stopped. But at the same time, Izzy didn't want them to know, didn't want to remind them that she was a burden to them. After all, Wesley was their son, their first born.

'No,' they chorused.

'Did you?' asked Mary.

'No,' Izzy replied. 'Sometimes the wind sounds like voices. Let's find John and Charles. Where do you think they are hiding today?'

They found John and Charles inside the well of a large coil of rope at the stern of the ship. They were reading and it was their voices that betrayed their hiding place, Charles' faltering reading and John's encouraging tone. 'Do you see how the q is always followed by a u? It can't be used alone. Heigh Ho! It's the others, climb on in. It's cosy in here.'

And so, the morning passed with tales of faraway knights and dragons, brave deeds and rescued princesses as John read to them from his favourite book *King Arthur and the Knights of the Round Table*. Izzy noticed that John never included sea monsters or pirate ships or shipwrecks and she was glad of that.

But what Izzy liked best was when John explained the natural world; how the rain formed or why the sun rose and set each day. Although she had been tutored in the growing season and the raising of vegetables, the skill of harvesting and the art of preserving, she had never considered these wider influences and she found that the way John explained things was easy to understand. His love of reading meant that his head was full of information that he would share readily if someone only thought to ask him.

John also knew about New South Wales, about the strange animals, about the natives and about what he said were the poor, sad wretches who were sent there as convicts. Although there were no convicts on their ship, they had seen them on the decks of other ships in Rio de Janeiro and The Cape. She never felt foolish asking John questions. He was thirteen, just a year older than Izzy but he was small and thin and looked much younger. Charles on the other hand was younger but bigger. His chubby body and ginger hair and jovial nature made a sharp contrast.

The thirty days passed and they rested in Hobart Town for a few days before the run up the coast to Sydney. The family stood on the deck with the other passengers as their ship glided into Sydney Harbour. Low trees hugged the shore, the occasional hut or plume of smoke the only evidence of settlement, until they reached the Cove and the bustling town of Sydney. The sun burnt down on them so fiercely that the Colonel, dressed in his full military attire, went below to find Mrs Peabody's parasol for her and insisted that she sit as the sailors secured the ship with ropes. Izzy was trying to remember what John had said about the seasons, trying to reconcile how it could be Christmas next week when it was so hot. She would have to ask him again.

There was a great crowd gathered on the wharf. Even forty years after the first settlement, any ship from England was welcomed for its news and link with home. Colonel Peabody spotted his friend Major Sullivan in the crowd, and his normally stern face broke into a smile. His eyes were dancing as he waved but he was too dignified to shout his greetings.

Major Sullivan had secured a suitable residence for them in Sussex Street and he had a wagon and cart to transport the family and their goods through the streets to their new home. The town of Sydney boasted a population of over 36,000 souls, almost half of whom were convicts, and Major Sullivan pointed out some fine buildings as the cart trundled along the dusty but wide road; St James' Church, the School of Industry, the Scotch Kirk. They saw some natives in the distance, on the edge of the road, and Izzy was relieved that they didn't come closer, watching as their lithe bodies melted away into the shadows.

~ ~ ~

They settled in quickly. The house was large and comfortable and caught the afternoon breeze that came from the south to dispel the heavy, humid January atmosphere. Mrs Peabody was confined and baby Jane was born without incident. Izzy continued in her role as nurserymaid to Thomas and Mary while the boys were enrolled in the nearby school.

Shortly after their arrival, near Izzy's thirteenth birthday, she was in the garden playing with the children when she felt an uncomfortable wetness between her legs. She could see Nancy, the housekeeper, in the scullery supervising the convict servants who were washing clothes and she called for her to watch the children for a moment and made her way hastily to the privy.

It was blood. Her undergarments were marked with the dark red. Where had it come from? She was not injured. Perhaps she was ill or injured on the inside. But she didn't feel ill. She decided to change her clothes and see if it went away and when there was an opportunity, she would ask Mrs Peabody.

But it didn't go away and that evening, when Mrs Peabody had kissed the children goodnight, Izzy asked her to come into her adjoining bedroom and told her of the bleeding.

'Oh,' said Mrs Peabody, and instead of her face clouding

with concern as Izzy expected, her eyes lightened and her voice lowered to a whisper. 'It is all right, my dear. Has it happened before? Oh, this is the first time, and you didn't know anything about it? That must have been worrying for you but it's nothing to be concerned about, it just means you are growing up and becoming a woman.'

'What?' asked Izzy blankly. She couldn't see how the two were connected. Mrs Peabody motioned for Izzy to sit on the bed while she sat on Izzy's small wooden chair.

'A woman's body is different to a man's. Men work with their bodies and the evil humours inside them are dissipated through their sweat. For women, who are used to a gentler way of life, the dissipation comes through bleeding. It will last for three or four days and it is important that you do not exert yourself too much during this time, otherwise the flow might stop and you will have an excess of blood in your body and that can cause hysteria which can lead to madness.'

'Madness! Will I go mad?'

'No, no, my dear, of course not, this happens to all women. It is thought that the flow has to do with bearing children because when a woman is with child, the flow ceases. In the olden days they called the flow "the flowers" and they said "without flowers there can be no fruit".'

'Mrs Betts told me about how babies come about, about the woman receiving the man's member into her body.'

Mrs Peabody shifted her feet and inhaled deeply. She straightened her back and held her head erect and Izzy saw a scarlet flush move up the side of her neck.

'Good, well we will not need to discuss that further. When you are older and married you can have that private conversation with your husband.'

Izzy lowered her eyes and felt foolish for her ignorance.

'Izzy, these are private matters and not to be talked about loosely. God has made your body for bearing children. Think back to the story of Eve. Her weakness, her disobedience of

God's law, has become the burden of all women. It's something we simply must suffer. But now child, wait here and I'll get some linen rags for you to wear to absorb the flow. You'll need to launder them privately and keep them for the next time.'

'The next time, you mean it will happen again?'

'Yes, my dear, it will happen every few weeks, sometimes up to six weeks in between, sometimes only two.'

When Mrs Peabody returned with the linen rags Izzy realised that Mrs Betts had already given her some. They were packed deep in her sea chest and Izzy had taken no notice of them, thinking they were some sort of bandages in case of accident. She showed them to Mrs Peabody, who was pleased because she said they were difficult to get in the colony. Mrs Peabody showed her how to pin the rolled-up rag to the inside of her undergarment to keep it in place. She said goodnight to Izzy, reminded her to say her prayers and shut the door.

Izzy lay in the dark thinking of all that had passed this day. She thought of her parents, of how her father had not yet written to her and how her mother had died, and her whole body heaved with sadness. She knew that the Colonel and Mrs Peabody had known her mother, had employed her in their home, and she resolved that one day she would ask them about her. Now that she was so far away from her father, they were the only link she had with her mother. They were good people, their kindness was reserved, quiet and practical and it was strange that their son, Wesley, was able to trick them into believing he was the same. Wesley, ugly-faced with hate, who scorned and ridiculed her at every chance, always did so out of earshot of his parents, the venomous, biting tongue turning silvery at his mother's approach.

The bed was comforting but she made herself kneel on the wooden floor, felt the nip of the night air on her heels, smelt the strange pungency of this new blood issuing from her body. She prayed for her dead mother, for her father and Miss Paul who would be married by now, for Mrs Betts, for the Colonel and Mrs Peabody. She paused before finishing and then prayed fervently that she would be a good woman, and in time, a good wife and most of all, that she would not go mad.

~ ~ ~

Three years passed and the children grew and Izzy, now sixteen, was confident in the role of governess, supervising their learning in the nursery every morning. Izzy often thought of Mrs Betts, her gentle ways and her concern that Izzy completed her lessons thoroughly. Mrs Betts had insisted that Izzy speak clearly and without trace of any common accent and Izzy found herself insisting on the same with Thomas and Mary. 'Your voice shows your breeding' was the adage Izzy now passed on to her young charges.

She missed Mrs Betts. Sometimes she cried for the feel of her comforting arms around her. There were so many things she missed about home; Honey especially and the garden, the sea, the grey skies and the rain. It never seemed to rain here in Sydney and when it did, it came in torrential bursts, not like the soft and gentle misty rain of home. But most of all she missed her father. He had never written to her as he promised and she had no news of whether he was married or not, whether he was alive or dead. She felt cast out of her own life and into the life of the Peabody family. Without them she would not survive, so she did her job as well as she could; she made herself as useful as possible.

It was quiet in the house during the day with the boys at school. John and Charles attended the Methodist School, while Master Wesley and Master William, as they were now called, were old enough to transition to the newly opened and prestigious Sydney College. For Izzy it meant that Wesley's taunts were now in Latin as he struggled to master the ancient language.

'Are you "filius populi" or "filius nullius"? Either way, your father was "ignotus".' He laughed sneeringly at Izzy's confusion. Later that week she saw the strange words listed in his primer: filius – son of or child of; populi – the people; nullius – no-one; ignotus – unknown.

You're a fool, thought Izzy looking at his large and immature handwriting and she suddenly felt more confident. She prepared her response, which she delivered tartly at the next taunt.

'Unknown? I know exactly who my father is. He is Edward ... Marchbank ... Duke of Winton.' The pauses between the words worked to stop Wesley in his tracks. 'And if you dared to ask him, he would confirm it. You stupid boy!'

She quickly strode off, smiling secretly at the look of shock on his face, rejoicing in her small victory, never considering that it may have consequences.

~ ~ ~

January had been hot and Janet Peabody welcomed the evening breeze as she sat on the veranda and arranged her mending. She found the thread and smoothed the rough serge of Charles' torn trousers. With five active, outdoor sons there was always mending, but Janet embraced the task as a simple excuse to sit and enjoy the end of the day. For the moment her needle flashed efficiently through the weave bringing the frayed edges together but soon it would be too dark to see the stitches and she would cast it aside. The Colonel would join her and Nancy would bring a tray with her small sherry and the Colonel's whisky, and they would talk as they had every evening of their twenty years of marriage.

The house was built on the side of the hill, like a theatre designed to capture the drama of the sky. The sun was low, suspended it seemed forever with its promise of sunset, its fire washing the clouds orange, pink and purple, before dipping below the horizon and bringing down the curtain of twilight. Every evening was different; different colours, different patterns in the clouds, different intensity of light. This Sydney sky was so big, so much bigger than in Cadiz or Scotland and every evening Janet marvelled at the artistry played out on its canvas.

Colonel Kenneth Peabody strode towards his chair, greeting her with his familiar formality. He was over ranked for his position of Major of Brigade in this outpost but after the active service he had seen in the Peninsula Wars he welcomed the relatively quiet and predictable work. His tall, thin frame, always immaculately dressed, was ageing however, and Janet's sharp eye detected a wince of unspoken pain as he gripped the arm and lowered himself into the chair. Nancy was behind him and quietly left the tray on the table and withdrew.

'I had some news today.' She saw his eyes were bright and young.

'Oh, tell me, please.'

'Governor Bourke has directed me to go to Van Diemen's Land with instructions for Sir George Arthur.'

'Oh, that's such a long journey. Is it important?'

'Aye, it's important. It's rumoured that Sir George is entertaining ideas about extending his Governorship to the mainland around Port Phillip. Apparently, there are residents of Van Diemen's Land who're making preparations to settle there. Governor Bourke is clear that Port Phillip is part of the colony of New South Wales and he wants to impress upon Sir George that he will not tolerate any private settlement of the area.'

'I see. That is important. When will you leave?'

'In about ten days.'

'I'll write to my cousin Douglas and tell him of your visit. He'll want to extend his hospitality to you.'

'Aye, I'll visit him but I'm sure that suitable accommodation will be provided as I'll be on official business and representing the Governor of NSW.'

'You're right of course.' She paused, reflecting on her meagre knowledge of the only other major settlement in this part of the world. 'Douglas has much praise for Hobart Town and its business opportunities, although in his last letter he was concerned with the lack of domestic help, especially as he mentioned that his wife is with child again.'

'Douglas was always a canny lad, with an eye for profit. I worry about you though, my dear. You'll be alone with the children for nearly three months by the time I make the journey to and from Van Diemen's Land.'

'I'll manage. I have plenty of help and Wesley and William are hardly children anymore. With their school days at Sydney College nearing an end, they are becoming responsible young men.'

'Yes, I'm confident that they will be able to look after things in my absence. They're good, sensible boys. I'll set out my plan for the garden as it will be autumn while I'm away and there will be much to harvest.'

'We'll manage, my dear, but we'll miss you just the same.'

~ ~ ~

That evening after she had washed the children and they were saying their prayers with their mother before bed, Izzy descended the back steps to the vegetable garden, as she did every night, to discard the two buckets of warm water she had used for their bathing. The light had faded and she sensed rather than saw the dark shadow spring towards her, felt him roughly push her to the ground and heard the buckets rolling away. He was on top of her, his hand covering her mouth, pushing the back of her head into the soft soil of the garden.

'You bitch. You bitch,' Wesley was saying in a frenzied voice, 'you think you are as good as us. You are nothing.'

He was heavy on top of her, pinning her down as she struggled to get out from under him. His knees found the space between her legs, and her dress pulled taut over her legs, making a tightening bond, preventing their movement. He was able to free his other hand to pull at her bodice and he ripped it viciously, exposing her breasts to his rough touch. 'Bitch you are, baseborn bitch, you're not good for anything, I'll show you all you're good for.' And he reached down to pull up her skirt with his free hand, keeping her mouth covered all the time, strangling the screams in her throat. His free hand was snaking up her leg, grabbing at her undergarments, clawing at her skin. She could smell his hand on her mouth and suddenly it slipped forward and she was able to bite down hard, as hard as she could. He let out a yell and jumped back, cradling his hand in pain. 'You whore, bitch,' he cursed but Izzy was up and running up the steps to the safety of the house.

Just as she reached the top Mrs Peabody opened the back door and Izzy was caught in the shaft of light. Mrs Peabody saw her immediately. 'What's going on?' she called, and her first glance took in Izzy's bodice, her dishevelled hair and wild eyes. Izzy wasn't crying, she was panting with anger as she pulled her bodice together to cover herself. She pointed to where Wesley was in the garden but could not speak and went to move past Mrs Peabody into the house.

'Just a minute young lady, what have you been up to? Who's down there in the dark?'

'He, he attacked me,' she stammered. 'I was emptying the buckets and he attacked me, threw me to the ground.'

'That's a lie,' came the innocent voice of Wesley. 'Mama, I am sorry you had to witness this, but now I am glad you have.' He came up the steps slowly, his injured hand slack at his side; his face was smooth and untroubled and he was able to inflect his voice with innocence. 'She has been taunting me for weeks, Mama, wanting me to kiss her, to meet her in the dark, and tonight she pulled her dress apart to reveal her body, asking me to touch her.' He shivered, as though with revulsion. 'I didn't know what to do. I was shocked and tried to run away but she kept pulling me back.'

Mrs Peabody turned to Izzy. 'Go to your room and tidy yourself.' And then she moved towards Wesley, her arm around his shoulder, her voice murmuring comfort.

~ ~ ~

Izzy was panting heavily as she stared at the wall. What could she do? Mrs Peabody would never believe her. She held the torn bodice in her hands, the sound of it ripping, the feel of his hands on her skin, his sickening words thundering in her brain. She squeezed her eyes closed and held her breath to calm her fury. The attack was bad enough, it was frightening and degrading, but worse was his use of the situation; that he could turn it to his advantage, convincing his mother of his innocence. Izzy writhed with indignation. Her tears for herself would have to wait. Overwhelming anger was all she could feel.

Mrs Peabody entered Izzy's room and shut the door behind her. 'Well,' she said, 'what have you to say for yourself?'

'He attacked me.' Izzy eyes blazed, their dark centres luminous against the candle light. 'I know you don't believe me, but he attacked me and tore my bodice.' In her excitement she shook the garment in front of Mrs Peabody like a snake.

'I should think if you were wronged you would be upset and crying, but you are dry eyed and certainly this tantrum, this display of anger, does nothing for your case. It seems to me that you are angry because you have been found out!'

'Found out? He has been taunting me for years and tonight he attacked me with such force that I had was lucky to escape. I bit his hand to escape.'

'Enough of this. My son is the gentlest of boys and I will

not have you speak of him in this way. I will speak to the Colonel and we will decide what should be done with you.' And she left the room.

~ ~ ~

Mrs Peabody spent the next day considering her options and when she had made her decision she confided in her husband as they sat on the veranda at sunset. Izzy had spent the day going about her usual chores but she knew that this would be the time and place for Mrs Peabody to discuss the incident with the Colonel, so she made an excuse to the maid, securing her supervision of the children, and stood behind the heavy curtain of the French doors which were open to the veranda and the cool evening air. Izzy listened in horror as Mrs Peabody's interpretation of the incident was accepted by the Colonel.

'It sounds just like her mother,' he said. 'We have never seen her behave like this.'

'I always thought that wilful nature was just below the surface of her gentility. I knew that one day her mother's recklessness would show, but not with my son as her victim. I won't have it, I tell you.'

'What can we do?' said the Colonel, sounding lost in this emotional battleground.

'You could take her to Hobart Town. My cousin Douglas would take responsibility for her and she would be of use in his household. I can employ someone here to take her place.' There was silence between them. Izzy's heart was beating so hard, she was sure they would hear it.

'Aye, I see what you mean. She is, what, sixteen years old now? We have had her as part of our family for the four years since we left home. The others will miss her greatly, especially the younger ones, but you're right. Perhaps the time has come for her to make her own way in the world.'

'I'll write to Douglas and tell him. Yes, she is old enough.

We've fulfilled our responsibilities. It is time she made her own way in the world.'

Izzy slipped from behind the curtain into the darkness of the room and silently made her way to the door and back to her charges. So many things were in her head, she had no time to think them through; the children would be getting restless without her.

~ ~ ~

The anger still burned inside Izzy at the dinner table that night as Colonel Peabody told the children that Izzy would accompany him to Hobart Town next week. She looked at the faces, these people who had been her family for four years. Wesley was smug and silent, his face arranged in a serious expression. William, always in his shadow, was listening intently. John and Charles were visibly shocked, their eyes wide. It was the little ones who voiced everyone's surprise.

'But why is she going?' cried Mary. 'Who will teach us?'

'Izzy is going to help my cousin Douglas in Hobart Town,' replied her mother.

'But why?' said Thomas. 'Why can't she stay here?'

'Douglas and his wife Edith need her to go and help them.'

'When will she come back?' asked little Jane.

No-one answered that question and Izzy felt the tears well up in her eyes as she moved to clear the plates away. She was being cast adrift again. John looked at her sadly but said nothing.

Later that night she lay in bed thinking about what Mrs Peabody had said about her mother; *wilful nature* and *recklessness* sent shudders through Izzy's body. It was clear that Mrs Peabody's low opinion would mean that she could never ask her about her mother. She heard a thud at her door and found *King Arthur and the Knights of the Round*

Table had been left there. Written on the flyleaf in John's neat handwriting was, 'To Izzy, I'm sorry you are going away, from your friend, John Peabody, January 1834. P.S. Charles is sorry too.'

Chapter 3

Hobart to Launceston 1834

The midday sun exposed every crag and gully in the rocky cliff face of Mount Wellington as Hobart Town baked in the February heat. The River Derwent was busy with local craft and visiting ships anchored in the small deep harbour. They were resting after the long voyage from Britain and before the final run up the coast to Sydney, their masts and ropes like a forest, their sailors lazily cleaning or mending nets or sails or ropes. Izzy remembered the place from their stop here four years ago, remembered the relief that the long and tiresome voyage was over and they were only days from their final destination. She looked past the wharf to the town straggling along the edge of the river and she could see how it had grown, and she counted six more substantial buildings added to the town centre.

Douglas Hamilton was on the wharf waving his hat, his smiling face much younger and more handsome than Izzy had expected. Colonel Peabody stood upright and reserved and on reaching the wharf he greeted Douglas with his usual formality. Douglas led the way to a waiting cart. While their belongings were loaded Izzy watched a nearby group of convict men cutting stone into blocks; the noise of their chisels tapping incessantly, the smell of their unwashed bodies wafting towards her in the breeze, the downcast attitude of their bent backs contrasting with the rigidly straight stance of the four redcoats guarding them. The distance to Douglas' house was short and as soon as they had alighted, Colonel Peabody took his leave of Izzy, reminding her to be a good girl and say her prayers, and then he departed for Government House and his official business.

Douglas was directing a man to take her sea chest into the house and Izzy turned to watch the Colonel's stiff back as he withdrew from her life, her last link with her father fading. The humble cart that carried him seemed to catch his formality, the horse holding its head a little higher, the wheels turning a little quieter, the driver ramrod in solemn silence. Izzy stared after him. Will I ever see him again? Why did they send me here? What wrong have I done? Is it my birth, my unnaturalness that provokes such distaste in others? Am I to live my whole life with this secret? She looked up at Mount Wellington's ugly, rocky face atop its enormous bulk, like an animal crouching, like her shameful secret that seemed too big to be hidden. Her thoughts were interrupted by Douglas' cheerful voice.

'I'm sorry that you have found us in rather a state of confusion, Izzy,' he said as they entered the house. 'As I explained to Cousin Janet in my letter, we are to leave Hobart Town next week for the journey overland to Launceston, where I am to take up the official position there as Post Master.'

'Oh,' stammered Izzy, confused by this news. 'They didn't tell me. Where is Launceston? Is it far?'

'It will be a week's journey, but cheer up! The road is good and there will be much to see on the way. It will be an adventure. Here is Edith. Look, my dear, Izzy has arrived, but you missed Colonel Peabody. He's gone immediately to Government House.'

'Oh, that's a shame. I had luncheon ready for him. Come in, my dear, it is good to see you and to welcome you to our humble little home. I expect you will find it quiet here after all those Peabody boys. How many are there, five or six?' Her voice was bright and matched her eyes, her small, round figure welcoming and comfortable.

They entered the house, which was cool and dark after the glare outside, and Edith did not pause in her talking as she led them into the small parlour and indicated the sofa with a sweeping gesture, inviting Izzy to sit.

'Douglas is very fond of his cousin Janet and has happy memories of his childhood visits to their cottage in Peebles. Janet was older of course but she had several younger brothers and I think there was much mischief made there. Am I right, my dear?'

Edith smiled broadly at her husband and he laughed and nodded. Izzy could only smile and try to keep up with Edith's chatter; there was no chance for any reply, and it seemed no reply was expected, but she remembered her manners and before she sat, she extended her hand to Edith.

'I am pleased to meet you, Mrs Hamilton. You are so kind to welcome me into your home.'

'Mrs Hamilton! No, no. You must call me Edith. Edith and Douglas, do you agree, Douglas? If Izzy is to be part of our family, she must call us Edith and Douglas.'

'Yes, yes of course. We are sadly lacking in family members, coming to the colony as a married couple, with no parents or brothers or sisters. So,' his eyes were laughing, 'we decided we shall make our own. Family, that is.'

They had just sat down when a little head peeped around the door.

'Oh, now here's our little Fanny, come in my dear and meet Izzy who is going to be like an aunt to you. Say good afternoon to Izzy, there's a good girl.'

Fanny stepped forward and curtsied rather clumsily, saying 'Good afternoon, Izzy.'

'Good afternoon, Fanny. I hope we are going to be friends,' said Izzy. The child did not reply but quickly returned to her mother's side followed by the indulgent smiles of her parents.

'You must forgive her Izzy, we have so few visitors,' laughed Edith. 'We have little opportunity to practise the niceties of society. I know you will be such a good example to Fanny. In her letter, Cousin Janet spoke very highly of your manners and bearing and your articulation of speech. We are very glad that you have come.'

Izzy wanted to think about that sentence. No, that phrase; very highly. Mrs Peabody spoke very highly of her. Was that so that these people would take her? Was it to convince them that it was to their advantage?

The child stood beside her mother and rested her head on Edith's arm. She was about two years of age, a pretty fair-haired girl with her mother's lively blue eyes and her father's slim build. Douglas clapped his hands and Fanny ran to him and snuggled onto his lap, burying her face in his chest as he wrapped his arms around her. Izzy was reminded of her own father in that gesture, the strength of his arms, the smell of the raindrops on his woollen jacket, the knowledge that nothing could harm her. Fanny wriggled into a position where she could observe Izzy and her contented expression clearly showed that she had felt those same feelings that Izzy remembered. A pain of sorrow, dull and thudding, rose up inside Izzy. She missed her father so much, so much. She fought the pain down, pushing it back inside an imaginary box inside her, clamping the lid shut, concentrating on it until she was in control and then she dragged her attention back to Edith, who was talking again.

'Of course, you know that we have recently welcomed another baby girl. Our little Augusta, or Gussie as we like to call her, is asleep at the moment. She is only three weeks old but is doing well and now that you are here my days will be much easier. We have one servant only, Nell, and she is a convict, and as Douglas told Janet it is impossible to find any help in this town. But my dear, let's be clear on one thing, your position here is not as a servant. You will be part of our family and I will expect that you will assist me with the children and the running of the household. However, we are able to give you a small allowance, not much at the moment because we have very little, but as our prospects improve, so shall yours.' Edith laughed heartily at the last part of this sentence.

'An allowance.' Izzy was stunned. 'You mean you will pay me?'

'Of course.' It was Douglas who answered. 'Although we hope that you will consider this as your home and us as your family, our agreement is basically a business one. You will help Edith with the children and in return we will provide for all your needs and give you a small allowance to spend as you wish.'

'I am most grateful for your kindness. I never expected to be paid.'

'Well now, no more talk of money and work.' Edith stood and held her hand out to Izzy in such an affectionate way that Izzy took it without hesitating. 'Let me show you your room.' Edith continued her chatter without pause. 'It is very small but we have heard that the house that has been secured as the Post Master's residence in Launceston is a good, solid house with several bedrooms and day rooms. Douglas' first task will be to supervise the renovation of the front rooms into the Post Office itself. There is no official Post Office there at the moment, so Douglas will have the honour of being the first Post Master of Launceston. There will be plenty of space for us all, with Douglas and his staff quite separate from us in the Post Office section that faces the street. I'm sorry these chests and boxes are cluttering the hallway, but we have been packing whenever we get the chance. We have been in this house for the five years we have been married and we seem to have gathered such a great number of possessions.'

The room was indeed small, her sea chest taking up all the floor space, but it was neat and bright and Izzy was thinking that she would be happy to sleep in a cupboard if it meant she could stay with these cheerful, welcoming people.

'Now, I will leave you to freshen up and change from your travelling clothes and then please join us in the dining room for a light luncheon in fifteen minutes. I'm sorry to rush you but Douglas will need to return to his place of work this afternoon. His superiors are very strict about the hours he keeps and some of his colleagues are more than a little jealous that he has secured such a prestigious position as Post Master in Launceston and that he will be leaving next week. All I can say is "good riddance" to those stuffed shirts, and I'm glad that I shall never see them again. Oh, I think I have shocked you, Izzy. Pray, forgive me. I know I talk too much and sometimes I am a little careless. However, I know we are going to be like sisters. Do you have any sisters?' Izzy shook her head. 'Neither have I, so I am glad now to be able to call you my sister.'

And with that she embraced Izzy robustly and left the room. Izzy was a little dazed and had to concentrate on opening her sea chest and finding her house dress and apron. She was not used to this much information, this much talking, or embracing.

~ ~ ~

The week was busy with packing and preparations for the journey. Douglas had hired two bullock drays, one of which was covered at one end to provide shade for the ladies as they travelled and could double as sleeping accommodation, if necessary, although Douglas had assured them that coaching inns were plentiful on this, the main road north. The other wagon contained all their furniture and boxes.

'We will look like a travelling circus I think,' laughed Edith, her hands on her hips and her face beaming up at her husband stacking the last boxes on the dray.

'Circus indeed, my love, I am just glad that I don't have to manage the beasts that pull the drays. Your suggestion of hiring the bullockies and their vehicles was a sound one.'

He jumped to the ground and caught her round the waist and danced her in a circle. Izzy was bringing a box of vegetables through the door and stopped in astonishment at Edith's squeals and Douglas' long legs dancing in time to his breathless pah, pah, pah imitation of music.

~ ~ ~

It took them three days to get to the village of Ross. It was a lazy pace; the lumbering bullocks, a team of six for each wagon, swayed in the summer heat and seemed to find their household burden light. The road was busy with carts and gigs and other bullock drays of varying sizes. Izzy counted twenty-four bullocks in one team whose dray was loaded high with wool going to the ships in Hobart to be transported to England. It was pleasant under the shade at the back of the larger vehicle. Douglas had stacked mattresses and pillows for their comfort and baby Gussie's basket lay next to Edith, while Fanny and Izzy had an uninterrupted view over the tailgate. Nell rode in the furniture wagon and Douglas spent most of the time walking or perched on the tailgate talking to them, or up the front with Joe or Frank, the bullockies. The road was fairly flat, but whenever they came to a hill it was a pleasant change to jump over the side and walk, to stretch their limbs while the bullocks laboured up the incline.

As they drew close to the village of Ross, they could see the half-completed Ross Bridge; its beautiful curved shape rising from each side of the river to eventually meet in the middle, its sandstone luminous in the afternoon light. The wagons halted and the bridge cast a spell on all the watchers, softening even the hardest heart; its shape, curving so perfectly, a memory of bygone home.

They crossed in the shallows downstream and stopped on the wide grassy banks of the Elizabeth River while Douglas went in search of lodgings for the night. He returned with bad news; the inns were full and they would have to pitch camp by the river. The bullocks were unyoked and watered and left to graze, their heavy bodies plodding even without their load. Izzy had never slept outdoors and was uneasy about it, imagining the dangers it could bring. She and Nell were watching the pots on the fire when Douglas brought the big tin box containing bread and tea and some salted beef. It was heavy and he was puffing. He put it down and sat on it as Izzy spoke.

'Douglas,' she began, 'is it safe? I mean, to sleep outdoors? What about the natives? Will they come near us in the night?' She was aware of Nell moving closer, feeding small sticks into the flames and positioning herself to hear his answer.

'No need to worry about that, lassie. There are none left. The Government cleared them all out. The last of them have recently gone to join the others at Flinders Island. After thirty years of battles for the land, the Government made it official policy that all natives were to be removed. It took a few years to round them up, but the roving parties did a thorough job.'

'So, did they go willingly?'

'Well, no. There were reports of resistance and bloodshed. I expect there were many more deaths among the native population than was reported.'

'Are they fierce, warlike people?'

'No, it seems they are just the opposite. They live in family groups and move through the land according to the season.'

'Isn't it possible then, for all of us to live in peace together?'

'No, Izzy. The settlers want the land and they don't want the natives. Simple spears are no match for guns and the settlers have won this battle. It is over.'

'I feel so sorry for them, losing their homes and their loved ones and at the same time, I am relieved that, as you say, the battle is over.'

'I always thought it was sad to see the remnant groups camped on the outskirts of Hobart Town, dejected and poor, sometimes drunk, so I suppose removing them to Flinders Island was the best solution, best for them and best for us.'

Izzy was reminded of John in the way Douglas took her question seriously and was willing to give her a full answer, so she continued. 'What about bushrangers?'

'Now bushrangers are another matter.' Douglas looked serious and Izzy felt her pulse quicken. 'There are bushrangers, mostly escaped convicts, living in the surrounding hills and sometimes they make raids on lonely farmhouses or vehicles travelling alone. You will have noticed that the road has been fairly busy since we left Hobart, but from now on we will need to travel with as many other vehicles as we can. It will be security in numbers.'

'Do you think they will attack?'

'I think it unlikely. The bullockies know the road well, and the most likely places for attacks. Also, we are obviously a family travelling with children and not exactly rich.'

'What about here in Ross, tonight?'

'No, we are perfectly safe here. With the large cohort of convicts constructing the Ross Bridge, there is an equally large cohort of soldiers at hand to control them. No bushranger would dare come into Ross.'

'And the convicts; will they be a danger to us?' Izzy was aware that Nell might think her rude for asking such a question when she herself was a convict, but Izzy needed to know the answer. Anyway, there was a great difference between Nell and the men of the chained road gangs she had seen, their hair matted and dirty, their eyes hollow, their backs bowed.

'No,' said Douglas, 'they are well supervised and restrained.'

He stood and stretched his long, thin body, looking towards the wagon where Edith was feeding the baby and Fanny was playing.

'I hope you will be comfortable sleeping outdoors. We are lucky we have clear weather because you will not only be dry, you will have a fine view of the stars. But for now, would you help Nell to gather some more sticks before the light fades? This fire is going to need quite a bit more fuel.' And with that he rose and strode to the wagon clapping his hands as Fanny ran towards him. He caught her and swung her high and her squeals filled the air.

Izzy and Nell walked towards the bush. The tall grey trunks grew close together and the warm, late afternoon air was heavy with eucalypt scent and Douglas was right, the light would soon fade. Although Nell was only a few years older than Izzy, she rarely spoke and Izzy was always a little nervous in her company. There were few servants in the Peabody household and her memory of those at Blackrock House and Winton was dim. Nell had a pleasant face and smiled often and seemed to love her master and mistress and the children but, thought Izzy, she is a convict, I wonder what crime she committed. As they began to gather the twigs and smaller fallen branches, Izzy decided to try to engage Nell in conversation.

'I'm glad Douglas has reassured us that we are safe.'

'Yes, Miss.'

'How long have you worked for them?'

'Three years in July, Miss. Mr Hamilton picked me in a line up at the Cascades – the Female Factory, you know.'

'Oh,' said Izzy. She imagined Nell, small and vulnerable, standing in the cold July wind, waiting for a man to 'pick' her. Was she handcuffed? Did she have a coat? What if the man wasn't Douglas, but someone rough and horrible? Izzy couldn't think of anything to say so they gathered the sticks in silence, holding them in the wrap of their skirts.

'I was that glad, Miss, that Mr Hamilton was the one what picked me, and he had a wife and family, and they are so kind.'

'Yes. I am also glad of that.' Perhaps it was because they were alone or perhaps because Izzy had asked the right question, but it seemed that Nell was only waiting for the invitation to talk.

'Can I ask you, Miss, are you related to them? Only I know you're not a servant and you have a nice way of talking, but at the same time you never mind getting your hands dirty.'

'In a way,' was all Izzy could say. They worked in silence and then she added, 'Douglas' cousin and her husband were my guardians, but they decided I should come to Van Diemen's Land and I had no choice.'

'Why did they do that? Oh, sorry Miss, I shouldn't pry, it's none of my business.'

'It's all right, Nell. I don't know. They said that Douglas and Edith needed help and so I guess that was the reason. Anyway, I'm very glad I came. I love being here. Douglas and Edith are so much younger and more light-hearted than the Colonel and Mrs Peabody and I am lucky to have found them.'

'Both of us, Miss,' said Nell, straightening her back and smiling broadly at Izzy.

In that moment Izzy knew that she wanted to know more about Nell, why she was a convict, what she had done, what it was like to be her. She would have to think about all that they had said. 'I think we should return. We have enough now.'

Their skirts were ballooning with the gathered firewood as they turned and made their way back through the trees towards the camp. Maybe it was because she couldn't see

Izzy

where she was putting her feet, or maybe it was because of the fading light or a combination of the two, but Izzy felt the shock of her foot sliding into a hole, her ankle twisting as she toppled forward, her hands flying up to break her fall and the firewood sticks scattering, some of them piercing her dress as she hit the ground.

'Miss, Miss! Are you hurt?' Nell had dropped her load and was gently tugging at Izzy's shoulders.

'Yes. It is my ankle. Help me up.' The pain was immediate, shooting from her ankle, up her leg, like fire. When she tried to put weight on it, she collapsed in a heap, the tears coming involuntarily with the groaning as she grasped her ankle as though touching it would stem the pain.

'Wait here, Miss. I'll run and get help.' Nell was gone and suddenly Izzy was alone in the darkening bush. She would have been afraid, but the pain was so intense that she could not focus on her surroundings. She put her hand on the ground to steady herself and felt the outline of the hole. Was it a burrow? Maybe it was a snake hole? As she dragged herself away from it, she heard Douglas calling her name.

'Where are you, Izzy?'

'I'm here,' she tried to call loudly.

'Keep talking so we can find you.'

'Over here, over here.'

'We're coming. Keep talking.'

'Over here, over here, over here,' was all she could say but it worked because suddenly Douglas and Joe and Nell were beside her. Joe picked her up as though she was a rabbit, his bullocky frame strong with outdoor work, his touch as gentle as a girl as he carried her back to the camp.

They laid her on the wagon and Edith examined her ankle by the light of the lamp.

'It looks bad, Douglas. It may be broken in which case we should fetch a doctor so he can set it properly so that it heals straight. Otherwise, she might have a limp or she may not be able to walk at all.'

Izzy could hear everything but the pain was so intense that she couldn't respond. It was as though they were talking about someone else, someone else who may never walk again.

Next, she heard Joe's deep voice. 'Dr Carrick looks after the convicts here in Ross. He comes from Campbell Town each week and stays at the Man O' Ross Hotel. He's probably having his supper about now.'

'Yes. Go and find him, Joe, and see if he will come here. It would be better if Izzy was kept still and not moved. She will probably go to sleep. The shock of the fall and the pain will take their toll.'

~ ~ ~

Izzy awoke to a firm hand holding her foot, rotating it gently and pressing expertly on the pain. The doctor's head was bent, his long curling hair obscuring his face.

'Is it broken? Will I be able to walk?' she asked.

He looked up. 'Yes, sorry, I hope I am not hurting you too much.' His face was young for a doctor, maybe twenty-five. 'It is not broken, but it is very badly sprained. It will heal in time but you must look after it.'

Dr Carrick put her foot on the top of the pillow and stood up straight. In the dim lamplight Izzy could see that he was stocky and clean shaven although his hair was long, falling beneath his collar.

'I will bandage it tightly and you must stay off it as much as you can. No more gathering firewood and certainly no dancing for a while. I expect you like to dance. All young ladies like to dance.' His Irish accent was strong and when he smiled Izzy was surprised that he was rather handsome. 'I will show Mrs Hamilton how to apply the bandage and she will be able to assist you.'

Dr Carrick bandaged her foot while discussing the benefits of different bandaging patterns with Edith and it was quite dark before he took his leave.

'Remember to take care of your ankle. Stay off it completely now for the next few days and then the pain will be your guide as to how much use you can give it. Good night now, Miss Marchbank.' The way he said her name made her sound grown up. Izzy watched him mount his horse and ride away.

Chapter 4

Launceston 1834–1835

Izzy wasn't sure what she was expecting of Launceston, or that she had even thought about it at all, but she was not prepared for the overwhelming welcome they received. The coming of the first Post Master was a milestone for Launceston. It declared that the town was important in its own right, that it was more than an adjunct to the military encampment of Port George, forty miles away. Launceston was finally its own place with an official Post Office and Post Master to prove it.

The building was on the corner, with the Post Office facing busy York Street, the main thoroughfare of the town and the Post Master's residence being accessed from the quieter St John's Street. It was, as Edith had hoped, a large sprawling house with room for family and business alike. Everyone in town knew who the Hamiltons were. For the first week people came to the house to pay their respects, some bringing welcome gifts. A basket of fruit; 'You won't find better 'n Tamar apples, Miss.' Cakes and baked sweets; 'Just something fer the little 'uns, Sir.' And even fresh meat; 'Best lamb in the colony, Ma'am.'

Along with these gifts came invitations for Edith and Izzy to take tea in some of the surprisingly fine homes in the district, and for Douglas and Edith to dine with the leading settlers of the area. These men had made their fortunes from the wool, fruit and dairy industries of the fertile Tamar Valley and their wives were well equipped to spend those fortunes. Launceston boasted five milliners in 1834, and they could not keep up with the demand for their services.

Two months after their arrival, with Izzy fully recovered from her ankle injury, Edith and Izzy were at afternoon tea in Mrs Underwood's garden. Mrs Underwood, smiling and hospitable, introduced them to Madam Foveaux, the leading milliner and couturière in Launceston.

'It is a pleasure to meet you, Mrs Hamilton.' Madam Foveaux was small and dark, with a French accent that she used to its best advantage. Her trim figure was highlighted by the perfect fit of her simple black dress. Her eyes widened when she saw Izzy. 'And who is this, may I ask? She has such beauty, such youth!'

'This is Miss Isabel Marchbank, my companion, Madam Foveaux, but we call her Izzy.' Edith was smiling and stood aside as Madam Foveaux took Izzy's hands and greeted her. Every inch of Izzy's body was appraised in that one sweeping glance.

'And do you like our little town, Izzy? I myself have only been here for less than one year but I like it very much. It is not the rough frontier that the people of Hobart think. We are quite gentrified here.'

'Yes, I do like it, Madam Foveaux. I am pleased to meet you. I have seen your shop in York Street. The pink and gold lettering, "Robe et Chapeau Boutique, the latest fashion styles direct from Paris", always catches my eye.'

'Ah, a young lady of great taste, I see.' Her expression was merry. 'Mrs Hamilton, where did you find such a treasure? She has such breeding, such clear and unaccented speech, such grace in her movements.'

'Izzy's guardians are related to Mr Hamilton, but she and I have become such firm friends we have declared that we are sisters. Isn't that so, Izzy?' Edith's face was beaming and genuine in her love for Izzy.

'Yes, it is so. I am very fortunate to have found such happiness.'

They chattered together and were soon joined by Mrs Underwood, the hostess, who brought with her two soldiers, their red coats and white trousers stunning in the afternoon sunlight. They were young and clearly ill at ease in this social setting.

'May I present Mr Underwood's nephew James and his friend Robert Beath? This is Mrs Hamilton, Madam Foveaux and Miss Isabel Marchbank.'

After they had formally bowed, it was Madam Foveaux who attempted to put the young men at ease by turning the conversation to them. 'You are stationed at Port George?'

It was James Underwood who answered. 'Yes, Madam, we are allowed very little free time, but we come to Launceston whenever we are able.' His eyes had drifted to Izzy's face and seemed to be caught there. There was silence.

'We are part of the 45th Regiment, Madam,' said Robert, covering for his friend's speechlessness. 'Our work involves the supervision of convicts and the building of roads and bridges in the area.'

James had recovered enough to add, 'It is not pleasant work, but the attractions of Launceston are reward enough.' Again, his eyes went to Izzy.

Robert looked sternly at James and quickly added, 'I hope you will not think us forward, Madam. We are simply unskilled in society.' James lowered his eyes as a flush moved up his pale neck and brightened his soft, childish cheeks.

Mrs Underwood arrived again with two more young ladies, Julianne and Genevieve Hardwicke, daughters of a local landowner, and again there was a formal round of introductions. Izzy was glad that the attention of the young soldiers was dissipated by these two girls who were radiant in their summer dresses and shading bonnets. Izzy was also glad to meet some girls of her own age and these two, although of a wealthy family, were easy to talk to and eager to meet Izzy, being part of the Post Master's family. There was no need for any further explanation. She was part of the Post Master's family and that was enough. No-one need know of her shameful birth and the fact that this was her third family in five years. Everyone she had met had accepted her without question. Her thoughts were interrupted by Genevieve, who was reaching for Izzy's hand as she laughed at a witticism by the tall and handsome Robert Beath. 'Oh, Izzy did you hear that? Can you believe that such things happen at Port George? A soldier's life is so adventurous!' Genevieve drew Izzy back into the conversation and she noticed that James had recovered his confidence and was eagerly imitating his more experienced friend.

Edith and Madam Foveaux wandered away from the group and sat in the shade chatting while the five young people were left to make their own conversation under the seemingly casual eye of their elders. The young soldiers attended to their needs, bringing them refreshments and telling amusing anecdotes about life at Port George. During the conversation Izzy realised that she had never done this before. She had never spent her time so frivolously, so enjoyably, without a practical outcome to be achieved. It was two hours wasted, but wasted so wonderfully. When Edith returned and Izzy realised that it was time to go, she was shocked that the time had passed so quickly.

They walked the short distance to their house, Edith plying Izzy with questions about the young people and teasing her about the look on James Underwood's face when he was introduced. 'Stunned he was,' said Edith, 'he looked as though he had seen a vision from heaven. He couldn't believe that he was talking to a girl and one of such beauty.'

'Oh, stop it Edith,' said Izzy, 'he was just shy, and anyway, I am not beautiful, I am just ordinary. Now, Genevieve Hardwicke is beautiful. Did you see her skin? So smooth and pale and her eyes are such a light shade of blue; I have never seen that before. But both she and Julianne have a very strict life and their mother is very particular about the way they dress and behave.' How wonderful to have a mother like that was the thought that came to Izzy, but she pushed it away. Her secret sadness would not spoil today and so she continued, 'They said she fusses about bonnets and gloves and shawls every time they leave the house. But despite that, they are lively and eager to enjoy themselves. Oh, it was such a lovely afternoon. I love Launceston, I love living here with you and Douglas.' And without thinking she linked arms with Edith and truly it did feel as though they were sisters. Perhaps Edith was the closest she would ever have to such a mother. 'I love it here,' she said again, and Edith responded with an affectionate squeeze of her hand.

'Izzy, young James Underwood is not the only one who noticed you today. I had a long conversation with Madam Foveaux and it was mainly about you.'

'Oh, why would she be interested in me?'

'She asked me to put a proposal to you. She would like you to help her in her shop, just for a day or two. She was very impressed with the way you conduct yourself, with the way you speak, and she feels that you could assist her in dressing the fine ladies of Launceston.'

'Oh, I don't know. What would I have to do? What about you and Fanny? It's an exciting proposal, but I would not want to desert you and Fanny.'

'Well, one or two days each week would be manageable. Nell and I would carry on as we did before you came. Think about it, Izzy, it could be a great opportunity for you to meet people and to learn some new skills. I have heard women talking about the dressmakers in Launceston and Madam Foveaux is, without doubt, the best in her field. Her fabrics and patterns come directly from Paris, from the family business, the *House of Foveaux*, which is quite famous in Paris, apparently. I have heard it said that the ladies of Launceston are better dressed than their sisters in Sydney. Do you know I heard that there are ladies in Hobart who order from her here in Launceston? She was there for quite some time and now those ladies cannot live without her fine skills. Her creations cost a fortune of course, but dresses and hats are all these ladies have to think about, and why should she not benefit? And you, why should you not benefit? She has offered you a handsome enticement, ten pounds per year for only two days' work, that's more than Douglas and I can give you for the other five days. I think it would be lovely to work with all those materials, the laces and beading, the fabrics, silks, linens and cottons, the best in the world, the feathers and bonnet trims and the styles, the catalogues she imports from Paris with the latest fashions. You would love it, Izzy. Well, I know I would love it.'

In the face of Edith's enthusiasm Izzy could not refuse, and so she went to work for Madam Foveaux. Mrs Betts had taught her basic stitching, joining fabrics together hemming and running stitch; and Mrs Peabody had shown her many of the skills in mending, how to join frayed edges, how to weave a patch that was indistinguishable from the fabric, how to turn collars and cuffs. But the work that Madam Foveaux did was nothing like that. It was fine and detailed, the tiniest stitches holding firm the lightest fabrics. 'The garment must be strong, Izzy, it is going to be tugged [she said "tug-ged"] on and off, and at the same time it must appear to be whisper soft like a fairy's breath, delicate and fragile.'

Over the following months Izzy found herself looking forward to Tuesdays and Thursdays when she would spend her days under Madam Foveaux's tutelage. As winter blew in from Bass Strait, the fires were lit and the rooms were always warm. 'How can one sew finely with cold fingers?' Madam Foveaux asked. One fireplace had marble surrounds and was in the room that Madam Foveaux had created for the comfort of her clientele. It adjoined a small dressing room and was like a parlour with armchairs and low tables, the windows richly draped in pale mauve velvet, but it had two huge mirrors positioned so that the lady could view the new garment and her figure from all angles. It was a delicate, feminine room with every fabric and piece of furniture chosen carefully. 'Your patron, Izzy, must feel she is visiting your home and that you are her friend, but most importantly the room must be a suitable backdrop to the creation you are presenting to her. She must feel beautiful when she looks in the mirror. She must fall in love with that mirrored image.'

The workroom at the back of the shop was a different matter. It was spacious and bright with several skylights and the centre of the room was dominated by an enormous table. It was the cutting table and Izzy could barely reach across it. It was smooth, almost soft, with the years of fabric that had skimmed it, the light blond of the Huon pine matching that of the four large cabinets standing side by side along the back wall. These cabinets were the heart of Madam Foveaux's creativity, their tiny drawers holding threads and beads and other small requisites, their deep shelves cradling bolts of cloth of different textures and a myriad of colours. 'My dear husband made all of this furniture when we first arrived in Hobart Town, some ten years ago. He was a great craftsman,' she said tenderly as her hand traced the brass inlay of the yardstick embedded on the side of the table. Her eyes cleared and she was once again her merry self, with her arms wide motioning to the four full-bodied wooden models and six hat stands. 'And these, my dear, are your most important advantage. See how they can be adjusted to your client's figure, meaning she does not have to endure tedious fittings.'

Izzy learned how to draft a pattern, how to lay out the pattern pieces on the table, checking the nap and grain of the fabric. Madam Foveaux's standards were the highest but her way of teaching was so encouraging that Izzy did not resent the many stitches she was asked to unpick, and when Madam Foveaux was finally satisfied, Izzy was elated.

The shop was busy on Tuesdays and Thursdays because with Izzy's help it was convenient for Madam Foveaux to schedule her consultations with her clients for those days. Izzy was nervous at first, but soon found that the chatter and laughter that characterised these planning or fitting meetings was relaxing and Madam Foveaux, always gracious and deferring, was nonetheless held in great respect by the ladies of Launceston. They asked and heeded her advice about colour, style and fabric and Madam Foveaux always managed to add something extra, some lace or beading or for younger ladies a bow, which made the garment truly individual. In the planning meeting Madam Foveaux elicited desired details from the client while she sketched quickly and accurately, making notes and suggestions, with Izzy bringing samples of fabric and lace for inspection. And when the garment was complete there were always at least two women, the client and her friend, daughter, mother, aunt or sister who came for the fitting. It was Izzy's task to assist with the fittings and to make sure the ladies were comfortable, offering refreshments and attending to any interruptions from the front of the shop to ensure the privacy of the ladies.

Then one day, almost six months after her first lesson, as she smoothed the fine yellow silk on the cutting table, Madam Foveaux handed the scissors to Izzy. 'It is time, my dear, you are ready.' And she stepped back and let Izzy take control.

~ ~ ~

It was shortly after this that Launceston received news that the whole of Van Diemen's Land rejoiced in. The *Strathfieldsaye* was only weeks away with its precious cargo; 280 skilled and free, single female emigrants, all of them under thirty years of age. The matrons wanted servants and nurserymaids, the single landowners wanted housekeepers (and if all went well, wives), and the business owners like Madam Foveaux wanted skilled workers.

'It is wonderful, I tell you Izzy,' said Madam Foveaux as she read the account in the *Launceston Advertiser*. 'The London Emigration Committee has done a fine job. This is the third ship they have financed, and they plan many more. The other two went to Sydney, but the *Strathfieldsaye* is bound for Hobart.'

'But who are these women, Madam Foveaux? Are they prisoners? Why else would they agree to come all this way?'

'No, no, they are free. Their only crime is that they are poor. This newspaper article describes how each woman has been interviewed and selected and the Government has given a subsidised passage in return for their willingness to work in their field when they arrive here. There are dairymaids and servants and cooks and, and,' she paused and raised her eyes to the ceiling in delight, 'needlewomen and seamstresses and embroiderers. Oh Izzy, we shall be able to expand the business with the help of these women. I will need to go to Hobart at the end of the month and appraise their skills and select the best to come and work for us.'

'For us? But it is your business, Madam Foveaux, I am merely helping you.'

'Yes, but you are more than an employee, Izzy, you are my right hand. The ladies like you. You are one of them. You speak the same language. You are of their class. I don't know how I ever managed without you. You have learnt how to create wonderful garments but with skilled workers employed to do the difficult and mundane work, you can concentrate on the more interesting aspects, the design, the adaptation of styles, the overall effect. You have a good eye, Izzy, you can see what each client needs to show off her figure and her best assets, what colours and styles suit her, and I would like to capitalise on your talent.'

Izzy was stunned with Madam Foveaux's words. It reminded her of Mrs Peabody's comment in her letter to Douglas, that she 'thought highly' of Izzy. That night she repeated the conversation to Edith.

'Well of course she spoke well of you. You are a good worker and you have helped her business quite a bit in the last six months. She obviously thinks you are suited to the business and would like to keep you. The coming of the *Strathfieldsaye* will certainly be of advantage to you. Douglas has already made arrangements to go to Hobart to employ a nurserymaid and possibly a cook, so your workload here at home will be lessened which will mean that you can spend more time with Madam Foveaux.'

'Really? You really think that this will be possible?'

'Yes, I do. Douglas has made quite a bit of money privately on land transactions here in the last six months and we can easily afford to employ two women to help in the house. Nell of course will stay with us for another four years when her time will be up and she will be free. Her work in the house will also be reduced so I thought I would expand the garden and buy some chickens that she could look after. I think it is best if we are quite clear about the boundaries of each person's work. Each person should be in charge of their own area, don't you think, without having to answer to each other?'

'I have some knowledge of gardens and the growing cycle. The Colonel and Mrs Peabody were expert gardeners and their son John explained much to me. It was also a focus of my education as a child in Ireland. I could help to plan and plant a garden and teach Nell how to look after it, if you like.'

'Yes, wonderful. We shall have to wait and see what the

Strathfieldsaye brings us. Perhaps our hopes and plans will be in vain, but if these women are as reliable as the Government has promised, then our lives will take an upward flight.'

'Yes,' sighed Izzy and she thought how her life had been soaring upwards since coming to Van Diemen's Land. She had never been so happy. She loved Edith and Douglas and their two little girls, and even Nell, although she didn't see that much of her. She loved working for Madam Foveaux, the complexity of the work and adult chatter and understanding that she experienced with the older woman.

That night, before she drifted into sleep Izzy tried to pinpoint the feeling, what was it that was so different here? In the end she decided it was that they all treated her with respect, Douglas, Edith, Madam Foveaux, even the clients at the shop treated her as though she was important, as though she was someone. She thought back to the years with the Peabody family, the kindness restrained and unaffectionate, charity perhaps, the days dull and uneventful, the ever-present threat of Wesley's vindictive attacks, her position in the house as, was it daughter? Was it servant? Was it poor relation? The two little Peabody children loved her and depended on her, but the only person she ever thought about, the only one she ever missed was John, and it was for that same reason, he treated her as if she was important, as if she was someone. Here in Launceston she was an adult, Edith's companion and no-one knew or cared about her past. She could make her own life here and maybe meet and marry a good man like Douglas and have a happy family of her own. It was a dream she had never had before.

~ ~ ~

The New Year saw life at the Post Master's residence greatly changed. Anne Southey ran the kitchen in a cheerful and efficient manner, her large round body streaming with perspiration as she laboured over steaming pots and pans, calling out to Nell to bring some eggs or singing as she opened the fiery furnace that was the heart of her domain. Her cakes were light and sweet, her meats tasty and tender, and she could make the dullest vegetable spring to life with sauces and condiments that she seemed to conjure from nothing.

'How do you do it? Douglas asked, pushing away his empty plate and smiling as Mrs Southey entered the room to clear the table. 'That was delicious. The lamb was as good as any I have ever had.'

'Thank you, Sir. I'm glad that you are pleased. The lamb is of excellent quality and I merely cook it and watch it carefully.'

Mrs Southey took the plates to the kitchen and the diners settled at the table in what had become a heavenly interval between a satisfying meal and the expectation of the coming sweet surprise. Sometimes there were only Izzy and Edith and Douglas for dinner, but since Mrs Southey had come, Douglas had taken to inviting guests and this evening it was Dr Bryn Carrick, the doctor who had treated Izzy's ankle at Ross.

'A rare find in the colony, Mrs Hamilton, a good cook is to be prized.'

'Yes, Dr Carrick. We are very pleased to have Mrs Southey and also Eliza, the nurserymaid. They have made our lives much more interesting, giving Izzy and myself time to attend to things other than domestic duties.'

'And what things do you do, Miss Marchbank, in your spare time?' He turned to face Izzy and his expression was difficult to read. Was he seriously asking the question or was there a hint of laughter about the corners of his mouth which was mocking her?

'I work with Madam Foveaux, Sir. She has been teaching me the skills of millinery and dress design.'

'Oh, I would think that is a skilled area indeed. Are you

hoping to make it your life's work?' He was serious, the playful smile dropped and his eyes were intense.

'Yes, Madam Foveaux is in much demand in Launceston and now since she has employed three women, also from the *Strathfieldsaye*, I am learning new and more interesting aspects of the business.'

'It seems that the *Strathfieldsaye* has brought a great boost to the colony.' It was Douglas speaking, although Izzy noticed that Dr Carrick's gaze remained just slightly longer on her face before shifting towards his host.

'Yes, everywhere people are singing the praises of the three hundred women aboard, now they have settled into regular employment, although I have heard they had an unfortunate beginning in Hobart, on arrival.'

'Yes, I was there,' replied Douglas, 'it was as bad as the newspapers reported. The behaviour of the men in the crowd was disgraceful; whistling, shouting, jostling each other and the women as they disembarked and made their way to Belle Vue, where they were to be housed while awaiting disposal. There must have been two thousand men on the wharf. Those poor women were subjected to scrutiny and insults that not even convict women have had to suffer in the past.'

'I'm surprised more propriety was not observed. Even convict women disembark at night, under the cover of darkness, to save them this trauma. I understood that this was the usual practice.'

'Yes, that is correct Dr Carrick, that has always been the case but the authorities, for some reason, decided on the midday disembarkation of these free women. You can imagine the distress it caused. Some of them fainted, many were crying and all of them were upset to be subjected to such scrutiny from the unruly mob of men. Then they had to walk almost a mile up Davey Street to Belle Vue, and although the house is large and fairly suitable, it was overcrowded in the beginning before the women were matched with their employers. And then,' continued Douglas, his voice expressing his disgust, 'the mob followed and dozens of men could be seen loitering around the house for the next week or so. It was badly done I tell you, Dr Carrick; those responsible for the disembarkation should be held to account for their lack of planning.'

The conversation continued pleasantly as Mrs Southey served an apple pie with fresh whipped cream, sweet and light and satisfying. Izzy and Edith retired to the parlour as Dr Carrick and Douglas relaxed on the veranda in the summer evening to smoke and drink their port and to discuss recent land deals, a topic of mutual interest to them, both men having made much profit from recent transactions.

'He's very handsome, don't you think?' whispered Edith as she rifled through the sheet music, looking for her favourite.

'Who, Dr Carrick? I suppose so, I didn't really notice.' She could feel the embarrassed flush surging up her neck to her cheeks as Edith giggled at her discomfort.

'Oh, Izzy, don't be so coy. He had trouble concentrating on the conversation, so taken was he with your pretty face and figure. I'll wager that Dr Carrick will find many excuses to be a regular at our table, and it is not all about Mrs Southey's cooking.'

The men returned and the next hour was pleasantly spent with Edith playing the small pianoforte that Douglas had procured in Hobart on his last visit. She had played it in every spare minute since its arrival, practising her favourite pieces, so long had it been since she had had the opportunity to indulge this interest. Edith played naturally, without effort, her fingers finding the notes and filling the summer air with the sweet sound.

'And you, Miss Marchbank, will you play for us?' Dr Carrick asked politely.

'I think not, Dr Carrick. My skill at the keyboard is poor at the moment, though Mrs Hamilton has been very generous in her efforts to teach me. Our lives are so busy it is difficult to find the time to practise. My repertoire is limited to the childish pieces I learned in Ireland, so I would rather wait until I can perform something more sophisticated.'

'Indeed, as you wish, Miss Marchbank. Ireland you say, may I ask what part? It is just that I did not distinguish any accent in your speech.'

Perhaps it was the pleasantness of the evening, or the security that Edith and Douglas offered in this now familiar drawing room that gave Izzy a strange feeling of confidence. She would tell him of her birth. He could make of it what he wished.

'I was born in Spain, Dr Carrick, my father being a military officer with the 52nd Regiment. My mother died at my birth and my father took me to Yorkshire where I had my first years. Then I was raised at Blackrock House near Dublin.'

'Blackrock House?' Dr Carrick's eyes widened as he connected Izzy with her surname. 'I know it well. It is part of Irish history now. Lord Marchbank, the revolutionary leader, lived there and was reputed to be very fond of the place. He used it as his local base when planning his attempt to unite Ireland against her English domination.'

It was Izzy's turn to look stunned. 'Lord Marchbank? Yes, he was my grandfather. My father told me a little of him, but I don't think he was so proud of his father. "A dreamer" he always called him.'

'Yes, a dreamer is true, but his memory is held dear by many patriotic Irishmen to this very day. It has been thirty or so years since he died of the wounds inflicted on him by English soldiers when they arrested him for treason, but his memory lives on, his sacrifice held dear by those who still fight for the cause. In Cork, where I grew up, his name is spoken with great respect.'

Edith and Douglas and Izzy were silent as Dr Carrick spoke, all of them stunned not only by the information that he imparted about Izzy's grandfather, but by the reverence which was inescapable in his voice.

'My father never told me any of that,' breathed Izzy, 'only that he was a dreamer who had nearly lost the family fortune. I remember his portrait at Blackrock, in father's study.' The memory of the last time she had seen her father came clear and sharp to Izzy, how she held his hand and looked into his clear blue eyes, and how his decision to send her to New South Wales seemed so simple, with Colonel Peabody standing at the door and her sea chest packed and Mrs Betts waving sadly. The images crowded her mind, images she had not considered for so long. She put her hand to her forehead as her eyes filled with tears.

'Forgive me, Miss Marchbank, I have upset you, I had no right to trespass on your memories.' Dr Carrick was standing, reaching for the glass of water that Edith was handing him. 'Here, drink this, Miss Marchbank. Please accept my apologies.'

'Thank you, Dr Carrick,' she said after a few sips, 'I am quite recovered. You were not to know that such comments were to remind me of the sad circumstances in which I left Ireland. My father was to marry and Colonel Peabody became my guardian and took me to New South Wales and then here to Van Diemen's Land. My life has never been so happy since I met Douglas and Edith, so please, do not alarm yourself. I am quite reconciled to my new life, and quite happy to leave the old one behind.'

'I admire your tenacity, Miss Marchbank. Many young ladies would have less courage and determination.'

'A young lady has few options in this world, Dr Carrick, especially if she has to make her own way without the benefit of family connections. I am grateful for the protection that Edith and Douglas offer me.'

'Izzy is part of our family and always will be,' said Douglas.

'I will take my leave,' said Dr Carrick, rising to his feet.

'My thanks to you Mrs Hamilton for a delightful evening and such a superb dinner. Good evening, Miss Marchbank. I hope I will be able to visit you again.'

'Certainly, Dr Carrick, you are welcome.' Izzy spoke quietly as Dr Carrick bowed formally and withdrew with Douglas accompanying him to the door. The women sat silently, listening to their voices as they farewelled each other on the step, Dr Carrick mounting his horse and clip clopping away and Douglas locking the door as he returned to the parlour.

'Are you all right, my dear?' said Edith. 'It was a little clumsy of him to speak like that.'

'Yes, Edith, he was not to know how delicate the memory was and I confess that as I am growing older, I am less affected by it.'

'He is a good man,' Douglas said. 'I believe he is always ready to attend his patients no matter who they are; gentry, poor, convict, it doesn't matter to him.'

'If you do not wish him to come again just say so and we will not invite him,' said Edith.

'No, I would be happy to see him again. He is a gentleman and even though he is old his looks are tolerable.' Izzy looked for the surprise on their faces at the word 'old' as Edith and Douglas were about the same age.

'Old!' they exclaimed together and the three of them exploded into laughter, their voices filling the house.

'Well, he is at least ten years older than me. But you are right he is a good man and I would be happy for him to come again. I am sure that Mrs Southey's cooking is another incentive for him to accept any invitation that you offer.'

Chapter 5

Launceston 1835

Nell was almost completely hidden among the corn stalks at the end of the garden as she searched for the hens, calling them by name and clicking her tongue, herding them out towards their coop as the sun dipped below the horizon. It was their favourite scratching place, the soil cool and rich with tasty insects and even some plump worms. But Nell knew that the night brought the danger of dogs and the occasional light-fingered passer-by who would happily twist a silent feathered neck to enjoy a good meal. 'Go in now, my lovelies,' she said as she counted them in and locked the door of the coop and stood straight, stretching her back and legs.

She looked around proudly. The corn was nearly ready for harvest and the neat rows of vegetables that she and Miss Marchbank had planted were maturing; the pumpkins and potatoes would see them through the winter, the lettuce and other greens had become their daily fare. 'Who'd have thought,' she whispered to herself, 'that Eleanor Cotter, convicted thief, sentenced to seven years, could ever produce something as beautiful as this.'

She sat on an old upturned box and pulled the basket of peas towards her. She had collected them earlier, their fine bright green pods luminous in the setting sun, the flesh of the pods firm and snapping fresh as she broke them open and the peas themselves, neatly lined snug inside, sweet to her tongue. The taste took her back, not to Banton, Cork, where she was born, but to London, where she worked and where her freedom had ended. Peas were common food even for servants; although smaller and less tasty than these, they were nonetheless a treat for a poor Irish girl so far from home.

She let the taste linger with her thoughts of London, of Johnny thrusting the dress into her arms and running away up the street, of the pawnbroker, red-faced and gasping as he called 'Stop, thief, thief', of her heart racing as she dashed after Johnny, of the Peeler's long legs catching up with her, his rough hands on her arm, his yellow teeth showing as he snarled 'Not so fast, my pretty'. Johnny had disappeared and she was left holding the evidence. Yes, she had stolen the dress from her Mistress and yes, she and Johnny had tried to pawn it. Her mistress had dozens of dresses and Johnny had assured her it was foolproof. 'It's an easy way to make five quid, Nell. We can have a slap-up time for that.' But the pawnbroker asked questions and Johnny's nerve gave way and suddenly he pushed the dress into her arms. If he had just dropped it on the floor, she might have had a chance. She might have run in the opposite direction and melted into the crowd, but he pushed it into her arms to save his own skin. He left her to take the blame, he disappeared and the Peeler caught her.

She was charged with theft of a blue gown, value £5, and sentenced to seven years transportation. Johnny had come to the court looking downcast and guilty and she had stared straight at him. Let him squirm, she had thought, leaving me to take the blame. Never again would she trust a sweet talker like him. Seven years. At first, she thought she would never survive. Every day of the voyage on the *Lucy Davidson* with two hundred other convict women was sickening, every glance of the leering, lecherous soldiers was frightening, every minute of her incarceration at the Cascades Female Factory with its thick, cold walls under the gloom of Mount Wellington was dispiriting.

But she kept out of trouble, she minded her manners to the matron, she made herself useful to the other women and kept away from the drunkards and those among the inmates who caused trouble. Finally, she was reassigned to Class One which meant she was employable. After a year in the system she found herself in the gig beside Mr Hamilton, wrapped in the blanket he gave her against the July chill of Hobart Town and hoping that Mrs Hamilton would be as fair and kind as Mr Hamilton appeared to be. And now she had completed nearly four years and was sitting in the garden that she had grown and London seemed such a long way off, Johnny seemed unimportant, her life was here, now. In three years she would be free and she could have her own garden, maybe marry a nice kind man and have a family. She would never go back. There was certainly nothing for her in Banton, her parents but a dim memory surrounded by her siblings, young and crying with hunger. None of them would know where she was or what had happened to her. Did they know? Did they care?

Suddenly she realised it was quite dark and she roused herself from her thoughts, picked up the basket of peas and felt her way towards the kitchen door, light flooding onto the back step as she stepped into the warm fug of cooking, sweet smelling and rich and Mrs Southey's cheery voice. 'Oh, there you are Nell, I thought you were lost out there in the garden. Fine looking peas, my dear, can you shell them for me, there's a good girl, wash your hands now, I'm in a bit of a rush, visitors again for dinner tonight. Heigh Ho.'

~ ~ ~

Nell's work finished after the last dishes were clean and dry and packed away in the kitchen. She had overheard snatches of the conversation at the dinner table as she served and cleared the dishes. It was Dr Carrick again; he was becoming a regular and it was clear to everyone, including Nell, that Miss Marchbank was the reason for his attention. He made the journey from Campbell Town regularly as he always had business to attend to in Launceston. Tonight the conversation had been about a plan put forward by John Batman, a local landowner, to sail across Bass Strait and establish a settlement at Port Phillip.

'The Cornwall Arms was at bursting point last night when Douglas and I arrived,' declared Dr Carrick. 'Every man in Launceston was there, and JP Fawkner kept the spirits coming, though I'm sure he was watering them down as the night wore on. But John Batman is a great drawcard. An entertaining speaker and a fine-looking man, he convinced the crowd that the expedition would go ahead.'

'His scheme seems to have merit, don't you think?' asked Douglas. 'After all, he is acting on behalf of some of the most respected men in the colony. The Port Phillip Association includes some of the most prominent landowners and it is rumoured that it even has the unspoken blessing of the Governor.'

'Governor Arthur could never publicly endorse such a venture.' Dr Carrick shook his head as he spoke. 'Port Phillip is part of the colony of New South Wales and as such lies outside his jurisdiction.'

Douglas nodded in agreement and continued. 'But do you agree, Dr Carrick, it is the landowners of Van Diemen's Land who will settle the area? It is reputed to be excellent grazing land for their expanding herds of sheep and the price of wool never looked better. The woollen mills of England and Scotland are clamouring for a secure source to lessen their dependence on European flocks.'

'Yes,' said Dr Carrick, 'I read only recently about the

application of the steam engine to drive the woollen mills. Many mill workers are finding themselves unemployed as the mills become mechanised and more efficient. But I fear we are wearying the ladies with our conversation.'

'No,' said Izzy, 'far from it. The steam engine is of great interest to me. My friend, Douglas' cousin John Peabody, explained much to me and Stevenson's Rocket was one of his favourite topics. He showed me pictures of it in newspapers and explained how it worked. I understand that it is a great advance and from what you say it is changing the world, as John had predicted.'

'Yes, you are right, and your young friend is right. It is the greatest advance of the age and the Government will have to ensure the supply of raw materials, which will make the sanctioning of expansion a necessity here in the colonies. John Batman recognises this and plans to make a treaty with the natives to buy their land on behalf of the Association, so that expansion will follow in an orderly manner.'

'And the Association will own all the land and sell it at high prices. When is he due to go?' asked Edith, who had been listening intently.

'He leaves in June to explore the area and see if the natives are amenable to his suggestion.'

The evening progressed and the talk of expansion gave way to more personal topics, with Dr Carrick inquiring about Izzy's work with Madam Foveaux and the progress of the garden that she and Nell had planted some months ago. Douglas was quick to point out that the success of the garden was entirely due to Izzy, her knowledge of the growing cycle exceeding his own and her training of Nell being thorough and detailed. Dr Carrick left the house later than usual, his hand slowly letting go of Izzy's as he made his final farewell and mounted his horse.

~ ~ ~

Throughout the winter Izzy worked with Madam Foveaux for four days of the week and spent her spare time in the garden, showing Nell how to lay it fallow and then how to prepare the soil for the spring planting. Douglas had employed a yardman, Jacob Reardon, who came two days a week to help Nell with the heavy work and to chop and stack the firewood. He was young and strong and a good worker, but he never spoke to any of the women. He did his work as directed, took his pay and went home, never chatting. After several weeks the women of the household simply accepted his brusque manner and gave up trying to engage him in conversation. Mrs Southey brought his plate outside at lunch time and was rewarded with a husky 'Thanks Missus', the most anyone ever heard him say. 'The cat sure has got his tongue,' Mrs Southey said to Nell.

In less than a year Eliza Bull, the nurserymaid, had taken complete charge of the children, and for Fanny and Gussie it seemed that there was never a time when Eliza wasn't there. The children were happy and it was in the last days of winter that Edith whispered her news to Izzy; there would be a new baby at the end of summer, perhaps a boy this time. With Mrs Southey in the kitchen, Eliza with the children and Nell completing other tasks, the household was running smoothly.

~ ~ ~

In October, with the garden at the height of its spring growth, Dr Carrick was again in Launceston, though this time it seemed, on a more permanent basis. Izzy was not sure that she understood the reason for his move but it seemed there was some problem that he was involved in with the convicts at Ross Bridge and there was a hearing in Launceston Magistrates Court that he was to attend. Dr Carrick and Douglas had sat on the side veranda in serious discussion for an hour before dinner and Izzy had only caught snatches of their conversation. But at the table Dr Carrick was his usual cheerful self and the conversation turned to John Batman and the now failed attempt to convince the Government that the treaty he had signed with the natives of Port Phillip back in June had any legal value.

'Null and void, it has been declared,' said Dr Carrick. 'It is not worth the paper it is written on, but I can't see that stopping the Port Phillip Association.'

'Do you think they will go anyway?' asked Douglas. 'I mean, to start a settlement, to occupy the land against the Government's directive.'

'Yes, I know they are going. Batman has contracted the *Norval*, a brig of 200 tons to take five hundred sheep across for Joseph Gellibrand, the lawyer from Hobart who drew up the Association rules and worded the treaty. They leave in early November. Gellibrand has asked me to be his agent, to see the sheep safely delivered and to act on his behalf in Port Phillip.'

'Are you going?' asked Izzy, more quickly than she would have if she had thought ahead.

'Yes, I have finished my time as the Government surgeon in Campbell Town and this venture will be something new for me. Batman thinks it important to move quickly before other groups take a hold. Johnny Fawkner, for example, listened to all Batman said, and there is a rumour that he then bought the brig *Enterprize* and his group has already made camp near the land that Batman had selected as the place for a village.'

'Fawkner's a cunning fox,' said Douglas, 'always looking out for a way to get on. He pretends innocence but is always scheming. I don't trust him and I don't blame Batman for wanting to move quickly.'

'Is it dangerous?' asked Edith. 'I mean, with the natives there?'

'Batman says not. He spent much time with them and finds them friendly although shy of the white man. And of course, we have the advantage of William Buckley as a go-between. His is a most interesting story. Batman told it to me and if Douglas agrees I think it is not too much for you to hear.'

'Yes, I too heard the story. I'm sure Edith and Izzy could cope with the details.'

'Please tell us, Dr Carrick. We females are not so delicate as some men seem to think,' replied Edith. Izzy said nothing but the thought of John Peabody and his stories flashed into her mind.

Dr Carrick put down his glass and began. 'Buckley is a Cheshire man. He had been a soldier with the 4th Regiment, that's the King's Own Regiment, but had been convicted of receiving stolen property and sentenced to fourteen years in New South Wales. This happened a long time ago, about 1802, I believe. He is a giant of a man, at least six foot seven inches tall, with an enormous beard and ruddy complexion. He was among the three hundred convicts on board the *Calcutta* and two other ships that Lieutenant Colonel David Collins took to Sullivan Bay near Port Phillip to set up a convict settlement. They were only there four months when Collins decided that the place was unsuitable, with little fresh water and poor soil, so he made the decision to move the settlement to the Derwent River, and of course that was the beginning of Hobart Town.

'Now, here's the interesting part. On the morning that the ships were to leave the settlement, Buckley and three others escaped into the surrounding bush. The soldiers shot one dead and searched for the others but with departure imminent, they gave up the chase and sailed away and left them there.'

'Oh, how awful,' gasped Edith, 'to watch the ships sail away, knowing you are so totally alone. I think I would rather stay bonded than face such isolation.'

'Well, they were hardened convicts and I suppose they thought that any freedom was better than none. Anyway, the other two inmates decided, over the course of the next few days, to walk overland to Sydney, thinking it was close, but Buckley stayed in the area, living in a sea cave and eating shellfish and berries.'

Douglas stood to refill Dr Carrick's glass. 'It sounds rather like the tale of Robinson Crusoe, except I know that this story is not fiction,' he said.

'Quite so,' said Dr Carrick, 'Buckley lived like this for some months and then left his sea cave to venture further afield. He found a grave, a native grave freshly dug, with a spear embedded in the soil. He removed the spear and was making his way through the bush when he came across a native camp. The inhabitants of the camp were shocked to see him, but not hostile. In fact, they welcomed him and made a great fuss of him. It came to pass that Buckley found out that they believed him to be the reincarnation of a beloved warrior whom they had recently buried, and whose spear Buckley carried. He, of course, let them believe it. He was given a wife and became part of the family, and lived with them for thirty-three years.'

'Thirty-three years? Really? Thirty-three years?' Izzy was incredulous.

'Yes,' Dr Carrick continued, 'he forgot his mother tongue and everything about his former life. Then just a few months ago he walked into the camp at Indented Head where Batman had left a small group of men while he returned to Hobart with the treaty. These men, Todd and Wedge and Smith, were shocked to see this giant, dressed in animal skins like a native but obviously a white man, who couldn't remember the English language, except for the word "bread", of which Todd gave him and he ate ravenously. He had the letters "WB" tattooed on his lower right arm and a mermaid, a sun, a half-moon and a monkey on the upper part. He stayed in the camp for a few days and gradually remembered his name and more of his own language.'

'A remarkable story,' said Edith. 'I wonder that he was

brave enough to return to civilisation, as even after such a long time he could face punishment for his escape.'

'There is a move afoot to plead for a pardon on his behalf,' said Dr Carrick. 'John Wedge was at Indented Head when Buckley came there, and he has already written to the Governor.'

'He will be very valuable in dealing with the natives; his understanding of their language and customs will be of great benefit to the first settlers,' said Douglas.

'Do you think you will meet him?' asked Izzy. 'I mean when you go to Port Phillip?'

'Yes, I expect so,' said Dr Carrick, 'I will be interested in talking to him. However, the hour is late and I fear that I have tired the ladies with such a long story. Thank you, Mrs Hamilton, for another delightful evening.' And with that, Dr Carrick rose, collected his hat and coat and took his leave of them.

~ ~ ~

It was ten days later that Dr Carrick called unexpectedly at Madam Foveaux's shop and asked to speak to Izzy.

'What is it, Dr Carrick?' asked Izzy as she came through the door from the workroom, discarding her apron as she entered the public part of the shop.

'I am sorry to call without invitation, Miss Marchbank, but I am leaving with Batman on the *Norval* tomorrow and I will be away for some weeks or months. I wanted to ask permission to write to you while I am away. The *Norval* will return promptly and there will be other ships that can bring your reply. Douglas, as the Post Master, will know which ones.' He paused, his voice unsteady. 'May I write to you?'

'Yes, of course, Dr Carrick. I will be most interested to hear of your adventures.'

'Thank you. Good-bye then.' His eyes were fixed on her face; he seemed afraid to let go of her gaze.

'Good-bye, and may God go with you.'

'Thank you.'

After formally bowing, Dr Carrick left and Izzy returned to her work but she found it difficult to concentrate. Her mind kept going over his words, seeing his face, his eyes so serious, so nervous, as he asked the question 'May I write to you?' What if she had said 'No'? She thought he would have been wounded to the quick, and that surprised her.

Chapter 6

Launceston 1835–1836

The spring progressed into summer and the garden flourished, with the quality of the produce surpassing any that Izzy had seen. The tomatoes, beans, peas, potatoes, pumpkins, lettuce, radishes, carrots, cabbage, onions were all larger, firmer and of a better colour than Izzy had seen in the Blackrock House garden, or in the Peabody's garden in Sydney. She and Nell carefully weeded and tended the garden, securing the escaping bean tendrils to the frame, spreading the hen's manure to every corner of the garden, carrying bucket after bucket of water to ensure that each plant had enough.

After Dr Carrick left for Port Phillip, Douglas continued to invite guests to dinner, mainly older men who were his business associates or partners in land deals and all entrepreneurs in the growing town of Launceston. Their conversation was lively and usually included some reference to the illegal settlement across Bass Strait as it became increasingly obvious that the Government's lack of action could only mean that sanctioning the settlement was inevitable.

It was a month after his departure that Dr Carrick's first letter arrived, addressed directly to Izzy, his hand strong, but studied and careful, the envelope robust and slightly stained with travel. It was the first letter she had ever received and something about the privacy of the small envelope, that it was directed to her, sealed awaiting her eyes only, prompted her to withdraw to her room, to read it alone.

28th November 1835

Port Phillip

Dear Miss Marchbank,

Thank you again for giving me permission to write to you. This is the first opportunity I have had since we arrived two weeks ago. I find my life completely changed, the hard, physical work and outdoor living contributing to a sense of wellbeing I have not experienced in years. The place we are in abounds with all kinds of birds, fish and animals and the growth of forest, woodland and grassland is plentiful and rich.

We arrived after an uneventful crossing of Bass Strait and anchored at Indented Head in the evening. Mr Gellibrand's five hundred sheep and fifty Hereford cows had weathered the crossing without incident. We were greeted by the party of four men that John Batman had left here after he signed the treaty with the Chiefs in June and they had much praise for the native inhabitants who had supplemented their supplies with greenery and animals from the surrounding bush. They had completed the enclosure for the animals and we could all see that John was right; the pastures here are green and deep and will suit the livestock well.

The willingness of the natives to welcome us was helped by their respect for their adopted brother William Buckley. I met him in the course of the first few days and he is, as Batman had described to me and I, in turn, to you, a giant of a man and a valuable asset to the settlers. He tends to live more with the white men now than with the natives, but his knowledge of the surrounding area is as good as any native and their language runs freely from him.

After landing the livestock, John was anxious to proceed upriver to the place he had selected for a village. However, upon arrival we found that Fawkner had preceded us by three weeks. John and his brother Henry Batman were abusive and angry that the Fawkner camp was on land that John had purchased for the Port Phillip Association. Johnny Fawkner, sly fox that he is, let them vent their anger and simply shifted his camp to the southern side of the river, saying they had no authority over him there, and demanding that John pay him £20 for the ploughing and crops already planted. Their camp is made up of ten souls, including Jem Gilbert, a blacksmith, and his wife Mary who is late with child.

My contract as overseer for Mr Gellibrand means that I must be responsible for his investment of five hundred sheep and therefore tomorrow Buckley and I will walk back overland to Indented Head to check that the shepherds have been vigilant in their duty of care. I plan to enlarge the enclosure and so our work of felling saplings and digging post holes will be gruelling. John leaves with Captain Robert Coltish who is taking the Norval *and this letter, to Launceston with the early tide tomorrow. That will mean that Fawkner's ship, the* Enterprize, *is the only vessel here in the settlement.*

I trust that you are in good health and that your work with Madam Foveaux continues to give you satisfaction. I think often of the pleasant evenings spent dining with you and Edith and Douglas. The civility of Launceston seems so far removed from this frontier but the possibilities here are obvious and I hope to obtain my own sheep and set myself up for the future. I have selected some land about ten miles from the settlement on the Salt Water Creek and hope to begin building a cabin there soon. Perhaps one day you will come and see it.

I hope that the next vessel that comes will bear your reply.

I remain your sincere friend, Dr Carrick

Izzy shared the letter with Edith and Douglas and over the next few days began to compose her reply in her head. She had written very few letters in her life but Dr Carrick's letter caused her to consider that perhaps she should initiate a correspondence with some people of whom she often thought, her father perhaps. He had never written to her and the thought of writing to him was overwhelming, like climbing an enormous mountain, too difficult and with the possibility of further failure. No, not yet, maybe she could think about that. John Peabody was an easier subject. His parting gift, *King Arthur and the Knights of the Round Table*, was on her shelf, next to her only other treasured possession, her doll Alice. So often she had traced his words *'sorry you are going away'*, her only childhood friend, the closest she would ever have to a brother. He would be eighteen now and finished school. Was he working? Or perhaps he had entered the army like his father. Or perhaps he had travelled back to England to further his studies. Yes. She would write to John. No, that would be too forward. She would write to Mrs Peabody and ask for news of all the family. That would be more suitable and from her reply Izzy could ascertain John's whereabouts and position in life. But Mrs Peabody had sent her away and never tried to contact her through Douglas. She would think about that but first she needed to reply to Dr Carrick.

Perhaps it was because she had spent time thinking about it, or maybe it was simply the mood she was in at the time but Izzy found that the letter was surprisingly easy to write, the words flowing easily from her pen, the small, neat script filling line after line on the paper.

22nd December 1835
Post Office Launceston

Dear Dr Carrick,

Thank you for your letter which arrived last week. We are all pleased to hear that you are in good health and that you are adapting to such difficult living conditions. I would think that the weather has been kind to you, that although the summer heat may bring some discomfort, it is far more pleasant that the cold and wet days of winter.

Thank you for your enquiry as to my health, I am happy to say that it is excellent and that Edith and Douglas and the children are also in good health. Edith will go into confinement in the autumn.

Since you have been gone not much has changed in Launceston. I continue to work with Madam Foveaux who is most kind and is teaching me many aspects of her work. The garden continues to thrive and I think that Nell has a particular aptitude for the work. She is from Bandon in County Cork. Do you know the town? She does not remember much of it as she was young when she transferred to London, like many of her age, to find work as a servant in a wealthy house. It was from there that she came to Van Diemen's Land. I have yet to discover the reason for her sentence, as I do not like to press her or pry into her privacy. She is a good person and loves to work with the chickens and in the garden.

I hope that the conditions in which you are living are not too tedious. Are there any home comforts for you in that wild place? Your walks with Buckley must be informative and interesting. Does he see his native family? You said that he had a wife and children. It must be very strange for him to be back in society.

I trust that the coming feast of Christmas will be pleasant for you and that God will bless you and protect you.

Your Sincere Friend, Izzy Marchbank

~ ~ ~

The celebration of Christmas and the coming of the New Year meant that Madam Foveaux's shop was extremely busy. Izzy worked long hours helping out with the stitching and more mundane work. The women from the *Strathfieldsaye* that Madam Foveaux had employed were fast and efficient and their experience in such fine work was obvious. Izzy felt herself a little amateurish by comparison but Madam Foveaux dismissed that thought instantly.

'Piffle!' she said. 'That English word is exactly right for what I think of that. Piffle. Your work is second to none and added to that you have skills above and beyond the mere mechanics of stitching. One day they will invent a machine to do the stitching but never will there be a machine to choose the colours and styles that suit a woman's particular shape and personality. That is a gift, Izzy, and you are blessed.'

Even though the work was exhausting Izzy always went home with a sense of satisfaction, Madam Foveaux's confidence in her occasioning her own increasing confidence, not only in her work but in other aspects of her life. But when she received Dr Carrick's next letter that confidence seemed to desert her and she was very glad that she had taken it to her room to read in private.

28th January 1836
Port Phillip

My dear Miss Marchbank,

Thank you for your letter which came on the Mary Anne *yesterday. I am happy to tell you that life is not so tedious here as there are many new settlers arriving in our little village, Bearbrass we call it and more comforts of life are becoming available each day. We eat well, with swan and other birds as well as a great variety of fish as our daily fare. The vegetables that were planted by Fawkner's party are growing well and there is much game in the surrounding bush.*

We had cause to celebrate the coming of the New Year with the birth of the first white baby in the district. I attended Mary Gilbert, wife of Jem Gilbert the blacksmith. They are both employed by Fawkner and their son, John Melbourne Gilbert, was born in the early hours of December 29th. The whole settlement toasted the newborn and Fawkner gave him his name; John (after himself, of course) and Melbourne as it is assured that when the settlement is legalised, it will be named for Lord Melbourne, the Prime Minister, so far away in England. For the moment we call it Bearbrass, which is close to the native name for the area. The river, which they call the Yarrow Yarrow, is wide and deep enough for the Enterprize *to anchor beneath what we call 'the falls', a small ledge of rock which separates the river into two; above the falls is fresh water, and beneath it is salt. The settlement is situated at this very point of the river and fish are abundant in its waters.*

We have several small craft with which to cross the river to the Fawkner camp. I dined pleasantly with them last night but Henry Batman (John's brother) is causing enmity between the two camps as he dislikes Fawkner intensely. Myself, I find both of them rather irritating. Fawkner is verbose and arrogant, but essentially harmless but Henry takes every opportunity to provoke him. Mrs Fawkner is a kind and gentle soul and welcomes visitors warmly. They have no children but have opened their simple home to the four children of Captain Lancey and his wife, and are especially fond of Amelia who is four years old. Now with the birth of the first baby here, the signs are that the settlement is bound to grow. It is the place for the future.

I trust that this finds you in good health, Izzy. May I call you Izzy? I think of you frequently and hope that our friendship will endure. With your permission I would like to send instructions and payment to the artist, Mr Bardolino, in Launceston to paint a miniature of you that I could keep with me as a comfort in this lonely place.

I hope that the next vessel that enters the Yarrow Yarrow River will bear your reply and that you will address me as Bryn, as a sign of our friendship.

Your sincere and true friend,
Bryn Carrick

Izzy felt the heat rise up her neck and settle on her cheeks. She had been standing by the window to read the letter and she gripped the bedpost as she lowered herself to sit on the bed. Her hands were clammy and she felt hot and a little dizzy. A miniature? He wants a miniature of me? She read the words again: 'as a comfort in this lonely place'. Her cheeks were burning and she tried to cool them with the palms of her hands. 'As a comfort in this lonely place.' She could not believe he had written those words of her. She stared at the page, at the handwriting. Was that last word 'place' a little shaky, wobbly? She imagined him labouring over the letter by the light of a candle in his tent. How many times did he crush that last page in his hands and discard it, working the phrasing so that it was exactly as he wanted it? Not too forward but definite enough. What would she say? What could she write to him? She would have to think about that. Should she tell Edith? Douglas had brought the letter in from the Post Office in the dinner hour and so they would both be expecting some news of Dr Carrick. She read the letter again and decided that she could share most of it with them. The last part she would keep to herself for the moment.

Edith and Douglas were pleased to hear more of Dr Carrick's adventures as Izzy read the relevant pieces to them in the drawing room after supper and they did not press her for any further information that the letter might contain.

However, Izzy found herself irritable and out of sorts over the next few days as she struggled to find a way to reply to his advances. At Madam Foveaux's she was unusually silent as she concentrated on her work and in the garden Nell had to ask her three times to show her how to cut and store the pumpkins. Her sleeping hours were troubled and restless and her waking moments were full of questions. Should I encourage him? Is he serious or is he playing with my feelings? Do I want him to pursue me? Is he too old for me? Would my life be secure with an older man who knows the ways of the world?

Eventually Edith, whose body was swelling with her unborn child, took her aside and said, 'Izzy, are you quite well? You have not been yourself these last days.'

'Oh Edith, I am sorry. I am anxious and worried and not sure what I should do. May I confide in you?'

'Yes, of course. After all, we have sworn to be sisters and care for each other. What is it my dear, what is troubling you?' Edith led her to the drawing room where they could talk in private.

'It's Dr Carrick. He asked me in the letter if he could have a miniature painted of me. I think he means to court me and I am not sure if I want that or not. I do not know what I should say to him, what I should write to him.'

'Oh, I see. You are troubled because you are not sure of your own feelings or of his, am I right? This is very understandable, but you are nearly seventeen and men will be looking at you with an eye to marriage and you must be aware of this. Do you like him, Izzy?'

'Well, yes. I like him. He is a gentleman, and he is amusing and considerate and his vocation as a doctor shows that he is generous and good and kind.'

'I think you should not worry too much. What harm can be done by allowing a miniature to be painted? My advice would be to agree to his request, but not to commit yourself too enthusiastically at the moment. Point out to him that you are still young and inexperienced in these matters, and that Douglas is your guardian and any formal relationship should have his blessing. Let time season his desire. If he wants to pursue you, he will. He will find a way to come back to Launceston for a visit to see you and then you can test his feelings and yours. Write to him of general news in Launceston, of the family and the garden and end with a few simple sentences on the topic that troubles you.' Edith embraced her and smiled. 'Don't be sad, Izzy, this is a happy occasion. There will be many such happy occasions for you in the future.'

'You make it seem so simple. Thank you, Edith. Yes, I will write to him tonight. I feel so much better now. I will do as you say. Thank you again, Edith. You are my valued friend.'

~ ~ ~

Moira McAlister

Dear Bryn,

It seems strange to address you in this fashion, but since you have requested it, I will oblige. All of us are well, the children grow taller by the day and the autumn coolness has refreshed us and is providing us with a harvest of such proportions as I have never seen. Apart from the abundant produce from our own garden, the district is proving to be an excellent source of fruit. The soil and climate and a plentiful supply of water has ensured that the orchards of the Tamar Valley are producing excellent apples and pears, and they are available in such quantities that they sell very cheaply. The children eat them enthusiastically and I confess that I join them, along with everyone else in the house. Mrs Southey, of course has been presenting us with delicious adaptations each day.

I am pleased to hear that you have the opportunity to dine with Mr and Mrs Fawkner and that Captain Lancey and his wife and children are providing some semblance of the life you are used to. It must be very difficult for the ladies in the camp as they have few conveniences to assist them and they are exposed to the elements by living in such primitive conditions. How is the newborn baby progressing?

As to the miniature, I am a little perplexed as to your intentions. I am happy to comply with your request, but I must remind you that I am not yet seventeen and I would expect that, as Douglas is my guardian, you would ask permission of him if you desire to make our relationship a more formal one. As for me, I am inexperienced in these matters and will seek counsel from Edith and Douglas.

Please let me know what to do about the miniature.
I know where Mr Bardolino's studio shop is situated
but it would be more discreet if he were to come to the
house for the execution of the miniature.
May God bless you and keep you safe.

Your sincere friend, Izzy

It was though a weight had been lifted off Izzy when she sealed the letter in its envelope and gave it to Douglas. He took it without comment as he went into the Post Office at 9am, but Izzy saw the look of recognition on his face and knew that Edith had told him of the contents of both letters. She was not troubled by that. It was comforting to think that they cared enough about her to worry that Dr Carrick should be well intentioned and act with propriety; that he should not trifle with her feelings. She vowed silently that she would keep them both informed, that she would return the honesty and openness with which they treated her.

24th April 1836
Port Phillip

My dear Izzy,

We have had great excitement here at Port Phillip
with an influx of new settlers. Chief among them is the
family of John Batman. His wife Eliza and their seven
daughters arrived on the Caledonia *just four days ago.*
Several of us have spent the last two weeks preparing
a dwelling for their arrival as the slab hut which John
brought on the Norval *back in November is far too*
small. Over the last two months since John returned to
Launceston to prepare for his permanent removal to
Port Phillip, I myself had been living in the hut but now
I am happy to say that my own hut at Salt Water
Creek is complete. It is a humble dwelling but it is

serviceable and keeps the weather out. I have my own canvas which I take with me on my journeying, though the natives are adept at building temporary shelters and many settlers have learned the skill from them.

I thank you for consenting to having the miniature painted and I want to reassure you that I understand your hesitation. I am to make a journey to Launceston within the next month or two to secure more livestock for Mr Gellibrand and would be grateful if I could visit you to reassure you and Douglas and Edith of my good intentions. I do not wish to bind you to any formality as I know that my situation here is rather precarious and compares poorly with the opportunities for you to meet eligible young men in Launceston. Please excuse my forwardness on the subject but the rough nature of our living here has not only sharpened my appreciation of the comforts of Launceston but encouraged me to speak plainly and honestly about the future.

We have discarded the name Bearbrass in favour of Melbourne and I am convinced that in a few years it will eclipse Launceston, and even Hobart Town and Sydney, in its growth and wealth. There are so many opportunities here and I intend to make my fortune through land and sheep. My medical practice is already in great demand as there is no other doctor here, although Dr Thompson has just arrived and has made his base on his land claim at Indented Head, which they are now calling by the native name, Geelong.

I thank you again for consenting to having the miniature painted and assure you that I hold our friendship in high esteem. I look forward to your next letter.

Your sincere friend, Bryn Carrick

~ ~ ~

Mr Bardolino came to the house on three consecutive days to complete the miniature. Izzy was amazed that something so small required such effort and detail, Mr Bardolino frowning with concentration as he firstly sketched her face in pencil, noting the depth of her eyes and the height of her cheekbones. The following two sittings were completed on the miniature itself and when it was finished Izzy was shocked to see that the likeness was so true. It was like looking in a small mirror; nothing had escaped Mr Bardolino's scrutiny. He had captured every detail of her hair, thick and curled and held in place by Edith's ivory comb, her eyebrows arched in a questioning shape, her lips delicately defined, her dark eyes looking straight at the viewer, her neck and the ruffled collar of her best pale blue dress balancing the lower portion of the portrait. There was so much detail in such a small space. She and Edith held the portrait at different angles, letting the light fall and illuminate each aspect, and Edith declared, 'It is beautiful, Izzy, it captures you so well. Dr Carrick will be delighted when he receives the package from Mr Bardolino next week.'

~ ~ ~

The welcome coolness of autumn boosted Edith's final reserves of energy as the time approached for the birth of her third child. She slept late each morning and sat in the parlour or the garden in the afternoon. Now that the busy summer season was over Madam Foveaux suggested that Izzy finish at an earlier hour each day so that she could keep company with Edith during those long afternoons, reading to her, sewing and chatting, tempting her with Mrs Southey's cakes. Finally, the day came when Edith stayed in her bed, the pains becoming more regular, and Nell was sent to get Mrs Leith the midwife and the household held its breath and waited through her pain, longing for the sound of the newborn. Douglas paced the hallway, Elisa distracted the children with walks to the river and Izzy did as Mrs Leith directed, filling that basin, removing that sweat soaked sheet, holding Edith's clenched fist, building up throughout the day to the final excruciating, screaming push as the child was born, her thin, mewling cry piercing the air and Edith collapsing back on the pillows, sweat-drenched and exhausted. Izzy had no idea that childbirth would be so violent, so painful, and then that it would be over so suddenly; from screaming agony to exhausted silence.

She gently wiped the child's face with a cool soft cloth, wrapped her in the waiting cotton sheet and placed her in Edith's arms. She held the door open for Douglas and left them together with their newborn daughter and went into the evening light of the garden, feeling the tension of the afternoon lift like a blanket. She closed her eyes and breathed deeply, the vision of so much pain still raw in her mind. Could I do that? Could I be that strong? Could I endure that suffering? This is what killed my mother. Perhaps it might kill me too. She could see how Edith could have died, how her own mother had died in the very act of giving her life. The tears came without warning and she was glad of the dimming light and the seclusion of the garden. There was so much ahead of her. She still had so much to learn.

Chapter 7

Launceston 1836

The last weeks of autumn brought a crisp morning chill and clear skies, blue and still and the Post Master's house rang with the sound of children. Fanny had her fifth birthday, sitting on her father's knee, delighting in the knowledge that she was his favourite. Gussie at two years also knew she was his favourite in the magical way that parents have of directing their love towards each, making it seem singular. Izzy knew that feeling. The baby Marianne bathed in the great tide of love that surged through the house, knowing instinctively that hers was the life they had all, always been waiting to welcome. This world of love had at its centre Edith, strong, smiling and gentle and Izzy saw how she gave herself in a thousand ways each day to her family.

April brought the news that most of Van Diemen's Land had been waiting for; that Governor Bourke in Sydney had authorised that a settlement be formed at Port Phillip. Douglas sat at the breakfast table reading the account to Edith and Izzy, his newly acquired reading glasses half way down his long slender nose.

'It is forecast that 1836 will see the arrival of a resident

Police Magistrate with accompanying soldiers, the surveying and dividing of land to form the heart of the settlement and the official Government sale of that land to interested individuals. Now listen to this part, this is the most important. The land will be put up for auction with a minimum price of five shillings an acre and no priority of purchase will be given to any individual or association. It will be a fair and equable sale of land and Vandemonians, especially those from Launceston, will be in a prime position to benefit. Melbourne may be sanctioned from the north but it will be settled from the south.'

'Ho, ho!' said Edith, 'that means the Port Phillip Association members will have to get in line with ordinary members of society. No priority of purchase will mean that the Association has no power. Do you think it will be dissolved?'

'Yes, exactly, this article is quite explicit that the sale of land will be fair,' said Douglas. 'There are great opportunities here to acquire profitable acreages and I will watch the developments very carefully.'

He folded the newspaper and his glasses and stood, pushing his chair into the table and moving to stand behind Edith's chair. His arms enfolded her and he bent to kiss her good-bye even though he was only going through the door to work.

'Do you think you are ready for another adventure, my dear? Shall we go across Bass Strait and make our fortunes in this new paradise?'

Edith wriggled around to face him. Izzy held her breath but could not take her eyes off them, for they seemed like two parts of one being. Douglas was merry with the idea but Edith's usually smiling face suddenly paled and her eyes widened giving her a frightened look. 'Are you serious, Douglas? Are you really serious?'

'Well,' he said straightening up, 'perhaps I might go alone first and survey the situation and assess the possibilities.'

'Yes,' said Edith, with determination, 'that would probably be wise. I don't want to pack up the children and the household and go and live in a hut, no matter how profitable it is. What about the natives and the animals? It would be fearful. And there's nothing there, no shops or conveniences.'

'Don't upset yourself, my dear,' said Douglas evenly, his smile still playing in the corners of his mouth, 'I would never put you to that discomfort. Our journey to Launceston was adventure enough.'

He bent and kissed her cheek and looked up across the table at Izzy. 'And you Izzy, would you like to go there?'

'Me? Well, I'm not sure. It sounds exciting from what Dr Carrick has told us, but I'm not sure I want to live there. Not yet, anyway.'

'No.' Edith said firmly. 'We women will stay here and you can go off and assess the profitability of such a move. The idea of living in a hut terrifies me. You'd best go to work as the clock is striking nine, my dear.'

~ ~ ~

It was not until the end of July that Dr Carrick made his visit to Launceston and Izzy found that she was nervous with the thought of him coming to dinner that evening. The hint of intimacy she had experienced through his letters was one thing, but how would it be face to face? Would he call her Izzy? Would she call him Bryn? Would he have the miniature in his pocket? Would he ask whether she had seen other young men? Would she have to tell him they all seemed like boys?

As he entered the house and Nell took his hat and coat, he shook hands robustly with Douglas, who clapped him on the back and welcomed him like a returning brother. He greeted Edith heartily, presented sweets to Fanny and Gussie and admired the new baby. When he turned to Izzy, she could see that he was as nervous as she. His face was weathered with outdoor life which made his eyes bluer and more intense. He seemed taller, no not taller, he seemed stronger. Months of axe and spade work and walking had been good for his body.

'Miss Marchbank, Izzy, I trust you are well?'

'Yes, thank you Dr Carrick. Please forgive me. I will grow used to calling you Bryn. It just sounds strange to me now.'

He smiled and ran his hand through his curling hair, stumbling for something to say.

'Perhaps it would help if Edith and Douglas also used my Christian name?'

It was Edith who rescued them both from their discomfort. She nodded to Eliza to take the children and stepped forward and Izzy was again struck by the ease with which she spoke. Edith was a natural talker; she could put people at ease with just a few sentences. Her face was always a smile, something about how the lips never quite covered the teeth and this gave her an openness that made people relax.

'Yes,' said Edith, 'after all, we are not strangers to each other and we do not need to have such formality within our own home. Come into the parlour, Bryn, and tell us of your adventures before Mrs Southey asks us into the dining room. How goes the settlement in Port Phillip?'

'We hear it is to become official,' said Douglas, 'as was rumoured all along.'

Izzy and Edith settled themselves on the sofa, with Bryn and Douglas taking the armchairs, and their attention turned to Bryn.

'Yes, Governor Bourke has made such a proclamation after a petition from the settlers there already. A Council had been set up by Batman, Wedge and Dr Thompson to hear complaints and settle disputes between settlers but it was clear from the start that it had no real authority and decisions could not be enforced.'

'Oh,' said Douglas. 'What sort of disputes?'

'They were just petty complaints and squabbles, mainly between Henry Batman and JP Fawkner. Fawkner had drawn up a "constitution" on how the settlement should be run, but of course no-one would take any notice of it. The man is a fool. He abhors liquor and makes a great noise about settlers drinking too much but he is the one who sells it to them and he has already made a great profit. He doesn't see the paradox.'

'And the natives?' asked Edith. 'Do they come into the settlement? Do they threaten the peace of the village?'

Bryn looked up sharply and was about to answer when he suddenly seemed to think better of it. He reached into his pocket for his neatly folded kerchief and ran it over his forehead.

'There is no use pretending that all is well, you will read about recent events soon enough. A settler called Charles Franks and his servant, a shepherd, were both murdered by the natives near Indented Head.'

Edith and Izzy gasped and Douglas said, 'Oh, how terrible, this is exactly what John Batman sought to avoid by entering into a treaty with the natives. Were you involved, in a medical capacity, I mean?'

'Yes,' said Bryn, 'that is why I have come to Launceston. I was the first to discover the bodies and I have written a deposition which I must present on Tuesday next when there will be a hearing at the Magistrates Court.'

Bryn looked at the three silent faces. 'I'm afraid that the details are too terrible to impart to the ladies, but I wonder Douglas, as my friend and as one who has had some experience with bureaucracy and the law, if you would look over my deposition and guide me. This is the first I have written. This is the first murder I have encountered.'

'Of course I will, my friend. I am sure your evidence, especially with your medical expertise, will be welcomed for its great value. Tomorrow is Saturday. Shall we say ten o'clock in my office?'

Just as he spoke, Mrs Southey entered the room and indicated to Edith that dinner was ready and they rose and proceeded quietly into the dining room.

The mood of the evening was subdued with the news of the murder overshadowing the conversation. Mrs Southey's baked trout however lifted their spirits and Dr Carrick made an effort to move the conversation on to pleasanter matters with anecdotes of life in Port Phillip. In a way the news of the murder, although terrible in itself, meant that Izzy was able to retreat a little from the conversation. It seemed to lessen the intensity of Bryn's visit, to make his presence somehow brotherly. He was clearly affected by the details of the murder and his vulnerability showed a different, more approachable side.

~ ~ ~

The next morning the two men were sequestered in Douglas' office for several hours. Dr Carrick left without entering the house and Douglas came to luncheon alone, reporting to Edith and Izzy that the task was complete and Dr Carrick had left the deposition with Douglas for a final reading and he would return on Sunday after church to finalise it.

That afternoon while Edith was resting and Eliza had the children in the garden, Douglas settled into his armchair in the parlour to review the document. It was quite by chance that Fanny fell heavily on the path outside the parlour, her cry piercingly close, and Douglas rushed to her aid. Her knee was badly grazed and he carried her round the side of the house to the kitchen and attended to her wounds himself, taking his time and making a game of it in an attempt to restore the little girl's cheer. It was also quite by chance that Izzy entered the parlour at that time and saw the deposition, saw Bryn's strong and now familiar script filling the pages, saw how it was lying on the side table where Douglas had cast it in his rush to help Fanny. Izzy had her sewing box with her and settled onto the sofa. It was only an arm's-length for her to turn the pages so they were facing her and read:

Dr Bryn Carrick, being sworn, deposes and states the following: On the morning of 9 July last, as near as I can recollect, I was on board the schooner Adelaide *then at anchor off Gellibrand's Point, Port Phillip. Mr Smith, overseer to Mr Franks, came on board and said he had been to the station on the evening before and found the tents deserted and no-one about the place and feared Mr Franks had been murdered. He requested me to give him assistance and go to the station to ascertain the facts.*

I immediately went in company with some other gentlemen and reached the station the same afternoon. I was the first of my party who discovered the body of Mr Frank's shepherd which was lying between 50 and 100 yards from the tents. I got off my horse and turned the body over. I observed death had been caused by some sharp instrument which had inflicted a very long wound in the skull: some of the brain was protruding. The ground under the head was indented evidently from the head being beat into it. I think the wound was inflicted with a tomahawk.

I waited until the rest of my party came up and then made a further search for the body of Mr Franks which was found near the sheep yards lying on the face. It was turned over and we searched his pockets and found a watch and guard chain and 15 pounds in notes and sovereigns, or thereabouts, a pocket book and one silver pencil case. The face was covered in blood and there was a blow on the temple and two cuts to the head. The tent Mr Franks had occupied was torn down, and his boxes opened, and a good deal of property scattered about. It appeared as if Mr

*Franks was about partaking of a meal as some mutton
was left in the saucepan which had been cooked, and
I should think the transaction occurred in the morning
as the shepherd's boots were quite clean and Mr
Franks had nothing on his feet but stockings.*

*I enquired repeatedly among the blacks to discover
who had committed the above murders and they told
me two blacks, one named Cullen; but that many
others were with them or at a short distance from
them.*

*I returned the following day (the 10th) to the
settlement and remained there or in the immediate
neighbourhood ever since. My station is about ten
miles from the settlement.*

*Signed: Dr Bryn Carrick; Given this day, Tuesday 24th
July 1836 at Launceston Magistrates Court in the
hearing of Judge Richard Roberts.*

Izzy was frozen to the spot. She had never read anything
like it. No wonder Dr Carrick seemed to be in a state of
shock. Imagine having to do that, having to see that. She
realised she needed to leave the room now, before Douglas
returned, because he would be upset if he knew she had
read it. She took her sewing box and made her way quickly
to her room. She lay on her bed thinking about the details
of the deposition and listening to the sound of Douglas
swinging Fanny in the garden, her wounds healed and her
laughter restored. Then the garden was quiet as Eliza took
Fanny to the nursery for her rest and Douglas returned to
the parlour.

~ ~ ~

The Sunday service was over and the good people of
Launceston filed out of the sturdy little wooden chapel and

mingled on the small adjoining grassy patch to catch up with news of the week. Bryn found the Hamilton family and accepted Edith's invitation for luncheon and he managed to position himself next to Izzy as they strolled the short distance home, Edith and Douglas and the children walking just behind.

'Do you have a clergyman in Port Phillip?' asked Izzy. She had been praying for the dead men during the service and wondered about their spiritual fate.

'No, not yet, Dr Thompson performs the role of catechist to the natives, and leads prayers every Sunday, but we are hoping for the appointment of a permanent clergyman soon.'

'The men who died, were they properly buried?

'Yes, I can assure you they were. John Fawkner and myself and several others selected a suitable site for a burial ground. It is on Flagstaff Hill. We also started a fund for the erection of a chapel on the site.'

'And did Dr Thompson lead the prayers for the men?'

'Yes. The whole of the settlement attended and they were buried according to the Christian tradition.' He paused and they were silent as they walked. 'I hope I have not upset you Izzy, with news of this tragedy?'

'No, Bryn. It is just that new settlers seem to be so vulnerable. The natives can attack without warning. It could have been you that died.' She was careful not to hint that she knew any details of the event.

'I do not think it will happen again. A group rode out after the culprits and came back assuring the settlement that justice had been done.'

'How did they know who was to blame?'

'They didn't, they just had a few clues and hearsay. Dogs and spears are no match for horses and guns. But I do not want to distress you. I have taken a vow to preserve life so I did not participate, but that is not to say that I disagree with the retribution that was dispensed. My father was the Police

Magistrate in our village of Millstreet in County Cork and I grew up witnessing a great many incidents where justice was best dispensed immediately. This is such a case.'

Izzy had nothing to say. Her experience and knowledge on the subject was non-existent. The thought of the two men lying dead in the dirt gave way to the thought of innocent natives being shot in revenge. Was that justice, an eye for an eye? She didn't know.

They had reached the front gate and Douglas and Edith caught up with them and they proceeded into the house and spent the rest of the day pleasantly with no more talk of murder and retribution. The many victims of this crime were far away and silent.

~ ~ ~

The court heard the evidence of several witnesses and concluded that the settler Franks and his shepherd were murdered by the Goulburn Aborigines Cullen and Dundom on the 8th July 1836. These men had accompanied John Batman and were supposed to act as a go-between with the local natives. No mention was recorded of any reprisals against the local Kulin people but everyone knew that they had occurred. The mood of the now steady stream of settlers was buoyant; the natives had been taught a lesson and would not cause any more trouble.

~ ~ ~

The frost was still on the grass as Izzy worked alongside Nell digging the rotting compost into the now bare stretch of soil between the gate and the house. This part of the garden had proved to be the most productive; its aspect providing both nurturing morning sun and protection from the hot and drying winds of summer. The garden was lying in its winter fallow but that did not mean that nothing was happening or that there was no work to be done. Izzy knew from her lessons in Ireland that the winter months were just as important in the life of the garden as the exciting months of spring and summer or the harvest months of autumn. 'This is the soil's rest time,' Mrs Betts had said to Izzy, and Izzy now said to Nell, 'We must feed the soil and make sure it is in good condition for all the work it will have to do in the spring.'

Izzy straightened her back and was waiting for Nell to bring the water bucket when Douglas suddenly opened the kitchen door and came towards her down the path. It was mid-morning so Izzy was surprised that he was not in the Post Office.

'I'm sorry to interrupt your work, Izzy, but could I have a few words with you in the parlour? Say, in five minutes?' His voice was light and excited.

'Certainly Douglas, is something wrong?'

'No, nothing is wrong.' He laughed but did not offer any more information as he turned and retraced his steps to the kitchen.

Izzy handed Nell the spade and directed her to continue while she took off the coarse thick gloves. Whatever could it be she wondered as she sat on the back step and removed her boots, heavy now with the rich and thick mud. She put on her woollen slippers, washed her hands and face in the scullery and hurried to the parlour, remembering to take off her apron before entering. Douglas was sitting in his arm-chair; the light was behind him and she couldn't make out his expression. She was reminded of the same light in her father's study the last time she saw him.

'Sit down, Izzy. Please stop looking so worried. I have pleasant news. Well, it is important news and I hope you will find it pleasant.'

Izzy could think of nothing to say, so she sat nervously on the sofa facing Douglas.

'Dr Carrick is to return to Port Phillip tomorrow and he is coming to supper with us tonight.'

'Is that all?' asked Izzy. Could Douglas seriously have called her in to the parlour to tell her this?

'No. That is not all,' he laughed. 'I have just spent the last hour with Dr Carrick and he is very earnest in his request. This evening, when he comes, he wants to ask you for your hand in marriage.'

There was silence. The clock ticked. 'What?' Izzy said blankly. 'Marriage already? Marry Dr Carrick?'

'Yes Izzy, how do you feel about that? He is a good man and a gentleman. He has approached this correctly by asking permission of me to speak to you.'

Izzy was silent as the thoughts tumbled around in her head, marriage, Dr Carrick, babies, pain, Port Phillip.

'Would that mean I would have to leave you and Edith and go to Port Phillip?'

'Yes, of course it would.' He paused, looking intently at Izzy. 'Izzy, there is plenty of time for you to think about this. If you have any reservations, you do not have to see Dr Carrick tonight. I will speak to him and ask him to delay his proposal.'

'Thank you, Douglas. You are the best of guardians. Can you tell me when this would happen? I do not want to go away immediately.'

'No, no, no.' Douglas seemed relieved. 'Dr Carrick envisages a long engagement as he will need time to prepare a suitable home for you. Port Phillip is a rough and tumble place at present but with the recent arrival of the Government representative, Captain Lonsdale, the place will soon be subject to law and order and it will grow. If it helps, I have been persuading Edith that our future lies there too. She is not easy to convince, as you know, but she is far more positive now than she was. Do you want me to send a message to Dr Carrick to tell him not to come this evening?'

'No, thank you Douglas. I would like to hear what he has to say and I will tell him that I need some time to think about it. Would that be suitable? He will not be expecting an immediate answer, will he?'

'No, I'm sure he will be happy to wait for your decision.'

~ ~ ~

Izzy spent the afternoon at Madam Foveaux's. It was a quiet time in the business, the winter skies unconducive to thoughts of new dresses and hats and the few orders they had were easily completed. Izzy was glad that she could sit quietly sewing and think of what life would be like married to Dr Carrick. Bryn. My husband. Mrs Carrick. Mrs Bryn Carrick. Would there be children? Thoughts of the pain that Edith endured in childbirth flashed before her. Could she make him happy? What would the marriage act be like? Mrs Betts had briefly described the mechanics and Mrs Peabody had been overcome with embarrassment, but watching Edith and Douglas it seemed to Izzy that the married state was something to be desired. As the afternoon progressed she felt more and more confident that she did have an immediate answer and that the answer would be positive. The long engagement was the key. It would give her time to adjust, to prepare.

~ ~ ~

When Dr Carrick arrived promptly at six o'clock, Nell took his hat and coat and showed him into the parlour. Edith and Douglas were nowhere to be seen and his nervousness was obvious as he bowed formally and approached Izzy.

'Good evening Miss Marchbank, Izzy. I know that Douglas has spoken to you and I thank you for seeing me.'

'Good evening, Dr Carrick. Please come and sit down.'

He sat on the spare armchair near the window.

'I know that we have known each other for some time and that I am much older than you but please listen with an open heart to what I have to say.'

Izzy waited. Her breath was light.

'Since I have been in Port Phillip, I have thought of you constantly. I have lived for your letters and waited impatiently for this visit to see you again. Your miniature has been my constant companion, my only comfort. Now, before I return to that lonely place, I want to declare my love for you and ask you for a pledge.'

He slid to his knee and took her hand. 'Izzy, would you do me the honour of being my wife?'

'Dr Carrick, you do me a great honour,' she said softly. 'I thank you for your proposal. I am young and inexperienced and I am flattered that you have chosen me.'

His grip on her hand was firm and as if he was expecting the worse, it seemed to tighten as she continued.

'Douglas said that you envisaged a long engagement and that would be agreeable to me as I think I will need some time to adjust to such a change in my life.'

'Yes, I will need time to put things in order and prepare a home for you.' His grip was still firm. 'Does that mean you will consider my proposal?'

'Dr Carrick, Bryn, yes I will accept your proposal.'

He dropped her hand and was suddenly sitting on the sofa beside her, encircling her in his arms and kissing her lightly, gently on the lips. Her whole body seemed to soar with his touch. She could have stayed there forever.

'You do not understand how happy you have made me. I expected that you would need longer to decide.'

'No, I too have missed you and waited for your letters and this visit. I trust that over the coming months of our engagement we will continue writing and will include our hopes and plans for our life together.'

'Yes, yes that we shall certainly do.' He fumbled in his pocket and produced a ring in a small cloth bag. It was a poesy ring, engraved with decorations on the outside and a verse on the inside. 'Before I left Ireland my mother gave me this ring. It had belonged to her mother and she said I was to give it to the woman I chose as my wife.' He placed it on her finger. It fitted easily. 'Will you accept this as a token of my love and my pledge to make you my wife?'

'Yes Bryn.' Izzy felt lightheaded with excitement welling up inside her. 'But let me read the verse inside.'

She made to remove the ring, but his hand closed over hers and he said, 'No need to take it off. The verse says "You never knew a heart so true". I have waited to say those words to you,' and he kissed her again. Then they stood and he led her out of the parlour to the dining room. Douglas and Edith looked towards them and Izzy saw their clouded faces clear in an instant as they understood what had taken place. Bryn held her hand high, showing the ring.

'Izzy has consented to be my wife,' said Bryn. 'I am the happiest man in Launceston.'

Chapter 8

Launceston 1836

When Dr Carrick returned to Port Phillip Izzy found that the news that they were affianced spread quickly. She wondered how such a small thing as the ring on her finger, plain and simple as it was, could cause such excitement, especially among her friends. Julianne Hardwicke was ecstatic. 'Was it romantic?' she giggled. 'Tell me what happened.'

Izzy was stunned. 'Romantic? Well, yes, I suppose so,' she said.

Madam Foveaux congratulated her and Izzy hastened to tell her that the long engagement would mean that she would not be leaving Launceston for some time, that she wanted to continue in Madam Foveaux's employ. She also shared her secret thought that if things didn't work out for Dr Carrick in Port Phillip, then there would be no reason to leave Launceston at all.

'But I should think that Dr Carrick may not want you to work after you are married. Most men want their wives to stay at home. Some however in this new world are like my Phillipe and rejoice in the skills of their wives. But do not worry Izzy, your engagement is wonderful news, my dear. I am so happy for you. Dr Carrick is well known for his care of the sick and injured. I heard recently that he gave evidence in that shocking murder that occurred in Port Phillip.'

'Yes,' was all Izzy could say, the details of the deposition still fresh in her mind. 'He has to deal with many such difficult situations.'

'You will be a great comfort to him. A man needs to have such comfort when he returns from his work. My Phillipe was always so happy to come home to me. He would say that sunset is made for lovers, the day is done and the long night lies ahead.' She smiled and her eyes twinkled with the memory.

'You must miss him so much, Madam, after spending so many years together.'

'Yes, my dear, I do miss him, he was a wonderful husband and father. When we came to this country, we had hopes that our two boys would marry and settle here but they both returned to France. I had set up business in Hobart Town and was doing so well and Phillipe's craft in wood was popular, so we stayed. It was only five years later that he died as the result of an accident with a saw. He suffered much, my poor Phillipe.'

Again, Izzy felt her youth and inexperience and could find nothing to say so she remained silent, watching the tapestry pattern on the cushion, following the weave in and out. When she was ready Madam Foveaux lifted her head and smiled.

'Thank you for asking, Izzy. Not many people know about Phillipe and it is good to bring back happy memories even if they are tinged with sadness. I have survived these last years without him and my thoughts are increasingly turning to the land of my birth. Your news has come at an opportune time. My sons write frequently urging me to come home. They are in business together in Paris, importing and exporting fabrics, and as you know it is they who supply me with the best and most fashionable materials. The *House of Foveaux* was Phillipe's father's business, and that, of course is how we met; I was a humble seamstress and he supplied my employer. But Phillipe was never suited to the business. He was a craftsman and loved the outdoor life and the adventure of new places, and so we came to Van Diemen's Land. The business in Paris was run by his brother who had no sons and that is why my sons have taken it over in the last few years. They have both married and have children and I have an increasing desire to spend my old age among my own people, especially my sons and my grandchildren.'

'Oh,' said Izzy, 'you will leave, go back to Paris? You will sell the business?'

'Well, I would give the business to you if Dr Carrick would allow you to work. You would be the only one I would trust to keep the high standards that make it appealing to these ladies. Would you consider discussing this with him?'

'I am indebted to you for such consideration, Madam Foveaux, but I cannot see that it would be possible if I am to make my home in Melbourne with Dr Carrick.'

'Yes of course my dear, I understand. You must follow where he leads you. I will close the business and see my employees have work in other shops. I do not need the money gained through selling and I would be uneasy that my name might be associated with a drop in standards. I have prided myself on the very highest.'

'Thank you Madam Foveaux, for your offer, I will always remember your kindness to me.' Izzy was fighting the tears, holding them back. Another change in her life, another person she loved would be gone. Just as she thought she could depend on her life, it changed again. That old familiar sadness welled up inside her again and she was overcome. Madam Foveaux reached out and encircled Izzy in her arms.

'Don't be sad, Izzy, especially don't be sad for me. It is time I went home and I am happy to make the decision. We cannot live in the past. My life must move on and so must yours. You have been a boon to my heart, Izzy, because you remind me of my youth. From the day I met you in Mrs Underwood's garden I knew that you were special, that you had such talent, such grace. And now you are to be married and live in Melbourne at a time when that town will be rising, rising to great heights. Remember Izzy, that when men make money, their wives spend it. You could easily set up such a business in Melbourne. Use my name as a reference if you wish. You have all the qualities to be successful.'

~ ~ ~

In October Mrs Underwood held another garden party and this time it was to farewell Madam Foveaux. The ladies of Launceston did her the honour of wearing one of her garments to the event. Izzy was dazzled by the variety of the gowns, their perfect fit and individuality and how they matched the personalities of the ladies. She had worked on so many of these gowns that it was like meeting old friends as they swirled around on the perfectly manicured lawn. Mrs Hardwicke in the olive-green silk, Genevieve in her pretty blue cotton with matching bonnet, Julianne in a similar cotton of palest pink, with the bow that Izzy had fashioned herself. And there was dear Mrs Stevens in the yellow silk, Izzy's first cutting task. Izzy herself wore her cream cotton with the delicate rose print, with a matching band on her bonnet, and Edith looked stunning in the deep blue silk that Izzy had made at home for her.

'They are like the butterflies of spring,' laughed Madam Foveaux as she stood with Mrs Underwood and welcomed more and more ladies. 'How delightful and what a lovely parting gift; to see so many of my creations in one place. I am truly overcome and I thank you for thoughtfulness.'

It was a week later that Izzy waved her handkerchief forlornly as she stood with Edith on the roadside and watched the coach for Hobart disappear from view. She clutched in her hand the address in Paris of Madam Foveaux's sons, should Izzy ever need to be in contact. 'Just in case you do go into business and need to order the very best of everything. You will find me there; my sons are encouraging me to advise them.'

Madam Foveaux had given Izzy the cutting table and the cabinets as well as the adjustable models and the mirrors and some of her parlour furniture, saying, 'There may be an opportunity in the future for you to use them.'

These items were securely stored in a shed belonging to Mr Booth, a furniture importer in Charles Street. In return for ten shillings a year, Mr Booth had guaranteed that the items would be safe from the weather and unlawful hands. Izzy would be able to take them with her to Melbourne if Bryn agreed, but she had not yet had the chance to discuss the idea with him. He was always interested in her work and asked her the details of it, but setting up a business was another matter and she was not sure that he would approve of his wife doing such a thing. His wife. She would be his wife and would be obliged to follow his directions.

~ ~ ~

Izzy missed Madam Foveaux. She missed the work, the deadlines, the excitement, the satisfaction of a completed garment, the society of both the workroom and the fitting parlour. She found she had time on her hands and Edith suggested that she turn her attention to assembling her trousseau, the household linen and quilts she would need along with personal garments, underwear and night dresses for her married life. Izzy set about the task enthusiastically, using all the skills Madam Foveaux had taught her along with some she had picked up from the *Strathfieldsaye* women; embroidery and lace making in particular. Edith gasped at the beauty of her creations, transforming simple cotton muslin and coloured thread into items so delicate and pretty that they looked as though they had cost a fortune.

She continued her correspondence with Bryn of course and told him of Madam Foveaux's departure. She did not mention the furniture as she wanted to talk to him face to face about it so that she could gauge his attitude. His letters were full of anecdotes of the life in the new settlement and Izzy read them with an eye to the detail; these would be the people and places that would constitute her new life and she was eager to learn as much as she could.

14th December 1836
Port Phillip

My dearest Izzy,

Your letter arrived yesterday and I am replying immediately as the Vansittart *sails for Launceston at first light tomorrow. I felt your sorrow at the departure of Madam Foveaux. She has been a good and true friend to you and you will miss her. I am glad to hear you have begun preparing for married life by collecting and making those items that you will need. Your position as my wife will require you to sometimes act as hostess and I intend that we shall mix with the best of society. However, do not despair, there is much available here. Every day here sees the arrival of more settlers and more conveniences on sale in the market square.*

Captain William Lonsdale arrived on 29th September bringing with him his wife and children and three constables; Robert Day, Joseph Hooson and James Dwyer. The constables have already had a profound effect on the village with a curfew being imposed and the publicans being advised that they must apply for licences to run their establishments. It is much quieter at night and safer too, as the rabble rousers are at last under control. Captain Lonsdale seems a reasonable man and his wife is charming.

Then, a week later a second Government ship, the Stirlingshire, anchored in Hobson's Bay. It brought the surveyors Robert Russell, Frederick D'Arcy and William Wedge Drake. This is exciting for these men will prepare a plan for the division of land to be sold. Other officials – Skene Craig the Commissariat Officer who has responsibility for government stores and the Customs men, John McNamara the Tide Waiter who inspects the incoming ships, and Robert Webb, the sub collector of Customs. These men will ensure that imports are regulated. So, you can see that we have the beginning of an official bureaucracy in our little village. Much has changed since I camped on the banks, of what we now call the Yarra, with the first handful of settlers.

Also on board were thirty soldiers from the 4th Regiment under the command of Ensign King and thirty convicts. The settlers here had asked that Melbourne not be considered as a convict settlement but these men have been brought here to assist with road works and the construction of official buildings. Their first task was to unload the supplies from the ships and the small crowd assembled to watch was delighted to see large quantities of timber, a great number of bricks, assorted tools, dozens of blankets and other provisions, and clothing in the form of canvas trousers, shirts and even nightcaps (red in colour!). Also, I saw twenty-five brass plates with chains which will be hung around the necks of co-operative natives.

One of the first tasks of the convicts was to build a public oven so that large quantities of bread can be baked daily. Captain Lonsdale has wasted no time in appointing officials. William Buckley has been *appointed a constable and interpreter to the natives at £60 per year. I had hoped to be considered as medical officer but that position was given to Dr Thompson, even though most of his time is spent at Geelong.*

John Batman, although debilitated and crippled through sickness, is a happy man at the moment, for his wife Eliza has given birth to a boy. After seven girls John finally has a son and he celebrated in great style, offering drinks all round at Fawkner's hotel last night.

So, you see Izzy, our little village of Melbourne is becoming more and more like home. My hut is becoming quite comfortable as more provisions become available but I would not expect you to live in the wilds as I am at present. By the time we are married I will have bought land in the town and will build you a beautiful house. I am confident that my private medical practice and my position as overseer to Joseph Gellibrand and my own modest flock of sheep will provide ample income for you to have the best of everything. Nothing will be too good for you. I think of you constantly and pray for the day when we will be together again.

From your loving fiancée, Bryn

Izzy shared her letters with Edith and Douglas and it was now becoming plain that they too would cross Bass Strait. Douglas read the newspaper reports constantly and there was an air of growing excitement in the house as Christmas came and went and the new year of 1837 dawned and Douglas prepared for his exploratory trip.

'This is the year,' said Douglas, holding his glass high, 'this is the year for great things to happen. Raise your glasses ladies and make a toast to Melbourne. Have I convinced you my love that we should go?'

'Yes Douglas. You know that I will follow you anywhere.

If you return from Melbourne in March and tell me that it is suitable then I shall believe you.'

'I am so happy, Edith, that you will be there,' said Izzy. 'The thought of leaving you is too much.'

'I couldn't let my sister go alone, could I?' she replied. 'From the newspapers and Bryn's letters it seems as though all amenities will be available. Nell has one year left and will come with us and Mrs Southey and Eliza have also agreed to accompany us. It will be a new adventure for us all.'

~ ~ ~

Bryn's next letter arrived before Izzy had had a chance to reply to the last. It was hurriedly written and betrayed his excitement.

> *15th January 1837*
> *Port Phillip*

> *My darling Izzy,*

> *Wonderful news has just been disclosed to me. Dr Thompson has resigned his position in favour of his private business interests in Geelong and Captain Lonsdale has appointed me District Surgeon with a salary of £200 per year. With this certainty of income, we can be married sooner. I await your reply with great happiness.*

> *Your loving fiancée Bryn*

Izzy too was excited at the idea that Bryn would hold a government position but she was not so sure about the marriage taking place sooner. The long engagement was still important to Izzy, giving her the time she needed to grow used to the idea.

~ ~ ~

Douglas returned from Melbourne full of excitement at the prospects offered there. He had spent some time with Bryn and had met many of the other local settlers, some of whom he knew from Launceston.

'I went with Bryn to his log cottage at the Salt Water River. It is a comfortable little place, weather tight and cosy. The land is excellent, undulating and lightly treed with pastures suitable for Gellibrand's two thousand five hundred sheep. Bryn has three horses and two acres under cultivation with potatoes.'

'Is he well?' asked Izzy. 'I worry that he has over committed himself taking on the role of District Surgeon.'

'He is quite well, though I agree with you. His days are stretched between his responsibility for public health, his own private practice which now includes the very ill John Batman, his own property ten miles out of the settlement and his position as overseer for Mr Gellibrand. It is a wonder that he ever finds the time to write so many letters to you,' he teased.

'And did you see Governor Bourke?' asked Edith. 'We read in the *Advertiser* that he came from Sydney on an official visit while you were there.'

'Yes indeed, he arrived as I was leaving and is to spend the month there. Preparations were in order for his official welcome dinner, which will proceed tonight, if I am not mistaken,' answered Douglas. His first task will be to inspect the settlement and instruct Surveyor Hoddle and his assistants to plan the town. The date of the land auction has been set for June 1st.'

'Is it possible to imagine what the town will look like?' asked Izzy.

'The present village straggles along the banks of the river as you would expect. There is some speculation about the shape the future town will take. Some say these surveyors lack imagination and will just impose a standard grid without reference to the natural features of the place. We shall have to see about that, but there certainly is much interest in the development. I believe the auction is being advertised in Sydney.'

Douglas was quiet for a moment, looking out of the window as if he could see the new town there. He cleared his throat.

'As I looked at the surrounding countryside I became convinced that there is a fortune to be made as a landowner. Thousands of acres to the north of the settlement are available to run sheep and I am certain that I could be successful.'

He waited, searching Edith's face for her reaction. Izzy remained still and silent and saw the effect that his words had on Edith. Her eyes widened, her lips parted and she gasped a small breath of air.

'To the north? How far out of the settlement? You would be a farmer. You don't know anything about farming.'

'Well, I would own the land. There are plenty of labourers to work it. And I could learn. Men from all walks of life are going to take up this challenge, men like Bryn who can turn their hand to anything.'

'Are you serious, Douglas? How far away from civilization would we be? What about the natives? Have you considered the dangers we might face?'

'Yes, yes, I know that there are difficulties but don't worry, my dear. By the time we actually get there the area will be settled and civilised. Even now there are very few natives in the area, most of them preferring to go further north. The most important thing to do is secure a land grant now, before there is a rush.'

'How do you do that?'

'All one has to do is simply set the boundaries and apply to the Governor for permission to take up the land. Bryn showed me how to do it, as he had done it at Salt River.'

Izzy quietly rose and left the room as she knew that Douglas and Edith would need to talk this through without her. And she was right, it took all night, but eventually Edith was not only convinced of the financial opportunity but excited at the prospect of being the wife of a country squire.

~ ~ ~

Izzy did not receive a letter from Bryn for the next two weeks although she had written two. As the days passed, she began to worry that he was unwell or injured or perhaps that his affection was waning. It was a shock to all of them therefore when he arrived after dark unannounced, obviously agitated and a little dishevelled.

'Come in my friend,' said Douglas, 'what has happened?'

'I apologise to all of you, especially you Izzy my love, for this intrusion.' He kissed her on the cheek and gave his coat to Nell. 'I am sorry Edith and Douglas that I was unable to advise you that I was coming, but there was no time. There has been a catastrophe and my presence is required in Hobart Town as soon as possible.'

'What is it?' asked Douglas. 'Come in and sit down. Nell, could you ask Mrs Southey to prepare a plate for Dr Carrick. You look exhausted, Bryn. Tell us what has happened.'

They entered the parlour and the familiar room and surroundings seemed to calm Bryn as they took their usual seats. Izzy could see that he was unshaven and his eyes were dark rimmed and tired. His hair was shorter. He took a deep breath.

'Joseph Gellibrand, my employer, has disappeared,' he announced as the eyes in the room widened with surprise. 'He was to attend the welcome dinner for Governor Bourke two weeks ago, but he didn't arrive. He and his friend Hesse had anchored at Indented Head and were to progress overland to the settlement. He is an excellent bushman and the journey should have only taken a day or two. When he failed to arrive, I went with several others in search of him. We followed his horse tracks from Indented Head as far as possible into the bush but then they petered out and we could find no trace of him. We spent three days camped in the bush looking for him. It cannot be that he became lost, so we must conclude that they were attacked by natives. We have scoured the area and with Buckley's help we have questioned the natives but to no end. They have simply disappeared.'

Mrs Southey entered the room quietly with a tray which she placed on the table beside Bryn.

'That is terrible,' said Douglas. 'What is your plan now?'

'Now I must go to Hobart and impart the news to Mrs Gellibrand and wait for some direction from her as to his assets in the settlement. She will be distraught with the news and will need to seek advice. I expect I will be there for some days or weeks.'

'You must stay here tonight and rest so that you are ready for the journey. The coach leaves early, at six, and there is no more that can be done tonight.' It was Edith speaking and she stood to leave. 'Come Izzy, we will see to setting up a bed for Bryn in Douglas' study. Douglas, you might offer Bryn some brandy before he has his supper. We will not see you in the morning, Bryn. Douglas will see you to the coach.'

'Thank you, Edith, for your hospitality. I am sorry again to impose on you this way.'

Then to Izzy he said, reaching for her hand, his fingers tracing over the tiny ring, the symbol of their love, 'You will understand why I was unable to write. I had hoped that my next visit to Launceston would be one filled with the joy of making plans for our future.'

'I understand, Bryn. You have been through much with the loss of your friend and I am sorry that you have such a sad task ahead of you in Hobart. Goodnight now and may God protect you.'

Izzy lay awake for hours. The thought that Bryn was under the same roof was unsettling. He had been away so long and now he was just a few rooms away. Would he be sleeping or would he be thinking the same? In a year's time she would be beside him in his bed. What would that be like? He was exhausted as Douglas had said and he needed to sleep. She prayed for Mrs Gellibrand, who did not yet know how her life had changed. She prayed for Bryn that his task would be completed soon and she prayed for herself that she would be a good wife to him.

~ ~ ~

Bryn did not return to Launceston as he was able to go directly by ship from Hobart Town to Melbourne. In his letter of apology, he explained how this route was increasing in popularity as more and more settlers were making the move north and that although he would have liked to have lingered in Launceston, his work both government and private demanded that he return post haste to Melbourne. He wrote of Mrs Gellibrand's despair at the disappearance of her husband and that he had instructions to sell the entire flock.

Douglas was growing impatient to leave Launceston. Bryn's visit, the newspaper reports and the general talk around the town all pointed to a bright future for Melbourne. Douglas was not an impulsive man but he sensed that those who arrived well before the land sales, with the opportunity to familiarise themselves with the countryside, would be in a better position to choose. As always, he shared his thoughts with Edith.

'So, when you say "soon", what do you mean?' asked Edith.

'I think as soon as we possibly can. I see that the schooner *Lowestoft* is available for charter at present. If I can secure it then we can begin deciding what to take with us and what to leave behind. There will be much to do, but we should take the opportunity to charter a vessel as soon as possible for there will be a terrible rush when the land sales are on. Our living conditions will be uncomfortable for a short while but if I can secure a landholding to the north of the town then our fortunes will be made.'

'Yes, I can understand the need to act quickly if we are to acquire land on which to build our house.'

'You shall not just have a house, my dear. You shall have a country mansion. It will be the envy of all, with gardens and lakes and as many servants as you like. And sheep, you shall have thousands of them. The wool trade is the future of this colony and we are well placed to take advantage of it. But we must act now. Do you agree?'

'Yes, I do, my dear, but what about the Post Office?'

'My assistant will be able to run things here for a while. I will return after our purchase to finalise our move from here. For the moment we need only take the basics with us.'

'I saw Mr Booth's shed when Izzy stored her cutting table there. It is spacious and well-constructed and waterproof, so we could arrange to store our belongings there until we have built this wonderful mansion.'

'So, you agree to come adventuring with me again?'

'Of course, Douglas,' she sighed. 'I trust your judgement in all things.'

He kissed her.

~ ~ ~

3rd April 1837
Post Office, Launceston

My dear Bryn,

There has been much activity here in the last weeks as we prepare for our departure to Melbourne. Douglas has hired the Lowestoft *to take ourselves and our immediate and personal possessions and is arranging for the storage of larger items until their house is built and ready for occupation.*

When Madam Foveaux left Launceston, she gave me her cutting table and cabinets along with her wooden models and hat stands. These I have had stored in Mr Booth's shed in George Street until I decide, in consultation with you, of course, what to do with them. With your recent rushed visit to Launceston and the distressing news of Mr Gellibrand, there was no time to tell you about the furniture or discuss my use of it in the future. Madam Foveaux suggested that I have the skills to set up a business of my own in the new and growing town of Melbourne. Her husband Phillipe, who was renowned as a fine cabinet maker, built the furniture when they first arrived in Hobart. It is constructed from the beautiful light-coloured timber, Huon Pine, and I am very proud that she gave it to me as she was so fond of it, especially as her husband had built it for her.

Mr Booth has been paid for two years storage so there is no need for an urgent decision. I wanted, however to tell you about Madam Foveaux's gift and ask your advice on its use and how you feel about me using it to set up a shop in Melbourne. One of Madam Foveaux's favourite sayings was 'When men make money, their wives spend it!' If Melbourne is going to be as progressive and prosperous as you suggest, then perhaps providing a dress and millinery service for the ladies of Melbourne will be an opportunity for me to contribute to our future.

I trust that God will bless you and keep you for the next short weeks until we are together again,

from your loving fiancée, Izzy

28th April 1837
Port Phillip

My dear Izzy,

Your letter reached me this afternoon and I am replying immediately as I do not know when I will have another chance in the next few weeks. My position as Colonial Surgeon is taking up much of my time. There have been several accidental deaths which have required my attention and I have found many of the convicts affected by scurvy. I have written to Captain Lonsdale recommending an increase in their vegetable diet.

But life is not all work here. Recently we held the first race meeting on a beautiful course at the base of Batman's Hill. The first race of the day, the Town Plate, was won by John Batman's horse Miss Dagatella, while Johnny Fawkner was furious when his mare, Yarra Lass, was beaten soundly. Edward Umphelby, the publican, suffered the greatest loss when his mare Miss Fidgett broke her neck at the final jump in the steeplechase and I had to put the poor creature out of her misery with a rifle shot. My horse was narrowly beaten by that of Mr Brown in an exciting end to a day's racing. There are many sporting men here and all keen to wager a pound or two.

As to your suggestion of setting up a shop here in Melbourne, I am not entirely sure it would be a good idea. I expect that once we are married much of your time will be taken in making our home a comfortable place. As you say, there is no urgency in making this decision, so we should just leave the furniture where it is and make the decision later.

I hope that you are well and wait with anticipation for your arrival,

from your loving Bryn

~ ~ ~

Izzy folded the letter and slipped it under the ribbon that held Bryn's other letters. She was disappointed, not so much in the fact that he did not like the idea of a shop, but in that he did not seem to give it much thought. The day at the races seemed far more important to him. Was she foolish to think that she could contribute? That she could do something like this independently? Other women did. Madam Foveaux did. It was something she would have to think about. When she married Bryn, she would have to abide by his decisions and she accepted that. But living with Edith and Douglas had shown her that married people could come to important decisions together, that a wife's opinion could be taken seriously by her husband. Yes, she would trust that Bryn would be that sort of husband.

Chapter 9

Port Phillip 1837

The smell of boiling mutton assailed her nostrils as Izzy stepped ashore from the *Lowestoft*, its rich pungency issuing from an open fire next to the wooden wharf. A woman bent low over the pot, her face hidden from view as she stirred, oblivious to the crowd. The noise and bustle and the tents dotted along the riverbank gave the appearance of a holiday place. Children skittered past, laughing and chasing each other, mothers were calling, men were shouting directions, men carrying timber on their shoulders, men hammering. Izzy saw the woman straighten her back as a worker approached and gave her a coin. She filled a bowl with the mutton and handed the bowl and spoon to him as she pocketed the coin and resumed her stirring.

Suddenly Bryn was beside Izzy, his eyes shaded by a broadbrimmed hat, his jacket buttoned against the April chill. He took both her hands and said, 'At last, at last you are here.' She had no chance to reply as he turned to greet Douglas and Edith who were making their way towards them. The children and the servants followed, eager to be on land again and anxious to explore the new settlement.

'There is not that much to see,' said Bryn. 'If we walk this way, we can avoid the muddiest patches.' There were certainly a lot of them; Edith, Douglas, Izzy, Fanny, Gussie and Marianne, Mrs Southey, Eliza and Nell with Bryn leading the way. The road was boggy after some recent rain and they stepped carefully. There were several mud huts lining the road with a few more substantial houses behind them, and on the rise of the hill, dominating the skyline stood a square two-storey building whose roof reminded Izzy of a pyramid in one of John's books. 'Johnny Fawkner's tavern,' said Bryn when Edith enquired. The gardens near the road were small and poor but as they progressed away from the wharf, they noticed the plots becoming larger and many people working to secure the last of the harvest. They passed a cart laden with corn cobs and pumpkins and Izzy looked immediately to the soil they had come from and saw that it was rich and dark. She pointed to it and Nell nodded and smiled.

The *Lowestoft* was to be their home for the next week or so until Douglas needed it to return to Launceston and transfer the five hundred head of sheep he had purchased. They could see it now being pulled a little further upstream where it would be secured and a wooden ramp erected so that they would have direct access to the shore. There were many such ships acting as temporary homes for families awaiting the land sales on June 1st, their masts forming a small forest along the river bank.

During the following days Douglas spent much of his time with Bryn, meeting other settlers and exploring the surrounding area with a view to selecting a site on which he would build their permanent home. The area to the north looked promising and he and Bryn and the surveyor John Wedge walked the selected area for days at a time and then spent the evenings perfecting the maps that John Wedge had sketched. When the claim was ready, Douglas relaxed and moved to the next step; erecting the canvasses for the family so that the *Lowestoft* was free to return to Launceston.

'Bryn has secured a suitable site on the curve of the river. It is a flat, open space, part of the Government Paddock, and there are one or two families there already, so you will not be alone.'

Edith wondered whether it might have been more sensible for the rest of them to remain in Launceston while Douglas and Bryn attended the land sales and began building some permanent structures. But it was too late to return; the Assistant Post Master had taken over Douglas' position and with it, the house. There was no going back. Douglas was determined to acquire land here, lots of land and she would support him. She would just have to make the best of it but she was concerned about the winter weather and Marianne already had a cough. 'Oh Douglas, I'm not sure that sleeping under canvas is good for the children. Is there any other arrangement we could possibly make?'

Douglas took her in his arms. 'I'm sorry,' he said. 'I'm sorry that you have to live this roughly, that things are so primitive here. You were meant for better than this. You were never meant to sleep under canvas and to eat outdoors like a tinker. But I promise you that it will only be for a few short weeks until I have secured the land and we can have our own home and not be dependent on anyone ever again. I know I can make this work. Will you be able to put up with these conditions for a little while longer?'

'Yes Douglas,' she said, the comfort of his arms and the strength of his confidence reassuring her. 'You know I would follow you to the ends of the earth.'

He kissed her tenderly. 'I know, and I promise it will be worth it.'

As Douglas walked the short distance to meet Bryn at Fawkner's Hotel, he wondered whether it may have been more sensible to leave the family comfortably in Launceston while he secured the land and began building. Certainly, it was not the best time of year to be in transition but the weather had been remarkably calm and moderate so far. Edith never complained about anything. She was always up for adventure, always encouraging him to pursue his dreams. He would talk to Bryn about it and see if there wasn't something better he could offer her.

~ ~ ~

Izzy and Edith stood outside Buckley's hut, the morning sun glinting on the river, the smell of fish cooking nearby. It was a small hut, the ground around the doorway had been swept clean and the one window had a neat red cloth pulled across it, giving it a cheerful look. Douglas puffed up, pushing the handcart filled with necessities as Buckley emerged from the open door.

'Welcome Mrs Hamilton, you and your children and of course, Miss Marchbank, are most welcome to have my hut for a few weeks.' He nodded to them and his enormous frame towered over them, his words slow and deliberate as though he had practised them. 'Can I help you with the cart, Mr Hamilton?'

As Buckley reached forward and shouldered one of the boxes, Izzy saw the muscles on his right arm quiver and his tattoo move. It was a mermaid, twitching and rippling along with a monkey, a sun and half-moon and several stars, she didn't have time to count them. His body was like the trunk of a large tree, straight and tall, nearly seven feet tall Bryn had told her, his hair and beard unkempt, but his demeanour was gentle and respectful and he was not frightening. Both Izzy and Edith were overawed by his presence, his physical characteristics only emphasising his recent past, the story of his history that Bryn had first related to them.

'Thank you, Mr Buckley. It is most kind of you to give up your dwelling for us,' said Edith, and indicating the swept path continued, 'and I see that you have gone to some effort to prepare for us.'

Buckley immediately looked wounded. 'I learned from the natives, Ma'am, that it is always good to keep your home clean. They are careful to always sweep.'

Edith realised she had offended him and immediately began repairing the damage. 'Quite so, Mr Buckley, I'm sure there are many in this settlement who could learn much from our sable cousins, especially about hygiene. The river seems to receive much abuse from the settlers.'

'Yes,' replied Buckley. His eyes regained their softness as he looked at Edith. 'Many of the fish have already gone. My native family no longer comes here.'

Douglas emerged, having placed the last things from the cart in the hut. He shook hands with Buckley and slipped some folded notes into his hand.

'Too much,' said Buckley, unfolding them, 'too much, Mr Hamilton.'

'No,' said Douglas, 'I appreciate your generosity and the inconvenience this will cause you. Where will you go?'

'I am used to the outdoor life, Mr Hamilton. But your lady and her young ones need shelter and if my poor hut can be of service then she is welcome. She is a gentlewoman and has an understanding heart.' He smiled and bowed to Edith in a formal gesture, swung his swag over his shoulder and marched erectly down the dusty road like the soldier he had once been. They watched him go in silence.

~ ~ ~

The hut proved to be a satisfactory solution. Izzy and Edith and the children spent their nights there, sleeping snugly in the small space, and their days at the campsite on the Government Paddock, where Mrs Southey, Eliza and Nell had set up a pleasant space for cooking and eating and the biggest tent made a comfortable day room. Eliza took the children to the river and played games with them along with the children of other settlers. It did not take Mrs Southey and Nell long to find the most reliable suppliers of food in the settlement, nor did it take long for the suppliers to recognise that Mr Hamilton's family could pay their way. There were plenty willing to sell freshly caught fish and ducks and to supplement their meals with fresh vegetables and bread. Every morning Nell would walk the short distance to the town and return laden with the produce that Mrs Southey had asked for.

Bryn was a constant visitor and Izzy looked forward to his cheerfulness. One day he borrowed Mr Fawkner's neat little gig and took Izzy and Edith on a jaunt to the Salt Water Creek to see his log cabin. It was ten miles through rough bushland, but a track was already evident and the drive was pleasant in the fine cool air. As they approached the clearing a native boy who had been sitting under a nearby tree jumped to attention and ran to greet them, his teeth white against his skin, his hair tousled and dirty, his body lithe inside the too big clothes. He ran along beside the gig laughing and shouting something incomprehensible until Bryn brought the gig to a halt. Then he ran back to where he had been sitting and returned immediately, with a dead snake stretched between his two hands, as wide as he could. His face was alive with pride as he offered it to Edith as she alighted from the gig. She froze when she saw it and let out a small squeal. The smile vanished from the boy's face and he looked at Bryn.

'It's all right, Tristan. Missus is not used to snakes that's all.' And then turning to Edith, Bryn said, 'He is my servant, though very unreliable, but he would like to cook it for you. Would you taste a little for him? It is quite good, perhaps like fowl or fish.'

'If you recommend it, Bryn, although I never expected I would eat such a thing. I wonder what Mrs Southey would make of it.'

Izzy had alighted from the gig and watched the snake in the boy's hands. Its deep brown skin shone lustrously, and its tan scales glistened in the morning light. She reached out to touch it and the boy stepped forward smiling and talking excitedly, his shyness giving way to her interest. The skin was cold and softer than she expected, the scales overlapping in perfect precision, the head lolling harmlessly in his hands.

They didn't eat the snake. Bryn spoke to him in a jumble of words and the boy laughed and disappeared into the bush taking the reptile with him, back to his own people Izzy guessed.

The day was cold and still, the smoke from the hut rising upwards in a single column against the solid, pale blue sky. Izzy sat alone on a log watching Bryn and Edith in the distance walking among the sheep. She listened to the silence of this place. Not silence exactly because there were occasional birds and in the distance was the low music of the sheep, like a line drawn far away. There was a deep stillness, a voicelessness to this place. Her life was full of voices but here there was room for other sounds, the buzzing of an insect, the beat of a passing bird's wing. She felt at peace but wondered what it would be like to live in a place like this, to live with all this silence. She was not sure and found herself shivering a little at the thought and she drew her shawl around her and walked towards the others, welcoming Bryn's voice as it dashed the silence, 'There you are Izzy, come and meet my woolly charges.'

~ ~ ~

A week before the land sales Bryn came unexpectedly to the Government Paddock with a visitor. Izzy and Nell were chipping logs for Mrs Southey's fire when they heard male voices approaching. Izzy recognised Bryn's voice but the other was deep and rounded and matched the stout body alighting from the fine black stallion.

130

'Izzy, look who is here. Someone you know well is to become another settler in Melbourne.'

Izzy craned to see who it was but there was no clue. He was young, maybe eighteen or twenty, corpulent and very well dressed and his whiskered face was full of recognition of her.

'Izzy,' he laughed, 'don't you know who I am? It's me, Charles. Charles Peabody.'

'Charles? Charles?' She could only think of the boy, snuggled with John, listening to stories, struggling over his letters. 'Oh Charles,' she said, 'you've grown up. You've changed.' She felt her voice choking with the joy of seeing him.

'I've certainly grown, as you can see, a little too much,' he laughed as he patted his belly, 'but you, you have changed little, I would have known you anywhere. And I hear you are to be Dr Carrick's wife. This is a wonderful day. And we are to be neighbours. I have come for the land auction next week and I mean to secure myself a block and build a house and settle down.'

While he was talking Edith had come out of the tent and Bryn introduced them and they sat in the warm winter sunshine and the talk continued. Izzy was full of questions, the questions that she had thought about writing to Mrs Peabody but never had the courage. She had questions about John. Where was he? Did he know why she had been sent away? What about the little ones; Mary and Thomas? All those questions came flooding back to her but now was not the time for them. She helped Mrs Southey prepare the tea and sat beside Edith as she poured it and listened to Charles talking about life in Sydney and how he had done well in business there, even though he was still so young. He had a head for land and had made some lucrative deals and that had prompted him to come to Melbourne for the great land auction. Edith listened too, and gradually edged the conversation towards more personal matters.

'And your parents, Charles, are they well? Douglas will be sorry that he missed you for he is very fond of his cousin Janet, but we are expecting him to return from Launceston next week with his purchase of sheep. Tell me about your parents.'

'Yes, by Jove, they are well. Although my father ages, he is still active in government service, having spent some months this year as Acting Governor of Van Diemen's Land after the departure of Sir George Arthur and before the arrival of Sir John Franklin. My mother keeps an even keel, she is the foundation rock of our family, and is now enjoying the fruits of her labour. Her children are grown, except for the youngest, and she is looking forward to being the matriarch with the promise of many grandchildren. William has found the ministry to be to his liking. He married a vicar's daughter last year and they have settled to raise a family. My brother John has lately returned from England where he studied the Law with great success. He was always the clever one in our family. Do you remember, Izzy, the stories he used to tell us?'

'Yes, of course I do. Is he well?'

'Yes, since he returned to Sydney he has been devoted to his work, and although my mother invites the best families to tea and picnics, John doesn't seem to be interested in any of their daughters. He has the looks and I daresay the girls are willing enough, but despite my mother's persistence, John shows no interest.' It was strange to think of John as a man, a grown-up brother, and Charles, a piece of her past, here sitting beside her.

'And Wesley? What of him?' Izzy was curious and forced her voice to be even, to disguise the anger and hate she still felt at the thought of him, even after so long.

'Ah, Wesley.' Charles inhaled deeply and shifted in his seat. 'Wesley is in India. My father secured a commission for him in the 51st, his own Regiment. It was all rather a rush.'

I wonder what that is about thought Izzy, but it was clear that Charles did not wish to expand on this topic with people he did not know, so she would have to wait for an opportunity when they were alone.

Charles kept them entertained for the next hour with talk and reminiscences and finally took his leave, accepting Edith's invitation to come to dinner on Sunday. He linked arms with Izzy and drew her close as they made their way towards the grazing horses, Bryn and Edith still talking where they sat.

'Wesley broke my mother's heart, Izzy.' He was speaking quietly although they were out of earshot of the others. She said nothing, unsure of what Charles knew about her departure from Sydney and what his feelings were, but he didn't seem to notice and continued. 'There was a scandal, a public scandal. The newspapers reported that he had attacked several young women in Sydney, some of them from respectable families and during the investigation, it was revealed that he had enormous gambling debts. My mother was distraught and my father, in order to salvage the family's name, arranged for him to leave with the 51st on their tour of India. My mother did not want to believe the allegations but the evidence was overwhelming. I think he is just a bad egg. He was always nasty when we were children, do you recall how he would tease?' They had reached the horses and Charles was rhythmically stroking his horse's mane.

'Yes, I do. He was unpleasant but your mother could never see it.' She paused, her fingers twisting the bonnet ribbons under her chin, and his silence encouraged her to confide in him. 'Did you know that is why I left Sydney?'

His hand stopped and he turned to face her. 'What? He attacked you too?'

'Yes'

'Why didn't you tell my parents?'

'I did, but they didn't believe me. Your mother accused

me of trying to seduce him. He was always so convincing and in your mother's eyes he could do no wrong.'

'I'm sorry, Izzy. I'm sorry that happened to you.' He seemed to have run out of words and there was silence between them, a comfortable, amiable silence.

'Well,' she sighed, 'it was three years ago now and since I left Sydney, I have never been so happy. Edith and Douglas have welcomed me and soon I will marry Dr Carrick and have my own family. The news you bring has given me some satisfaction in that he has been found out and now your mother knows the truth.'

'Can I apologise on her behalf? She is a proud woman, but if she was here, I know she would want to admit that she was wrong.'

'Yes, of course,' said Izzy. She knew that would never happen but it would make Charles feel better and she wanted to maintain his friendship. The other reason for Mrs Peabody's accusation had nothing to do with Wesley. Izzy was Rosita's daughter and Mrs Peabody transferred those words *reckless* and *wilful* from Rosita to Izzy without thought. Nothing would ever change that.

The others had joined them and Charles kissed Izzy in an affectionate, brotherly way and he and Bryn both raised their hats in farewell as the horses clip-clopped away towards the town.

~ ~ ~

The coming land auction had caused a great flurry of activity in Melbourne, with the surveyors working to finish measuring the blocks and teams of convicts brought in to remove the trees from what would become streets and thoroughfares. Finally, Surveyor Hoddle's plan was published and there was much discussion as to its merit and otherwise. That the streets were unusually wide was appreciated by the potential townsfolk, but it was noted by some that the grid bore no relationship to its surroundings, to the Yarra or the undulating landscape, to the swamp on the eastern side or the gully that ran a torrent after rain and now had the words Elizabeth Street etched over it.

June 1st dawned bright and clear, the light frost had dissipated and the settlement was alive with expectation as the crowd of about two hundred men gathered around the single large gum tree in the market area beside the river. Some had already begun drinking. Fools thought Bryn, today of all days is the day to keep a clear head if I am going to get one of the one hundred blocks on offer. He edged his way through the jostling crowd closer to the log on which Surveyor, now Auctioneer, Robert Hoddle stood. Bryn knew most of the settlers in Port Phillip, so he was surprised to see such a number of unfamiliar faces. He found himself standing beside a middle aged, slightly built man whose sandy hair and fair complexion were protected by a broad-brimmed hat. An outdoors man, who by the look of his plain but expensive clothes had done well. Bryn introduced himself and the Scots accent of the man's reply did not surprise him.

'Macalister, Lachlan Macalister,' he said shaking Bryn's hand, 'I arrived overland from Sydney yesterday and I am hoping to secure some town blocks here today. The country we came through will suit sheep very well.'

'Are you experienced in raising sheep, Mr Macalister?' asked Bryn.

'Yes, yes. My property at Camden adjoins Macarthur's. You have no doubt heard about the progress he and his sons have made in the development of the Merino in this colony.'

'Yes,' said Bryn. He was conscious that his eyebrows were raised in an expression of surprise. Macarthur's name was legendary in terms of sheep and the way in which Macalister spoke showed a personal relationship with the man.

'You know the family personally, Sir?'

'Yes, I am lucky enough to call his sons Edward and

James my friends. They have taught me much about sheep. And you, Dr Carrick? Have you an interest in sheep?'

'I was overseer for Joseph Gellibrand and brought two thousand head of sheep here with John Batman in '35. I have just sold his flock on behalf of his widow. Have you heard that Gellibrand disappeared?'

The crowd around them was becoming noisier and Macalister raised his voice in reply.

'Yes, bad business. Killed by the natives I believe. Were they taught a lesson?'

'I believe so. There has not been any trouble lately, though you can never tell.'

'That's right, laddie, never trust them. There is only one solution to the black problem; make sure they know who's boss. There's not too many left around Camden but on my property near Goulburn they occasionally cause trouble, stealing livestock, begging for flour. Come down heavy is my solution. Otherwise, they will never know who's boss.'

'You don't think they can be educated, Christianised to live in our society?'

'No, from what I can see they are savages, simple of mind and little more than animals. They don't use the land and they make trouble for those of us that can make it productive. Better off without them, we are. And it won't take them long to die out. They are weak, easily sickened.'

Bryn was about to ask about diseases when a sudden pistol shot split the air and the crowd was immediately stilled and silent. The voice of Robert Hoddle rang out across the crowd, welcoming them to the first land auction and introducing his assistant Horatio Cooper, Comptroller of Customs at Sydney, who was to act as clerk and receive the deposits at a makeshift table in his tent nearby. Hoddle proceeded to set out the rules of bidding, and it was not long before the auction began with Johnnie Fawkner buying the first two blocks on offer.

~ ~ ~

It was mid-afternoon by the time Bryn had waited in line outside the clerk's tent, paid his deposit, completed all the paperwork and been issued with his official Bill of Sale.

He could feel the paper folded neatly in his breast pocket as he hurried to the Government Paddock. He had resisted the invitation of Lachlan Macalister to join him in a celebratory drink at Fawkner's Hotel. Macalister had bought three blocks in Flinders Street facing the river but Bryn could not wait to share his news with Izzy. His step was so light that he was almost running. The land was his. The half-acre known as Block 12, Section 11 on the south-west corner of Bourke and Swanston Streets was his and he had the paper to prove it. Now they could make plans for their marriage. Now he could begin building their house.

She saw him coming and dropped her kindling axe and ran towards him, her hair escaping from her bonnet, her shawl trailing as she ran. Her eyes were fixed on him and she was on the verge of a smile, a smile which became a laugh that he released as he caught her up in his arms and swung her around. 'I have it, I have it,' he said breathlessly, 'at last we can make our plans and build our house.'

He brushed her lips with a light kiss and set her down and reached inside his jacket to retrieve the folded paper. He handed it to her and was suddenly still, serious. 'All I have is yours, Izzy. I love you and I want to be with you forever.'

'Oh Bryn, I feel the same. This is a wonderful day. We have waited long enough for this day. Can we go there now?' She indicated the paper. 'Can we see it now?'

'Yes, why not? Come and get your warmer cloak and we will tell Edith and Douglas the happy news before we go.'

Chapter 10

Melbourne 1837

It was during the spring when all of Melbourne seemed to be building and the air was full of optimism for the future, when Izzy and Bryn were at their happiest, that Edith realised she could not ignore the pain any longer. It had begun its spiral two years earlier, slowly gaining intensity, like a vine encircling and choking.

She spoke to no-one about it and prayed silently that it would go away, but Mrs Southey's old and experienced eyes saw. She warmed stones in the fire for her and when wrapped in cloths these provided a comfort, seemed to calm the long, probing fingers, those red-hot pokers stabbing her very core. But even Mrs Southey didn't realise the full extent of the pain. 'It's a woman's lot,' she would say, thinking it was simply due to the regular monthly issue.

It was easy for Edith to hide the pain. Izzy was spending most of her days with Bryn, watching the construction of their house in Bourke Street, scouring the increasing shops and stalls at the market place for furniture and homewares. Douglas was away at Box Hill for weeks at a time, caught up in the building of their own home and the care of the newly arrived sheep. When Eliza took the children for their lessons or to play, Edith would retire to the sofa in the day tent and rest, the warmth of the stones pervading her body, allowing her to relax and gain strength to live the rest of the day normally. In the winter an hour's rest in the late morning had given her the whole afternoon to live her normal life but now those pain free hours were becoming shorter.

Izzy was startled in the night by Edith's muffled cry. She could see her hunched form outlined in the gloom of Buckley's hut, the girls asleep beside her.

'Are you ill?' Izzy asked softly.

'No, I have some pain. It seems to be more severe tonight. It will subside. I'm sorry I disturbed you. No need to worry. Go back to sleep.'

But Izzy could hear the pain in those short bursts of words, words that gasped. She stood and felt her way towards Edith, stretching her hand out in front until it came to rest on Edith's forehead. It was like touching a cooking pot, hot and moist, as though an internal fire was producing heat and steam.

'Edith, you are ill. You have a fever. Let me help you.' Izzy returned to her bed and pulled the cover off her pillow and doused it with water from the jug by the door. She gently wiped Edith's face, feeling the cloth warming with the touch. More water, more soothing application, Izzy was thinking ahead. Should I leave her to get help? Not yet, perhaps she will sleep again, but what if she should pass into delirium, then I couldn't leave her, not with the girls asleep here. Izzy went to the door of the hut and looked out. It was dark, no moon, no sign of dawn, no movement. She would just have to wait it out, cool Edith's fever, hope that sleep would come to her. There was nothing she could do about the pain that seemed to come in waves, causing Edith to writhe and groan and clutch her stomach as though she could push it away, contain it somehow. Izzy thought about the birth of

Marianne and the agony Edith had endured to achieve that final joyful goal. If only this was the same. Izzy knew it wasn't. The darkness worked for both of them, hiding their faces; Edith's contorted in pain and Izzy's betraying her fear.

And as the night wore on Edith fell into an exhausted sleep. The fever seemed less severe but Izzy continued to apply the cool cloth. It seemed to soothe them both. It was something to do. Izzy looked outside many times as the night dragged on, always dark and silent, no movement, no people. She felt totally alone in the universe, the stars, small pinpricks of light offering no solace. She thought about shouting for help to bring someone running from the surrounding huts but she didn't want to alarm Edith. She had been sleeping now for several hours, so perhaps the worst had passed. The minutes and hours limped by and Izzy dozed fitfully.

At last she heard a horse slowly clip-clopping down the street and opened the door to see the first faint rays of dawn. She wrapped her shawl around her, and lighting the lamp, went outside to speak to the rider. He was a young man making an early start north to his brother's selection and yes, he knew Dr Carrick and yes, he would go that way and ask him to come to Buckley's hut to attend to Mrs Hamilton. Relief poured over Izzy as she watched him go. Bryn would come and everything would be right. He would know what to do and Edith would be herself again.

Izzy must have dozed again for suddenly there was knocking at the door and Bryn entered, putting his medical box on the table and taking off his overcoat as he listened to Izzy's account of the night.

'Has she been asleep very long?'

'I don't know. Yes, for some time now, I think. She was awake and in great pain for many hours. She had a fever and I tried to cool her. Will she be all right?'

'Yes. You did the right thing, though I wish you had sent for me earlier.'

'I couldn't. There was no-one to take a message to you and I couldn't leave her.' Izzy's voice was trembling.

'Of course, I see. You did the right thing. Now, I think it would be best if you roused the children and took them to the Government Paddock where Nell and the others can care for them, and then come straight back as I will need your help for I must perform some bloodletting to balance the humours in her body. Please bring clean bowls and towels with you, and water, clean fresh water.'

~ ~ ~

It was towards the end of the week that Bryn decided to send a message to Douglas in Box Hill. He had been visiting Edith twice and three times a day but could see no improvement. The usual practice of daily bloodletting seemed ineffective, 25 ounces, enough to fill a wine bottle; perhaps he should increase the amount. The pain seemed to be increasing and he was concerned that the increasing dosage of laudanum also seemed ineffective. He had physically examined Edith and detected a large mass deep in the abdomen, a tumour perhaps, but the pain that the examination occasioned prevented a more precise diagnosis. Douglas would have to know how serious his wife's condition was and so Bryn wrote to him and paid privately for a rider to take the message to Box Hill.

Douglas came immediately and took up Izzy's position by Edith's bedside. Buckley's hut had become a sickroom. The children had permanently relocated to the canvas accommodation at the Government Paddock in the care of Nell, Eliza and Mrs Southey and they were allowed to visit only for very short periods. Izzy had spent every waking moment attending to her friend and now she and Douglas took turns to share the vigil. But still there was no improvement. Mrs Southey made broths and poultices but nothing could bring comfort, not even her hot stones.

'Just take a little, Edith,' coaxed Izzy as she offered the spoonful of broth. 'It's Mrs Southey's best vegetable broth and will give you some strength.'

'No Izzy, I cannot.' Edith tensed as the wave of pain approached, her teeth clamped together and the beautiful mouth distorted as she struggled to smother the scream of agony. Izzy was now familiar with the pattern of pain; the long approach, the tensing build up, the fever pitch, the height of the pain and then the long slow withdrawal and then perhaps an hour's rest before the next cycle.

It was in the rest time that Edith took Izzy's hand and said, 'Thank you, Izzy, for all you are doing. We promised so many years ago to be sisters and you have been faithful to that promise, even to my deathbed.'

'No, this is not your deathbed, you will recover. You are young and strong and you will—'

'No Izzy, I think not. I can feel that the end will come soon for me, maybe tomorrow, maybe next week. You are my sister and I ask just one thing of you now, now while I am able to speak privately and coherently to you.'

She paused and wiped the tears away and took a deep breath. Izzy could feel their grip tightening and knew her own eyes were welling with tears.

'Make sure that Douglas and the girls are all right. Make sure that they know how much I loved them. How much they meant to me. How I loved them, Fanny and Gussie and Marianne, their little bodies coming from mine, their little faces smiling, laughing, crying. They are my blessing. They made my life complete.'

Izzy put her arms around Edith and they clung together for several minutes until Edith pushed her away to look into her eyes. Her voice was even and strong as though she had rehearsed this moment.

'And Douglas, my darling, gentle husband, make sure he is all right. He will be distraught; he will need your help. Promise me, my sister, promise me you will do this for me.'

Her grip was tight and her eyes burned forever into Izzy's memory.

'Yes, yes. Of course, I promise. You have been a sister and a mother and a friend to me and I will do anything for you. But please don't leave me. Get better. Stay with me, Edith. Oh, Edith stay with me.'

Edith relaxed and lay back on the pillow. She smiled thinly, her voice a whisper. 'Thank you, Izzy. I feel so much better now. We will see what the Lord has in store for me and I will accept it willingly. Bryn is doing all he can and I am grateful for his care. He is a good man, Izzy, and I know you will be happy with him.'

~ ~ ~

Three days later Edith asked to see the chaplain, Mr Grylls, and he gave her his blessing. Buckley's hut had become a focal point of the town as people stopped by with food or wildflowers or just a kindly word for the lovely Mrs Hamilton. Eliza brought the children in individually as Edith found it easier that way, Nell with her eyes swollen and red, waiting with the others outside. Douglas spent his days at Edith's bedside and Izzy took over during the night.

'Will nothing improve her situation?' Izzy sobbed as Bryn walked with her back to the Government Paddock in the early morning.

'I cannot see any solution. All we can do is keep her comfortable, keep the fever at bay and lessen the pain as much as we can.' His arms were around her as she buried her face in his shoulder.

'She thinks she will die. Will she die, Bryn? Tell me the truth. Will she die?'

'She may die for her body is weakening and the tumour is growing larger. You must prepare yourself, Izzy. It is a possibility that Edith may not be able to overcome this.'

'She is so good. Why would this happen to her? She never did a wrong thing.'

'There is nothing fair about sickness and death, Izzy. I know. I've seen it so many times. You have been a good friend to Edith and you will stand by her as she faces this.'

'I don't know if I am strong enough to help her.'

'Of course you are. Would you see her face it alone? Or would you leave Douglas to be her only mainstay? No Izzy, you will support them both and you will accept whatever comes. The children will need to have stability and love and Douglas will need you if the worst were to happen.'

'But Edith, Edith, I do not want to think about a future without her.'

'Do not upset yourself, Izzy. It may settle and she may return to some normality. For the moment we will do everything possible to make her comfortable and relieve her distress. We must present an optimistic face for both Edith and Douglas. Be strong, Izzy. This is what they both need now.'

But the light that was Edith flickered and could not be sustained no matter how strong Izzy tried to be. Finally, her pain was over and she was still.

~ ~ ~

Izzy could hear the children as she approached the river. She stood at the top of the rise and watched them as they played in the shallows, the towering gums casting their cool shadows, robbing the fierce December heat of some of its impact. They didn't notice her approach, so intent were they on their game. Eliza with her back to Izzy was watching them, vigilant from the tiny sandy beach. Nell was a little closer downstream, her basket on the bank overflowing with washed clothes. Izzy had come to call the children and Nell and Eliza home for luncheon. Every day she helped Mrs Southey prepare the midday meal and then went to call the children home. It was a routine that Izzy liked, one that was useful and kept her busy.

Today marked exactly one month since Edith's death and Izzy had woken with a sadness that she couldn't shake off throughout the long morning. Watching the children laughing and playing lifted her spirits a little, and she could almost feel Edith laughing with them. The breeze rustled the leaves and grass nearby and tossed Izzy's hair and she paused to listen, not to the breeze or the laughter, but to a voice that was growing stronger inside her. 'Let me go,' it said, 'let me go, for I live through them.'

Izzy clutched the trunk of a nearby tree to steady herself. Yes, it was definitely Edith's voice. Was she going mad, hearing voices? Hearing Edith's voice? Perhaps it was the sun or the walk to the river. But there it was again. 'Let me go, for I live through them.' The tears she had withheld all morning flowed uncontrollably as she sank onto the hard, dry ground. She was aware of nothing until a hand grasped her shoulder and shook her gently.

'Miss, Miss, what's wrong?' It was Nell, her hands cold and still wet from washing.

'Oh Nell, I'm sorry. I thought I heard Edith's voice.' Izzy paused, her chest heaving with her sobs. 'It's stopped now, but I'm sure it was Edith's voice. So strange, but it was so real, so close, so like Edith. And more than a voice, it was as if she was here, as if she was present, standing here with me, watching the children.'

Nell said nothing but helped Izzy to her feet.

'I must be going mad, Nell, hearing voices.' Izzy bent and used the hem of her petticoat to dry her eyes. 'But it was so real.'

'Was it frightening?' asked Nell.

'No, not at all, it was ... it was ... comforting. Yes, comforting, that's the word. It was as though she wanted to tell me something to comfort me.'

'And what did she say, Miss?'

'She said, "Let me go. Let me go, for I live through them."'
Izzy began to sob again, but Nell's hand was firm on her arm.

'Miss, Miss, listen to me. In Ireland, in my village of Bandon in Cork, that would be said to be an omen. It's an omen, Miss; a sign, a sign that you must listen to and obey. If you ignore it, you will always be unhappy and your life will come to naught.'

'Obey, what do you mean? How can I let her go? I miss her so much, I want her to come back, I am so wretched without her. And for a minute I felt her presence, just like it used to be.'

'You must let her go. That is what she wants. It means she wants you to live your own life. My granny would say that those words come from heaven. Mrs Hamilton is happy and she wants you to be happy. Sometimes messages come from the fiery depths and there is only despair for those left behind. But this message is from heaven. She is giving you permission to be happy again, to live your own life. That's what it means.'

'Do you think so, Nell? I can't imagine living happily ever again. I will think about what you say. Let me sit here a while in the cool. Can you and Eliza take the children home for luncheon? Mrs Southey is ready. I will stay a little while and come home later. I need some time to think on my own.'

~ ~ ~

It was six weeks later, on 15th January 1838, that Izzy and Bryn were married. They exchanged vows in front of Mr Grylls and a small gathering of Melbourne residents. It was a simple wedding. Izzy wore her best dress and Mr Grylls recorded their marriage in the register. Douglas and the whole family, including the servants, were there of course. Izzy gazed at the space beside Douglas that should have been Edith and she knew that Edith would be smiling on her today.

After the ceremony they walked to Fawkner's Hotel where Bryn had arranged refreshments for the group. Bryn engaged a fiddler, the only one in town, and they danced the afternoon away, with many people stopping by to wish Dr Carrick and his bride happiness in their future together. Bryn consumed much brandy during the long afternoon and when it was time to make their way to their newly completed home in Bourke Street he could hardly walk. Douglas brought his dray to the front of Fawkner's and they were farewelled with shouts and songs and a scattering of flowers.

The house had been finished for a week or so, and Izzy stood on the street looking at it, her home, as Douglas helped Bryn to open the door and took him inside and seated him in the parlour. She could hear Bryn singing as Douglas returned to bid her goodnight.

'Will you be all right, Izzy? He asked, his eyes shifting back to the parlour. 'He's had a fair amount to drink, more than he should have, and he may fall asleep. Not the most romantic of wedding nights.'

'Thank you, Douglas, I will manage. We will have many nights together, so there is plenty of time.' She pushed her disappointment down with a smile.

'He is a good man, and you have chosen well. I feel that my duty as your guardian ends this evening as you now belong to Bryn and you will have many long and happy years together.'

'Like you and Edith,' Izzy said, 'I will always treasure the time I spent with you both. It was the happiest of my life. You showed me how love can bring such happiness. I only hope that I can be such a wife as Edith was.'

'Yes,' said Douglas sadly, 'she was everything I ever wanted. I miss her terribly, but I must look to the future, to the future of our daughters.'

'When do you leave for Box Hill?' asked Izzy, knowing that the answer would be too soon for her.

'Next month. The house is almost complete and I would like to move while the weather is dry. Mrs Southey and Eliza and Nell will come with me to look after the children. The house is large enough for everyone. You and Bryn will have to visit when you can.'

'Thank you, Douglas, we certainly will do so. Now, goodnight, I should go in for I think Bryn has, indeed, fallen asleep.'

'Good night, Izzy. May God bless you.'

~ ~ ~

Izzy spent her wedding night alone. She lay on the linen she had so carefully sewn, so carefully spread on the bed upstairs just yesterday, when she was full of expectation as to what this night would bring. A warm breeze floated the curtain but the house remained still and silent for hours. It was first light when Bryn stumbled into the room, his hair dishevelled, his stubble rough on her cheek, his penetration efficient and short-lived. He rolled away to her side and slept again, the reek of stale brandy and cigars on his breath, the silence of the act deafening.

They had not yet employed any servants so the house was empty and private and quiet and it was nearly midday when he awoke, toileted and came downstairs to find Izzy sitting in the parlour. She was facing the window so he could not gauge her expression. Her embroidery lay on her lap untouched.

'Izzy, my darling, can you ever forgive me? I behaved abominably.' He knelt beside her chair and touched her arm.

She turned towards him, her pale skin contrasting with the red of her eyes, the harsh light from the window leaving no shadows.

'I didn't know it would be like that,' she stammered. He took her in his arms and held her close.

'It shouldn't have been like that. I'm sorry, I'm sorry,' was all he could say. 'I'll make it up to you, Izzy, please forgive me.'

Izzy was still. She was exhausted and had no more tears to shed. Yes, of course she would forgive him. What choice had she? As Douglas had said, she belonged to Bryn now.

'I didn't know what I was doing. It was the brandy.' He drew away from her and held her at arm's-length trying to look into her eyes, but she kept them downcast. 'I promise it will never happen again, Izzy. I will join the Temperance Society. I will make it up to you.'

'Thank you, Bryn.' She lay limp in his arms.

'You are exhausted. Let me take you upstairs. You should sleep and then you will feel better.'

He carried her upstairs and laid her on the bed, straightening the coverlet and pillows for her. Then he drew the shutters and immediately the room was darker and cooler. He kissed her on the forehead. 'Sleep, my darling and we will talk later.'

~ ~ ~

Bryn didn't join the Temperance Society, not at first anyway, but the disregard with which he had treated her on their wedding night became a faded memory. He was loving and attentive and their lovemaking was mutual and both of them looked forward to the intimacy it provided. In those early months Izzy understood why Edith was so happy, how wonderful it was to have your own home, to be respected as Mrs Carrick, to be in charge of servants, to have a generous husband who loved you.

Bryn worked long hours as he was juggling two roles; that of Colonial Surgeon attending to the convict gangs that had been brought in to clear the trees and build the streets of the new settlement, and also his private practice, a lucrative business as the settlement was attracting more and more settlers of a better class. He also had his own land at the Salt River, with sheep and horses, and although he had employed an overseer, he liked to check on it regularly, staying overnight. Izzy grew used to his being away as he sometimes rode miles to attend victims of accidents in the outlying settlements. She suspected that he enjoyed staying away, camping roughly with other men and drinking brandy without the restraints of home.

Far away in England it was early summer and the lovely young Princess Victoria, aged nineteen, became Queen, and began an era that would bear her name. In Melbourne, as winter blew in from the south, Izzy, also aged nineteen, began to feel unwell. Not sick exactly, but nauseous and tired. She noticed too, that her monthly issue stopped. She wished that she could ask Edith about it and she realised that she had no other women friends that she could call on for advice in these matters. But she did have a doctor for a husband so one night as they prepared for bed, Izzy told him of her problems.

His face lit up and he laughed and laughed. 'You're with child,' he said, embracing her and lifting her off the floor, 'we are going to have a baby. This is wonderful news, my darling.'

'Oh, a baby, of course, how foolish of me not to have known.' She felt the familiar flush rising up her neck to her cheeks.

'Foolish? No, never. Why should you know? You have never felt this before. You are young and inexperienced in these things.' He enfolded her in his arms and kissed the top of her head. 'My darling, this is wonderful. Thank you. I will look after you both. You will want for nothing.'

With some questioning Bryn calculated that the baby would probably be born in January. He explained much to Izzy about conception and the growth of the baby. She knew a little from her childhood nanny, Mrs Betts, but Bryn was both experienced in the practical aspects of childbirth and knowledgeable about the biological development of the unborn. She would be in good hands.

As Izzy grew bigger with child Bryn became more attentive to her, staying home as much as he could, buying gifts and furniture for the baby as more and more items became available in the markets of Melbourne. He insisted that she rest at regular intervals and taught her about the process of childbirth and what she would go through when her time came. It was true, she was young and inexperienced and grateful that he was so caring. She remembered the birth of Marianne and the pain that Edith endured and looked forward to January with a mixture of fear and excitement. This would be her baby. Boy or girl? Bryn said it didn't matter.

The labour was long and painful but Bryn was there throughout it all and Izzy knew that she was safe. With the last of her strength, she pushed the baby into the world. 'A girl!' shouted Bryn, his face elated. 'Izzy, we have a daughter.'

'Edith,' whispered Izzy, 'I want to call her Edith.'

Part 2
Mrs Carrick

Chapter 11

Melbourne 1839

Edith or Edie, as they called her, was an easy baby, nuzzling and sleeping, sleeping and nuzzling. Izzy wondered how she had ever lived without her, this tiny scrap who depended so entirely upon her. If she was awake Izzy cradled her, sang to her and played with her. If she was asleep Izzy gazed at her in wonder and thought about all the other mothers who had gone before her, thought about her own mother, Rosita, who had not lived to know this joy.

Perhaps it was because she was so besotted with Edie, so preoccupied with her new role, that Izzy did not mind Bryn spending less time at home. The township of Melbourne was growing rapidly and he was making many successful land deals. He spent much time at Fawkner's new Shakespeare's Inn meeting business partners and planning ventures for the future. He would come home late with the evidence of brandy on his breath. He would not go near Izzy but sleep in one of the back bedrooms.

About this time a small group of settlers, Bryn, Charles Peabody and Henry Batman among others, decided to form a club; the Melbourne Club. It was to be styled on the gentlemen's clubs of London and membership was to be restricted to the elite of the town. One of the prime purposes, they decided, would be to provide accommodation for members who came into Melbourne from the surrounding areas. It would also be an easy and convenient way for the gentlemen of Melbourne to meet, transact business and socialise with other men of their class. The first meeting was at Fawkner's new Shakespeare's Inn, a fine two-storey building that they had in mind to lease for the purpose, but the second was held at Bryn and Izzy's Bourke Street home with the aim of drawing up a list of potential members. A dozen or fifteen of the leading citizens were invited to attend and clearly Bryn was excited about the opportunity to impress them.

'It is important that we present ourselves well, for these are the most important men in Melbourne and I am transacting business deals with some of them. Will you help me make it a success, Izzy?'

'Of course, Bryn, what do you want me to do?'

'We will need to arrange for refreshments to be served after the meeting. I would like you to preside over that.'

'Yes, of course. You mean I will fill the role of hostess, making sure all the gentlemen are comfortable, with food and drink as they desire?'

'Yes, I know you will have to leave Edie with the nursemaid for the evening, but it is important that they see you, that they accept me as a stable member of this group with a wife and family and a home of my own.'

'I understand, Bryn. Will I be the only woman present?'

'Yes, of course, this is a gentlemen's club. All you really have to do is be present, and look your best of course. Gentlemen of every age are impressed by a pretty face and they are sure to be impressed by yours.'

'What about the refreshments? How will I do them beforehand?'

'No need to worry. I will have the refreshments brought

in from the Shakespeare and you can arrange them as you please. We can hire plenty of servants to help for the evening; you will not need to do anything other than welcome the gentlemen and keep an eye to their comfort.'

Izzy looked forward to the evening. She had not had a chance to wear any of her Launceston dresses over the last year of rough living. She chose the cream organza, which she managed to squeeze into, the evidence of her recent confinement hidden under its soft folds.

~ ~ ~

The evening was a huge success with the carriages coming and going in the driveway, the gentlemen with their expensive top hats and soft hands, every candle burning in Dr Carrick's fine townhouse. Izzy saw their eyebrows raised in approval when she was introduced, saw the long looks they gave her and saw how proud Bryn was of her, of the house, of his new status as part of this elite set. She was relieved to see Charles Peabody make his way towards her, kissing her in his clumsy, brotherly way and introducing her to several other young gentlemen. Among them was George Arden who had just begun the new newspaper, the *Gazette*, in opposition to Johnnie Fawkner's, *The Patriot*. It was while Izzy was making polite conversation with the Police Magistrate, Captain Lonsdale, that Charles returned with another young man. He was tall and wore the uniform of the 28th Foot Regiment, with its distinctive red jacket, cuffed with yellow.

'Mrs Carrick, Captain Lonsdale, may I present Lieutenant Chevalier.'

Izzy curtsied and extended her hand. The young soldier bowed from the waist.

'Madam, I am delighted to meet you. Sir, we have met before. I visited you officially when I arrived last week.'

'Yes, of course, Chevalier. You have taken charge of the iron gang, if my memory serves me correctly.'

'Indeed Sir, my regiment is tasked with an orderly clearing of the scrubland to the north of the settlement to build roads and bridges which will open up the interior. Madam, may I congratulate you on an excellent table. I am pleasantly surprised to find such refinement in this far-flung place.'

'Did you come from Sydney, Sir?' Izzy faced the young soldier as Captain Lonsdale's attention was taken by Charles, who had business on his mind.

'Yes, I was only there for a few weeks and I can assure you that your hospitality rivals the best that town has to offer.' He was smiling, his grey eyes dancing, and Izzy was not sure whether he was serious or not.

'Thank you, Sir, I trust that my husband and the members of the Melbourne Club will continue the tradition of fine hospitality, so that gentlemen of the Corps are always comfortable when they visit.'

'I am glad to say that I will be staying here for at least a year. Perhaps I will have the pleasure of meeting you on other social occasions. I hear that Melbourne is a lively town; there is to be a Racing Club and a Cricket Club set up soon. Your husband is a leader in society and apart from the good work he does in his profession, he seems to enjoy a very active social life.'

'Yes, he is keen to participate, although he is very busy and often away when injuries or accidents call him out of town.' His eyes never left her face.

'That must be hard for you, Mrs Carrick, being left alone, I mean.' He stumbled over the last part of the sentence.

'I have a small child, Lieutenant Chevalier, so my days are busy and fulfilled.'

'And your nights?' he whispered, then faltered, eyes downcast. She looked at him blankly and thought she had misheard. She gave him her hand and he kissed it as he stepped back quickly and took his leave. Charles was already introducing her to someone else.

She had heard but she was so shocked that it did not register for a moment. By the time the scarlet flush was rising up her neck, he was well away. She saw him take his leave of Bryn and stride through the front door, his back straight in his uniform, his figure slim. He moved quickly, his youth evident in his step, in his lithe body. Several other gentlemen were leaving too, so it was not awkward for Izzy to feign a headache and retire from the room. Bryn and half a dozen men would spend the next few hours drinking brandy in the parlour.

~ ~ ~

In the next few weeks Izzy found herself daydreaming about the young lieutenant, and the words he had so foolishly uttered. Each time her mind turned to him she would push the memory away and busy herself about some task. She did not see him in the town when she was walking, although sometimes she imagined what their conversation would be if they were to meet.

One morning just after the feast of Easter, Bryn came home unexpectedly from his shop in Queen Street. He slammed the door and Izzy could hear his voice raised to Mrs Stanbury, the housekeeper. Izzy hurried downstairs to find him red faced and shaking with rage.

'Bryn, what is wrong?' She ran towards him. 'Are you all right?'

'No, I'm not,' he shouted at her. 'It's Batman, he's gone over to Dr Cussen for care. Told me not to bother coming back, that the mercurial potion is ineffective and he is not going to pay me for the attention I have given him over the last six months. I'll have him in court if I have to, he owes me and I will be paid.'

'Is there any way you can reason with him?'

'Reason with him? What a ridiculous notion. Reason with him? The man is half mad with syphilis, that disease of decadence, and now he blames me for his suffering. I'll have him in court. I have right on my side. I'll go immediately to the Magistrate.'

With that he slammed the door and was gone. Izzy sank to sit on the bottom step. He was like a hurricane, noisy, swirling, uncontrolled, and now that he was gone, she listened to the quiet of the house and heard the thin mewling of Edie upstairs. She rose and went to attend to her.

The court case found in favour of Bryn and so his humour was restored. John Batman was becoming increasingly decrepit, his nose having been eaten away by the disease and his body crippled. He relied on his servants, Aboriginal men from Goulburn, to push him in a wicker basket. His wife had left him, leaving for England, his daughters were cared for by Mrs Cooke who ran a school for girls in Flinders Street and his finances were in turmoil. The man who once boasted that he was the biggest landowner in the world was reduced to a state of pathetic poverty. By the time he died Bryn was reconciled with him, having settled the debt by transfer of land into Bryn's name.

It was at Batman's funeral, on a blustery, cold day in early May 1839, that Izzy caught a glimpse of Lieutenant Chevalier. He and several fellow officers followed the casket up William Street to the cemetery on Flagstaff Hill. Behind them followed a crowd of sixty or seventy people, including notable members of the community who listened to the prayers read by Mr Grylls and saw the casket buried. The crowd jostled and moved and she lost sight of Bryn. After the burial Izzy was looking for Bryn in the crowd, her cloak and hood pulled against the cold, when Lieutenant Chevalier was suddenly in front of her.

'Mrs Carrick, we meet again.'

'Yes, Lieutenant, sadly the circumstances are not as pleasant as at our last meeting.'

'May God rest his soul. I hear he was a strong and vibrant man in his youth.'

'Yes, I believe so, my husband knew him well.' She paused and they both stood silently hemmed in by the crowd. He was very close to her; she could feel his nervousness. Slowly the crowd began thinning out, wandering in groups down towards the town. She wanted to stay there, so close to him. There was something about him drawing her close, it was as though there was a bond between them, something unspoken that she recognised; perhaps he was like herself. She didn't have time to think it through. Bryn would be waiting for her.

'Have you seen my husband?'

'Yes, he left with a group of men some time ago, as soon as Mr Grylls had finished the prayers.'

'Oh,' was all she could say.

'May I escort you home, Mrs Carrick?'

'Thank you, Lieutenant. That is kind of you.'

He took her elbow and guided her past the last of the crowd. She felt his hand on her arm; her heart was beating wildly. What foolishness is this, she thought. He is only doing what any gentleman would do in the circumstances. Bryn had obviously forgotten about her and the Lieutenant's good manners decreed that he should see her home safely. The feel of him walking beside her was so different to Bryn. Bryn walked quickly, his stocky frame just a head taller than Izzy herself, his face creased with years and rough living. Lieutenant Chevalier was languid in his movement, slow and deliberate as though he didn't want to arrive. He was tall and Izzy had a feeling of safety, of protection that she couldn't fathom. Even the wind seemed calmer. He talked of Sydney and his home in Kilkenny, Ireland, where his father was a minister. Too soon they arrived at the Bourke Street house and he took his leave of her.

That evening Bryn again shocked her. She was in the parlour with Edie when he burst in, his face dark and brooding.

'What is it, my dear?' she asked.

'What is it? You might well ask "What is it?" It is slanderous, that's what it is. I have just come from the Club where I heard that John Wood has been entertaining a group of rich young layabouts with stories of my wife on the arm of a soldier, in broad daylight as brazen as you like, like any young hussy.'

'Oh. No, no it wasn't like that. Lieutenant Chevalier simply escorted me home. You left without me. You left me alone. You had forgotten me as you went off with your business associates to the Club.'

Izzy could feel the tears and anger welling up inside her. She was determined not to weep, but Edie felt the tension and let out a loud bawling cry. Izzy gathered her up and rocked her. Bryn was immediately silent and Izzy felt rather than saw him step towards her and put his arm around her.

'I'm sorry, Izzy. You are right. I did forget about you and I'm sorry. Please forgive me.'

'I need to put Edie to bed.'

'Will I see you later? I need to return to the Club as I think I have a buyer for the land in Collins Street. It will fetch a pretty penny and I shall spend it all on you to make up for my transgressions.' He kissed her neck but she could not relax. Her anger was quieter now but still burning.

'I am tired after a long day and I think I will sleep with Edie.'

~ ~ ~

The next morning Bryn was blustering around the morning room as he explained to Izzy what had happened at the Club last night.

'I met Wood as he was coming out of the Club last night and I asked him why it was that he was slandering my wife. He was drunk and his answer was that I should take better care of my pretty little wife or other people will, especially those in uniform. Then he reached forward and pulled my nose. The insult was too much for me, but I did not retaliate with violence. No, I will see him in court for my retribution. I will not have my name slandered by anyone, especially the likes of John Wood, and to think that I have known him so long. I think he is jealous of my success in life and means to make trouble for me. Well, he has met his match for I will not be taken as a fool by the likes of him. Court it shall be and I shall have satisfaction.'

He slammed the door and stormed down the front path, oblivious to Izzy's silence throughout this tirade. She ate silently, grateful that he had gone. She allowed herself a small moment to remember the feeling of excitement she had as she walked beside Lieutenant Chevalier. Then she pushed it away and went about her daily chores.

~ ~ ~

Two weeks later the matter was heard in court and Izzy was shocked to read in the morning paper that Lieutenant Chevalier had also pressed charges against Mr Wood.

15th May 1839

Today was a somewhat remarkable day in court on account of two trials which created quite a storm of sensation in the public mind. There were two well-known residents, sporting men and favourites of the people viz Dr Bryn Carrick and Mr John Wood. There was also (a not unusual occurrence) a lady in the case, from whom the medico considered himself justified in warning all trespassers, which so annoyed Mr Wood, that one day meeting Carrick in the street he not only gave him a sample of his tongue, but wrung the professional nose, and even resorted to rougher treatment. Doctors don't like to be 'nosed' in this way though some of them deserve it, and Carrick prescribed for his assailant by pulling of another kind, viz, bringing him before the Police Court, where he was sent to trial to the Sessions. Here he was convicted, fined £100, and imprisoned for a month. Mr Wood was also prosecuted on the same day for libelling Lieutenant Chevalier by writing a defamatory epistle to him. The proof of the handwriting broke down, so in this case the defendant scored a victory, as a partial set off to the other.

She had not seen Lieutenant Chevalier throughout this time and she wondered if she would ever see him again, so humiliating was all this public coverage of the issue. No, she decided, he would run a mile rather than see her again. Bryn, although satisfied with his court action, was brooding and short-tempered. It was towards the end of May that he was again involved in a public argument, this time with the young George Arden, publisher of the *Gazette*. Again, the argument took place at the Melbourne Club when both participants were charged with brandy and it ended when Bryn challenged his young rival to a duel, the usual alternative to an apology. It was the first duel in Melbourne and it took place on the racecourse at the base of Batman's Hill with the quietly spoken solicitor William Meek acting as Bryn's second. The coverage in the papers was again humiliating for Izzy, though Bryn was portrayed as the offended participant with Arden described by many as 'offensive' and 'quarrelsome'. No-one was injured and the matter finally blew over and Izzy breathed a sigh of relief when Bryn began to settle back to normal.

~ ~ ~

As the winter of 1839 approached Bryn and Izzy became lovers again. He seemed more settled and with the proceeds of the sale of several blocks he was generous in his gift buying. One morning as she entered the morning room, he folded his paper and said, 'At last, I have been waiting for you to come down.'

'Oh,' she said, 'I was attending to Edie. She was restless but is asleep again now.'

'Don't sit down,' he said, pushing his chair back and rising to his feet. 'I have something to show you. Come with me.' He took her hand and led her through the entrance and around the back of the house. Then he took from his pocket a blindfold. 'Put this on. I have a surprise for you.'

'What is it, Bryn?' she laughed.

'You'll see. Come over here. There, stand still, give me your hand.' Izzy could hear breathing, loud breathing and an animal smell as she touched soft hair.

'Oh, how beautiful,' Izzy exclaimed as she pulled the blindfold down and looked into the lovely dark eyes of a young mare. Honey coloured with a pale mane and tail, she was a young horse and in this town was worth a fortune. 'Oh Bryn, she is beautiful, thank you, she is beautiful.'

'And look, I have indulged and bought this stallion for myself.' They walked towards the stable and the large black horse looked up at them and whinnied, his hoof pawing the ground, anxious to escape the confines of the stable. A young man was brushing him.

'This is Paddy Lonegan, a groom. He arrived on the *David Clarke* last week with his parents and family from Scotland. He is to be a yard man with special care for the horses. Paddy, please saddle him as I need to go almost immediately.'

'They must have cost a fortune,' said Izzy.

'They did,' replied Bryn, 'but they are worth it. Yours has a quiet nature but we will take our time as I teach you to ride.'

'I can ride.' Izzy was stroking the fair mane and the mare turned her head towards the gentle touch. 'My father taught me, but I haven't done it for such a long time.'

'Well, let's take it slowly. In the meantime, you will have to name them both. Think about it.'

'No need to think. This is Honey and yours is Ajax.'

Bryn laughed out loud. 'Perfect!' he said. 'Perfect names. Paddy, saddle Ajax and I will be gone.'

Chapter 12

Melbourne 1839

She did not see Lieutenant Chevalier for the next few months and the memory of those words, his courteous attitude and his young face faded as her life spiralled with activity. She was delighted to find that Genevieve and Julianne Hardwick had come to Melbourne and their parents had bought a large house in Collins Street, not far from Izzy. There were afternoon teas and picnics and Izzy began to enjoy a social life of her own. The Hardwick girls twitted about the eligible young men in Melbourne, and introduced Izzy to other young women, some of them with small children which meant that Izzy was able to seek advice whenever necessary.

Izzy began to enjoy the friendship of women again, and although no-one could ever replace Edith in her love, one new friend, Harriet Weston, became especially close. Harriet was companion to Mrs Fawkner and was quietly spoken and gentle, with auburn hair and hazel eyes. She had come to Melbourne alone in the hope of setting up a school, but so far was not able to afford the premises, and so contented herself in keeping Mrs Fawkner company. She was well educated and spoke easily of history and literature and Izzy enjoyed her company immensely. Harriet loved Edie and sang to her and told her stories. She and Izzy became firm friends and it was Harriet who first heard the news that Izzy was to have another child.

'That is wonderful, Izzy. I am so happy for you. Is Dr Carrick pleased?'

'I have not told him yet as he has been away at his cabin at Salt River for three weeks. He sent a message to say that he would be home on Tuesday, so I will tell him then.'

'Are you pleased?' Harriet asked directly.

'Yes, of course I am. A little play friend for Edie. How could I not be pleased?'

Harriet nodded and smiled. 'Let's walk to the river,' she said. Harriet, like Edith, was able to judge when silence was preferable, and Izzy loved her more for that. One day, Izzy thought, she would truly confide in Harriet, tell her about Lieutenant Chevalier's attentions, but not yet.

~ ~ ~

It was some weeks later when Bryn was pushing Edie on the toy horse in the garden, with Izzy watching from the window and catching her breath at every upward swing, when the leaves were ready to fall from the young peach trees in the front garden, that Charles arrived unexpectedly. He was out of breath, hurrying his portly frame through the gate, lifting his hat to nine-month-old Edie, greeting Bryn with his usual good humour and deference. He had come from his property at Maribyrnong for the livestock sales and planned to stay a few days at the Melbourne Club, and perhaps catch up with Izzy and Bryn and the family. Bryn clapped him on the back and called him 'old chap' and invited him into the parlour. Izzy knew that meant brandy, so she hurried downstairs and called for tea as she passed the kitchen. Edie was passed to the nursemaid and Bryn suddenly found he had work to do, leaving Izzy with the teacups and Charles in the parlour.

'So, is it only the livestock sales that have brought you to town, Charles?'

'No. You see through me, Izzy. You know me too well. I am lonely living on my own and I have come to town for the company it brings.'

'Do you mean female company?' she persisted.

'Oh no, women make me nervous.'

'Really? I never thought that, Charles. You are such a man of the world, I can't believe that we women, harmless creatures that we are, innocents who know nothing of the world, would have such an effect on you.'

'Well, you don't have that effect on me because, well, you are more like a sister, more like family. I never think of you as a woman. I mean as a woman I might have to compete for, one that I might have to win over or impress. You are part of my life and I don't have to worry about what you think.'

'I'm pleased that you are comfortable and I too enjoy knowing that we have such a platonic, reliable friendship, one that is not clouded by the double meanings that romantic attractions bring, not complicated by feelings of inadequacy.'

'That's it, inadequacy! That is just how I feel when I am around women. I am stout and I do not cut such a fine figure on a horse or on the ballroom floor. I have not been endowed with great wit or with fine features. There is nothing about me that a woman would find attractive.'

'That's not true, Charles. There is much about you that women would admire. You are kind and generous and although Melbourne is becoming more civilised it is still a frontier town and those are still qualities that a woman will cling to. You come from a respectable family and you are a gentleman, not only by birth, but in manner.'

She stopped talking and observed him closely.

'But I wonder, is there a particular woman who has sparked these feelings of inadequacy?'

Charles lowered his head to avoid her gaze. He twisted his fingers as though he had been caught out. He stood and paced towards the window, his back to Izzy, his shoulders visibly drooping so that she knew his downcast expression without seeing it.

'There is someone,' she said. 'Who is it, Charles? Won't you tell me who it is?'

'I fear you will laugh at me for aspiring to such beauty and wit.'

'Who is it? Tell me, who is it?'

'It's Miss Weston, Harriet Weston. I meet her every time I visit the Fawkner residence and I cannot drive her from my mind. There I've said it. See you are laughing at me.'

'No, Charles, I'm smiling with great pleasure. Harriet is my dear friend. She is gentle and kind like you and yes, she is possessed of great beauty and wit, but that, surely is no barrier to true love?'

'The barrier is my fumbling inexperience, my inadequacy. I have no ready words of love, no compliments roll off my tongue, no smooth flattery comes to my mind when I am with her. I am all fluster and stutter. I am a portly, whiskery, young fool who has no chance of winning her.'

'Don't be so sure, Charles. What do you suppose women talk about when they are together?'

'I don't know. Dresses, parties, men?'

'Of course, men! And love. And the future and who they might want to spend the rest of their lives with. And it is not the false flatterer who wins their heart. There are ten men to every woman in Melbourne and I have learned that women need to be careful in their choice.'

'Exactly, that's what I mean. Why would a beautiful woman like Harriet Weston choose me, when there are so many others to choose from?'

'Give her a chance. She may have beauty and wit, but she

has no social standing to speak of, no family background, and you would offer her respectability and a secure future.'

He was silent as Izzy continued. 'Give her a small indication and see what happens. Do you want me to help? I can arrange for you to meet by chance, for whist perhaps in the afternoon, or a picnic by the river?'

'Yes, whist, indoors is better, I think. But do not tell her of my feelings. I want no sympathy from her. If there is no hope, I do not want to be a laughing-stock.'

'Oh Charles, you would never be that. Harriet is the kindest and most gentle person in the world. Just give her a chance. She too is reticent in matters of the heart and will need encouragement to show her true feelings. Be here next Saturday at four o'clock for whist. A party of eight can be easily arranged.'

Izzy embraced Charles and watched as he descended the steps of the veranda. She fancied that his gait was a little lighter, that he looked taller and slimmer than before. This will be interesting, she thought. Charles and Harriet a match? Who would have thought that bumbling, brotherly Charles would be smitten with love? Certainly, Harriet could do worse, with no connections to speak of. Her position as companion to Mrs Fawkner allowed her access to the better society of Melbourne, and as Charles said, she is much admired, but a match with Charles Peabody? Is it possible?

Izzy glanced at the clock in the hallway as she ran lightly up the stairs to collect her hat and cloak and gloves. Nearly two o'clock, she thought. Mrs Fawkner will take her nap at two o'clock and I can have Harriet to myself for an hour. Charles is naïve if he thinks I will not prepare Harriet for what is coming.

~ ~ ~

The following spring marked two years since Edith's death but Izzy's sorrow at the approaching anniversary was tempered by three celebrations. First, the marriage of Harriet and Charles brought great joy to her, especially knowing that she had been instrumental in bringing it about. The wedding was a simple affair with no family members present from either side. They set sail for Sydney shortly afterwards so that Harriet could meet Charles' family and were gone for several weeks.

Then the visit of the Hamilton family from Box Hill was a cause for great celebration. The girls had grown of course but they greeted Izzy with all the love and joy that she remembered. Mrs Southey was still with the family but had declined the invitation to travel, owing to her arthritis.

Nell, although free from her bondage, had chosen to stay with the family and greeted Izzy with great affection. She had become engaged and was to marry in the summer. It was Jacob Reardon, the silent yard man from Launceston, who had stolen her heart.

'Oh Nell, that is wonderful news, I am so happy for you.'

'He suits me, Miss. He don't say much, but he's steady as a rock. I've had enough upset in my life but my seven years of bondage is over now. We'll make a good go of it here in the colonies, Jacob and me.'

'What are your plans? Will you apply for farming land?'

'Not us, Miss, we're city folk. Jacob's a blacksmith by trade and there's plenty of work in Melbourne and we are both saving every penny so we can buy a house. But he has an eye for business and says there's money to be made in importing tools, good strong tools from Birmingham. He says a growing city needs workmen and workmen need tools.'

'So, you've no desire to return to Ireland?'

'Heavens no, Miss. Melbourne's the place for me. A nice simple house of my own, a good husband and family is what I want. You, Miss, you gave me the skills to plant and care for a garden to help feed a family, and I'll always thank you for that.'

'Thank you, Nell. Mrs Betts, my governess in Ireland

taught me, and I think she would be pleased that we have both been so successful in such a faraway place.'

Eliza still cared for the children and Douglas confided in Izzy that he had asked her to marry him. Her quiet ways and the stability that she offered the family suited him and she had accepted his offer. Izzy was surprised that she wasn't upset, that it didn't seem as though Eliza was taking Edith's place. Edith would want what was best for Douglas and the girls and Eliza was providing that. Edith was in the past and her memory would always be sacred to Douglas and their daughters. Izzy knew that Douglas' decision was the right one.

And the third cause for celebration was the birth of Helena, a small bundle who looked so like Izzy but was named for Bryn's mother. Bryn professed his love time and again during her confinement and spent the evening of her birth at the Melbourne Club in celebration.

Chapter 13

Melbourne 1840

The room was brightly lit, the polished floor reflecting the softness of the oil lamps. Izzy stared at the boards. The room was the pride of Melbourne and the reason this ball was possible. Suddenly her mind flooded with forgotten images of the ballroom at Winton, an enormous expanse of polished wood, the intricate pattern of the tiny, interconnecting pieces that formed it. She could smell of the polish that brought out its deep and lustrous shine. She saw the chandeliers, heavy with crystal and candles, and the gilded mirrors, reflecting the richness of the room. She gripped Bryn's arm to steady herself as she came back to reality. This floor was small and plain and sad.

But most of these people had never seen a ballroom like the Winton ballroom, and heaven knows her own memory of it was like a faded dream. Yes, embrace it, it was beautiful for what it represented, beautiful for what it offered – a ball, just like at home. Might it be that the dusty outpost of mud huts and flyblown meat, Bearbrass as they called it only five years ago, was finally a thing of the past? That the civilising, other worldly magic of music and formal dance was truly heralding a new beginning?

For weeks, all of Melbourne had talked of little else. The floor was finished and a ball would be held to welcome in the New Year of 1840; a new decade and with prosperity on the rise, the future was promising. The ball was a bright spot on a dull horizon, an opportunity to make and wear a new dress and yes, to dance. And looking around at the crowded ballroom, it was clear that the ladies of Melbourne had prepared well, resurrecting dresses long ago packed in sea trunks, airing, pressing or remaking them, adding some lace here, some embroidery there, critically appraising mirrored reflections after what had been for most, years since they had had this opportunity. There were precious few social occasions here, especially for women. The men had their Melbourne Club, which seemed to Izzy an excuse for drunken foolery, playing practical jokes on each other and on the more sober members of the settlement. Last week *The Patriot* reported that it was members of the Melbourne Club who had sawn through the veranda posts of Mr Cashmore's store and put fireworks under the door of Mrs Umphelby's Guest House. Bryn, although not participating in such frivolities, quietly smiled at the audacity of the younger members. She thought them fools.

She brushed off her gloom as her focus returned to the ballroom and the music as Bryn led her towards the floor. They had only danced together once, at their wedding and that had been a jig because the only musician available had been old Harry, who played the fiddle. The sound of the trumpet announced the beginning of the dancing and the violin, cello and other instruments swirled the dancers onto the floor, lifting their spirits with the waltz as the music soared and filled the room. Bryn bumbled and they stepped out the waltz carefully, like school children. Most of the others were doing the same, self-conscious with their lack of recent experience.

But time and refreshment eased the tension and the merry makers began to relax in their new entertainment.

The musicians had come from England recently and news of their arrival had fuelled speculation about the grandness of this occasion. They were known to be in great demand in the south of England, not in London of course, but they were well respected for their musical presentations in the grand houses of the southern counties. The Committee of Managers who were in charge of organising the New Year's Ball assured everyone that their talents were unsurpassed in the southern hemisphere.

The refreshments were served in the adjoining room. There was tea and coffee as well as biscuits and cake and stronger refreshments like wine and champagne. The tables were scattered with heavier meats, tongues, hams and fowls, all carved and tied prettily. The guests crowded around the tables jostling and laughing and devouring the delicious portions. Izzy's memory returned to Winton and the tables laden with the very best and most delicate of foods, and the dainty manners of the gentlemen as they served their ladies. It was too long ago and so far away and she had been only a child, peeking from behind the side door. She sighed and turned her attention to her friends Julianne and Genevieve Hardwick, who had just arrived. She was not really listening as she surveyed the room.

What she noticed first was the yellow of his cuff. His hand moved as he spoke to Charles and the yellow cuff seemed to be a flag, waving against the crimson of his uniform, against the music and movement of the dancing. Charles was craning his neck to listen and the young soldier had his head bent towards him. Suddenly they both threw their heads back and laughed at whatever joke they had shared. It was in that instant that Izzy caught his eye; his glance was like an arrow. So, when Charles led him through the crowd to where Izzy was standing, she was stunned, as though she had been shouting out for him to cross the floor and come to her. The women in her group held their fans against their faces, but Izzy forgot. She was bare, naked before him, her eyes staring, no words to say. Charles was introducing him to the ladies in the group, Izzy was conscious of their small fidgets and giggles.

'Lieutenant Chevalier, you know Mrs Carrick, I believe?'

'Mrs Carrick, it is my pleasure to meet you again.' His grey eyes held her gaze a fraction longer than expected. Charles introduced his wife Harriet, and Chevalier turned and extended his hand to her.

'Mrs Peabody, may I have the pleasure of this dance?'

Harriet glided beside him as he led her to the floor, her tall, graceful figure matching his, and they circled away but Izzy saw him glance back towards her, over Harriet's shoulder and knew that her own eyes had betrayed her.

Charles Peabody bowed in front of Izzy and swept her away to dance, his feet surprisingly light, given his bulky frame. Izzy relaxed in his brotherly presence and listened to his chatter as she followed his movements, but her mind was across the room where her friend Harriet danced. She knew he would dance with all the ladies, as was expected. She also knew that he too was longing for the few precious minutes that the waltz would provide for them.

~ ~ ~

The next morning Izzy awoke to an unsettling feeling in her stomach. Her fingers quivered as she pulled the shawl around her shoulders and she moved in a dream towards the nursery where she could hear Helena wailing, despite Mary Parkins' efforts to calm her with a lullaby. The servant patted the baby gently and handed her to Izzy.

'Little girl, baby, baby, stop your crying, Mama's here,' Izzy sang, thinking not of the words or even of this baby in her arms, but of the grey eyes that saw her soul as they turned and turned to the music on that polished floor last night. No-one else had noticed it, it was too close, too private to allow anyone else in, but to the two of them it was so obvious. No words were necessary. Only the feeling of his hand on her waist mattered, of being guided, completely at his command. It was just the one dance; he was too discreet to persist.

'I think it's her teeth, Ma'am. I've given her gums a little rub.'

'Thank you, Mary, I'll stay with her.'

The lullaby moved imperceptibly towards a waltz. Eyes closed, the baby embraced on her shoulder, Izzy retraced the steps, the flowing movement and the memory of the music engulfed her whole being. Anyone watching would see a young mother soothing a fractious infant, but in her mind, Izzy was immersed in the memory of his touch, in the very essence of him, so close to her, as close as the baby's warm, now sleeping body. How long she danced with the baby she could not say. A noise made her stop. Bryn stood in the open doorway, one hand on the doorknob, his hat and cane in the other.

'I'm going now. Out to Salt River – there's been an accident with a bullock cart.'

'Oh, yes.' Izzy immediately focused on his face. 'Will I expect you home at midday for dinner?'

'No. Don't rely on me to be here. Mrs Stanbury has packed a basket. Who knows what I will find when I get there? It was quite serious I believe.'

He moved forward and gently stroked Helena's dark curls.

'Her cheeks are flushed,' he murmured. 'Is she teething?'

'Yes, I think so. She's been upset. I was just dancing her to sleep.'

'You do it so well.' His eyes were alight with the memory of last night. 'Your gown turned all the heads there. I was the envy of Port Phillip, my love.'

He kissed her on the forehead and then kissed Helena in the same way. He closed the door and Izzy put the sleeping child in her cradle. It's strange, she thought, how a mind can have two lives; one that others see and one that is secret. I should forget last night and not entertain thoughts of him. And then a creeping doubt wormed in; perhaps she was mistaken. Perhaps she had misread his good manners. But his eyes, she thought, the look of him. I'm not mistaken. I saw the way he looked at me.

Mary Parkins lumbered quietly into the room. Her soft bulk filled the doorway and her big moon face softened as she saw that Helena was sleeping peacefully.

'I'll just collect these soiled things and wash them, Ma'am. I'll listen out for her if you want to attend to your morning dressing.'

'Thank you, Mary. Can you bring Edie up? I haven't seen her this morning. She wanted me to tell her about the ball. Are you quite well, Mary? You look a little tired today.'

'Thank you, Ma'am, but I am well. There is nothing to worry about with me, Ma'am. I will bring little Miss Edie up when you are dressed.'

~ ~ ~

The house stood on the south-west corner of Bourke and Swanston Streets. It was large by Melbourne standards and being situated away from the noise and activity of the river it had a quiet, homely feeling. There were three bedrooms upstairs, and a drawing room, dining room and entrance room downstairs. The kitchen and servants' quarters were housed in a separate building at the back, along with a large storage shed for the carriage and other outside equipment and of course the stables for their two much envied horses, Ajax and Honey. Every time Bryn and the servants used those names Izzy felt young again, wrapped in her father's arms on top of the mighty Ajax as they led Honey home from the market.

Bryn had bought the horses at an exorbitant price from Mr Kirk through his expanding business, Kirk's Melbourne

Horse and Carriage Bazaar at the western end of Bourke Street. The business was a sign that Melbourne was on the rise and Mr Kirk saw the potential and could charge what he pleased. At Kirk's there were harness rooms and haylofts and granaries and the men he employed, mainly rural Irish workers, excelled as farriers, saddlers and grooms. To have such skilled tradesman was a luxury Melbourne had not known until now. He had even built a 'bull ring' for unbroken horses. There had been a welcome influx of new horses from Van Diemen's Land and the residents of Melbourne were beginning to grow used again to the forgotten luxury of travel by carriage or on horseback.

Izzy was dressed in her plain, green house dress when Edie slid silently into the bedroom. Mary Parkins fussed a little before leaving mother and daughter alone and Izzy sat on the dresser stool and held her arms open for Edie to clamber up onto her lap.

'Was it beautiful, Mama? Was Mr La Trobe there? What did Mrs La Trobe wear? I think you must have been the most beautiful one there in your new ball gown. You and Papa looked like a Prince and Princess when you were leaving.'

And so, Izzy spent the next hour or so recounting the detail of the evening to her three-year-old daughter. The food, the lights, the dresses, the floor were all easy to describe, but how do you describe the music of the ballroom to a child who has only heard the pianoforte and the accordion?

~ ~ ~

Later in the morning and holding Edie's hand, Izzy left the house for her morning walk. It would be reasonable to walk west towards Kirk's as Edie loved to see the horses, but Izzy immediately dismissed the idea as she would have to pass the Bourke Street Barracks. That would be unwise. So, she turned into Swanston Street and walked towards the river.

Even though it was not yet noon, the January sun shone fiercely. Izzy adjusted their broadbrimmed bonnets to protect their faces.

Catherine Kennedy, a young housemaid, accompanied them, pushing the baby carriage with Helena tucked up inside. Mary Parkins did most of the nursery work, and Izzy always found her gentle with the children and thorough in her duties but she was not able to walk very far because of her great weight. Catherine was young and strong enough to push a baby carriage safely along the potted and rough tracks that were the Melbourne streets of 1840. Tree stumps and pot holes littered the road but the chief danger was broken glass; green shards from the champagne auction lunches that were a feature of Melbourne life, pierced through the dust or wedged dangerously in the dried mud. Bryn insisted that Edie and Izzy always wore sturdy boots on leaving the house, having the best sent from London. Dogs were another danger, dozens of feral animals roaming the streets, some of them snarling and aggressive and all of them riddled with disease and ticks and fleas. Catherine was a match for them though. She carried a stout stick and would shout and wave it at them if they came near.

And that's exactly what she was doing when Izzy's heart stopped as a group of red-coated soldiers rounded the distant corner, marching towards the convict compound on the outskirts of the settlement. She knew it was him leading them, mounted on the only horse, long before she could distinguish his features. She saw him dig his heels into the horse's flanks and speed towards them. He pulled up just short of them as the dogs scattered in different directions and he jumped down in one fluid movement, taking his cap from his head and bowing shortly from the waist.

'Mrs Carrick, can I be of assistance to you? These wretched animals are a danger to the good people of Melbourne. I would like to rid the town of them.'

Izzy again heard a faint Irish accent there, similar to Bryn's. As he waited for her reply, she sensed the same intensity she had felt last night. His eyes, narrow against the harsh light, were concentrated not just on her, but on her being, her very self. No-one had ever looked at her like that. Was it brazen, or pleading?

'Thank you, Lieutenant Chevalier, we are quite safe.' Izzy regained her composure and at the same time realised she sounded a little harsh, a little stiff. 'I thank you for your attention, and I agree that the dogs are a great nuisance.'

The six soldiers had caught up and were standing to attention a little way off, waiting for direction from him. Their boots, although clean, were worn and shabby.

'I will accompany you home. The men can continue without me.'

'No, really, Lieutenant Chevalier, there is no need. Here in Melbourne, we are used to such inconveniences and Catherine is ample protection for us. Are you becoming familiar with Melbourne Town, Lieutenant?'

'Yes, I see much of it in the supervision of the iron gang, the worst of it, that is. It is a pleasure to see the finer and more beautiful aspects of the town. I hope to make Melbourne my home.'

There was silence between them then and to Izzy it seemed they were both considering the meaning of this statement. The horse pawed the ground and Izzy roused herself, conscious that Catherine was present and that holding his gaze any longer would be unnatural and the situation might become gossip among the servants.

'Thank you again, Lieutenant Chevalier. Your concern is appreciated, but we must be on our way. The sun is too strong for the children. We are going to the river where it is shady and the breeze is pleasant.'

'My pleasure, Madam, I hope to be of service to you another time.'

He seemed to understand the importance of finishing this

scene with propriety and took his leave of her, remounted his horse and lifting his cap to her, he moved off with the soldiers. The women watched him go and as they made their way to the river, each, servant and mistress, had the same thought; that his back was straight as he sat in the saddle and his bearing was that of a gentleman. Neither noticed his hand move over his breast pocket, checking the safety of its contents.

~ ~ ~

Two days later Izzy took out her ball dress and laid it on the bed. The deep rose-pink satin shone as she moved it, catching even the slightest light. The tiny pink roses embroidered on the bodice had taken her weeks, so exquisite were they. And still in the glass dish on the dresser were the twelve matching roses she had made for her hair. They were tiny and discreet but they complimented her abundant coal black hair and fair skin perfectly and she knew they would be the only ones in Melbourne. She also knew that others would think they had been ordered from London. Let them think it, the gossips of this colony, delighting in finding out and spreading the worst about a person. She counted eleven and set about looking for the twelfth, but it was not on the floor or on the dresser, she must have lost it at the ball or perhaps on the way. She would look in the carriage later.

Izzy glanced from her bedroom window and saw the now familiar figure of Lieutenant Chevalier leading his soldiers up Bourke Street. It was odd because a shorter route to the convict compound would be to turn left at Russell Street. There must be a reason, she thought, and she lingered by the window to watch him pass. As he drew level with the house and prepared to turn into Swanston Street his eyes lifted to her window and he looked directly at her. She drew back immediately and leaned against the wall, her face flushing as a wave of heat spread through her body. This cannot continue she told herself, I cannot entertain thoughts of him. I am a wife and mother and he is dallying with my feelings.

But continue she did. Each morning after Bryn left the house, she would find an excuse to be near her window as he rode by, and each morning he looked up in search of her. After a week she showed herself and his smile was her reward, or her punishment, she could not decide. I am weak was all she could think.

Chapter 14

Melbourne 1840

Izzy lived the week waiting for Sunday when she could attend church, with or without Bryn, knowing that behind her Lieutenant Chevalier watched her every movement. Each week as she left the little wooden structure that was St James, she was rewarded with the touch of his hand as he greeted her. The touch and his eyes conveyed the certain knowledge that he would rather linger with her than move on to others, as manners dictated.

The weeks passed in regular routine, punctuated by Bryn's movements in and out of the house. Izzy sensed that he was becoming disheartened with life in Melbourne and when he mentioned once or twice that he would like to return to Ireland, she noted it but made no comment and hoped that it would pass. He was often away for days at a time, camped in some mud hut, talking to the growing number of settlers about sheep and crops and attending to medical issues and then drinking himself to sleep at night.

Charles Peabody had told Izzy that Bryn was at ease too with the natives, squatting in the dirt with them and drawing on the ground, and warning them not to drink the settlers' potion, that it would make them sick. Izzy shivered at the thought. Only sometimes would the Aborigines venture into the town, their ghostly figures retracing their once familiar path to the river, their eyes wide with wonder and fear of the foreignness which had overcome it. Bryn always rode Ajax when he went out, the big, black stallion pawing at the ground, anxious to be out of the confines of the stable. They were well matched.

Izzy was growing used to the half-life she lived with him, but she felt a secret, deep resentment inside her when she thought about Bryn. Increasingly, sick convicts, injured farm workers, serving girls in labour, old drunks and of course, the wealthier residents of Melbourne all came before Izzy. And when he returned, he would spend his time at the Melbourne Club or at the new Racing Club, arriving home drunk in the early hours, expecting to be welcomed into her bed. She had never admitted her feeling of neglect, not even to herself, but that changed when the *Glen Huntly* sailed into Port Phillip on 24th April 1840, with 157 poor Scottish migrants on board and flying the yellow flag of typhus.

~ ~ ~

The arrival of the stricken ship required the Superintendent of the Port Phillip district to appoint a medical man to take charge of it. Charles La Trobe, gentleman, fine featured and charming, approached the idea of recruiting Dr Carrick with caution. He knew Carrick was respected as an original settler and the first doctor in Melbourne, arriving with Batman in 1835. But he had heard that the young doctor was a drinker and a gamester and that there was a whiff of scandal about his dismissal from government service in Van Diemen's Land. At the same time, any intercourse he had had with Carrick had shown him to be reliable and he had a reputation as a doctor of solid training and one who showed great care for his patients. He was also renowned as an outdoors man, one who would travel long distances and was not fussy about the accommodation available.

La Trobe drew his chair a little closer to the fire, his thin feet cold in his dainty shoes, his bony shoulders hunched over the desk. So, in considering a medical man to set up and take charge of a quarantine station on windy Point Ormond, Carrick seemed ideal. He needed someone who could leave immediately and could work in the harsh conditions for the several months that it would take to make sure the disease was under control. Yes, Carrick was his man.

~ ~ ~

It was shortly after Bryn left for Port Ormond that Izzy was shaken out of her preoccupation with her secret life. The new servant, Mary Parkins, seemed unwell, and certainly her weight seemed to be increasing, but it didn't occur to Izzy that she was pregnant. Everything about Mary was big and round and matched her body and Izzy had simply accepted her when Bryn hired her from the deck of the *William Metcalf* when it had docked in Port Phillip four months ago. Mary said she had worked at a large house, Mayfield Hall, near Cork and obviously she was very experienced in laundry and cleaning. Izzy was pleased to have her. Not only was she gentle with the children but she had an exceptionally clear singing voice and often Izzy would stop and listen as Mary worked alone in the scullery or the laundry, the notes piercing and true. Even Bryn commented on how pleasant it was to have Mary Parkins in the house.

So, when a newborn baby was found dead in the back garden, Izzy was distraught. Jane Stanbury, the cook, had discovered the little body half buried and in a terrible state as the feral dogs of the neighbourhood had found it before her. She sent for Izzy and at the same time sent Catherine

Kennedy to the army barracks for help. Izzy was in a state of confusion trying to think how this could be when Captain Scott from the barracks arrived to take charge of the situation. Behind him was Lieutenant Chevalier but Izzy could not look at him. It was Jane Stanbury who took Izzy aside and said, 'Mrs Carrick, I suspect that Mary Parkins knows about this.'

'Mary?'

'Yes, I have had my suspicions for some time.'

'Mary Parkins? Do you mean she has given birth to this child?'

'Yes, and perhaps caused its death.'

'What? Why would she do that? Where is Mary now?'

Catherine Kennedy was listening, her face streaming with tears. She blurted out, 'I seen her, Ma'am, she's in the stable. I seen her go in there about an hour ago. Shall I fetch her, Ma'am?'

Izzy felt herself overwhelmed and suddenly Lieutenant Chevalier was beside her, offering her his arm as she felt her knees weaken. He spoke to Jane Stanbury.

'Mrs Carrick has had a shock. Take her into the house and settle her while we deal with this. Make her some tea. Make sure she is comfortable. We will speak to Mary Parkins.'

Later that day Captain Scott came to the house to report on the events. Mary Parkins had indeed been charged with the murder of her own child and she was presently in the watch house. Izzy had been pacing the floor all day trying to make sense of what had happened.

'Thank you for your kindness, Captain Scott, this is a terrible business.'

'I agree Mrs Carrick, and with your husband at Point Ormond, it is more difficult for you to deal with it. The woman is saying that the child was born dead, and of course with the, ahem, damage to the body done by the dogs, it's difficult to tell.'

'I wonder, would it be possible for me to speak to Mary?'

'I wouldn't recommend it, Madam; the watch house is no place for a lady, and I cannot see that it would do any good.'

'I think it would do Mary Parkins a lot of good to see a friendly face, and I feel responsible. After all, she is in my employ and I want to help her, even if she is guilty of such a terrible sin. If she is not guilty, then I should help her even more so.'

'I feel that your husband would not approve, Madam.'

'My husband is not here Captain, and I will take full responsibility for my own actions in this case.'

'I see that you are determined. Tomorrow Lieutenant Chevalier will accompany you to the watch house, and stay with you the entire time. Will that be satisfactory? Can you be ready at nine o'clock?'

'Thank you, Captain Scott, that will be perfectly satisfactory. May I take some clean clothes for her and some food?'

'Yes, Mrs Carrick, of course. Your generosity is a credit to you. Not many ladies would be so kind to their servants. Good afternoon to you, Mrs Carrick.'

~ ~ ~

Izzy slept badly, her mind going over the events of the day, her body nauseous with horror at the crime she felt she could have prevented had she been a little more observant, a little less selfish. She was up at first light and ready when Paddy Lonegan, their yard man, brought the carriage to the front door. Lieutenant Chevalier was mounted beside the carriage but Izzy did not acknowledge him, swallowing her guilt that she derived pleasure from the fact that he was there. No, she must keep Mary as the focus and her own brave words to Captain Scott about taking responsibility for her own actions were ringing in her ears. Paddy gently tapped Honey and clicked with his tongue and the little company moved off down Swanston Street towards the watch house.

It was a small, dismal place. Mary was hunched on the floor in the corner in dull silence, her filthy dress caught up behind her, exposing her boots and lower legs. There was straw on the floor and Izzy noted with relief that it was clean, but still there was a smell of rotting and decay in the tiny enclosure. Lieutenant Chevalier had insisted that the four other women who occupied this space be taken out while Mrs Carrick was there. He was met with their curses in language which he didn't even hear in the barracks. He insisted that a chair be brought for Mrs Carrick and when it was slow in coming, his raised voice could be heard in the next room. Eventually the chair was brought, the women quieted outside and Lieutenant Chevalier stood at attention in the corner.

'You shouldn't have come, Ma'am. This is no place for a lady.'

'Mary, tell me what happened.'

'The baby was dead, Ma'am. He didn't make no noise or nothing. I went to the stable about midnight because I had such terrible pains, I thought my time must 'ave come. It didn't take very long. He just lay there, on the hard ground, not moving, not crying, not even breathing, and then I realised 'e was dead.'

Mary began to cry in great sobs, her mountainous body heaving with each intake of breath. Izzy moved forward to comfort her and at the same time, felt rather than saw Lieutenant Chevalier move closer, his knee-high black boots beside her. The sobbing continued for some time and then it subsided and Mary seemed to deflate into herself. A puff and the noise was gone, just a quiet rasping breath as she cradled her head in her hands.

'Mary, tell me how it came about. Who is the man who is responsible for this?'

'There ain't no-one but me responsible for this, Ma'am. I

knew long ago that he wouldn't care, fool that I am. Geoffrey Sandeman was his name, for what it is worth, in his smart uniform, fumbling away behind the grain sheds down by the river in Cork. He knew nothing to start with. And pleasant it was for me, with the sun on my face and the pretty gifts he would bring me, just lying back, pretending that it was real. But when he said it was over and his regiment had been ordered to New South Wales, I felt wronged. And then I realised that there was a baby on the way so I signed up for the assisted passage to Port Phillip. I guess I still thought Geoffrey would want us, but why would he want a serving maid, and a fat one at that?'

'Mary, how did you manage on the voyage?'

'It was easy, Ma'am. Everyone was seasick, so I didn't stand out. And my voice was my trump card. Everyone loves a song, especially women far from home, so I would sing for them and they were kind to me. Most of them were respectable women, just poor and in need of a steady job and some kindness. I was lucky when we arrived at Port Phillip and Dr Carrick picked me because he came from Cork too.'

'But why didn't you tell us about your situation?'

'I was afraid, Ma'am, afraid that I would lose my job. There is not even a workhouse in this town. No hospital, nowhere for a girl to go. I was too frightened to get rid of it and I guessed it was too late anyway. I reckoned I would just have it quietly and then leave it at the church. Some kind person would have looked after it.'

'Oh, Mary, I'm sorry that I didn't even notice.'

'I was never so pleased to be fat. It was my only comfort, that no-one knew. Although I think Mrs Stanbury had her thoughts about me. But, but, I didn't kill him, Ma'am. He was dead when he arrived. I didn't kill him.'

'There, of course you didn't. Tell me what happened after he was born.'

'I wrapped him up and took him out to the garden and

dug among the leaves and dirt near the back fence. And then I put his little body in the hole and covered it up. Then I wanted to mark the spot, so I took a fence paling that was broken and I pushed it down on top of him. So I could see where he was, you know. So I could come and visit him.'

'And then you went back to the servants' quarters?'

'No, I slept in the stable for the rest of the night. Honey was warm and seemed to understand, so I stayed there with her until I heard the dogs barking and the ruckus that was caused by Mrs Stanbury this morning. I'm sorry, Ma'am, I've made a terrible mess for you.'

'Thank you for telling me, Mary. We will see what can be done. Lieutenant Chevalier, I think it is time to go. Mary, be strong. I will be back again to see you.'

They returned in silence to the Bourke Street house and Izzy spent the day alone in deep thought. Captain Scott called the following morning to tell Izzy that the local magistrate had decided that infanticide was too serious a crime for the local court and that the case had been referred to the Supreme Court in Sydney and that Mary Parkins was already under guarded transfer.

'Infanticide? So, it seems that she has already been declared guilty.'

'Mrs Carrick, I do not wish to alarm you, but there was a definite stab wound on the child's chest.'

'Captain Scott, could that wound have been the result of the fence paling that Mary Parkins pushed into the ground to mark the place of burial? So she could visit her child's grave secretly?'

'I am sorry, Mrs Carrick. The body has been examined and a statement taken from Mary Parkins and the matter is out of my hands.'

Izzy was left bereft. Nothing she could do would ease the pain she felt for Mary. She knew that most of what she felt was guilt. There was the guilt that she hadn't noticed Mary's predicament, but mostly there was guilt that her life and her babies were whole and healthy and the difference was simply the matter of who she was and who Mary Parkins was.

She stayed indoors for days with the curtains drawn, never looking for Lieutenant Chevalier. She felt sick with the knowledge of how much she missed him when she should have been missing her husband. She realised with a shock that she hadn't missed Bryn at all and it occurred to her that with all his medical experience he too hadn't noticed Mary's condition. I cannot take refuge in that, she thought. He is so rarely here. She knew Bryn would be furious with the gossip that the incident had caused, and when Catherine showed her the detailed and gruesome newspaper articles, she was physically sick. Bryn's greatest fear was scandal and even a servant's indiscretions would infuriate him. He was going to reprimand her severely for her visit to the watch house, but at least Captain Scott was her witness that she only wanted the best for Mary.

Slowly her thoughts returned to Lieutenant Chevalier and a week after she had last seen him, she opened her bedroom curtains and waited for him to pass. She began to entertain thoughts of ways that they could meet. Nothing underhand of course, it would have to be in the company of others and carried out with propriety. But she did nothing. Then one afternoon Genevieve Hardwick called to tell her that her mother had organised a luncheon party for the following Saturday to bid farewell to the Reverend Grylls, who was to take up a senior appointment in Sydney. Reverend Grylls was the clergyman who officiated at the marriage of Izzy and Bryn, and was a well-known, if dour, member of early Melbourne society. The party would be held in the Hardwicks' garden and the children were welcome to attend with their nurse. Izzy was sure that Lieutenant Chevalier would attend. He was so regular at church that Mrs Hardwick was sure to invite him, but she did not dare to risk confirming his presence with Genevieve.

Chapter 15

Melbourne 1840

He was there.

Izzy felt an overwhelming relief when she saw him shaking Reverend Grylls by the hand, smiling at Mrs Grylls and his eyes skimming the garden as he moved away from the elderly couple. He was coming towards her but he stopped at several groups along the way, delaying the pain or pleasure of their few minutes of conversation. Izzy was sitting on the veranda with Mrs Fawkner. The old lady was bowed and arthritic but she always greeted Izzy with affection, recognising her as one of the original settlers, like herself. Mr Fawkner's voice could be heard nearby, strident and ceaseless as he harangued a group about the disgraceful state of the Yarra River. But Mrs Fawkner's voice was soft as she spoke the words that were on every lip at the party.

'My dear, what a ghastly business you have suffered with your servant girl. The poor girl is one among many in this town. She was a victim of our society's lack of care for those less fortunate. I have been harassing Mr Fawkner to use his newspaper to institute a workhouse for those in this town who are unfortunate enough to need it. It's disgraceful.'

When Izzy did not reply Mrs Fawkner asked after the children and Dr Carrick.

'I hear he is doing wonderful work on Point Ormond,' she said. 'I have read two of his reports in *The Patriot* and it seems as though his system of the two camps, the sick camp and the healthy camp, is working, with the number of deaths decreasing rapidly. But you must miss him, my dear.'

Izzy was about to answer when Lieutenant Chevalier stepped lightly onto the veranda in front of them. He greeted Mrs Fawkner formally, bending low from the waist and taking her hand. Then he turned and addressed Izzy with the same formality. Mrs Fawkner's eyes were as bright as her greeting. 'My dear Lieutenant Chevalier, it is such a pleasure to see you here. Come, sit here next to Mrs Carrick and tell us all the gossip of the barracks. We poor ladies are never exposed to the fun you have down there. Tell us some stories, but only those you think suitable for us.'

They laughed at this and Izzy felt the lightness of the moment with a smile. Lieutenant Chevalier launched into an account of a young soldier who was recently lost in the bush, only to return half-starved and find that he was to be punished for his absence. Their three chairs were facing each other, and Mrs Fawkner's back was to the garden and the rest of the guests. Izzy and Lieutenant Chevalier had a clear view of the party and the activities in the garden. After two or three stories Mrs Fawkner's head began to nod and her eyes closed, but this was not obvious to anyone except her two companions and they remained safe against scandal because they were accompanied by a third person. Izzy realised that they would have some precious moments to speak. Lieutenant Chevalier's voice drifted off in mid-sentence and the distance between their bodies suddenly diminished. He looked at her and said softly, 'I am dying, Mrs Carrick. I cannot go on like this, seeing you and not knowing how you feel. Give me a small sign and I will be content.' His fingers traced the cane weaving of the chair.

'I cannot, I have a husband and family.'

'I know that it is impossible for us, but I sense that your heart is straining to be free. I watched your kindness pour out for that unfortunate woman, and yet no-one sees the angel that you are. Meet me somewhere while we have the chance, while your husband is away.'

'No, we must not be indiscreet.'

'Then let me come to your house late tonight. I will be discreet, no-one will know. I will come to your side door at midnight. I have examined your house and know that the side veranda is screened from the street and prying eyes. We can meet there safely.'

Izzy was silent, looking out across the crowded lawns, and her silence was her consent. Lieutenant Chevalier rose and bowed to her as he took his leave and mingled among the other guests. Izzy sat for a few minutes thinking about what was to come and then she rose and roused Mrs Fawkner gently and they continued their conversation.

~ ~ ~

Izzy wrapped her heaviest shawl around her and tiptoed downstairs. Catherine Kennedy was snoring in the nursery and her rhythmic breathing continued as Izzy reached the bottom step and made her way through the dining room and quietly unbolted the side veranda door. Bryn was the only one who ever used this entrance and he would leave his muddy boots there when he entered the house, rather than come through the front door. The servants had no reason to ever go there as they came and went through the back door. Lieutenant Chevalier, Francis, as she now thought of him, was right; it was a private place. The roof was low and the area was screened from the street with a lattice and climbing rose, although now it was May, the rose leaves were yellow and falling. There were two cane chairs but Izzy could not recall ever sitting there because it was on the cold side of the house and there were other, more pleasant places to sit in and around the garden. She looked out into the blackness but saw no-one. Perhaps he won't come, she thought. I wonder how long I should wait.

Suddenly he was there in front of her. He held out his hands and came towards her, enfolding her gently in his arms. He felt warm and she could hear his heart racing. He was tall and had lowered his face to touch the top of her hair and he held her without movement, both of them immersed in the perfume of the other, the closeness of their bodies. He didn't kiss her until he sensed that she was ready. Izzy lost track of reality and could not have said how long she was there in his arms as though it was the place she had always longed to be.

Every night for the next week they met. It was for less than an hour and there was never more than the embrace and the kiss. He treated her gently, as though she would break. They rarely spoke, content to hold each other close in the cold night. He did show her that he had the tiny, single pink rose from her hair.

'You lost it at the ball,' he said. 'I carry it next to my heart always.'

Izzy was deliriously happy and over the next few days she hugged her secret to herself. She wanted to shout her joy to the world, to tell everyone, to tell Harriet, to confide in Harriet. But she knew that Harriet would counsel her to end it, to remain true to Bryn. She imagined the conversation; the look of disappointment in Harriet's eyes, her concern for scandal, her sensible approach to such a non-sensible situation, that Izzy was in love with a soldier. No, it was better that Harriet didn't know, better for Harriet, better for Izzy.

Then Izzy had news that Bryn was returning and their meetings ceased. Bryn did indeed reprimand her sharply for her visit to the watch house, but she sensed that he was not too disturbed. Three weeks had passed since the incident and other items of gossip had supplanted it in the bars and bedrooms of Melbourne. In fact, he treated her lovingly on his return and it was not until the second week that he resumed his nightly sessions at the Melbourne Club.

Then one night he returned early from the Club, his eyes bulging, stammering without making sense, his anger flowing hotly. Captain Scott, at the Club, had told him privately that he had reliable information that there had been an indiscretion between his wife and an officer from the Bourke Street Barracks. Bryn could not contain his anger and came within inches of striking her as she cringed away from him. She did not deny it and that seemed to make him angrier. Then he stormed out of the house into the night.

The house was suddenly silent, though Izzy's heart was clamorous. She reached for the sofa and felt it soft around her, its red damask cloth so familiar and welcoming. I am a fool, of course he was going to find out. What will I do? She sat there all night going over what Bryn had said. In the morning she went about her routine with a heavy heart.

~ ~ ~

Two days later he returned.

'I have arranged our passage on the *Rookery* departing on June 22nd.'

'Am I to have no say in the matter?'

'No. You lost that privilege when you chose to turn your back on your marriage vow.'

'But nothing happened. I promise nothing happened. It was all innocence.'

'Innocence! I will not be played for a fool, a cuckold, publicly, here in Melbourne, where I have worked so hard to make a name for myself and to secure our future. You have thrown it all away. And for what? For a dalliance with a soldier. I was hoodwinked by a pretty face and figure, but by God, I will make a proper wife of you.'

'I didn't know it would happen.'

'Your choice is clear; your children or your lover. You may accompany us back to Ireland and you will have a second chance to prove yourself a satisfactory wife. Most men would throw you over and be done with you. I am generous in allowing you this opportunity. It will save face and if you are away from him maybe you will devote yourself as a proper wife. We will speak no more of this and no-one is to know the real reason we are leaving this damnable town. My standing as a respected surgeon and the first of my profession in Melbourne may yet be salvaged.'

'This choice is no choice. I cannot give up my children. I will forget him. I will become a proper wife for you. I will forget him.'

'In the meanwhile, you will not leave the house. I have arranged for the sale of the furniture and household goods through Mr Purvis, the auctioneer. He will be here this afternoon to assess the value and the auction is settled for June 4th.'

'So soon?'

'You will have plenty to do in arranging the contents to be shipped to Ireland. You will need to pack the children's clothes for the voyage and the warmer ones required for Ireland and of course your own and mine.'

'May I not see my friends?'

'They may come to the house to visit you, but you will not speak of the divide between us. You will tell them I have had a letter from Ireland informing me of my brother's death and requiring me to return to take over my family's property in Cork. That should satisfy the gossips in this town and will account for our abrupt departure.'

Chapter 16

Cork 1840

Izzy looked back at the ship from the gangplank. The *Rookery* had been their home for four months and faithfully brought them from the other side of the world. The ship looked large, its masts towering above them as their feet welcomed the touch of dry land. There had been times on the voyage when it had felt like little more than a toy in the ocean, battered and tossed by enormous waves, speeding with sails full before the wind, at other times helpless and becalmed; their progress always at the mercy of the wind.

Captain Bourne had managed not only the ship and its crew, but also the passengers housed in the fourteen cabins on board. He knew everyone, even the children, and never failed to enquire as to their health and comfort. He was particularly aware of Izzy and Edie and Helena because he had had reason to call on the medical skills of Bryn once or twice when the ship's own doctor was in a drunken stupor. Bryn had been surprisingly gracious in attending to the medical needs of the ship. Izzy saw how important it was and her old jealousy of his work fell away.

The September sun was surprisingly strong and Izzy bent

down to adjust the girls' bonnets. She swayed a little and had to steady herself against Edie's shoulder. She was pregnant again, conceiving early in the voyage, and Bryn estimated that the baby would be born in the New Year. The journey from Melbourne to Cork had been long, in both time and distance and this had had an unforeseen benefit. The long days and nights of the voyage had given them ample time together and Bryn, never mentioning Lieutenant Chevalier or the indiscretion which prompted their departure, was young again. For the first time he shared with Izzy his plans for their future in Ireland. A future made possible by the fortune that he had amassed in land deals in Melbourne. A fortune which would continue to grow because he had invested in property in the city centre, and it was obvious to everyone that Melbourne was on the rise. She could not fault Bryn on this voyage. He was attentive to her, choosing to spend time with her, sitting in the cabin or on the deck, playing games with the children. He was sociable with the other passengers, enjoying the status that his newly acquired riches gave him. He occasionally shared a drink with the Captain, but Izzy recognised that it was the lack of brandy which made Bryn a pleasanter man, a loving husband and father. Perhaps she could fall in love with him again and let her infatuation with Francis die through lack of contact. It would be the sensible thing to do.

'Sit here my dear, on the sea chest. Hopefully they won't be too long in unloading our belongings.' Bryn opened her parasol and handed it to her. Then he swung Edie and Helena up onto the sea chest to sit either side of her. 'I'm going to find a wagon to transport our goods and then a carriage which will take us to Flintfield House. Wait here. Maria will fetch you some water. Get it from the ship, Maria, not from any of these filthy places here.' Maria, Izzy's companion and helper, was staring around her at the noise and bustle. Having been born in Van Diemen's Land, this had been Maria's first ocean voyage and first time back home. Well, home to her was Melbourne not Cork, but even so, Izzy thought, she must have heard enough about Ireland to regard it as home.

There was no shade on the dock but a small breeze came off the harbour to relieve them as they watched the crew deposit more chests, boxes, bags, wooden crates and cases around them. Maria returned with a can of water and they all drank. The port of Cobh, just east of the city of Cork, was squalid. The smell of rotting garbage made Izzy nauseous. There were dogs, thin and mangy, filthy from their foraging. There were people too, also thin and mangy, who competed with the dogs among the rotting vegetation dumped by incoming ships. This produce was already rotting when it arrived and had been rejected by the merchants as unsaleable. They were mainly women, those foragers. Women with the thinness of poverty and the ghostly look of those already dead. Hair, face, clothes were all the same colour, all reduced to the brown of starvation. Izzy looked down at her fresh white muslin dress and the girls' pink ribbons, bright in the morning sun. She clasped the children closer to her as a group of sailors, singing and shouting, reeled their drunken way towards them. 'Got tuppence for us, Missus? What a pretty sight you are sitting up there, surely you got tuppence?' The speaker pushed his hands towards her, fingers extended, grimy spindles on the end of pitifully thin arms.

'Get away! Get away from us,' shouted Maria throwing the can and the remaining water at the group. 'Leave us alone!'

The sailors backed off laughing and cursing and sniggering as Tommy Payne, one of the crew from the *Rookery*, hurried up. 'I'll stay here with you, Ma'am; this is not a good place for ladies. I'm sure Dr Carrick will be back soon with a carriage.'

After an hour, Tommy Payne spotted Bryn weaving through the crowded wharf and went to help him guide the wagon and the carriage towards the women. The girls were calling 'Papa! Papa!' and Izzy had to quieten them, but she shared their relief at his return.

'I'm sorry, Izzy,' he panted, wiping his brow. 'I had to walk further than I thought and there was very little choice in vehicles, but I managed to find a brougham, so our journey should be more comfortable.' He stopped and took her hand to help her down from the sea chest. 'Are you all right? You look pale, even in this blasted heat.'

'Yes, I am quite well, although anxious to be on our way, away from this fearful place.'

'I am shocked.' He sighed and wearily looked around. 'It wasn't always like this. Ireland is suffering great poverty, I fear. Come out of this heat and sit in the carriage.'

Bryn guided the family towards the carriage and settled them inside the spacious interior while he commandeered some of the crew to load their belongings onto the accompanying wagon. Izzy knew exactly what was in each box, each chest, each crate, and she watched from the privacy and comfort of the enclosed carriage as her Melbourne life was loaded onto the wagon. Until now it had all been theory, just a plan, an idea, but suddenly Izzy realised that her life would be quite different here in Ireland. She had made a life in Melbourne and now there were only those goods on the wagon that would connect her with that life, and to Francis. Good-bye Francis, she thought, as she felt him slip further away from her.

~ ~ ~

The old road from Cobh to Cork was noticeably smooth, after the rough, colonial tracks they were used to, and the children were asleep within minutes. Helena was sprawled across Izzy's lap and Edie propped up neatly against Bryn's shoulder. Maria had elected to travel up the top and Izzy had noticed her smile as the young driver helped her up.

Even now Izzy could hear snatches of their conversation and Maria's excited laughter which floated past the window. Her thoughts were interrupted as Bryn leaned across and took her hand.

'Izzy, this may be the last opportunity I get to say this before we get to Flintfield House. I know the voyage was difficult for you and that beginning a new life in Ireland will also be difficult, but I promise you that I will try to make it as easy as I can.'

'Thank you, Bryn. I am confident that we will be happy here. There were many pleasant aspects of the voyage and your attention to us made it pass quickly. I only hope that your brother and his wife will welcome us lovingly for I would not like to feel that we are intruding on their hospitality.'

'I cannot speak for Sarah, but my brother William certainly sounded enthusiastic in the letter I received. He clearly would have no other arrangement than that we stay at Flintfield House for as long as we want. As he said, it is, after all, my childhood home and should be the place that we come back to. He is looking forward to our return, especially to hear news of the colony and to meet you and the girls. In his view Ireland is sliding towards disaster with poverty rising as more people leave the rural areas for work in the cities. He himself is considering emigrating and would be happy to sell his share of Flintfield to me to facilitate his plan.'

Izzy did not reply but turned the words over in her head. In the past Bryn had never confided his plans in her; perhaps, she thought, because he considered her, at twenty-one, still too silly and young to understand them. But she did understand that he wanted to make a success of this new life and more than that, she understood the importance of Bryn telling her what he thought. This was, then, the beginning of a new relationship. One in which she would be treated with respect, in which her opinion and feelings would be taken into consideration. She knew that her response was important and she chose her words carefully, the decision gelling in her mind as she formed the words to speak.

'Bryn, I too would like to use this opportunity to speak privately to you. I know that what I did was wrong and I want you to know that those days are over. You have been generous in allowing me this opportunity and I promise that I will be a credit to you and support you as much as I can. If your brother decides to leave Ireland then we can make our lives at Flintfield House but otherwise we will find another place together. I may be stronger than you think and I would like the opportunity to prove myself.'

Bryn's face had clouded slightly at her directness but he held her gaze and smiled as he squeezed her hand. Perhaps he had misjudged her, mistaking her youth and inexperience for being headstrong and wayward. The compliant, sensible Izzy that had emerged on the voyage was one that he could depend on, one who would help and not hinder his plans. And the fact that she was so damned pretty would always be a boon. He saw the way men looked at her and envied him his good fortune in having such a wife. Yes, the future was looking very bright. He patted her hand.

'Rest now, my dear, we have had a busy morning and will be in Cork soon. Then we have a two-day journey to Flintfield House and there will be much excitement when we arrive.' And with that, he settled back into his seat and closed his eyes.

But Izzy could not sleep. She shifted Helena's weight into a more comfortable position and turned her attention to the ever-changing scene through the window. Fields, stubbled and brown from the sun and an early harvest, dotted with the skeletal shapes of sheep and the occasional cow, women bent low digging in the dust, ragged children sitting in any shade looking too tired to play, deserted cottages with their thatched roofs neglected and collapsing, men working as animals pulling ploughs and carrying loads on their backs. The details were ever changing but the pattern was the same, and the pattern spoke of poverty, hardship and starvation. Where were the green fields, the soft rain, the fat lambs and dairy cattle? Bryn had told her that County Cork was famous for its deep yellow butter, thick and smooth and creamy with a taste beyond imagining. This place had been baked dry and stiff so that it seemed even movement was difficult.

A woman on the side of the road arose as the carriage approached, shaded her eyes and stared. Izzy saw that she clutched a ragged bundle that could have been a child, but there was no sound as the luxury brougham passed within feet of the woman, only the vacant, hollow stare of hopelessness which shot from her and pierced Izzy like an arrow. 'Oh' escaped from Izzy and looking back she saw the woman had turned to follow the carriage with her eyes, one hand supporting the ragged bundle and the other lifted in a pleading gesture. Bryn stirred and opened his eyes to see Izzy still staring backwards through the window.

'Oh, it's awful, Bryn, these poor people. Why are they so poor? I thought Cork was a place of plenty. "Butter fat" was how you always described it. But this is terrible, so poor, so hopeless and, and they look ... hungry.'

'There have been several crop failures in the last few years and the landlords have failed to take care of their tenants. These deserted cottages show that the people are no longer able to make a living from the land and are leaving for the cities or, more probably, to emigrate. It seems strange that we are returning just as so many are leaving. And it is quite obvious to us that life in Van Diemen's Land or Port Phillip is far richer than this.'

They fell silent as the story repeated and repeated on the other side of the window, glazed with shock that the Ireland they had both known as children was so changed.

Chapter 17

Cork 1840

They stayed overnight in Cork. The inn was comfortable and the innkeeper was eager to please Dr Carrick, who paid him well. There were many questions about their journey and about life in the colonies and Izzy began to feel a little overwhelmed by the interest. She did not feel brave or adventurous as these people seemed to think she was. She had gone to the colonies as a child, with no say in the matter, and had travelled back to Ireland because her husband had decided it. She had no say in where she was or what she was doing. Her role was to look after the children and in her new mode of thinking, to give comfort to her husband. Certainly, she thought of Melbourne as her home and Launceston as the place she loved most in the world. But she didn't think she would ever see either again. That would depend on Bryn and how things worked out in this strange land, this 'coming home' land that was, at once, both familiar and foreign to her.

Two more days of travel followed as they wound their way north, staying overnight in the village of Mallow before heading west to Flintfield House near the little town of

Millstreet on the River Blackwater. The scenes they had encountered on the first day followed them all the way and it was not long before they were accustomed to the poverty that surrounded them. Izzy found herself thinking less about the hardships she saw and more about the unknown that awaited them at Flintfield House. Sarah. What was she like? Would she welcome her like a sister? Would they become friends? Would their lives be linked forever because they had married brothers? Would Sarah become the sister that Edith used to be? Would Izzy look back in a few years and marvel that there was a time when she didn't know Sarah? Sarah and William had four sons, all older than Edie and Helena, so surely as a mother she would welcome these two little girls.

Bryn was growing excited as they edged closer to their destination.

'Look, Edie, here's the crossing of the Blackwater River. I played here when I was your age, perhaps a little older; fishing and building tree houses and once my brothers and I built a raft and sailed on the river.'

'Can I do that, Papa? Can we come here and build a raft too?'

'Yes, perhaps we can, maybe with your cousins. Look we are coming closer and I see the roof of the house. Look. There it is. There's Flintfield, just as it always was.'

And so saying, Bryn stood up and leaned out of the carriage window to get a better view. Izzy couldn't see from the inside, but he was waving his hat in wide semi-circular motions and laughing like a boy. 'Home!' he shouted. 'We are home!'

With Bryn blocking the view, Izzy slid across to the other window. They were trotting up a long, shady driveway, gravelled and neat, and at the end stood the grey, solid walls of a country farmhouse. Squat and low at one end and rising to three storeys at the other, the house had obviously been here for many years. It looked solid, stable, like a house that belonged to good people. Yes, thought Izzy, this could be our future home.

As she watched, the front door opened and people were spilling out onto the driveway. There were six, seven people. No, eight, ten? There was an older man, younger men and boys, servants and now women, maids and yes, finally walking slowly and reservedly, the obvious mistress of the house, pulling her sleeves down and buttoning her cuff. William was standing with his arms outstretched ready to embrace his younger brother and before the carriage had stopped Bryn had opened the door and leapt towards him. They were shouting and laughing at each other and then suddenly Bryn was taking Izzy's hand and helping her out of the carriage. The children tumbled out too and they were all caught up in the embrace of the jubilant William, red faced and portly, laughing and shouting, smacking his sides and declaring, 'This is a day to be joyful, for you are home, home at last.'

Suddenly he stopped and turned to where Sarah was standing. 'Come and greet your brother, woman.'

Sarah came forward hesitantly and accepted Bryn's formal greeting and then turned to Izzy. Her head was erect, her hair, brown and flecked with grey, was pulled into a severe bun. Izzy saw that her eyes showed no warmth and she felt all hope plummet in that instant. This is going to be difficult, she thought, but she smiled as she returned the greeting. 'I thank you, sister, for your generosity. You are so kind to welcome us. I have long looked forward to meeting you.'

Bryn brought the girls forward and presented them, but even they failed to raise a smile in Sarah. William was whooping and fussing and lining up his four sons to present them to the visitors. The boys all had their mother's erect, reserved demeanour and wore an air of youthful embarrassment at their father's enthusiasm. They were stepped down in height from eldest to youngest and Izzy noticed that their country clothing although of good quality was a little shabby.

'Here we have Daniel aged fourteen, my son and heir and very proud we are of him. Next is William aged twelve, who is proving to be quite a scholar. Then Bryn aged ten; I guess we will have to call you "young Bryn" now. He wants to be a doctor, like his uncle! And here is baby Michael aged eight, although I'm not allowed to call him "baby" anymore.' William laughed uproariously at his own joke as Michael squirmed with embarrassment.

'But that's enough of standing in the sun. Come along inside and see the old house again. You can see that not much has changed since you left.' William's arm was around Bryn's shoulder as he guided him into the coolness of the house. Izzy and the girls followed with Sarah and her sons behind. 'We have given you the top floor, the old nursery floor, as you would remember. There are three rooms there, so you should be comfortable. Daniel and William are doubling up downstairs with the younger ones while you are here. You'll remember that we grew up ourselves in those top rooms.'

~ ~ ~

The wagon bearing their boxes would not arrive for another three days, so after unpacking their small bags Izzy and Maria and the children spent the afternoon resting in their rooms while Bryn walked the fields and surrounds of Flintfield with his brother and nephews.

The accommodation was comfortable. Two bedrooms flanked a small sitting room that was furnished with soft lounges and rugs and was perfect for the family to relax in. Bryn was delighted to be back in his childhood rooms. He had slept in the room now occupied by Helena and Edie. It was a large room and Bryn asked that an extra bed be brought in so that Maria could sleep with the girls, thus relieving Izzy of attending to the girls at night. 'You need to rest and save your strength,' he said. 'A summertime confinement can be taxing. I will ask Sarah's advice on employing a village girl as a daily nurserymaid.'

'No Bryn, could I do that? Could I ask Sarah's advice? I feel that I need to have a reason to approach her. She did not seem very pleased when she greeted us, though I cannot fault her hospitality in giving us these rooms. She has obviously been preparing for our arrival for some time.'

'Give her time, Izzy. I'm sure she will soften as she becomes acquainted with us. My brother is a lovable buffoon, but I am sure he is not easy to live with, and he bullies her into action. Yes, I think that is an excellent idea. You approach her for advice about a village girl. It will give you a good basis for a relationship with her.'

'Thank you, Bryn. I can see why you have loved Flintfield and I am looking forward to exploring the village and the places of your youth.'

~ ~ ~

The months passed quickly. Izzy, her belly swelling steadily, welcomed the autumn coolness like a forgotten friend. She had missed winter this year as they travelled back to the northern hemisphere and another summer, but now she watched the seasons rescue the parched fields, firstly with the softness of autumn and then continuing colder and colder as Christmas came and went. Rain drenched the fields and garden and ran in small rivers down the gravel driveway and through the muddy lanes.

The cows stood in the misty rain, ghostly figures, their forlorn calls echoing as they waited for the milking maids to walk them to the shed. Twice a day, in the early morning and the late afternoon, five women huddled under shawls would walk from the nearby village of Millstreet to milk the twenty-six cows that William owned. Izzy grew used to hearing their voices as they called the cows by name and talked and sang to them as they strolled from the field towards the shed. Their lilting voices relaxed the cows and made the milk flow more freely, a simple trick that had given County Cork that nickname 'Butter fat'.

Izzy found that daily life at Flintfield was timed by many such small markers – the kitchen maid fetching water from the well, the stablehands exercising the horses, the gardeners digging vegetables or clearing the drains around the house, William noisily taking the dogs with him as he did his morning rounds, the housemaids' routine, the boys' routine of leaving for and returning from the village school. But when the sun was low on the horizon, either in its rising or its setting, Izzy loved to listen for the lazy, comforting voices of the milkmaids.

~ ~ ~

Izzy welcomed the new year of 1841, knowing that her confinement was nearly over. She ventured downstairs for the midday meal on most days but took her other meals in her room. It was late morning as she stood in the upstairs sitting room, her hand on the bedroom doorknob, listening for Helena stirring from her morning sleep. Her gaze fixed on the wood panelling of the sitting room wall, dark, knotted, walnut perhaps, each panel married perfectly to the next. She tried to imagine Bryn playing here as a boy, but she could only see Sarah's sons. Seeing him here with William over the last few months had given her some insights. Normally so confident and outgoing, the 'Bryn with William' she had seen had surprised her. He was circumspect, deferring always to his brother's opinion, easily following his brother's suggestion, laughing at his many jokes. Bryn was the charming, younger man of their courting days and Izzy puzzled over how the moody, self-righteous, demanding and critical man of their marriage could be so changed.

Her fingers traced the old knots in the wood. They were smoothed with age, as though others had stood in this very spot and unknown fingers had done the same. Was I really so bad? she thought. Enough to make him so unpleasant? She could see her younger self – sixteen, seventeen, eighteen, pretty, petite – responding to his favours and gifts, absorbed in her work with Madam Foveaux, jealous when his work took him away, completely swept away by the romance of Lieutenant Chevalier. Yes, no wonder Bryn saw her as petulant, moody, a spoilt child. She blushed with the memory. I'll not go back to being like that, she promised herself. Certainly, Bryn seemed to have forgiven her completely for her indiscretion with Francis. He never referred to it. It was as though it had never happened. He was also delighted with the progress of her pregnancy, attentive to her every need. She couldn't fault him and yet she still had doubts, but about what she couldn't say. She missed Edith, missed her knowledge, her certainty. Her hand moved over her swollen belly. Not long now, little boy. She was sure this one was a boy. She had felt the familiar tightening in her abdomen over the last few days and knew that her delivery would be soon. Childbirth held no more fear for Izzy. The pain was short-lived and Bryn was so experienced that she wondered how other women, whose husbands were not doctors, managed. Helena cried and Izzy opened the door. 'How are you, my precious?' She put her arms around the little girl, smelt the hot sleepy breath on her cheek and lifted her, burying her face in the mass of dark curls until Helena's cry became a whimper and within moments was forgotten.

Izzy was singing softly to Helena as she walked to the window overlooking the back courtyard. The rain had cleared and a weak sliver of sunlight lit the drops on the leaves and the puddles on the cobbled courtyard. Maria had taken Edie out for some fresh air earlier, but they were out of sight, probably walking in the gravelled driveway. The back courtyard was a practical place, part of the working farm. Izzy could see the kitchen maid, scrap bucket in hand, listening intently to the groom, his brush discarded and the horse patiently waiting, their bodies carefully placed so as not to betray their desires.

Izzy saw the kitchen door open and watched Sarah stride across to the well in the centre of the courtyard, saw the kitchen maid scurry towards the chicken pen with the scrap bucket, saw the groom pick up the brush and the horse jump as he briskly resumed his brushing, saw the very chickens themselves stand straighter and cluck quieter because Sarah was present. Without addressing them, Sarah kept striding to the vegetable garden on the far side to speak to the gardener, seemingly unaware of her effect on the scene.

A cold fish she is, thought Izzy. I hope I am never like that. William was, as Bryn had said, 'a lovable buffoon' but he did not extend his energy and humour to his wife. Their relationship was barely civil – a smouldering complexity of long-term resentment and blame on both sides – and Izzy felt that Sarah's controlled tolerance of their presence in the house was just another entry on the balance sheet. Izzy had tried to humour her several times, beginning with the employment of a village girl as nurserymaid. Sarah listened silently, then made enquiries and reported to Izzy that the cook's niece, Bridie, was a reliable girl who lived close by and would be a suitable candidate for the position. 'Of course, you and Dr Carrick will have to manage her employment, as her position here will have nothing to do with the running of the household.'

Everything Sarah did or said was business-like and direct, as though she was afraid of giving even a little away, of risking herself. Her angular frame had no softness, her clothing and hairstyle no glamour, her gait no grace. Her every move spelled efficiency and her every word was measured and spent as though it was her last.

Izzy thought about the other mistress of Flintfield, Bryn and William's mother, Helena. She looked at the small, modest poesy ring that Bryn had given her when they plighted their troth. It was home again here at Flintfield, on her finger instead of Helena's. It was one gift for another. Helena had told Bryn to give the ring to the woman he would marry and Izzy had named her daughter for Helena. Perhaps one day she would become the mistress of Flintfield.

The sitting room door opened and Bridie entered, flustered and rushed. 'I'm sorry, Ma'am, I wanted to be here when she woke up. I have laundered all their little things and put them by the fire in the kitchen. Cook says she loves to see the pretty baby clothes for little girls, after only having four boys grow up in this house.'

'Thank you, Bridie,' said Izzy as she handed Helena to her. As she did so she felt a sharp pain, low and deep within her, and she clutched the nearby chair to steady herself. 'I think I might rest a while. Do you know where Dr Carrick is?'

'Yes, Ma'am, he's at the river crossing with the Master. A cart has bogged and all the men have gone to help drag it out. Do you want me to fetch him?'

'No, not yet, it is nearly dinner hour and they will be returning soon. Perhaps you could ask him to come up to see me then. Take Helena downstairs to join Maria and Edie in the garden while the rain holds off. Thank you, Bridie.'

~ ~ ~

Charles Henri Bryn was born the next afternoon. The delivery was a little longer than expected, but Bryn gently encouraged her through the stages and made her as comfortable as he could. As the baby finally slipped from her, Bryn could not contain his joy, shouting the news and laughing as he held the baby for Izzy to see. 'It's a boy, a beautiful, healthy boy!'

Chapter 18

Cork 1841–1842

Life at Flintfield moved along timeworn tracks, punctuated only by the agricultural activities of the year. Charles Henri was a robust child and as Izzy grew stronger, she took him downstairs more frequently and began to participate in the life of the household.

Bryn was teaching five-year-old Edie to ride and Izzy re-discovered her enjoyment of horseback riding. When the weather allowed, she escaped the house on Lady, a quiet mare that the children rode. Lady was older and more sedate than Honey and it was easy for Izzy to explore the village and surrounding countryside. Sometimes Bryn accompanied her but she enjoyed it most when she was alone and could decide her own direction and speed. Lady seemed to enjoy cantering at a good pace on the lonely, barren hills around the village. Those opportunities came occasionally, but mostly Izzy spent the winter indoors, and as a guest in the house, had little to do.

'I want to feel useful, Bryn. What can I do to contribute? Sarah and William have been so generous in allowing us to stay here, so I want to help if I can.'

'There is no need for you to do anything,' Bryn said, folding his newspaper. 'I have an arrangement with William concerning payment for our lodgings, and a very generous arrangement it is. Our presence here is a help to him and he is considering staying in Ireland, not emigrating at all. I enjoy helping him oversee the farm work and our financial situation is such that we do not have to rely on my practice of medicine at all.'

'Shall we stay here for a long time, Bryn, or will we move somewhere else?'

'There is no need to move. My investments are sound and Michael McCarthy, my agent in Melbourne, reports that they are returning a healthy profit, so we can continue as we are. This house can accommodate us all, and it is a convenient location.'

Izzy felt her disappointment rising. Was she never to have her own home again? Was that her punishment? She ignored her thoughts and focused on her words.

'My needle skills are all I have to offer. Could I have some material and perhaps make some summer clothes for myself and the children? Maybe I could offer to make a dress for Sarah. I have Madam Foveaux's address in Paris. I could write to her and ask her to send some magazines and materials.'

'Send them from Paris? I don't think so. Irish linen and local materials are suitable for the task. I am going into Millstreet this afternoon and I will ask Mr Bolton, the draper, to bring a selection for you to see.'

It didn't matter anyway. Sarah dismissed the idea of a new dress with an expression that was somewhere between sneering and mocking. The flush that spread from Izzy's neck to her face brought with it the memory of Miss Paul's face ten years ago, when Izzy had offered her a posy. Her father's fiancé had turned her head and walked away in the same manner that Sarah rose and left the sitting room. I'm not good enough was the feeling then, and the feeling now. It seemed that for Sarah it was not so much the idea of a new dress but that Izzy was offering to make it. Frivolous and silly were words that Sarah never used, but her actions shouted to the entire household that this is what she thought of Izzy.

When she told Bryn of the encounter and its accompanying memory, he jollied her along, saying that Sarah was a busy woman, and she would have meant no harm. It was a few days after this that he suggested to Izzy that she should contact her father.

'But why, Bryn, what good would it do? I haven't seen or heard from him since I left Ireland twelve years ago. I was just a child when I last saw him.'

'Well, he might want to reacquaint himself with you, especially now that you are living in Ireland and have a husband and family. He might want to, for example, meet his grandchildren.'

So, Izzy spent several days composing a letter to her father, informing him of her marriage and children and their current living arrangements at Flintfield House. At Bryn's suggestion she hinted that the family would be able to visit Winton in the summer, if her father so desired it. The Flintfield House address was clearly written, the envelope sealed and the letter posted and the long wait for a reply began.

Spring came and Izzy found her life at Flintfield increasingly tolerable. Her days were full of her needlework and activities with the children and her regular escapes on horseback were her greatest joy. The feel of Lady's strong body under her, with the wind on her face as they cantered up the broad and treeless hill behind the house, brought an exhilaration of power and independence that Izzy had never experienced before. She could go anywhere, ride to the ends of the earth, be whomever she wished, do extraordinary things, love and be loved forever. Sometimes she rode so far that she was late returning and Bryn would scold her, saying that she must be mindful of her duties as a wife and mother and as a guest in his brother's house.

~ ~ ~

One rainy afternoon Izzy was browsing the Dublin newspaper that William had carelessly left on the sofa in the main sitting room when she saw a small entry, barely two inches square. It announced that Lieutenant Francis Chevalier, manager of the 28th Foot Depot at Chatham, Kent, had been made Captain by purchase. Her heart raced. Her finger followed the words a dozen times. He was here, so close, just across the Irish Sea. All her promises to herself evaporated. She truly had tried not to think of him and it had been so long since she had seen him but now his face, his hands, his voice, the very feel of his arms around her were so clear, every detail vivid in her mind and she saw that she was trembling.

Her first desire was to cut out the tiny square and keep it in her bodice, close to her heart. She dared not. What if Bryn found it? But she could not part with it, could not just wait for the maid to dispose of it, burn it. So, she folded the newspaper and took it upstairs, and placed it innocently in her needlework trunk. The broad sheets of newspapers were excellent for drafting patterns and she had a small collection of them for that purpose. She watched it lying with the other newspapers, shouting its small secret to her. She stroked it and felt its warmth, like a jewel in a pocket.

~ ~ ~

Izzy had not expected a reply from her father so quickly. The envelope was made of heavy paper and the red seal, although small, was enough to raise interest, even in Sarah's eyes. But Izzy did not share the contents with anyone but Bryn.

Winton, Yorkshire
3rd March 1842

Dear Mrs Carrick,

Lord Edward Marchbank has asked me to reply to your letter of 2nd February on his behalf. His Lordship read with interest of your marriage to Dr Carrick and your subsequent family and your recent removal to Ireland. He regrets that he cannot receive you at Winton as it would place Lady Marchbank and their daughter in an awkward situation. His Lordship reminds you that all responsibility for your welfare was transferred to Colonel Peabody when he agreed to become your guardian, and now that responsibility rests with your husband. His Lordship wishes you good fortune and does not expect to hear from you again.

I remain your humble servant,
William Starkey,
Private Secretary to Lord Edward Marchbank

Bryn's face contorted in rage, the letter shaking in his hand. 'It's an insult,' he croaked. It was the first time in a year that Izzy had seen him struggling to contain his anger, and although it was directed at the letter, Izzy knew she was the real cause of that anger. She shrank back into herself and lowered her head to focus on the lace that she was making.

~ ~ ~

Bryn did not refer to the letter again and life returned to normal as the summer progressed. Charles Henri grew strong and lively and loved to watch his sisters playing noisy games in the garden with their cousins. It was during the summer that Izzy first noticed the small changes that were happening at Flintfield. William sold ten of his dairy cows and now only three women came to milk the remainder. When the kitchen maid and the groom married and migrated to America they were not replaced, and the rest of the staff had to take on their work. There were subtle changes inside the house including poorer cuts of meat and fewer sweet desserts, and Izzy suspected that Sarah had sold the best tableware as they now only used the everyday set. Bryn had commented on the danger of another poor season, the soil was depleted and the crops returning only a fraction of their potential, and the long, dry days, although pleasant, now carried the threat of shrivelling the tender young plants before they could produce.

It was during the harvest that Izzy realised she was pregnant again. Her body, although small, was strong and she was able to bear pregnancy and birth without complaint. Bryn expressed his pleasure but Izzy noted that he was not as attentive to her in the early stages as he had been on the voyage. He was often distracted by business letters from Melbourne and he constantly searched the newspapers for reports of the economic situation there. He worried about the Irish crops and seasons and he seemed to worry too about how his investments in Melbourne were progressing. For as long as Izzy had known him, he had always been a confident businessman and she could see that he was on edge about influences that he had no control over. Then just before Christmas in 1842, Izzy was sewing in their sitting room when Bryn stumbled through the door, eyes wide, shaking the letters in his hand like a serpent.

'It's gone, it's gone.'

'What, what has gone?'

'The money, the property, everything has gone. He's sold everything.'

'Who, who do you mean?'

'Michael McCarthy, my agent in Melbourne. He's sold me out, and for a pittance. Look! For two thousand pounds! It's worth at least ten thousand, no twenty thousand. I am ruined, ruined.' He sank to the floor, shaking, sobbing. Izzy was beside him, her arms around him, cradling his head to her breast and rocking him gently.

'Can you get it back? Can you do anything?'

'No, look, these are the receipts. It's over, it's gone. I was a fool to trust him, a fool to trust the banks and their over-lending in the boom period. He has sold me out. I will have to go to Melbourne and see what I can salvage from this mess.' Bryn roused himself and shuffled through the papers in his hand. 'The house in Bourke Street is sold, and my investments in Flinders Street and Swanston Streets as well as the property I secured in Collins Street just before we left. I will have McCarthy in court, the dishonest, thieving scoundrel. I will see him pay for this.'

Bryn, in a cloud of blackness, spent the next few days organising his departure, leaving Izzy enough money to last her in the support of the children for one year and then he would be back again, or he would send for her. And then, three weeks before Christmas, he was gone.

~ ~ ~

The first six months without Bryn passed slowly and Izzy was surprised how much she missed him. The children asked for him constantly in the first few weeks, but their asking became less frequent and finally the word 'Papa' was rarely mentioned. Izzy grew heavy in pregnancy and could not ride Lady, and rarely ventured downstairs. William sometimes came upstairs to visit her, bringing her Irish newspapers with articles about Melbourne, but they were depressing as they were mainly about the effects of the financial crash.

William also brought two letters from Bryn, one written on board the *Argostina* and sent from The Cape and the more recent one from Melbourne. Bryn reported that the situation was dire. All his property had been sold for a pittance and there was no point remaining in Melbourne, nor of Izzy and the children joining him there. There was not even enough money for his return voyage and he would have to wait until he could get a position as ship's doctor. He did not tell her that he had been arrested for trying to enter the Bourke Street house and assaulting its new owner. She read the account of his trial some weeks later in the *Geelong Advertiser*, one of the many newspapers that Bryn had arranged to be regularly sent before they had left Melbourne.

MELBOURNE: CHARGE OF ASSAULT

Dr. Bryn Carrick was charged by Mr. J. W. Barlow at the police office, on Tuesday, with assaulting him on the previous evening. The defendant, conceiving he had a right to the possession of the premises situated in Bourke Street, occupied by the complainant, went there in a highly excited state, broke down the palings and destroyed the peaches and peach trees in the garden, in order to show that he could exercise the rights of ownership over the property. He eventually tried to dispossess the complainant both of the property and his life at the same time, by aiming a blow with a club at his head as he was coming out of the door, which, fortunately, did not take effect where it was intended, but on the site of the door.

The defendant admitted the charge, but pleaded in justification, that the property occupied by Mr. Barlow was his bona fide property, and had improperly passed into other hands, during his late absence in Ireland. Having been robbed of 13,000 pounds, he had not the means of making good his claim in a court of law, and had taken the only method in his power to procure restitution of his property. A good deal of cross-skirmish in the way of retort and mutual recrimination took place between the parties, which the bench bore patiently for some time, having evidently compassion on the defendant for the many and severe losses he had suffered, but at last put a stop to the case by fining the defendant 20 shillings and costs.

Izzy wrote to Bryn, pleading with him to come back soon or to allow the family to come to Melbourne, but she knew it was impossible. She was at the end of her pregnancy and would deliver this baby within a week or two. She was alone and responsible for her children and knew that she could not depend on the charity of William and Sarah for much longer. The wheat and corn crops failed again due to the poor season and it was quite obvious to everyone that once Izzy's money ran out, she and the children would have to go elsewhere. Already the Irish newspapers carried reports of a disease that had attacked potato crops in the eastern United States and was now reported in Europe, transported it was believed, by blighted potatoes used to feed passengers travelling on sailing ships. The poor Irish peasants grew only one strain of potato, the Irish Lumper, and this lack of variety would mean devastation of the entire potato yield if the disease should take hold.

~ ~ ~

One afternoon Izzy was coming downstairs slowly, as the weight of her unborn child demanded, when she heard raised voices from William's study and she knew that William and Sarah were arguing over her.

'What would you have me do? Turn her out with nowhere to go? She is my brother's wife. I am responsible for her.'

'No! You are not responsible for her. You are responsible for your own wife and your four sons, and your workers and this farm. I will not see my sons suffer for a pretty little ineffectual society miss who hasn't done a stroke of work in her life.'

'That is harsh, Sarah, even for you. She has been left in a very bad situation and she has no-one to turn to, and you would have me send her to the workhouse?'

'We cannot support them any longer. As soon as Bryn left, I knew there would be trouble. As soon as the money he left runs out she will be a beggar, and we cannot afford to keep a beggar, especially with four dependent children.'

'What is the solution, then?'

'Her father is the solution. Make her write to her father and obtain his help in her predicament. He is a wealthy landowner and can well afford to support her, even if she is a natural child and not welcome, as we suspect the letter confirmed. Make her write to him and make arrangements to leave us.'

'As you say, that might solve the problem. But even if her father agrees, it will take time. We must allow her the shelter of our home until she has delivered this child. It is the only Christian thing to do.'

'You must start immediately to hasten her departure, for I tell you, William, our farm has not looked so poor in years and the future looks even worse, with the whole potato crop of Ireland likely to fail.'

Izzy had sunk to a sitting position on the stairs and saw with horror that Sarah's hand was on the doorknob and she was leaving the study as she spoke. She swept across the foyer towards the sitting room, not glancing up the stairs to where Izzy sat. But William was right behind her and when he looked up, his face softened as he realised that Izzy had heard their conversation. He came up the stairs quickly.

'My dear, I am so sorry,' he said, 'there is little I can do. She is right in what she says. We are experiencing very poor conditions and our resources are very low.'

'I know, William, and I am sorry to be such a trouble to you.' She was sobbing uncontrollably and William helped her to her feet to return upstairs. 'I will do as Sarah says and write again to my father and plead for his help. Surely, he will not deny me, if only for the sake of my children.'

Chapter 19

Cork 1843

The baby had no name. Izzy could find no joy in him. She watched as he lay in an exhausted sleep. The three weeks since his birth had been a well, deep and dark, with no way of escape for Izzy. Her days and nights were dominated by this anxious, clinging child whose very existence set her teeth on edge. She was tired, so tired from constantly attending to his needs. His waking moments were fretful and demanding, his sleeping moments short and inconsistent. Poor little thing, I should love you, she thought, watching him in the cradle, his bottom lip quivering, his breath irregular, but his eyes and mouth were shut and the silence fell like a blessing on her face as she felt forehead and neck muscles relax from the tenseness that had become normal for her.

Bridie had said a tearful farewell as she took the last few shillings that Izzy could afford to give her. Maria had opted to stay. 'Where would I go?' she said, looking out the window at a land she did not know.

William had insisted that Izzy and Maria and the children stay until the baby was six weeks old. The atmosphere in the house was tense, with Sarah openly hostile. Izzy spent most of her time upstairs, away from her. While Bryn had been there and there had been a constant supply of money, Sarah had tolerated the family, never graciously, but at least with some restraint. Now there was no holding back. She criticised the children for their noise and muddy boots, she monitored every morsel of food they ate and forbad candles upstairs. Although she was afraid of Sarah's temper, Izzy knew that Sarah was reacting to the restraints of the season. The potatoes had failed again throughout Ireland and every day Izzy watched from the nursery window, watched the poor, huddled in their brown rags and dragging or carrying their dirty children up the driveway, to knock on the door, crying and begging for bread.

She would watch Sarah emerge from the house with a basket of bread and give it out and then roughly wave at them to be off. Sarah knew these people. They were villagers or farm workers, some of them crofters who eked out an existence in the dirt of the farms of absentee landlords. Those landlords, snug in their stately homes in rural England, or in their townhouses in London, extracted exorbitant rents from their tenants, and at the same time made great profits exporting the crops of oats and barley that could have been used to feed the starving poor. After all, it was only the potato crop that had failed. Potatoes were the staple food of Ireland's poor, but a few more seasons like this and they would be reduced to eating the grass like the animals. Sarah knew all this and she wept that she could not do more for these people, her people. She resented the fact that Izzy's father was one of those landlords and yet it was up to her and William to support his daughter and her increasingly large family with no assistance whatsoever.

The letter, on heavy grey paper, had arrived a month ago and it lay open on the mantelpiece like a shot pigeon, the wounded red seal leaking its foulness into the room. Izzy picked it up and read it for the hundredth time.

Winton, Yorkshire
4th August 1843

Dear Mrs Carrick,

Lord Edward Marchbank has asked that I write to you in answer to your letter of the 18th ultimo. His Lordship regrets that he cannot be of assistance to you at this time, and reminds you that, as a married woman, responsibility for your welfare belongs to your husband. He advises that you should stay in Ireland in the home of your husband's brother while your husband attends to his financial affairs in Melbourne. His Lordship emphasises that he does not expect to hear from you again.

I remain your humble servant, William Starkey, Private Secretary to Lord Edward Marchbank

As she turned away from the mantelpiece, she stared at the sewing trunk in the corner; the hidden newspaper cooed seductively ... Here I am, waiting for you. I will make you happy. I will not desert you like your husband, like your husband's family, like your father. Come to me.

No. No. I can't. Not yet. Where is Bryn? Why doesn't he write to me? Tell me what to do. Send me some money. How am I to manage? Sarah hates us. William is growing impatient with Bryn's silence. Is he dead? We will have to leave soon. Already the baby is three weeks old. Time is running out for me.

For the next four days Izzy resisted the temptation to write to Francis, but finally she tricked herself with logic. Perhaps he won't get the letter. Perhaps he has moved from Chatham. Perhaps he has left the army entirely. Perhaps he will simply ignore my plight. Therefore, there is no harm in writing to him.

And within a fortnight the answer came. The answer she dared not hope for.

Chatham
10th September 1843

My darling,

I am overjoyed to receive your letter, although your circumstances are dire in the extreme, being dependent on your husband's family, and feeling unwelcome in his brother's house. Of course, you must come to Chatham.

As manager of the Depot here, I have already secured accommodation for you in Clover Street which is a respectable area where the married officers with families live. The house I have requisitioned has ample accommodation and is situated on the outskirts of the Army Depot, close to the town.

You will be welcomed as my brother's widow and your children as my responsibility. There is a shifting population here and no-one will question such an arrangement. All propriety will be observed so that you and your children will be treated with the utmost respect.

As you have not heard from your husband in more than six months, it seems that misfortune may have assailed him, and I cannot but hope that the arrangements I have made are suitable to you.

I wait with impatience for you to write, giving me details of your arrival. The enclosed £100 should assist you in leaving your unhappy situation and making your way quickly to my waiting arms.

I remain forever at your service
Francis

~ ~ ~

William's farewell had been emotional, hot and flustered,

dominated by regret and guilt, questions about the 'friend' that they were going to, the suitability of an army depot, the forwarding address in case he heard from Bryn and finally, pledges to keep in touch. Since her contact with Francis, Izzy had found an inner strength, a quietness and certainty that a month ago was unknown. She wrote to her friend Harriet asking if she had any news of Bryn, and then describing the intolerable situation in the house and her rescue by Francis. She worked through all the chores required to pack up her family, safe in the knowledge that she was wanted by Francis.

Izzy did not know where they came from nor how they sprang to her lips so strongly, but her parting words to Sarah surprised them both in their graciousness. 'I thank you, Sister, for your kindness. I hope we meet again in better times.'

~ ~ ~

The first thing she noticed about Chatham was the bright colours; green fields, small neat white houses in rows, yellow hay nearing harvest. The people seemed to be dressed in bright colours and their ruddy faces showed good health that she had not seen in years. The busy shipyard rang with hammers and the whirr of machinery which produced the white plumes of steam, rising like clouds and vanishing into the azure August sky. Steam power always reminded her of John Peabody and she was grateful for its efficiency and its independence from the vagaries of the wind. The little steampacket took only two weeks to make its way around the coast from Cork, calling to deliver and collect mail and passengers at numerous ports on the way.

Chatham, the last stop before London, seemed to welcome her with its anthem of activity and its colour as she stood on the deck with Maria and the children. No dull brown here, no starvation, no guilt, no dependence on relatives. Francis wanted her. Francis had sent for her. Francis had paid generously to have her come to him. Bryn had disappeared without a sound, without a trace. She knew that if the situation in Ireland had been tolerable, she would have waited longer for him, but it was impossible to live with Sarah and there was no alternative. She had rehearsed the arguments she would have put to Bryn. Where were you? Why didn't you write to me? What was I supposed to do? We have four children and you deserted me. Left me to fend for myself, to do the best I could. Well, this is the best I could do. Francis offered me a home and I accepted. My choices were limited and I had nowhere to go.

She lifted her chin to the dockyard, to the wharf, and saw the tall, slender figure of Francis hurrying towards the little steamship. All her defences fell away and she knew in that moment that she loved him, that she had always loved him. She held the baby close to quieten the pounding of her heart but she could not drag her gaze away from his approaching figure, his uniform bright in the sunlight, his boots shining. Her eyes were filling with tears of relief at the enthusiasm in his stride and his purposeful expression.

Chapter 20

Chatham 1844

The house was just as Francis had described. Situated on a wide street with full grown shady oaks and opposite a public garden, there was ample accommodation for all of them. Francis employed a maid and a cook who came during the day but did not live in the house, which meant the servants' rooms at the top of the house were available for the children and Maria along with a nursery room for meals and play. Izzy was delighted with the large bedroom on the middle level, its bright bay window overlooking the garden at the back of the house. The drawing room was simply furnished but airy and comfortable, its large windows giving a pleasant view of the park opposite the house. Behind the drawing room was a small apartment which Francis took for himself, his few belongings occupying the space, well separated, as propriety demanded from his 'sister-in-law'.

On that first evening, after the children had settled, after their trunks and boxes had been unpacked, after Francis had bade her goodnight, Izzy sat alone in her new bedroom. She was exhausted from such a day, but she knew she would have trouble settling to sleep, her excitement and relief jostling with the worry that she had done the right thing. She unpinned her hair and let it fall, her thick curls dark in the soft gas light, her hair brush skimming her scalp, her hands separating the tresses, her eyes watching the woman in the looking glass. Yes, a woman, not a girl. Where was the girl who grew vegetables in Launceston, the one that Madam Foveaux had such regard for, the one that Edith loved so much? What would Edith say about this? About living with a man who is not your husband? But I had no choice. I have four children dependent on me. Where are you, Bryn? Are you dead? Have you forgotten us? Francis has rescued us and I am grateful to him. Bryn has deserted us. We are alone and I must do what I can for our survival.

~ ~ ~

So often in the coming weeks, especially late in the evening when she and Francis sat in the drawing room, comfortable and companionable like old people, did she desire to give herself entirely to Francis. She knew he would respond, could see the yearning in his eyes, but the possibility of another baby and the complications that would bring stopped her. She was honest with Francis.

'I cannot make the same mistake my mother made. I cannot give birth to a child without the protection of marriage.'

'But we will marry. It is not like your parents. I love you and I only want what is natural when people are in love.'

'Not yet, Francis, give me time.'

She developed the habit of removing herself, of giving Francis a sisterly kiss and wishing him goodnight, of leaving him alone reading his newspaper. Weeks turned into months and the days shortened and the weather turned bleak.

The approach of Christmas marked a year since Bryn had

left. She had not heard from him for eight months. Her memory of those lonely, frightening months in Ireland, Sarah's hostility, her father's cruel rejection, her growing realisation that Bryn had abandoned her or was dead, all crowded her mind. She saw again the longing in Francis' eyes and worried that his patience might run out, that he too might abandon her. All her good intentions came to naught. It was in the week before Christmas when the snow was thick and soft, when the hour was late and the house had settled to slumber, that she took his hand and led him to her bedroom. 'Are you sure?' Francis asked.

She nodded and smiled. 'You have made me so happy, Francis. I desire this more than I can say. I have waited so long to give myself to you and you have been so patient with me, but I cannot wait any longer. Bryn is never coming back and you ... you are my one, true husband.'

She was submerged in his embrace, his kiss, his hands caressing her skin, his tall, slim body surrounding her, consuming her and she knew she was right. This is where she belonged, this is what she was made for. Their scattered clothes marked the path to the bed and as their passion intensified, Izzy realised that this lovemaking was totally different from her experience. She was in this lovemaking, she was not an observer or the object of someone else's activity. She was in the act, she wanted to be in the act, she wanted to be fully one with Francis. And Francis seemed to sense her desires and her joy.

Francis was her saviour and she clung to him, loved him and she could feel no guilt. If a baby resulted from their lovemaking, well, so be it. Every night after that first, she allowed herself to feel only delight and relief that she was away from Ireland, that she was mistress of her own home again and that Francis loved her, wanted her. She noticed how young he was compared with Bryn. She noticed his soft whiskers, his fair skin, but mostly she noticed his tentative lovemaking, how gentle and concerned he was for her. She remembered the disappointment of her wedding night, how Bryn had used her roughly when the brandy had hold of him, how foolish and inexperienced she had been. Francis loved her. Francis talked to her, telling her of his love, of how she was safe with him.

~ ~ ~

The weeks slipped by unnoticed and suddenly it seemed that the sun had deserted them completely. The wind howled up the river in fitful gusts, battering the shuttered warehouses and houses with horizontal rain. And when the rain stopped the fog hugged the town for days at a time, seeping its cold into the streets and the park opposite the house, into the very bones of the people huddled inside their overcoats. The snow buried the garden and mounted around the house. An hour's exercise in the garden for the children was as much as they could manage and going further afield became almost impossible so unpleasant were the conditions.

Izzy loved it. It seemed the house was like an island, snug and safe in a sea tossing violently around it. It meant she didn't have to meet anyone, she didn't have to lie about her situation, didn't have to pretend. The fires burned brightly in each grate and she would sit at the window and watch the rain and play with the children, especially the baby, whom she had taken to calling Frankie after Francis. But best of all she would wait for Francis to come back from the depot and at night she would lie in his arms listening to the wind and rain. It was in these quiet months that she returned to sewing, remodelling dresses, making clothes for the children, creating small, decorative items for her new home. It was a winter of peace, of reflection, a chance for Izzy to gather her strength, to think about her life and the few choices she had. One choice was the name she would use publicly and with no news of Bryn for so long she was beginning to think he would never return and that Chevalier was the most obvious choice. Francis was surprised when she mentioned it.

'Why, I should think you would use my name.' He sounded as if it never occurred to him that she wouldn't. 'After all, I have told people that you are my brother's wife, so our names would be the same.'

'It seems wrong to me, to take your name without any formality.'

'We have no choice. We cannot marry yet. You must live apart from Bryn for seven years unless we receive news that he is dead. Then of course we will be free to marry. But for the moment there is no legal reason why you should carry your husband's name. There are only social reasons here in Chatham and to have the same surname is simpler and raises fewer questions.'

'And the children, will they follow suit?'

'Yes, of course.'

'I am concerned that the baby has not been baptised and he is ten months old. We cannot truthfully baptise him with your name and yet giving him Bryn's name will tell all of Chatham the true story.'

'Yes, I see.' He was silent for a minute. 'Perhaps we need to go to a larger place, to London and have him baptised there with his father's name. That way the problem is solved. When the weather improves you and I will take the baby north and have him baptised.'

'Oh, of course, that is an ideal solution.'

'Izzy, you must understand that Chatham has a very transient population. Soldiers and their families move frequently and the social relationships in a place like this are shallow and short-lived. You must not trouble yourself about this detail.'

'What if Bryn was to return and find me living here, with you and with your name?'

'Then I would expect that he would understand that you

have had no choice. He left you in a very bad situation and it is only through his rash actions that you are here. If he is alive, he must know by now that Ireland is approaching famine with the complete failure of the potato crop and that any money that he left with you ran out long ago, that your father has rejected you and that his brother was ready to turn you out onto the street.'

'I am so grateful to you Francis for your protection. What would have become of us if you had not taken us in?' She could not fight the tears and gave into them. Francis held her close, whispering his love to her.

~ ~ ~

Easter brought the first signs of spring to the garden. Izzy and Maria ventured out with the children for walks in the park and by the river. Other doors opened and other families came out to greet the first rays of the milky sun. Leaving Maria and the servants to care for the other children, Francis and Izzy took the baby to London and he was baptised Francis Henry Durell Carrick. Francis stood as his Godfather and Izzy insisted that not only his Christian name be given to the child, but also that his mother's name, Durell, which Francis carried as well, be included, thus recognising the special relationship between them. Their few days in London were like a holiday. To the casual eye they were just a young married couple with their first child.

They were back in Chatham for less than a week when Francis brought home a letter from Bryn which had been readdressed by William and forwarded to Francis at the depot. It had taken nearly seven months to finally reach Izzy. Her hands shook as she opened the battered envelope.

25th September 1843
Melbourne

My Dear Izzy,

I regret that I have no good news to share with you. I have delayed writing this letter in the hope that fortune will turn my way but at every turn I am met with disappointment. My investments have come to naught and I am ruined and I see now that the trust I placed in my agent Michael McCarthy was ill founded. He has sold me out and I have little to show for all the fortune I had made in my land deals here.

Many others are in the same situation but those who remained here at the time of the financial crisis were able to salvage a little more. Charles Peabody has been the essence of kindness to me, allowing me to use his house, horses and his name to establish myself once again in my practice of medicine in this town. I estimate that if I work for the next six months, I will be able to send you enough money so that you can all return to Melbourne. It seems that a better life is to be had here, especially for the children. I hear that the situation in Ireland is worsening, that famine is imminent and I thank God that you are safely under the protection of my brother. Life must be difficult there for you. Were you safely delivered of our child? I would estimate that he or she has already had three months of life.

You can write to me care of Charles as I will be staying here for the next few months, saving every penny I have to send to you. Charles and Harriet have welcomed their second child, a girl, and frequently ask after you.

I remain, your loving husband, Bryn

Izzy crumpled the page in her hand as she sank onto the sofa. What would she do? It was one thing to think of him as dead or not caring, but to read his words took her right back to where she was when he left her in Ireland. But she was not back in Ireland. She had to make a decision for her four children and now she would stick by that decision. She had chosen Francis and she would have to let Bryn know her situation. She sat at her desk composing a letter. It took many drafts but finally she felt her words reflected her true feelings. She shared the contents of both letters with Francis and he agreed that she was right to be so direct.

15th March 1844
24 Clover Street
Chatham, Kent

Dear Bryn,

Your letter of September last year has just reached me. I am sorry to hear that the financial situation is so desperate and that you have lost your fortune.

You do not seem to be aware that we were cast out of your brother's home after the birth of our son. Sarah demanded that we leave and William was not strong enough to withstand her arguments. I wrote to my father for protection but was once again rejected. My salvation came in the form of a friend. Captain Chevalier was the only person I knew and could appeal to in this part of the world. He has kindly taken us in and we are living near the Army Depot in Chatham, Kent.

Having not heard from you for a year I supposed that you were dead or that you had deserted us. I had no choice but to accept his kindness as I have four children dependent on me, your four children. Maria Batman has stayed faithfully with me as she has nowhere else to go. Captain Chevalier has been a true gentleman in his actions and I am grateful to him for his kindness. I do not know what you will make of this arrangement but I declare emphatically that I am not to blame. You left me in a very bad situation and I had to act in the best interests of our children.

This letter will not reach you until June but I shall be here in Chatham and living under the name Chevalier, as Francis' brother's widow, so that all propriety is observed. But I will tell you truthfully that Francis and I intend to marry in the future and I have no desire to return to Melbourne. You, however, will need to send me money to support your children, for without the help of Francis your children and I would have been reduced to penury, with the workhouse our only option. Can you imagine what that would be like, your children and your wife begging for entry to that most fearful of places, the workhouse?

I remain in anticipation, Izzy

Chapter 21

Bass Strait 1844

Bryn looked at his possessions. All he had in the world fitted into one small sea chest; a few clothes and his medical documents which enabled him, in haste, to secure this position as ship's doctor on the *Isabella*, bound for London. At the bottom of his sea chest lay that last and poisonous letter from Izzy. How dare she, the hussy, run off to her lover as soon as my back is turned, while I watch my assets dissolve into nothing, while I struggle to earn money for her, while I suffer the indignity of bankruptcy.

He could not help comparing this with his last departure to London three years ago. It had taken all day to move the full wagon of crates and boxes and sea chests from the Bourke Street house, with the children and Izzy conveyed to the ship by carriage. Their departure, although privately troubled, was publicly triumphant; the humble doctor returning to his homeland, a rich and successful man. Now he was a humble doctor again. The final sale of all his assets in Melbourne had netted him £536 and he opened the envelope and stroked the banknotes thoughtfully. He would not need to spend any until he arrived in London, and then he would visit Izzy without warning, catch her unprepared, see what the situation was and make his plans for the future. He had not replied to Izzy's letter, and he told himself it was because he wanted to keep the element of surprise, but he wondered as he sat on his bunk whether it was also because he didn't know what to write. He closed the envelope, returned it to the leather wallet with his medical documents and locked it in the sea chest.

The *Isabella* sailed from Port Phillip at daybreak on 18th June. The ship's name was an omen that all would be well. The wind was strong and cold and filled the square sails of the three masts so that the ship moved through the dawn like a phantom, silent and sleek. Bryn leaned on the rail and sighed with satisfaction as he watched the faint outline of Melbourne, the place of his humiliating financial downfall, disappear forever. His attention turned to the activity on board, the crew, fresh and lively from their respite in Melbourne, responding to the shouted commands of Mr Legg, the first mate. Captain Bradley was coming towards Bryn.

'We're away, Dr Carrick. I've set the course for the islands known as Kent's Group, but I need to retire to my cabin as I find this wind very chilling. Mr Legg will look after things here.'

'Are you unwell, Captain Bradley? Can I bring you a draught?'

'No, Dr Carrick, I am not ill. I am never ill. I just need to get out of this wind. It travels about my ears in a most disturbing way, making me suffer a painful whistling that I cannot shake.'

As he spoke, the Captain hopped from foot to foot, his hands clasped to his ears and his head thrust down into the folds of his greatcoat. Bryn was intrigued, thinking back to syphilitic John Batman and their arrival together on the banks of the Yarra in November 1835, nearly nine years ago. John had moved in a similar way as his leg muscles randomly and painfully contracted and the movement brought some kind of relief. John's nose was eventually eaten away by the disease and he lost all use of his legs, ending his days being pushed around the small settlement in a wicker chair.

'Are there any other symptoms, Captain?'

'No, Dr Carrick, I told you I am not ill.' Captain Bradley pushed roughly past Bryn, heading towards his cabin. The hopping movement lent a comical appearance to his otherwise staid figure and Bryn watched him go, summoning up his knowledge of the effects of syphilis; muscular dysfunction, tremors, skin diseases as well as those which softened the brain – confusion and disorientation, moodiness and melancholia. Bryn made a mental note to check the ship's medical chest for mercury, the usual remedy for this condition.

Over the next twenty-four hours the wind whipped the sea into a grey, heaving mass, the ship rolling and pitching, sometimes so low that the waves were mountains surrounding them, and sometimes so high that no water could be seen, until the downward movement began again and the ship found the bottom of the trough before it began its next upward climb. It was like riding an enormous horse, the pattern of movement lulling and predictable while at the same time each body was stiff with knowledge of the danger.

The passengers, seasick and frightened, turned their backs to the wind and cowered away from the stinging, icy points of the driving rain. The noise was deafening and as the black night descended, movement on the deck became impossible and Mr Legg instructed the passengers to stay below. But Bryn found it claustrophobic, the smell of vomit and fear assaulting his nostrils, and using his position as part of the crew, he went above. He found Mr Legg on the deck calmly issuing orders to the crew, his collar turned up against the wind and rain, his feet planted wide to balance against the constant rolling of the ship.

'Are you experienced with the sea, Dr Carrick?' Mr Legg shouted over the wind.

'No, not in any practical way, Mr Legg, I have had one or two voyages but they have been uneventful. Are you expecting this bad weather to last?'

'Yes, Bass Strait in June is never a pony ride, but this is of hurricane force. Captain Bradley expects we will see Kent's Group of islands tomorrow.' Mr Legg moved closer to Bryn and lowered his voice. 'I fear this wind will put us off course and the Captain will need to be extra careful with his readings.'

'Captain Bradley's a strange man, don't you think?' Bryn risked his opinion, sensing that Mr Legg would agree.

'Yes, Dr Carrick. It's my first voyage with him. We brought the *Isabella* along the coast from Sydney before arriving in Melbourne.' Mr Legg looked around to check that he was not overheard. 'I think as the ship's doctor you should know that the crew lacks faith in him. This condition he suffers from makes him a figure of fun and I have had to discipline some of the younger crew members for their lack of respect.'

'And you, Mr Legg? What is your opinion? Do you share their lack of faith?'

'Dr Carrick, it is my business to run the ship efficiently and see that the Captain's orders are carried out. I do not indulge in gossip, but I will tell you privately that I check his course readings thoroughly and compare them with my own which I take independently.'

'And is there any variation?'

'I have noticed today that we seem to be running further east than he anticipates, but I have not approached him on the matter. I will wait until I take a new reading at dawn and if I think we are off course, I will have to confront him. We will be two days from Port Phillip by then and should be within sight of the Kent Group of islands.'

Bryn tossed in his bunk, but it was not the storm that

troubled him, so much as Mr Legg's words. The conversation left Bryn with an unsettled feeling. Never before had he doubted the ability of a sea captain, and never before had he realised the enormity of the captain's responsibility. Apart from the safety of the ship and the delivery of the cargo, the captain was responsible for the welfare of the crew and passengers. The *Isabella*, a medium sized barque of 400 ton, carried twenty-five crew members, mostly fit and active men in their prime, and fifteen passengers, specifically two women with infants, one family with three children and six single men travelling individually, including himself. Bryn shivered as he considered the possibility that their survival could depend on the decisions made by a captain who did not seem fit for the position. He heard the timbers creak in the wind and the ship groan as it tossed itself at the waves. The night would be long.

~ ~ ~

There was a hammering on his cabin door as the first light of dawn filtered greyly through the heavy clouds. The wind and rain had been remorseless throughout the night and Bryn had slept little. He stumbled from his cot and opened the door as Mr Legg, agitated and alarmed, pushed past him into the cabin.

'Dr Carrick, we must act quickly for I fear that Captain Bradley has put us all in danger. We are miles off course according to my calculations.'

'Have you spoken to him?'

'Yes, yes, he told me to hold my tongue. He said that he was the Captain and he would have no opposition. It is quite obvious that we are nowhere near Kent's Group and I fear that with this weather our lives will be in danger.'

Bryn could see that Mr Legg's concern was not to be taken lightly. 'What can we do?'

Mr Legg leaned towards Bryn, his voice low and husky,

his oilskin smelling of salt, of the huge expanse of the sea, concentrated into this tiny, cramped cabin.

'There is one solution, but we must be careful. You, as the ship's doctor, can declare him insane and the command of the ship, by law, will pass to me and I can at least try and get back on course. We must follow the law on this occasion, documenting our reasons and our actions, gaining the support of the senior crew members and following all procedures, for none of us wants to end up tried for mutiny. The men are not fools; they know we are off course and they are anxious to get the ship under control and headed in the right direction.'

'Right, then it is agreed. I have reason to believe that the Captain is suffering the effects of a long-term syphilitic condition and it has affected his judgement and decision-making ability. He should be confined to his cabin and command of the ship should pass to you.'

'Could you defend that judgement in court? You may be brought to account, and although I will support you, your medical knowledge will be the crucial factor in the court's determination.'

Bryn took a long breath and thought again of John Batman, the handsome, charismatic founder of Melbourne, his once strong back and legs reduced to crippling inactivity, his clear-thinking brain befuddled and confused. Captain Bradley showed the same symptoms and Bryn could see that this was their only chance. He would have to trust in his own judgement for the sake of the ship, and everyone aboard. Mr Legg would get them back on course and they would be out of danger.

'Yes, I am confident in my diagnosis. I will attend to the matter immediately.'

As he spoke there was screaming and shouting from above and they both rushed up to see waves breaking over the deck. When the mist cleared, they saw a cliff looming towards them, black and shining in the dawn light, streaked with luminous rivulets of water. They heard the terrifying noise of timbers crushed against rock, of the ship wedged, then breaking free to throw itself again at the cliff. They held on to the rails for dear life as the shudder went through the ship, and she broke free to be carried back away from the cliff, back into the swirling deeper water.

'She's listing. Get the anchors, men. Bow anchor, twenty, forty, sixty fathoms. Let it go. Hold tight. Tie it off. Second anchor, from the stern, forty, sixty, ninety fathoms. Hold tight. Tie it off. That's it, men. That should stabilise her for a while.' Mr Legg's voice was calm authority as he went about the procedure of securing the ship, and the men responded with the same calm and ordered sequence as they began inspecting and assessing the damage.

Suddenly Captain Bradley appeared, his eyes mad with fear, his face streaked with tears, his hands tearing at his hair as he hopped from one foot to the other. 'We are doomed,' he shouted, 'doomed to go to the bottom of the sea. A watery grave is yawning around us. There is no hope for any of us.'

'Take him below, Dr Carrick, and keep him in his cabin, for our work here will be easier without him. Restrain him with rope to his bed if you must. And keep him quiet. The passengers will be alarmed enough without his ranting.'

For the third morning in a row, the light of dawn showed a sea that was a frenzied cauldron, whipped in every direction by gusts that could knock a man over. But now they were close to land. The comfort that gave was outweighed by the danger it presented. The cliffs in front of them were surrounded by rocks above and, more dangerously, below the surface of the water. The ship was still upright, her sails reefed tightly, her decks awash with rain and the constant waves breaking over the rails as she rode on her short anchor lines between the cliffs on one side and rocks on the other.

Bryn had administered a draught to Captain Bradley to calm him and he was now sleeping in his cabin. Rather than tie him to his bed, Bryn had engaged the cook's lad to watch him and he would call Bryn if necessary. The ship seemed relatively stable, wedged in its rock prison and riding on its anchor lines, so Bryn, hearing the cries and shouts of the passengers, took the opportunity to check on them.

'Dr Carrick, are we sinking?' Mrs French screamed wildly, her eyes were wide with terror, and she clutched her wailing infant to her breast. As she spoke several cabin doors opened and passengers filled the short corridor, anxious for news of the plight of the ship and the reason for this sudden stability.

'No, Mrs French, we have struck land.' Bryn addressed the crowded group of frightened passengers. 'I suggest that you all dress yourselves and your children in your warmest clothes, as we may have to abandon ship. You will not be able to take anything with you, but you should make sure you are warm.' As he said this, he thought of his leather wallet and its contents and vowed to return to his cabin to retrieve it and secure it firmly in his undervest in case the worst were to happen. But his attention was taken by Mrs French, who fainted, crumbling silently into a heap, the child screaming as they hit the floor together. Bryn picked up the infant, as Miss Scott helped Mrs French to her bed. As he picked up the baby, he realised that there was water swirling around the floor of the cabin, only an inch or two deep but, as he watched, it was deepening. The passengers panicked as they saw water streaming down the steps at one end of the corridor and welling up the steps at the other end, where Bryn's cabin was situated. Mr Legg's voice broke through the confusion. He was leaning into the stairwell from the deck, the water running over his hand in a small waterfall as he balanced there.

'All passengers on deck immediately,' he shouted. 'Come up slowly. You will need to assemble on the deck and board the longboat in a calm and orderly fashion. Bring nothing with you. Remember, panic costs lives.'

Mrs French rose dreamily, supported by one of the

gentlemen, and with Miss Scott carrying her infant the group proceeded up the stairs and onto the deck. Within minutes they were drenched and all looked to Mr Legg for direction.

'The hold has been stoved in and water is entering the ship at a great rate. There is nothing for it but to abandon ship, but we must do it calmly. My men are preparing the smaller crafts for that purpose. Women and children will go first in the longboat.'

'But where are we, Mr Legg?' ventured Mr Broadfoot, a merchant who had a considerable amount of cargo in the hold. 'Is there any chance that the cargo can be saved?'

Mr Legg searched his surroundings with a practised eye. 'According to my calculations we are about sixty miles off course, in the Furneaux Group of islands. This is Mount Chappell on Flinders Island,' he said, pointing past the cliff face to a broad hill rising behind, 'and just past these rocks on the starboard bow is Badger Island. This passage is notorious for its reefs and I cannot see that we have much choice than to get ashore before she breaks up, for the signs indicate that she will. I doubt that we will salvage much, but my priority must be to save the lives of the passengers and crew.'

The *Isabella* carried four craft that could be used for such an emergency. The biggest, the longboat, held about twelve people and with much exertion it was dragged from its covers and launched over the side. But in the launching it crashed against the side of the ship and fractured several of its boards around the prow. The damage, although worrying, was assessed as negligible and the women and children, trembling, wet and frightened, readied themselves to be lowered in. Suddenly Captain Bradley, with the cook's boy shouting behind him, pushed through the group and was first to clamber into the longboat. There was no time for anyone to object, the women and children, some crying, but others glazed silent with fear, were bundled into the

longboat and with four sailors straining at the oars were set
free upon the heaving seas. Bryn lost sight of them as the
waves rose and fell and then caught a glimpse of them in
the steely light as they floundered away from the ship, in
which direction, towards the shore or towards the ocean, he
could not say. 'God go with you,' he found himself saying,
for it seemed there was nothing else to say.

The gig was hoisted out and secured to the stern of the
ship. There was an enormous crash as a wave hit and the
gig was swamped, the two sailors handling her holding onto
the gunwales and desperately trying to bail the water by
hand. At the same time the ship twisted as though in pain
and rolled so that she was on her beam ends, lying almost
sideways with waves crashing over her. Those left were
thrown onto the deck and had to cling to the rails as the
ship convulsed hideously and finally settled enough for Mr
Legg to issue his command.

'Cut the mizzen mast, men, mizzen first and then the fore
and top masts; that will right her.' Bryn, his heart racing,
his entire body soaked and shivering, fear heavy as a rock
in his guts, again marvelled at the calmness and clarity of
Mr Legg's orders.

It did right her. The ship, without the weight of the masts,
slowly regained its balance, groaning and heaving, fighting
the wind and waves for its natural upright position.

The business of abandonment took all day. The cutter,
able to carry about eight people, was prepared for launching
but each of six attempts failed, the wind driving the craft
back against the ship, and the waves filling it with water to
the point that it seemed that it would surely sink. At last,
fully loaded, with the passengers bailing furiously and the
crew battling with the oars, it was finally cut free and left
the side of the ship.

As it bobbed away out of sight all efforts turned to
hoisting the last escape craft, the dinghy, into the water.
Again, the force of the wind made a mockery of the strength

of the crew, men straining with ropes and pulleys, the dinghy swinging wildly and crashing into the water, only to be swamped by the incessant waves, sailors in the water, bailing furiously while they held onto the gunwales for dear life. The simple command to 'abandon ship' had taken six hours. Six hours of intense labour and fatigue for the crew and there was no guarantee that their efforts would result in a single life saved. They just did as Mr Legg commanded, their complete trust resting in his decisions.

Bryn was supposed to be in the dinghy, but there were five injured sailors, including three with broken limbs, whom he assessed as needing to get to shore sooner, so he elected to stay on board. If they made it to shore, one of the boats was to return to take Bryn and Mr Legg and the six men who remained with the ship. And if they don't make it, thought Bryn, we will have to take our chances in the water. As the afternoon light faded, Mr Legg commanded that they lash themselves to the spar, a long pole secured for the purpose on the poop deck, to prevent them being washed overboard.

'It's the safest way, Dr Carrick, while she's still in one piece. It won't be for long. I have every confidence that my men will return shortly and we will be on solid ground before the night is through.'

Bryn was lashed beside the ship's carpenter, McNeil, and as they strained with every heave of the ship, he drew strength from the solidarity of the men around him and the encouraging words of Mr Legg which came fitfully on the gusts of wind. Every gust of wind could bring death. This is how people die. This day, this hour could be my last. Izzy! Her face came smiling at him through the darkness, her voice, merry and light as she sang, soft in the candlelight, the very smell of her enveloped him, soothed him as he braced himself against the stuttering of the spar as the ship heaved and groaned.

How long they were there he could not say, merging in

and out of consciousness, but it was light when he felt a different movement of the ship. It was being lifted up, up, higher and higher, higher than it had ever been, it seemed suspended in the air for an eternity and then it came crashing down at a tremendous speed, splintering and crashing onto the rocks. Men were screaming, the wind howling and throwing its final worst at the puny humans lashed for their lives to the spar and each other. McNeil somehow produced a knife and the lashings were sliced through, all eight men shaken and still holding the spar as they saw that the ship had been broken into four pieces. They saw cargo floating around them, bales of wool, casks of tallow, boxes and crates, and it was then that Bryn realised that he had not retrieved his leather wallet. All would be lost in this shipwreck. If he survived at all, it would be with only his life.

~ ~ ~

There was no time to think.

'We must take our chances in the water, men,' shouted Mr Legg. 'She's breaking up and we cannot wait for the boat any longer.'

McNeil let out a cry of despair and Bryn watched as he pulled a string from around his neck with a bag suspended from it. 'It's my sixty sovereigns,' he cried. 'I thought it would be safe if we escaped by boat, but the weight of it around my neck will be the death of me.' He held the bag high and with a scream threw it as far as he could into the broiling sea, towards the cliff. His face was contorted with rage and pain and despair as he threw himself into the water. Bryn watched the hole in the water and saw his head emerge, a tiny bobbing dot that came and went as wave after wave washed over him.

Bryn thought he couldn't be any colder or more exhausted, but he had to endure two more hours in the water, clinging to a bag of tanning bark that had escaped the hold, pushed and pulled by the waves, until finally the dinghy was beside him and other hands were pulling him on board. The dinghy and the cutter collected all eight men from the raging sea. They could not approach the ship because of the danger of it breaking up and the force of the waves. McNeil slumped in the boat, his face swollen and bruised from collisions with the rocks and debris, his spirit broken with the loss of his life savings.

~ ~ ~

The beach was windswept and cold and the women and children huddled together among some long grass which afforded meagre protection. The twelve passengers who had escaped in the longboat had spent a miserable night exposed to the elements. The men in the party had searched for a cave or overhanging rock as shelter from the wind, but there was nothing. Now the daylight showed the new arrivals sprawled on the beach, breathing and thankful to be breathing. Bryn, lying on his stomach, opened one eye and watched Mr Legg moving along the beach through the rain towards him, checking on each person, some sitting up, others attempting to stand. There was seaweed under Bryn's cheek, green and slimy, its rank, rotting odour filling his nostrils, turning his stomach. Bryn rolled onto his back, spitting the sand out of his mouth as Mr Legg reached him.

'No lives lost, Dr Carrick, we can be glad of that, though I think this place is inhospitable and we will have to survive on our wits here. Are you well enough to carry out your duties and attend to the injured?'

'Yes, Mr Legg.' In the face of Mr Legg's continued optimism and calm, any other reply would have been cowardly. Bryn struggled to his feet and set about his work, though he had nothing to work with, the medical chest having been left behind. Miss Scott asked the ladies to part with their petticoats, tore them into neat strips and then assisted him as they bandaged the broken limbs and cleaned and bandaged the lacerations.

They moved through the day like ghosts, saying little, moving only when they had to. It was mid-morning when Bryn first noticed that the wind had dropped, had lost its power. Although the rain still fell in torrents, the lack of wind brought a silence, a reverence, as though they had found shelter after suffering a brutal, physical assault, had crawled into a protected alleyway after being kicked senseless by heavy boots on the high street. The rain gradually softened and finally for the first time in five days they were able uncurl, to expose their faces and bodies to a world without the stinging, icy bite of winter rain hurled by cyclonic wind.

They could see the poop deck wedged between the rocks at the south end of the beach, but the rest of the ship had gone, smashed to splintered pieces. Rain had puddled quite deeply on a rock platform at the northern end, protected from the salty waves by a curve in the cliff. The rock formation was a natural well, deep and cool, and the five days of cursed rain now repaid them with clean, fresh, potable water. Hunger was the next priority and they searched for anything from the ship which may have been washed ashore, but all they found were pumpkins. They collected limpets from the rocks and ate them greedily, but having no fire, their existence, even without the wind and rain, was miserable. Are we to survive all that only to starve on the beach? Bryn's head felt light, his vision blurred, but he squinted and he could see Izzy and the children coming up the beach. Fanny was riding Honey and Izzy skipped along holding Helena's hand and their laughter floated on the waves. She reached out to touch his shoulder, to shake him …

'Dr Carrick. Are you quite well? You look delirious. I have some water. Here, drink this.' It was Miss Scott, plain, practical Miss Scott.

Mr Legg again took control of the situation, calling for the fittest men to accompany him on foot in search of a sealers' camp. He calculated that the Aboriginal Mission on Flinders Island was about seventeen miles north, and ordered that four of the best rowers set out in the longboat to see if they could procure supplies from Dr Milligan and his wife, who managed the Mission. He insisted that Bryn stay with the main party and attend to the needs of the injured as best he could. Captain Bradley had to be restrained, as he kept running into the waves, cursing them for the disaster. Bryn was amazed how few the injuries were considering the trauma they had been through.

Bryn embraced the idea of staying with the injured for it meant that he was able to scour the beach for his lost possessions. Maybe the entire sea chest would be washed up or maybe it split open and he would find the leather wallet, like a dead fish, on the beach. He ventured around the rocks near the shattered last part of the wreck, searching every crevice, every rock pool, balancing with bare feet on slippery, rocky platforms to stretch up while his fingers fruitlessly searched the eroded nooks in the cliff face. Others in the group did the same, their shadowy forms moving slowly, their eyes alert for anything they could salvage. Carpenter McNeil, being strong and fit, had gone with the sailors to the Aboriginal Mission but he had pleaded with Bryn and the remaining group to look for and return his sovereigns. Each day they searched until the light faded, but they found nothing. The sea had taken everything.

A melancholy came over Bryn, such as he had never felt. Am I to die here on this windswept beach at the bottom of the world? Am I never to be reunited with my wife and children? He thought of Flintfield House, not as the home of his youth, but the feeling of Flintfield House as he had left it so long ago, the feeling of living there as a rich man. He stroked the memory of having a loving wife and children, a warm and comfortable home, staff at his disposal, the admiration of the rural folk and the status amongst his peers that his riches brought him. If he could regain this, he would do anything. He wondered about God. Did He really control these disasters? Did He expect some recompense for past flaws? For the drinking, the gambling, the cruel actions he had inflicted on Izzy. If so, Bryn was willing, more than willing, to make amends. He would reform his wayward habits if only he could go home. If only he could go home, he would do anything.

The sea took two days to calm. The last of the clouds parted and the sun shone feebly on the beach as the sealers' boat, laden with food, blankets, skins and oil and flint for fire surfed the waves towards them. The seal meat and fish they cooked could have come from the finest kitchens of Europe and there was an atmosphere of celebration as they gratefully ate their fill. The longboat returned the next day with fresh mutton and vegetables for their consumption from Dr Milligan, and Mrs Milligan sent clean, warm clothes for the women and children. And then, two days later came the news they all craved; that the brig *Flying Fish*, en route from Hobart to Melbourne, was at anchor on the other side of the island and would delay its departure until they could board.

~ ~ ~

The weary survivors climbed the last hill in their five-mile trek across Flinders Island. The afternoon was clear and cold, and with the sun bright on their backs their spirits lifted with the thought that their ordeal was over. The men carried the children on their shoulders. The women carried the bundled clothes which had been replaced by the kindness of Mrs Milligan. They could have been a party of picnickers on a Sunday outing, chatting and laughing after a pleasant day in the fresh winter air. As they topped the ridge, they saw the *Flying Fish* lying at anchor in a small, protected bay. From this height the brig looked tiny, a toy bobbing in the great expanse of ocean. To the left they could see the four minute craft that had been their escape, the crew having brought them through the dangerous passage and around the south of the island to be hoisted aboard the *Flying Fish*. They were all that remained of the *Isabella*.

They were made welcome by Captain Clinch and set sail immediately. The *Flying Fish* was carrying six passengers and general cargo on its regular run between Hobart and Port Phillip. The crew gave up their quarters for the ladies and children and camped under canvas on the deck with the male passengers and the crew of the *Isabella*. The passage to Port Phillip was only twenty-four hours and there was an atmosphere of celebration and relief on board, the survivors held in awe, with a status they did not expect. Stretched out on the deck, Bryn looked at the stars in the clear black sky and thought of Izzy. His anger at her letter had subsided. In his brush with death, he saw his faults, saw how he had neglected her. He wanted nothing more than to be with her, to feel her softness, to listen to her chatter, to curl with her in the darkness of their bed, to play with his children, rolling on the grass with them, hearing their shrieks as he chased them. On the poop deck, lashed to the spar, he had thought he was going to die. He had prayed. On the beach he had bargained with God. He had promised that he would turn teetotal, devote himself to his family and his profession. Now it was time to fulfil those promises.

Bryn looked at the soft and gentle sea, shining in the morning sun as the *Flying Fish* entered Port Phillip Bay, and wondered that it could have such moods. The thought of Melbourne, unwelcome as it was, seemed to beckon him to begin again. He had arranged to meet Mr Legg the following week to write their account of the shipwreck and the reasons for the change of leadership on board. As they tied up at the wharf he watched as Mr Legg, solid and erect, offered his arm to Captain Bradley, who was laughing and chatting as he hopped erratically towards him along the deck. They disembarked and walked away together towards a cart that would take them to a public house in the town, where they would stay before Captain Bradley was called to account for the loss of the *Isabella*. Who knew what the outcome would be?

'He is as nutty as a fruit cake, that one.' It was McNeill and as Bryn turned to face him, McNeill grasped his hand. 'I want to thank you, Dr Carrick. You and Mr Legg were the saviours of the crew and passengers.'

'No. No. Not me, McNeill. Mr Legg is the man who saved us. He knew what to do and—'

'But you supported him, Dr Carrick. I know Legg. A good man but he's a stickler for the rules. He needed your support.'

'Thank you, McNeill. I'm sorry for the loss of your sovereigns.'

McNeill took a long breath and blew it out slowly. 'We all lost everything, Dr Carrick. But we are alive. We are alive. It is only when we make a new beginning that we can make a new ending. Good-bye, Dr Carrick. I wish you well.' And he was gone.

As Bryn walked to Charles Peabody's house he thought of McNeill's words; a new beginning and a new ending and a plan of action was forming in his mind. His friend Charles would welcome him and care for him but Bryn was determined to be as independent as he could. He would have to take advantage of the subscription list that would be started for the passengers by the good people of Melbourne. He had contributed himself often enough in the past, and now he had nothing, it was his turn to benefit from this public charity. The first thing he would need to do was travel to Sydney to have his medical qualifications reissued. Without them he could not work but the process was slow, so it was important that he begin immediately. He estimated that the shipwreck of the *Isabella*, as well as robbing him of his last funds, had put him behind by about two years. But first he would write to Izzy. There was much to tell her.

Part 3
Madam Chevalier

Chapter 22

Chatham 1845

A sudden sharp chill in the air told the people of Chatham that the seasons were once again changing. They had been there for just over a year and in her later life Izzy would count that year as her happiest. When she had had no reply from Bryn by July, Francis suggested that he let it be thought among the residents of Chatham that they had married in secret. It was just a small lie but it would ensure Izzy's reputation and full acceptance of herself and the children, in case a new child were to be born. As Francis had said, the population of Chatham was transient and nobody suspected the falsehood. The family was included in the society of Chatham, invited to picnics and parties, with the girls attending the village school and making their own friends.

Autumn brought familiar signs to Izzy; the swelling of her breasts, the halt of her monthly issue, the constant nausea. She had known of course that it would happen. She had been living as Francis' wife in all but name for over a year and each month she was surprised to find that she was not pregnant. Francis was delighted and Izzy looked forward to the birth of this child, born of her love for Francis.

Barely had she become used to the idea that she was to have another child, when a letter arrived from Bryn. Before she had even opened it, the envelope seemed to shout her secret – this is falsehood, I am your true husband, you are living in sin. Wearily she opened it and read.

5th August 1844
Melbourne

Dear Izzy,

I received your letter written in April and I was shocked with the contents. That my brother should have cast you out is monstrous. He should have found alternative accommodation for you in Ireland, even amid Sarah's complaining. I have had no correspondence from him, though I hear through others that things are deteriorating rapidly in Ireland with the failure of the harvest and the heavy-handed tactics of the English landlords. Your father's behaviour was also detestable; to cut you off without thought. It would have been only a small generosity on his part to allow you access to Blackrock House, your childhood home near Dublin. This is such meanness and all at a time when I am in the depths of despair, half a world away.

I cannot say that what you did was the right thing but I will say that I understand why you did it. However, I am disappointed that you have thrown me over completely for Captain Chevalier and that you are willing to risk your social standing and morality for his favour. I have been trying to get back to you but every step holds a trap, the latest being the worst I have experienced. I have enclosed a copy of the newspaper account of the wreck of the Isabella. *You will see that it was devastating and that I came close to losing my life. This will explain my delay in reaching you.*

I have lost everything now, even the few hundred pounds I had salvaged from my assets and most importantly my medical qualifications were also lost in the shipwreck. I cannot work without them, nor apply for a position as ship's doctor on a vessel bound for England and am at present in Sydney pursuing the means to have a copy sent from Glasgow. But all this takes time. It would seem that at least a year, maybe more will pass until I can send you enough money for you and the children to come back to Melbourne. I know that in your letter you declared that you did not desire that, but you are my wife and these are my children and your place is here with me.

The shipwreck taught me that I have much to change in my life and I have already set about making some changes. I have again joined the Temperance Society and have not indulged in brandy in the last weeks. I intend to devote myself to my family and to my profession and I resolve to build up my practice with perseverance and steadfastness, so that I am able to welcome you back to a life which is as comfortable as that which we had before.

I remain your true husband, Bryn

The newspaper article was long and described in horrific detail the five days of torture that the passengers and crew of the *Isabella* survived. It gave much attention to the role of Bryn; how he declared the Captain insane which allowed Mr Legg to take control, how he remained on board until the last and how he attended to the health of the bedraggled band once they were beached on Flinders Island. Izzy felt an old admiration, a pride in his upright and honourable nature and it took her back to the early days of her marriage and her realisation that he would ride twenty miles to attend a sick convict but he would not leave the Melbourne Club to come home to her. He would risk his life for these strangers but he had abandoned her on the other side of the world. Was it pride and admiration she felt or was it jealousy? She sighed as she folded the article and the letter and slipped them back into the envelope for Francis to read later.

Izzy did not reply to Bryn's letter. What could she say? He obviously wanted her to return to Melbourne, which she would not, and he would never accept another man's child as his own, as Francis had. Izzy caressed her swollen belly and imagined her new baby, a summer baby to be born in July, born to the man she loved. No, she would not reply, she would wait and cause him to wait, as he had caused her to wait.

Francis read the letter and agreed that there was no need to reply immediately. Bryn was half a world away; his pride was wounded but he was in no position to pursue Izzy and the children simply to satisfy convention. Time would tell if his good intentions would come to anything or whether the lure of brandy would triumph. There was only one small, niggling complication at the back of Francis' mind but he shook it away. It would resolve itself. No need to worry Izzy and upset her happiness. It might come to nothing.

But as the weeks progressed, he realised that it would not be ignored. It grew out of proportion and as Easter approached it demanded to be addressed, demanded that Francis shatter his domestic harmony, shatter Izzy's happiness. Izzy caught the downcast expression in his eye as he returned home from the depot.

'What is it my love?' she said, as she hung his topcoat in the hall cupboard.

'There is news today which I was hoping would not eventuate. There have been rumours over the last weeks, but until this they have only been rumours.'

'What rumours? Is it bad news?'

'Yes, I'm afraid so. A battalion of the 28th is to be deployed to India and will leave in mid-summer. I was hoping to avoid being called upon to lead such a mission but today,' he paused, not wanting to speak the words, 'today I received my orders.' He took a single sheet of paper from the breast pocket of his uniform, unfolded it and handed it to Izzy. 'I'm sorry Izzy, but I will have to follow orders and leave you.'

'No!' She sank to the chair, clutching the arms, her knuckles white with her grip. 'No Francis, please. Can't you do anything?'

'It seems not,' he said, folding the paper and replacing it in his pocket. His shoulders sagged. 'I have been pursuing every avenue for the last few weeks but the orders have come and they must be obeyed.'

'Have you been given a date of departure?' Her voice was barely audible.

'Yes, July 23rd from Gravesend on the *Claudine*. Seventy-eight men will accompany me.'

'But the baby is due in July! Could we not accompany you as well?'

'No Izzy, that is not possible. It is not a mission for women and children. There is war in the Punjab region with the Sikhs rebelling against British rule.'

'But why can't someone else go in your stead?'

'Izzy, I am a soldier. I must follow orders. It will not be forever and when I return we will consider our future together without the army. Farming perhaps; we could buy a small holding.'

'How long,' she caught her breath, 'how long will you be gone?'

He paused and cast his eyes to the floor, not wanting to see her face crumple.

'It will take at least a year, probably two.'

Izzy could not speak, so overcome with grief was she at the thought of their separation. He helped her to the bedroom and made sure she was comfortable then sat with her until her convulsive sobbing left her in an exhausted sleep.

They didn't talk about the possibility that he may be

killed or injured in the bloody conflicts that became the First Anglo–Sikh War and Francis kept the true extent of the risks well hidden from Izzy. He arranged for his pay to be made over to Izzy and any pension which his death would occasion was to be paid to her. He paid the rent on the house for the next five years, giving Izzy the document and assuring her of her security. He visited his bank and withdrew all his funds, just over £2,000, which he gave to Izzy. Then finally he wrote to his father, the Dean of Kilkenny, and explained the situation and asked for protection for Izzy, should the worst happen. The reply was positive but confused. Who is this woman? Why have you not brought her to Ireland for us to meet? Is she your wife by law? He answered as best he could; that she was a widow with four children whom he had married and that their own child was to be born in the summer, that there had been so little time to visit Ireland, that he was sorry for his parents' disappointment, that he asked their blessing on him as he departed to do his duty.

~ ~ ~

Three weeks before Francis was to sail the baby was born. Her hair was dark like Izzy's and her skin as faultless and fair and it was Francis who suggested that she be named for Izzy. Izzy agreed and added her own mother's name and so she became Isabel Rosita Chevalier. The children crowded around her whenever they could, singing to her, treating her like a doll and she seemed to enjoy the attention of her siblings. Francis was fascinated with her, picking her up and singing to her, feeling her grip his finger in her chubby fist, looking into her dark eyes.

Izzy was between ecstasy and despair. Every day the baby grew more beautiful, more loved and every day was one day closer to saying good-bye to Francis.

~ ~ ~

'What am I to do?' she said aloud as she watched the ship fade into the river mist. 'He is gone and I know not when I will see him again.' She retired to her bed and could only attend to the baby, Maria and the servants taking charge of the other children.

Chapter 23

Chatham 1846

Izzy was miserable. The whole household seemed to be miserable; this winter was interminable. Already it was March, with no sign of spring. Cold seeped under the doors, frost hugged the ground and rain hurled itself at the house. Izzy looked out the drawing room window at the park, the trees shrouded in fog, the path barely visible.

She thought wearily of last winter, her first in Chatham, and the long days indoors. How she had loved that winter, how cosy it had been, how secure she had felt with Francis, her beloved Francis. Was it only last year? Had he only been gone for three quarters of a year? How would she survive until he came back? She clasped his latest letter to her heart. Like all his letters it was full of love, of homesickness, of questions about the baby. He spoke little about the war but his disdain for its barbarity was becoming more obvious. 'I cannot reconcile,' he wrote, 'that I murder with my own hands. I hate this place, these deeds I do. I want only to run, to hide, to be with you and safe from this turmoil.' Izzy was lost in thought when Maria Batman, her long-time companion and second mother to the children came into the drawing room alone and asked if they could speak.

'Of course, Maria, come in and sit down. What is it? Is something wrong?'

'Yes Izzy, something is wrong. Something is very wrong.' Maria moved towards the single chair as Izzy settled herself on the sofa.

'What is it, Maria? You are distressed. I can see you are distressed.'

'Yes, I am distressed. I am distressed for your children. They are so unhappy. Forgive me if I am too direct, but they want you. In your grief you have no time for them. I have come to plead on their behalf. They need you. You cannot go on like this. Your unhappiness is causing them to be anxious.'

'Anxious? What do you mean? Are they sick?'

'Well, yes in a way. They think you don't love them anymore. They think you only love the baby. They think it's their fault.'

'Oh, I didn't think. Did you tell them it's not that at all?'

'Yes, of course I told them that. But they don't need to hear it from me. They need to hear it from you. They need their mother, Izzy.' Maria rose and sat next to Izzy on the sofa, her arm around her shoulder as Izzy convulsed into sobs again. 'There, it will be all right,' she said, patting Izzy on the back. 'You just need to come out of your room and be yourself with them again. You have been sad for long enough. Captain Chevalier would not want you to go on any longer.'

'But I miss him so much.' Izzy accepted Maria's handkerchief and dabbed at her eyes and running nose. 'He hates the war and wants only to return to us.'

'Of course, you miss him, but you must think about the children. They are your responsibility and they need you. You must look to the future. No good will come of this misery. You must think less of yourself and more of your children.'

'Do you think I have been selfish?'

'Forgive me but yes, in a way. I know you are sad, but that will not bring Captain Chevalier back. You must recognise that and then get on with life as best you can.'

The slow, deep ticking of the clock intensified as silence fell between them. Ticking away my life, thought Izzy, ticking the very life out of me. Maria is right, all these months it has been ticking, not only my life away but the lives of my children. How could I have been so foolish, so obsessed with my own sorrow? She could feel Maria's arm, still tight around her shoulder, and she turned towards her and took both her hands. They were small hands, plain and scuffed with the work of raising Izzy's children.

'Thank you, Maria, you are right of course.' Izzy took a deep breath and stared at her paid companion as though she was seeing her for the first time. 'It must have been hard for you with the children.'

'Yes, it has, but I am an adult and I understand your misery. Your children don't understand it and they need you.'

'Yes, I have been selfish. I have been indulging my own misery these past months; Francis has gone and I must make the best of it. Thank you for what you have said, I know it must have been hard to tell me. Give me an hour or so and I will wash my face and come up to the nursery with the baby. Thank you, Maria.'

Maria rose to leave the room, then stopped and patted her apron pocket, smiling as she handed the envelope to Izzy. 'A letter from Melbourne for you, from Mrs Charles Peabody.'

Izzy reached excitedly for the letter and was already reading before Maria had left the room.

4th January 1846
Melbourne

My dear friend,

I trust this finds you well and happy in your new situation in Chatham. It was with great relief that I read in your last letter that Captain Chevalier had so generously offered to care for you and the children by enabling you to leave the intolerable situation in Ireland. News is slow to reach Melbourne, but it seems that famine will entirely take over the south of Ireland so Charles and I praise God that your departure was so timely.

The financial crash here in Melbourne has seen many businessmen in the same situation as Dr Carrick, losing their fortunes with no possible way of regaining any profit. I understand little of it but it seems that Charles has been conservative in his investments and we are able to continue to live nearly as before. Dr Carrick had stayed with us but has been in Sydney this last year and Charles has not been in contact with him, so I am sorry I cannot give you any news of him.

The children continue to grow and enjoy good health. Little Kenneth is no longer so little, being now six years of age and beginning to learn his letters. Margaret is approaching her fourth birthday and is her father's favourite. Baby Alice had suffered some colic in the early months but is now much stronger as she enters her second year of life.

But, my dear friend, the real purpose of my letter is to tell you that we will be visiting England in October. Although this seems a long way off, I could not wait any longer before writing to you. Charles has booked our passage on the Euphrates *leaving Sydney on June 3rd and arriving in October in London. We will spend several weeks in Sydney with his parents before embarking. He has some business interests to attend to in London and Edinburgh and of course we will visit his family members in Scotland. My family is situated in Somerset and he has promised that we will also visit them.*

Of course, we both wish to spend time with you and the children; how lovely for our children to know each other. Charles will arrange lodgings in London for three months and then we will tour the cities of Europe – Paris, Rome and Venice in particular. In the New Year we will relocate to Scotland. We expect to be away from Melbourne for at least two years, maybe more, but it depends on Charles' business dealings. He is keen to negotiate directly with the woollen mills in Edinburgh and Bradford, so that the fleece produced in the Melbourne area has a smooth transition and attracts the best prices for the landholders in our region. I am mad with excitement and overjoyed that we will be able to have some time together.

Write back to me immediately so that we can plan how we will spend our days. May God bless you and keep you.

Your friend Harriet

~ ~ ~

Izzy waited two or three days to reply to Harriet. She needed to inform her friend of her true relationship with Captain Chevalier, the birth of baby Isabel and her present living condition, with Francis away in India. Although the letter was carefully composed, her enthusiasm for the approaching visit could not be stifled and the final missive reflected her excitement. Izzy was surprised with how much better she felt over the coming weeks. The joyful news of Harriet's visit did much to lift her spirits.

Every day she would play with the little boys in the nursery or in the drawing room. When the weather permitted, they would all walk out to meet Edie and Helena coming home from school in the afternoon. She examined the girls' lessons with pride and even though they were only seven and six years old, Izzy was amazed at their proficiency in writing and reading. She rejoiced in their singing and dancing and in their beauty, their bodies straight and strong, their perfect skin. Never again, she resolved, would they be ignored. She was their mother and they must be her first priority.

Izzy's heart ached for Francis. His letters came more regularly, almost every second day. Sometimes they rambled so much that Izzy could not follow his thoughts. She puzzled over this but tried to remain positive in her replies. She told him of the new focus in her life; that she would see the children educated and brought up carefully, with a view to manners and respectability, so that they could achieve the best that life had to offer them.

Francis had left her money and the security of this house. As spring slowly ripened, she silently thanked him again and made plans for the next twelve months; the girls would continue at the village school, and she would give over care of the baby to Maria so that she would be free to educate the boys herself in preparation for them entering school. She thought back to her days in the Peabody household and how she was governess to Mary and Thomas, the games they played and the manners that Mrs Peabody had insisted that she impart to the children. Yes, she would devote herself to this task.

Baby Isabel continued to delight the entire household as she learned to sit up, to hold a spoon, to make noises that could be imagined to be words. The warmer spring weather meant outdoor activities and laughter as the children pushed her carriage in the park and played with her on a rug in the garden, bringing her blooms, encouraging her to crawl, all four of them vying for her attention.

She still slept in Izzy's room, even though she had been trained to take the bottle and was eating solid food. Izzy held onto that last little luxury, her last link with Francis, keeping the baby for herself at night. She would lie awake listening to her breathing, slow and rhythmic, wondering about her dreams, describing her progress as she mentally prepared her next letter to Francis. This week had seen the anniversary of her birth and Izzy had drawn a likeness of her to send to Francis. It was quite good and she felt proud of it. She packed it into the bulky envelope, addressed it and took it to the depot to send to him.

Sometimes the baby would cry and Izzy would nurse her back to sleep, cradling her in her arms, singing softly to her. One night, though, Izzy awoke to find that when she picked her up her little body was burning hot. She stripped the baby's nightdress off and sponged her with cool water. The baby wriggled and cried, her little legs drawn up against the stomach cramp and the foul issue that exploded from her body. She relaxed enough for Izzy to be able to clean her and change her clothes but the cycle continued all night, three, four, five times until the baby collapsed in exhaustion, her delicate frame lying on the damp sheet, her forehead beading with sweat. Izzy was exhausted too and she and Maria took turns all the next day to care for her. Her body temperature seemed to rise and fall but never stayed at a normal level for very long. The doctor arrived after lunch, his portly frame climbing the stairs, his touch gentle as he examined the baby, his kind old face crinkled with concern.

'I'm sorry, Mrs Chevalier, there is little I can do.'

'Will she recover quickly, Doctor? I have been trying to get her to take some broth.'

'Good. Yes, broth is good. Sometimes these remittent

fevers right themselves. If we can get the body temperature to remain stable instead of fluctuating then we have a better chance of controlling it. I will give you some Syrup of Squills which will cause vomiting and release the evil humours from her body. In order to prevent too much inflammation in the stomach you can combine it with a few drops of opium.'

'Thank you, Doctor. How quickly would you expect her to recover?'

'We shall have to see, Mrs Chevalier. Keep using the cool cloth on her forehead but keep the windows shut against the moisture in the night air, for it increases the potency of the gases which cause the fever.'

'Is there nothing else I can do?' The old doctor was kind but he was already packing up his bottles into his medicine bag in preparation for moving on to his next patient. Izzy thought of Bryn and how lucky she had been to have him on hand when their girls were so little.

The old man shook his head. 'Perhaps you can try washing her feet in hot water. Some say it works. You could try that. I will call by tomorrow to see how she fares.'

The doctor called every day for a week. Sometimes Izzy thought the worst was over and baby Isabel was showing signs of recovery, but then the high temperatures would return and the cycle would start over again. The doctor proceeded to the next level of treatment which was two grains of calomel, a mercurial concoction, mixed with four grains of the purgative, powdered rhubarb. Izzy would mix it with treacle and spoon it into her baby's mouth. The baby's eyes were glazed and her body listless, drained of all energy. She had stopped crying and Izzy sat beside her day and night and helplessly watched her fade away. She prayed and prayed for her baby. She bargained with God for the baby's life. She offered her own in her place. She promised to give Francis up, to return to Melbourne, to be a good wife to Bryn if only the baby could live.

But it was not to be. Despite the summer warmth Izzy

wrapped her in a blanket and carried her out of the house to the church of St Mary in the main street of Chatham where she asked the pastor to baptise her. 'I fear she is going to die,' she croaked, her voice hoarse with grief, her body weak with lack of sleep. The pastor obliged sympathetically and Izzy returned home to wait for the inevitable. Two weeks after her first birthday, baby Isabel died.

~ ~ ~

Izzy returned to the blackness, her thoughts constantly recounting the pain.

I am holding her little body, so cold and still. I am weeping, I think. I wait for a sound, a cry. A pain stabs in my chest because I can't remember her cry, the sound of it, the feel of it. She stopped crying days ago and I knew then that there was no hope. Two weeks of sickness, her body emptying itself of all goodness until there was nothing left. Nothing would stop it, would calm her. I am wretched. It is my punishment. I know it is my punishment. Her birth was like mine, an accident. But her death, this is too unfair. I place her gently in the cradle. I want to believe she is just asleep. She is a doll, lifeless, limp, her dark curls around her tiny face.

Chapter 24

Chatham 1846

Bryn stood on the deck as the small barque *Dublin* tied up to the new dock at Southampton. He shaded his eyes against the intense August glare, marvelling that an English sun could have all the ferocity of that in New South Wales. The dock was alive with activity and he could see a line of hansom cabs on the edge of the dock. He had signed off as ship's surgeon after an uneventful voyage and now shook hands with the Captain. He signalled to a porter to carry his sea chest and picking up his medical bag he followed the porter to the cabs.

He stayed two nights in Southampton rejoicing in the forgotten familiarity of ordinary things, like the good cheer of a proper British public house and the sophistication of ordinary life; paved streets, closed sewers on the main streets and the wonder of the century – the railway. On the third day he made for the Terminus Station, a gracious three-storey building which had opened six years ago and he stood in amazement as the train chugged in noisily, puffing its steam and soot over the bystanders, metal wheels screeching to a halt before disgorging its many passengers.

He bought his ticket which was dispensed quickly by the clerk using the new Edmondson ticket system, a small, cardboard, numbered, colour coded ticket that had the date printed in it when it was inserted in the machine. He sat in the carriage waiting for departure and looked at the ticket in wonder. The whole process had taken only seconds, replacing the laboriously handwritten tickets he was used to for coach travel. There was no comparison now, the railway had replaced coach travel, halving the time and cost of journeys like his.

The carriage was full but fairly comfortable, roofed and enclosed, with open windows and the pleasant regular rocking was in stark contrast to the unpredictable lurching of a horse-drawn coach. As the train traversed the open fields, the speed increased to almost sixty miles per hour and Bryn watched as the trees and fields blurred by. He had read reports critical of the high speeds and the 'devilish' effect it produced for passengers hurtling through the countryside, but he found that he liked the sensation. What would have been a two- or three-day coach journey was over within the day. At sunset the train terminated at Nine Elms Station on the southern shore of the Thames.

His plan was to stay in London for a few days and then to make his way to Chatham to see Izzy. She knew nothing of his journey and his forthcoming visit and he wanted to keep it that way. From her only letter he knew she was living at 24 Clover Street and his plan was to observe the house for a few days before making his presence known to her. That way he could get a true picture of her new life and judge whether he did indeed want her back. It seemed she had made a cosy nest and had given herself entirely over to Captain Chevalier without a thought for her real husband, the father of her children. A few days of observation would determine what the best course of action would be.

~ ~ ~

He found lodgings in Chatham High Street in a respectable public house and used his mother's maiden name and his brother's Christian name without his title of Doctor, so he became, for these few days in Chatham, Mr William Hayes. He did not know why he took this precaution, but it felt safer, freer somehow to be without his true identity. He asked directions to Clover Street and found it close by, a broad, treed street with townhouses on one side and a park and garden opposite. An attractive street; no wonder Izzy liked it. He found number 24 and walked by quickly, his head bent and his hat securely on his head. He crossed the street to the park and saw that there were benches for seating but he passed them by as they were on the edge of the park and would be easily seen from the house. He walked deeper into the park and chose to sit on a bench that faced the house but was some distance from it, with trees and gardens in between. A gravel path wound its way through the park and people came and went, taking no notice of the gentleman reading his paper in the shade of the old trees.

He remained there for over an hour glancing across to the house regularly, the front door shut tight, the curtains drawn. Perhaps they have moved on, Bryn thought. It was late morning and he folded his paper and made his way back to his lodging for his dinner. He would come back in the late afternoon.

The next day he varied his observation times. In the mid-afternoon he gasped as the front door opened and a woman with two small children emerged. They were boys but the woman was not Izzy. Who was she? From this distance he could not make out any features, except that she was carrying a posy of flowers. He rose and followed the gravel path which brought him back to the street and he could follow behind the woman at a distance. The boys ran along the roadside skittishly and were admonished by the woman who called them back so the younger one could take her hand and Bryn decided from her clothing and voice that she was a governess or servant of some type. They stopped and waited outside the village school, Bryn finding interest in the church building opposite. Presently the school doors released a noisy flood of children and the woman was joined by two older girls, aged around seven and eight. Bryn held the church gate for support because he was looking at his children. That surely was Edie and Helena, how they had grown. And the two little boys would be Charles Henri and the new baby, born after Bryn had left Ireland. He stared, fixated, his hands grasping the church gate, his brow suddenly dripping sweat under his hat.

He moved into the church graveyard towards the shade of an old tree, its deep coolness caressing his skin. He leaned against the rough bark and took in a slow breath, steadying his shaking hands. He quickly moved around the other side of the old tree as he saw the woman and children cross the road and enter the graveyard. He could see now it was Maria Batman, an older, weightier version of the girl who had accompanied the family to Ireland. She was Henry's daughter, the niece of his old friend the original founder of Melbourne, John Batman. A good girl, steady like her mother. It was not surprising that she stayed with Izzy.

The little group made its way through the old headstones towards the back of the cemetery and stopped by a newly dug grave. It was so new that there was no headstone, just a pile of brown dirt baking to clay in the August heat. They knelt in prayer around the grave and then Maria emptied the flower pot of its dead contents and gave the children a fresh flower each to leave at the grave. Was it Izzy? Was she dead? Bryn was confused, wanted to shout out to Maria, wanted to replace the children's sadness with the joy of his return. But he stopped. He waited. Perhaps it was Captain Chevalier who had died. That would make his task easier. Izzy would be more likely to return to Melbourne if her lover was dead. He would have to wait and find out more information.

~ ~ ~

After a week of observing exactly the same ritual each day and no sign of Izzy or Captain Chevalier, Bryn decided he would have to approach the house and make his presence known. He had asked casually at the lodgings about recent deaths in Chatham but was not able to glean any information without raising suspicions. He timed his visit for mid-morning when he knew the girls would be at school.

~ ~ ~

Bryn waited in the simply furnished drawing room while the maid went upstairs to fetch Maria. He had thought it safer to ask for her, not knowing whether Izzy or Captain Chevalier were still living here, or indeed, whether they were alive at all. He had not given his name to the maid, so Maria would only be told there was a gentleman wishing to see her in the drawing room. The door opened and Maria came in, obviously curious about this visitor.

'Good morning, Maria,' said Bryn as he rose and took a few steps toward her.

'Dr Carrick,' she gasped, 'Dr Carrick, what are you doing here?' She curtsied quickly and came towards him. 'Does Izzy know you are here?'

'No, I was not sure of her circumstance and thought it wise to consult you. I saw you in the street with the children.' He fumbled, suddenly ashamed of his subterfuge.

'She is unwell. She is very unwell, Sir. Since the baby's death, she has not been herself at all. I fear for her, Sir. I am glad you are here as I don't know what to do, with Captain Chevalier away and all.'

'Away? Where is Captain Chevalier?'

'He's gone to India, with the Regiment, Sir. He left in July last year, just after baby Isabel was born and then, then ...' Maria rummaged in her pocket and brought out her handkerchief. 'Then just a few weeks ago, just after her first birthday, the baby got sick and there was nothing we could do, Sir. No matter what we did, there was no hope for the poor little thing. The children were distraught and Izzy has gone right back to the darkness she was in when Captain Chevalier left. I should not be saying all this to you, but I don't know what else I can do for her.'

'Maria, you have done the right thing. I have come at a very bad time. I can see that. Would you tell Izzy that I will come again tomorrow morning at eleven o'clock? I would like to see her to discuss the future, the future of our children.' He took a deep breath and considered his next sentence before continuing. 'Please convey my sympathy to her on the loss of the child, and impress on her the importance of this meeting. Even if she is unwell, it is important that we meet to discuss the future.'

He rose and bowed and left the house immediately.

~ ~ ~

It was a shadow sitting in the armchair as Bryn again entered the drawing room. His practised eye saw a melancholic young woman, small and vulnerable. Her face was colourless; lips, cheeks, forehead, startling against the black of her mourning gown. Her once lively eyes were vacant, slowly focusing on him as if swimming through fog. All the demands, all the recriminations he had prepared to hurl at her evaporated as he saw only a creature of pity, a mother who had lost her child.

'I am sorry, Izzy, that you have suffered so much,' Bryn said after he had kissed her hand and she had indicated that he should sit on the sofa.

'Thank you, Bryn.' Her voice was lower, more mature than he remembered. She cleared her throat as if to speak but then looked away as if she had nothing more to say, or had forgotten the words.

'Maria told me of your loss and that you are greatly affected by it.'

'Yes, I cannot see that life will ever be the same.' There was silence.

'And what will become of our children? Have you thought of them, Izzy?'

'Maria cares for them and I will be strong enough in time.'

'I cannot think that so much time in the company of a servant is beneficial to them. The girls especially are of an age where they need more refinement than she can offer.'

The silence was intense. Izzy closed her eyes and listened to the old clock again. This was Bryn, sitting here in her drawing room, talking about what would be good or bad for her children.

'And do you have a suggestion, Bryn?' Izzy sat a little straighter and turned her body to face him.

'I would like you all to return to Melbourne with me,' returned Bryn, missing the sarcasm in her voice.

'No, that will never happen.'

Bryn was surprised with the speed of the response and its definite delivery.

'Well,' he said, trying to suppress the anger that was rising, trying to keep an even tone in his voice, 'if you won't come, then I will take the children with me.'

There was no movement, no flicker in her eye.

'No.'

'I have every right to take them. They are my children as much as yours and the law would favour me over you, if it came to that.'

'No. I will not be parted from my children. You used that argument to get me to leave Melbourne six years ago. You will not use it again to get me to go back.'

Bryn suddenly felt foolish. Yes, she is right, I did exactly that.

'With Captain Chevalier away at war, you are in a vulnerable position. Have you thought what might happen if he were to be killed or injured?'

The mention of his name seemed to jolt Izzy into the present.

Suddenly she was on the offensive, as if fire was pouring though her body, giving her the strength to fight off this attack.

'Don't mention his name. You are nothing compared with him. You deserted us, Bryn. You left us for dead. You didn't care whether we lived or died. Francis was our saviour, our only hope. He loves me and he will come back to me. Go back where you came from, Bryn. Go back to Melbourne for you have no place with us anymore.'

Bryn was stunned that she was suddenly so forceful and he sat silently as Izzy composed herself once more. Then he spoke, the evenness of his voice barely containing his anger.

'I have tried constantly to make my way back to you. I was shipwrecked. I have overcome great hardship to be here. I have the best of intentions and you throw them in my face. I want to take the children and by God, I will have my way.'

'You don't want the children. You have not paid a penny to their upkeep in the last five years and never have you enquired of their wellbeing or happiness. You are only concerned with convention, with what is right and proper.'

'Yes, I am concerned with convention and it is fortunate I am for it seems that you are most certainly not. You, misbegotten as you were, you are being kept by a man who is not your husband and you have just buried his bastard child. Do the people of Chatham know—'

He had no chance to finish the sentence for Izzy flew out of her chair, screaming and scratching at his eyes. He caught her by the wrists and stood to fend her off. The door flew open and Maria entered, running to Izzy's side and lowering her back into her chair.

'Dr Carrick, perhaps you should leave,' Maria exclaimed.

'No, Maria, Dr Carrick will stay as we bring this to a conclusion.' Izzy was panting with anger. 'Perhaps, though, you could take a seat by the door so that he remains civilised in his speech.'

Maria took her seat out of their sight and again the room

returned to silence. After several minutes it was Bryn who spoke.

'Perhaps it is best if we continue our deliberations tomorrow, after we have both had a chance to think about the possibilities and difficulties of the future.'

'Yes,' Izzy murmured, 'come again at eleven o'clock.'

~ ~ ~

Bryn left Chatham a week later. Their arguments were fierce and angry but in the end he knew that Izzy was right. He hadn't thought about Izzy not coming back to Melbourne and he didn't want the responsibility or the care of four children; he couldn't afford it, having only just returned to solvency. Izzy was determined to stay in Chatham and wait for her lover, so to hell with her. She could do as she pleased and the children with her. She had demanded that he pay an annuity for the upkeep of the children and although he knew in his heart that this was the right thing to do, his anger was so aroused that he had shouted and declared that she could go to the poorhouse before he gave her a penny. It was the end of all his good resolutions and he returned to London and poured his soul out to the stranger in a public house who shared the bottle of brandy with him.

Chapter 25

Chatham 1846

Izzy had been in a whirlpool, buffeted and twisted and tumbled, disoriented in the world around her and unfamiliar with the faces that came and went in her dreams and waking moments. Maria's voice, calm and soothing, was the only constant, comforting her as she retched, encouraging her sips of broth, accompanying the cooling cloth. Now she opened her eyes and the realisation assailed her; the world was still, her body was still. The room was dark but the edge of the curtain revealed it was not night. She tried to sit up but the effort overcame her and she sank into the clammy sheet.

She may have dreamt or she may have just wandered through her thoughts, carelessly, flittingly, here and there, then and now. Images came and went; the children playing, Edith laughing, the smell of stale brandy, the softness of Francis' hand, the deep black pit that held her baby, the slam of the door as Bryn left.

But when she came back into the real world, into the now of her bedroom, the sliver of light at the edge of the curtain, the smell of sweat on her own body, she concentrated on the stillness, visiting each part of her body, legs, knees, hips, arms, neck, head. She moved her hand to feel her forehead. No fever. She pushed herself up and sat on the edge of the bed and slid her toes to the floor. The rug felt chilled and she wondered what the season was, what the month, what the day?

She moved towards the window and pulled the heavy curtain slightly. The brightness stabbed her eyes and she snapped them shut, steadying herself against the wall as she did so. How long had she been in this death-like phase? Cautiously she opened her eyes and looked out across the park. The trees were being whipped by the wind, their yellow leaves clinging stubbornly, their dead brown ones flying through the air and swirling along the path. The clouds skittered across the sky, across the face of the sun, milky white and weak. It must be autumn. When was Bryn here? Hot, it was hot – August, yes, it was August. Suddenly she felt an urgency to escape this room, this darkness.

She tottered towards the door and grasped the knob to open it. She had to use two hands and when the lock released the door itself felt heavy and sluggish to move. Was she so weak that opening a door was difficult? The hallway was silent and she moved towards the stairs tenuously, holding the wall before finally reaching the top step and grasping the banister. The stairs were steep, lowering away into the dim light of the entrance hall below. She called Maria but there was no reply, perhaps she had only whispered the name, she couldn't tell. She slid to sit on the top step, wishing she had brought her shawl to cover her thin nightdress. She was shivering when she heard Maria's voice and felt her strong arms pick her up and help her limp back to her bed.

'Izzy, you must stay warm. There, get into bed, your feet are freezing.'

'How long have I been ill? Is it autumn? The leaves are yellow.'

'Yes, it is September. You have been ill for three weeks. The doctor said you would recover your strength with rest and that the stress of seeing Dr Carrick so soon after the tragedy of baby Isabel would pass.'

'Oh yes,' said Izzy, remembering the interview, his insulting reference to her own birth, his arrogance and his intrusion on her grief. 'If only Francis were here or at least coming home soon, I could cope so much better.'

Maria smiled. 'There is a letter,' she said, moving to retrieve it from the dressing table. 'I brought it to you when it arrived last week but you were not aware of much. Izzy reached out and saw the familiar, almost feminine script as she fumbled to open and read his words.

Firozpur, Punjab, India
15th August 1846

My dear Izzy,

With what pain I read your words that our darling girl has departed this life. Such sadness has overcome me that I can barely raise this pen to write to you. Did you do everything possible? Did you make sure she had the best attention, the best doctors? If I had been there, I would have made sure she lived. I would have done anything to save her little life. She was all I had to live for, all I had to come back to England for. Nothing will cheer me. Nothing will lift my spirits. There is nothing left to live for. I cannot think about coming back to England. I will go somewhere else when my time here finishes – the Cape or Queensland perhaps, they say the land there is suitable for cattle.

Here the war goes badly. All wars go badly. Death is all around me. Every day I see the destruction we heap upon our enemy when their only fault is their defence of their homeland. I take life every day and now God has taken the only life that I created, my own little girl. It was not right for us to live as man and wife and this is our punishment. We must recognise that what we did was wrong and accept that we must live separate lives.

I would not see you and your children destitute so you may stay at Chatham as I have paid the rent in advance for the next five years. However, I would urge you to return to your husband as it is his responsibility to provide for you. I cannot be held responsible for another man's children forever.

I know it will pain you to read this as it pains me to write it, but we must recognise the sin we have committed and make amends by accepting the punishment that God has given us.

Forever here the war goes on, forever I will pray for forgiveness from God in Heaven and trust that our child was welcomed as an innocent victim of our selfishness.

In sadness, Francis Chevalier

Maria had been tidying the curtains but she turned sharply as Izzy groaned, low and long, an animal sound, a sound of hopelessness, of desperation. Izzy leaned back on the pillows, her eyes staring blindly, her fist beating the paper that lay beside her. Maria had expected gaiety, a smiling face, news perhaps of his date of return, cheerful news that would buoy Izzy towards full health. She picked up the letter and read it then sank to the bed and cried with Izzy, encircling her small body, sharing the pain, this new grief, this new loss.

Chapter 26

Chatham 1847

The weeks and months passed in a sort of daze for Izzy, wallowing in her sorrow, existing on a plane above the world. Her interaction with the children was minimal as Maria still carried the main burden of their upbringing. The cook and the two maids did the heavy work, but Maria was their nanny, their governess, their paid mother.

The autumn brought its biting wind, its hints of the darkness of winter to come. Izzy pulled her shawl around her against the chill and wandered in the garden. She noticed the work that needed to be done; the soil that needed turning, the seeds that needed collecting, the old plants that needed to be rooted out so that the soil could lay fallow for the winter. But she had no energy to address these issues.

She sat on the garden bench, out of the wind, and closed her eyes, lifting her face to the pale disc of a milky sun. In her misery Izzy allowed her mind to replay her life as she had done so often in the last few months. I am a leaf in a river, she thought, rushing headlong into who knows what. I am being carried, surging forward, struggling just to stay afloat, I have no power to stop the force that carries me. There have been eddies where I've been trapped, going round and round, repeating myself with no easy escape. I long for a backwater, to be calm, to feel the gentle, pulsating rhythms, to make my own decision, to set my own course. I am a leaf alone. I have lost my tree. I have no roots.

Always the same, it was a sort of comfort; she could immerse herself in her memories, feel the pain anew, see how she had progressed from one bad situation to the next, how for all her good intentions she had been used badly. Today, however, the comfort seemed less. She opened her eyes and stared at the garden, at the order of things – the back of the house, the kitchen garden, the grassed area, the winding path connecting it all.

She closed her eyes again and returned to her reverie. Slowly, slowly the jumble of memories aligned themselves into some sort of pattern, an order. The pattern wove itself around the four men in her life and she found herself looking from a different perspective, not from in the usual middle while it was happening to her, confusing, confronting, unexpected. No, she found herself watching from above, watching the swirls carrying her along. There she was, going from one disaster to another, from one man to another. She had the urge to shout. Instead, she picked up a stick and drew the pattern on the gravelled path; four circles with swirls in between connecting them. 'Four men, four men have abandoned me.' She whispered the words to herself and was shocked to hear that instead of the usual misery and regret, her words were tinged with something else. She stabbed each circle. The stick broke as the anger rose and the stabbing increased in violence.

'Here they are and all of them abandoned me, abandoned me when it suited them. My father was ashamed of me for I was the sin he had committed. My guardian saw me as a legal obligation. My husband traded me for brandy and then deserted me. My lover. Oh Francis, you were false and that is the hardest cut of all. You abandoned me for your conscience.'

She threw the remains of the stick with force and felt herself shaking and suddenly hot. She noticed she was dry-eyed. The sadness was gone, replaced by anger inside her like a bull, tossing, bucking, kicking to get out. She stood and opened her mouth but no sound came. Her silent scream shook her, her breath hot and panting. How dare they treat her as they did; they had used her, used her for their own purposes. And she, she had complied. Why had she let this happen? Why had she allowed herself to be such a victim? Was it because she had no choice, because she knew no better, because she trusted her happiness to them? She had been a child, an innocent, passing the control of her life to men.

She stood and strode back through the garden, stopping and staring at the neglected vegetable patch. Then she plunged in, tearing out the dead plants, kicking the roots to loosen their grip, her actions giving vent to her anger, the violence she inflicted on the garden fed by the energy that the emotion brought. She was blind to everything except the fury driving her. Dry stalks of corn taller than herself were yanked out and hurled behind her. Runners of pumpkin thick as rope and just as strong were ripped out of the earth, the soil rippling off as they emerged into daylight, coarse and brittle leaves were clawed up in her hands and cast on the lawn behind her. She could hear her voice now, roaring with the intensity of the work, her hands, cut and bleeding, her face crimson with effort. She snatched the aged vine of runner beans, ripping it from its frame, kicking at its stubborn roots and dragging it like a fishnet to the lawn. Then she uprooted one of the frame stakes and drove its pointed end time and again into the soil, the roar of her voice accompanying each strike. She could think of nothing, she could see nothing except the deadness around her. Six, seven, eight times she struck until she fell forward in exhaustion, just as the back door opened and Maria came running towards the garden, skirts in hand and shouting her name.

Maria dragged her to the lawn and Izzy lay there, heaving and groaning until she focused on Maria's voice and saw her face. Suddenly she went limp, a crumpled heap, dress ripped and dirt-stained, hands and face scratched, blood oozing from her lower arm. 'What are you doing? I heard the noise and saw you from upstairs. What are you doing?' Maria was shouting, holding Izzy's shoulders, shaking her.

'It's men,' Izzy blurted out, 'men have always controlled my life. All my life I have been controlled by men; by their desire, by what *they* wanted.'

Maria cradled her in her arms, rocking her to and fro like a child, and said nothing, just made hushing sounds as she stroked her dishevelled hair. It took several minutes but Izzy calmed herself, felt her heartbeat slow, her breathing regulate, and the heat in her body dissipate. She looked at her thin house shoes, ripped and mud-caked, ruined. She slowly pushed herself to a sitting position.

'I'm sorry, Maria, if I frightened you. I'm sorry for all the things you have had to put up with. I'm sorry for the work you have had to do and the burden you have had to bear. I'm sorry for shirking my responsibilities and leaving them to you.'

'Hush now, Izzy, come inside and I'll make some tea. I'll tell Mary to run a bath for you and then you can rest. Come now, stand up and we will walk together.'

Chapter 27

Chatham 1847

As Izzy watched the scratches heal over the next few days, she found herself hardening her resolve to survive. Francis' betrayal was her greatest source of anger. Each time she thought of him her blood seemed to boil. Over the days she developed an effective method of combat; she would stand, stretch her body and pace the room, breathing deeply and purposefully to regain control of her emotions. She found this method allowed her to consider her problems more rationally, to look again from that different perspective, to look from above and see the pattern that her life had been. She found herself drawing the pattern – four circles with the flowing lines between and then the stab wounds on each circle. There was a satisfaction in making her thoughts physical.

She thought of Edith, her bright eyes, that smile that always seemed to light her face, and wished she could talk to her. Maria had picked up the pieces so many times but she was a paid companion and Izzy could not truly confide in her. But Edith, Edith had been a true sister, a confidante and friend. What would she say about this situation? Would she have disapproved of Francis? Would she have counselled Izzy to return to Melbourne with Bryn and continue the lie of their marriage for the sake of the children? But Edith was dead and couldn't help her. Slowly her thoughts turned to Harriet, softly spoken Harriet and Izzy suddenly remembered the letter she had received just before the baby had died. They are coming, Charles and Harriet are coming, but when? She rushed up to her bedroom and threw open the desk, scrabbling among her papers to find Harriet's letter. October, they would arrive in just a few weeks. She read again the details; *passage on the* Euphrates, *arriving in October ... lodgings in London ... visiting Europe.*

Izzy examined the newspapers every day and finally found what she was looking for. The ship *Euphrates* had left Sydney on 3rd June and was due to arrive at Deal on or near October 15th. Izzy used these few weeks to think about the coming visit and also to reconnect with her children, to walk with Maria and the boys to the school, to visit the grave of baby Isabel every day, to cry with them, play with them. She was astonished how quickly they were growing, how clever they were, and found that every day her resolve to survive strengthened.

~ ~ ~

'All that you have told me points to such unhappiness, Izzy. I wonder that you are able to carry on at all.'

Izzy considered her reply as she gazed at Harriet, noticing how her friend's voluminous auburn hair framed her perfect complexion, how the lustre of her hazel eyes was accentuated by the jade silk bodice, how the tiny lines around her eyes lent a wise and sympathetic air to Harriet's speech and demeanour.

'I am so thankful that you are here, Harriet. I have not had a friend for so long. I longed for someone to confide in but I have had no-one. I suppose that is why I turned in on myself and let my melancholy possess me. But I feel stronger and stronger each day and now that you are here and have listened to my sad, sad story, I need you to help me. I need you to guide me in what I should do next.'

'Certainly, my friend,' said Harriet and she embraced Izzy. 'I am here. Tell me what it is you need to do.'

'I came to the realisation in recent weeks that I need to be independent. I need to provide for myself and for the children and I need to make our lives not just bearable but enjoyable again. I cannot allow the thought that my children are unhappy and that I have contributed to that unhappiness.'

'So, how can you do that? How can you provide for them?'

'Well, Francis left some money and he paid the rent in advance here for five years, so we are fortunate to have such a comfortable house to live in. Bryn has promised that he will send money in support of the children when he can, but I have not heard from him since he left here, in a rage, in August.'

'Do you have enough to survive on?'

'Yes, for the moment, but I need to think about the longer term. I need to be independent, to support my children and make sure they are educated. I never want to depend on anyone else again.'

'I understand, Izzy; your experience has been a harsh teacher. But the future is bright. Many women are of independent means these days. If you can identify the means at your disposal then you can make a plan to attain your goal.'

'I have been thinking much of Madam Foveaux lately. She was independent and held a place of respect in Launceston society through her needlework and millinery skills and because she was a good businesswoman, she acquired much wealth.'

'You were her long-term protégée, Izzy. Could you not use the skills she taught you to do the same?'

'Oh, I have been thinking of that. She had such confidence in me. I could write to her and ask her advice. I have the address of her sons' business in Paris. They deal in importing and exporting silks and cottons and provided her with her fabrics in Launceston.'

'That is one avenue you could pursue. Are there any others?'

'Yes, I have been thinking that I have several advantages that could work for me in choosing a path.'

'Shall we make a list? I know it sounds silly but I always find that making a list is helpful because it enables one to see things more clearly.'

They laughed and moved to sit together at the writing desk, Izzy organising paper, pen and ink, Harriet bringing a second chair.

'Before we start, it might be useful for us to make a list each, then put them together. That way we might cover a wider area. Agreed?'

'Yes,' said Izzy, 'you have such practical ideas. "A List of Advantages". I know this is going to work.'

They were giggling but settled quickly to their task and within the quarter hour were ready to compare their notes, Izzy sharing first.

'I have six on my list, but I am not sure that the order is correct:

1. I have skills in needlework and millinery.
2. I have this house rent free for five more years.
3. I have knowledge of gardening and can provide vegetables for my family.
4. I have worked as a governess and can do so again.
5. I took an interest in the girls' schooling before and trained the boys myself.
6. I could appeal to my father one more time.'

Harriet listened attentively. 'These are very practical ideas and I too have listed the idea of using your skills to set up a business, but I have also included some thoughts here that you may not have considered:

- You are educated and can mix with all levels of society.
- You are a Marchbank and can use that connection.
- You have friends who could help you; Charles is here and Douglas Hamilton is in Melbourne and Madam Foveaux is in Paris.
- You are still a young and attractive woman.'

Izzy smiled a sad smile. 'I don't feel particularly attractive,' she said. 'I feel I have let myself lie fallow like the garden.'

'Well, my dear, perhaps that is the place to start. Perhaps you will feel better if you attend to your skin and your hair and your wardrobe. Look through your dresses and see what can be remade. We could go to London and see the latest fashions or better still, you could accompany us to Paris.' Harriet's voice rose with her excitement and she clasped Izzy and danced her in a circle. 'Yes, Izzy, come to Paris with us. Izzy, you will be famous, you will make the most beautiful creations and the ladies of Chatham will adore you.'

Izzy stopped suddenly. 'There is no couturière in Chatham. You are right. The ladies of Chatham must travel to London to buy their gowns. I could set up my business right here. In Launceston the ladies came to Madam Foveaux's premises for their fitting, but here in England it is more traditional that the fittings are done in the lady's home. I will visit the ladies in their own homes for planning and fitting meetings, but I can do all the work right here. I can ... I can convert the breakfast room to a workroom – it is big enough and full of light and perfect for the task. Oh, do you think it is possible, Harriet, do you?'

'I am absolutely sure it is possible.' Harriet saw the excitement in Izzy's eyes, the liveliness that used to be there in Melbourne. 'You will need to purchase some items I would imagine – suitable furniture and of course materials, lace and ribbons.'

They were interrupted by a soft knock on the door and Maria entered the room. 'I'm sorry to disturb you ladies, but Mr Peabody has returned and is waiting for you in the parlour.'

'Thank you, Maria, we are coming down immediately.'

When they reached the parlour, Charles rose to greet them, his face flushed with his walk in the fresh air, but lit with a smile as he saw the state of excitement that both Izzy and Harriet were in.

'Well, I see you have had a happy morning.'

'Oh yes, Charles, Harriet is the best of friends. We have made a plan for my future, for my independent future. I am going to open a business, dressing the ladies of Chatham in the finest gowns, and I'm going to do it right here in this house.'

The next hour was full of talk of converting the downstairs rooms, of contacting suppliers in London, of a visit to Paris and of purchases that would have to be made.

'You know Madam Foveaux gave me her cutting table and her cabinets and dress models – everything I could possibly need, but it is all in storage in Mr Booth's shed in Launceston. Bryn would not hear of me taking it to Melbourne but I had paid the storage in advance, so it should be still there.'

'Write to him immediately,' said Charles without hesitation, 'that is a very valuable resource. Tell him to put it on the next ship to London. Within six months you can be set up properly to achieve your goal of a thriving business.'

'Do you think so, Charles? Should I not just buy a cheap table and save costs?'

'I am a businessman Izzy, so take my advice. If you are going to do this, you need to do it properly. Write to him and have the furniture sent.'

'I will if you say so, Charles. Will it be expensive to ship?'

'Now, that brings me to my next point. As I said, I am a businessman and I know a profitable investment when I see it. I would be willing to invest in this venture – a long-term loan with a small interest rate attached. Purely business, we would have a contract drawn up and you would be free to run the business as you wish and I would collect my repayment in, should we say, ten years, £2,000 over ten years?

'Oh Charles, really, you would really do that for me?'

'It is not a gift, Izzy, it is a business venture.'

'Ten years is a long time. What if it fails?'

'That's the risk of investment, but I can see it won't fail. You will make it work. You will be successful and with a sound investment to start with, you can employ skilled seamstresses to do the hard work and you can buy the best fabrics. I can see that you will repay the loan long before ten years has elapsed.'

Izzy had tears of joy in her eyes as she embraced them both.

'You are the best of friends,' Izzy was saying and as she drew back from them, she saw that Charles' eyes were moist too.

'Izzy,' he said holding both women in his arms, 'you gave me the greatest gift of all. Without you I would not have had the happiness that Harriet has brought me. I can never repay you for that.'

Chapter 28

Paris 1848

Just after Christmas they arrived in Paris. Izzy had heard the word 'Paris' so many times but never dreamed she would ever visit this city. She saw Notre Dame and Montmartre but her excitement was not for the buildings but for the living treasure this city contained. Madam Foveaux was her focus and she could not sleep for the excitement of seeing her old friend again.

Madam Foveaux held her outstretched hands in greeting towards Izzy, her small frame perfectly fitting the dark blue silk dress, her now silver hair complimenting its modest colour and lack of adornment.

'My dear, dear Izzy, how wonderful it is to see you.' Her body felt thin and frail in Izzy's embrace but her voice was still strong.

'Madam, I am overjoyed to see you, to be here with you. I trust you are well, Madam?'

'Yes, Izzy, I am quite well. My old bones are rattling a little with the aches and pains of the years, but I am in good health and my sons look after me admirably. But let me look at you.' She held Izzy at arm's-length and scrutinised her form as she used to in the old days in Launceston. Izzy had prepared for this moment and had remade her heavy blue cotton dress from her days in Ireland, reshaping the sleeves into the now fashionable bell shape and deepening the waistline to a pointed vee. The addition of some fringing gave movement to the dress. '*Magnifique*, still *magnifique*,' was her verdict. 'But your friends; come introduce me to your friends.'

The Paris winter hurled its rain at the windows as Charles and Harriet sat with Izzy and Madam Foveaux for an hour or more and talked of their past lives and people they knew in Launceston. 'So far away,' sighed Madam Foveaux, 'so far away, but the old world is giving way to the new world, both in the Australian colonies and in America. There is such youth and inventiveness there, and in Van Diemen's Land such enthusiasm for living.' Madam Foveaux laughed at her own comment and the others joined in but Izzy felt a pang of sadness. Thirteen years had passed since they last met. Izzy had grown from a young woman of twenty-one, unmarried and yes, naïve, to the maturity of thirty-four. Such a lot had happened to her in those years that Madam Foveaux knew nothing about.

As if sensing Izzy's thoughts, Harriet used the pause in the conversation to indicate their departure. 'Enthusiasm for living we may have, Madam, but we have little in the way of culture. Charles and I have been looking forward to seeing the old-world antiquities held in the Louvre Palace. We will come back for Izzy at four o'clock, if that suits you.'

They said their good-byes and Izzy and Madam Foveaux spent the afternoon retracing the years. Izzy remained completely honest and open in her recount of the events in her life; her joy of the children, her disappointment in her marriage, her fear in Ireland, her rejection by her father, her love for and betrayal by Francis, her devastation at the death of her baby girl and finally her determination to rise above it all and succeed. All the time Izzy found herself again looking from above, watching herself swirling between the now familiar pieces of the pattern of her past. 'But now is the time to stop and take a different path,' she said in conclusion.

Madam Foveaux had listened with an open heart and now she embraced Izzy lovingly, 'My dear, you have suffered so much. Any one of these things would be enough to break the spirit of most women. But you have conquered your fears and disappointments time and again and now I can see you are determined to set upon the path to financial independence. I know how difficult that is because I had to do it myself after Phillipe died in Hobart Town. But I will help you. If you can stay in Paris for a month or so I will teach you how to keep accounts, how to ensure that your clients pay – for you know, that is our greatest problem in this industry – many rich people neglect to pay their bills, but there are ways, subtle ways, to avoid such difficulties. I will also teach you about the suppliers in London and Paris, who to use and who to avoid. My own sons, of course are beyond reproach,' she was smiling and holding her hands in an open gesture, 'but many are unscrupulous, so you must be wise and always on guard.'

'Oh Madam, thank you so much, I will be indebted to you for your guidance. My friend Charles has offered to invest in my business, so I have enough money to set it up and ...' she paused so that Madam Foveaux's attention was fully focused, 'I have already written to Mr Booth in Launceston and he will send your cutting table and other furniture. I expect they will arrive in the summer.'

Madam Foveaux clapped her hands and laughed. 'How wonderful, Phillipe's table and cabinets are coming? I knew they would be useful to you but I never guessed that they would make the journey to this part of the world. Oh Izzy, you are going to be a great success in the fashion world.'

~ ~ ~

Izzy stayed on for the month of January while Charles and Harriet departed for Rome. Maria corresponded regularly, reporting on the children's progress and both Edie and Helena sent their own letters. The boys sent pictures and Maria wrote the words for them. Izzy examined the letters carefully and knew that she would have to be patient with their progress. She missed them terribly but knew that this period of instruction in Paris was vital to her success in the future. When I am established, she thought, I will send the girls to school in London and employ a master to prepare the boys for the same. Just wait my little ones, Mama will be home soon.

~ ~ ~

Madam Foveaux's sons and their families lived in the more refined outer areas of Paris but Madam Foveaux preferred to live alone in the old apartment above the family business in Rue de la Paix in the city centre. 'I love the centre of Paris,' she said. 'I know it is crowded and not so clean, but it is the area where I grew up. The business was Phillipe's father's and this apartment was my first home with Phillipe. It has such happy memories for me. You can see it is adequate and I have a spare room where you can sleep while you are here. My sons come to the business every day and so I see them and they drive me to stay with their families whenever I please. I have the best of all worlds, Izzy. I am so fortunate. And now I have you, my dear, to stay with me and learn as much as you can about this work.'

Madam Foveaux was the perfect host and instructor and began by introducing Izzy to her sons Michel and Anton, who explained the workings of the established and respected *House of Foveaux*.

The business was equally shared, they explained, with Michel, the elder brother in charge of importing materials from regional France and Spain and as far away as China and India. Anton had responsibility for the export of the fabrics to local buyers in France, across the borders to Italian and German cities and of course to London.

'It is important that Izzy has a broad understanding of the way that fabrics are produced,' Madam Foveaux explained to her sons. 'She needs to become familiar with the processes involved; the weaving, dyeing and printing techniques used in the Far East and indeed for our own silk from Lyon, of the difference in the weight of materials, of the hallmarks of quality merchandise. For this Izzy, you need to listen to what Michel says, he is an expert in this field and will teach you much. On the other hand, Anton knows all there is to know about prices, markets, and the leading fashion designers and dressmakers of Europe. He supplies the houses of royalty and the *House of Foveaux* is responsible for the fine dressing of ladies of good society everywhere. He will show you the magazines and the latest patterns and recommend the best fabrics for each style.'

~ ~ ~

The two brothers had inherited their mother's slight frame, neat dress style and quick intelligence. They welcomed Izzy and took her education seriously. She spent every day in the warehouse downstairs, asking questions and taking notes, as she familiarised herself with the immense variety of fabrics. She was mesmerised by the colours and patterns, by the intricacies that the work involved. There were floral sprays that were block printed by hand onto fabrics, there were fabrics with a mottled effect produced by an engraved metal cylinder or roller printer, striped fabrics which achieved their effect by combining silk and the lightest of wool. Muslins and cottons from India were diaphanous in their texture, light in colour and perfect for summer fashions. The ikat dyeing technique from the Far East meant that either the warp or weft threads could be bundled and dyed to form the pattern before weaving, producing an attractive, sometimes 'blurry' effect. There was so much to learn, so many new techniques and materials to work with and Izzy used all her energy to absorb every fragment of information that the Foveaux brothers could give her.

She spent every evening with Madam Foveaux and there she learned how to keep accounts, how to itemise the cost of a dress, taking material, under layers, trims and labour into account. She also learned how to insist subtly that payments be made before progress could be guaranteed on a new creation. 'Three times, Izzy, three times you may mention payment, but after that you must withdraw and take another patron. Once a lady has been refused service, her pride will ensure that it never happens again. But also, others in society will learn from her embarrassment and make sure they pay on time. It is a difficult thing to do, especially in the beginning when you are setting up your business, but take my advice and stay firm when it comes to payment. The ladies will want your high-quality product because it is the best and they want to be able to show their friends that they can afford to buy such luxury. And anyone who recognises your dresses will know that the owner has paid a great price for them. Nothing creates a demand like a high price. The ladies cannot resist it. But it has to be worth it. It has to be individually styled and of the highest quality, with the finest needlework and materials. There are very few who can do this, but I know you can and although it has taken you many years to return to this work, I am so glad you have. You have a natural gift which will work for you, if you heed my advice.'

Madam Foveaux insisted that Izzy practise her sketching. 'The sketch that you produce at the beginning of the process will determine whether a lady will proceed with the order. It is vital that you take her wishes into account and combine those with your own eye for detail to produce a sketch that is both flattering to the lady and possible to make into a dress. Sometimes that is more difficult than you think, especially when a lady has not, how shall we say, a fine figure.'

One evening as they sat comfortably in front of the fire, Madam Foveaux cleared her throat, laid down her magazine and began, 'Izzy, may I ask you a question, a personal question?'

'Of course, Madam, of course you may.'

'Your name, what name do you use in your daily life? Is it your husband's name or your lover's name or your birth name?'

'When I was married ten years ago, I was known, of course, as Mrs Carrick, and all in Melbourne knew I was the wife of Dr Carrick. Then in Ireland I kept that name as I was living with the Carrick family, my husband's brother. But when Francis and I lived as man and wife I took his name. I'm known as Mrs Chevalier for simplicity, to guard myself and my children against gossip and scandal. Do you think it is important, now that I have no husband and no lover?'

'Yes,' said Madam Foveaux, 'but not from any moral point of view. A woman has few protections from the evil tongues in society and you were right to protect yourself and your children. I am thinking from a business perspective. The sound of the name is important. Mrs Chevalier may be acceptable in England for daily use, but I am sure that Madam Chevalier is far better as a business name.'

'Yes, it does sound better. It's a good suggestion.'

'And this small town, this Chatham, do you intend to stay there?'

'I have not thought about that. I have no reason to stay except that Francis had paid the rent forward, so I have secure accommodation for two more years. The house is suitable to rearrangement; the breakfast room is light and airy and although a little small, would make a suitable workroom.'

'And tell me of the ladies of Chatham? Do you know many who would patronise your business?'

'No, I have led a very enclosed life since I arrived there four years ago. I have no friends there. I never visit or receive visitors. I would be beginning with no history at all. Francis said once that Chatham has a very transient population, simply because it is a port town and a military base. The people who were there four years ago have probably moved on.'

'I ask this because perhaps you should consider dismissing Chatham as a business base and go straight to London instead. It will be a bigger market and you will have more chance of success.'

'London would be a big step.' Izzy continued to consider this aloud. 'I could leave the children in Chatham until I was established and although I would not want to leave them, they would be secure and stable there with Maria in case things didn't work out.'

'Yes,' said Madam Foveaux, 'and if things do work out, they can join you in London.'

'Oh Madam, that has given me much to think about.'

'Well, my dear, here is one more thing to think about. My sons have been considering extending the business to London and would be glad to have you as a sort of forward ambassador. If you would consider it, the business name *Madam Chevalier of the House of Foveaux* could work for both you and my sons. It would be a partnership. They would gain a foothold in the English market and you would gain custom from the excellent reputation of such an established supplier.'

Izzy was stunned. It could work. To be associated with such a famous name she could hardly fail. As long as, of course, she was able to produce garments of the highest standard of needlework. She knew she could do that. But Madam Foveaux was talking again.

'My sons would secure a business address for you in the centre of London. Anton said that Bond Street would be best for its proximity to Mayfair. They would pay the rent on the premises and use part of it as a storehouse for their fabrics and convert the rest to proper workrooms for you.'

She paused and searched Izzy's face for a response. 'What do you think, my dear?'

'I am overwhelmed with your kindness, Madam.' Her voice was husky, swollen with emotion. 'I can hardly speak for the gratitude I feel towards you and your sons. You have taught me so much, both here and in Launceston and now you are willing to support me as I venture forth on my own.' The tears swelled in her eyes.

Madam Foveaux embraced her and then held her at arm's-length and looked at her kindly.

'Izzy, this is a business venture. My sons are businessmen and are confident of success here. It is certainly not charity. They will reap a huge reward from the work that you do, from your fastidiousness, from the creative way in which you will use their fabrics. They are confident that the association will work as much for them as it will for you.'

Izzy smiled and dabbed her eyes dry. 'It is strange but the two names seem to fit together so well.'

'In fashion Izzy, you know that the French have always set the path, the English look to Paris for the trend.'

'It is amusing because Francis' family is Irish, from Kilkenny. They were Huguenots who fled from France to escape religious persecution over a hundred years ago.'

They both smiled at this. 'Then that is even better,' said Madam Foveaux, 'for you do not have to pretend to be French. Your unaccented speech and perfect diction will work for you among the fine families of England. Just let people assume you are well connected in France as well.'

'And well connected I certainly am,' said Izzy as she embraced Madam Foveaux again.

~ ~ ~

As the month drew to a close, Izzy shopped with Madam Foveaux for *passementerie*, decorations in which the French excelled, trims, fringes, cords, tassels, buttons and laces, in the many small shops that her mentor knew. Michel guided her in selecting fabrics for the London warehouse and included dozens of bolts of the plain fabrics which would be needed for the under layers, especially the crinolines, those stiffened with horsehair which would enhance the shape of the skirt.

Anton plied her with fashion magazines, *Petit Courrier des Dames*, *Le Follet*, *Les Modes Parisiennes* and *Le Moniteur de la Mode*, which featured the latest styles and he promised to send her the new editions as soon as they were published. The voluminous 'Bishop' sleeves of just a few years ago had been tapered to the slender, more attractive bell shape, and waists were ever deepening, shoulders exposed and the innovation of 'organ' pleating, fine tubular pleats closely drawn together, enabled the skirt to cascade over the crinoline for a perfect dome shape. Piping made from material cut on the bias was used to effectively delineate the waistline and the use of whalebone supports accentuated the silhouette. 'All of this,' Anton said, 'has to be achieved without fuss or notice – the finished garment looking as light and fragile as possible while its structure is as sturdy as a sofa.'

Izzy smiled at the comparison. 'That is not so easy to achieve,' she said, shaking her head.

'It will be easier in the future. A machine will be invented that makes every stitch perfectly and takes the hours of drudgery away.'

Izzy felt her eyes widen in surprise. 'Really?' she said. 'Is that possible?'

'Yes, it has already happened, though it is not in use. You have probably not heard the story of Barthélemy Thimonnier. It is a sad story for it shows how ignorance can halt progress. Let me tell you what happened.'

Izzy settled herself on a packing chest, and Anton leaned against a row of shelving and began. 'Thimonnier is a tailor from Lyon and about twenty years ago, in 1830, he invented a machine in which a barbed needle pierced the fabric and hooked the thread bringing it to the surface to form a chain stitch.' Anton used his fingers to illustrate this action. 'The machine was powered by a hand wheel and made perfectly even stitches.'

'Oh, how wonderful.'

'Yes, it was wonderful. Thimonnier's friend, August Ferrand, was an engineer and he drew the requisite plans and a patent was issued to the two men for the production of the machines. The government offered them a contract to make army uniforms and they built a factory in the southern city of Saint-Etienne. Everything was going well and it looked as though the venture would be a success.'

'But what happened? How could they fail?

'They failed because the workers burned the factory down.'

'What? Why would they do that?'

'Because they feared they would lose their work; that the machines would replace them and they would be left without income.'

'Oh, that is so sad. What happened to Thimonnier?'

'As far as I know he is working as a tailor again in Lyon and has never had success with his machine. But you can be sure, Izzy, that in our lifetime someone will perfect that machine and the world of garment making will be changed forever.'

~ ~ ~

Izzy farewelled Madam Foveaux and her sons at the end of January and arrived home in Chatham to the joy of her children to begin her new life. Three weeks later, on February 22, Paris erupted into revolution; the streets were barricaded and the rule of law was abandoned as workers protested against lack of employment and government ineptitude. Izzy followed the newspaper reports and feared for the welfare of her friends, but the political instability had a positive effect for her. Anton wrote to her to say that they were bringing forward their plans to expand to London as a safeguard. A thriving business in London would ensure the survival of the *House of Foveaux* and they could rebuild the business in Paris when peace was restored.

Chapter 29

London 1850–1851

The early morning light reflected across the table, its Huon pine pale and smooth, its brass fittings and measuring line glowing. Izzy ran her hand across its surface, an action she performed several times a day, and felt the satisfaction that it gave her.

Three years had passed since she had moved to London, since she watched the carts trundle up the street from the dock delivering the furniture, the furniture that was not only part of her past life but her means to the future. Three years since she had come back from Paris, full of the enthusiasm and optimism that Madam Foveaux and her sons had instilled in her. They were years of long hard days, filled with endless stitching, aching fingers, tired eyes, and of nights alone finalising accounts or perfecting her sketching or poring over magazines searching for the ideal feature to distinguish her latest commission.

Her first great milestone was that she was able to repay Charles. In just less than three years she had saved enough to cover the debt. It was then that she truly felt she had launched *Madam Chevalier of the House of Foveaux*.

Success seemed to breed success as one commission rolled into another and the name *Madam Chevalier* came to mean quality and beauty and the high price of both. The rooms that Anton had secured for her in Bond Street were perfect; airy and light and well located on the edge of Mayfair. She corresponded weekly with Madam Foveaux, describing her problems and her successes and the older woman, always supportive and loving never failed to reply, to encourage, suggest and advise. It seemed she had a new life to live through the success of Madam Chevalier.

This success had enabled Izzy to employ three skilled seamstresses and several apprentices to take over the mundane work and free her to accept more clients. But her greatest asset was her personal assistant, the capable Mrs Holland, who with her Scottish accent and quiet manner projected a calm atmosphere in the workrooms. During the day the workrooms were alive with activity, the women working companionably together, Izzy insisting that the older women guide the apprentices with patience and excellent example. When work was worthy it was highly praised among the women and when it was not it was rejected gently but firmly. Izzy visited her clients in their homes, assisted by Mrs Holland. They worked well together and rotated the apprentices on these visits so that the young girls were able to practise their interactions with the clients under the watchful eye of Mrs Holland, who insisted on their cleanliness, neatness and excellent manners.

~ ~ ~

The success of her business had also allowed Izzy to secure a very comfortable house in Curzon Street, just a few blocks from Bond Street on the southern edge of Mayfair. Maria and the children had moved from Chatham and the house, although not grand, had a pretty garden and spacious rooms for a growing family. The girls were enrolled at Mrs

Appleby's Academy nearby and Izzy employed Mr Murdoch to tutor the boys for two or three years in preparation for public school. These were long-term changes in the family and Izzy was quick to include Maria in her plans.

'Maria, you will be relieved of quite a burden now that the children are taken care of.'

'Burden, it was never a burden, Izzy. But it is true that my days will be less busy now. Is it time for me to move on?'

'Oh no, Maria, please don't leave us.' Izzy stopped herself lest she presume too much. 'Unless you want to, of course. I have no right to keep you if you want to move to another family or, perhaps to return to Launceston?'

'No, I have no desire to return to Launceston. You and the children have been so much a part of my life that I cannot imagine anything different.'

Izzy embraced her fondly. 'Maria, I do not know what I would have done without you during my dark days in Chatham. You were so steadfast and I will be forever grateful to you for your care of me and of the children.'

'Thank you, Izzy. I would like to stay but what role would I have in the house? I cannot be idle and you have employed enough staff to run the house efficiently.'

'The work I have undertaken in the business requires long hours and much time away from the house. Would you consider carrying on as usual; overseeing the running of the household and the progress of the children? It would not be as onerous as it was in the past and you would have more time to yourself. The children love you as, indeed, you have been a mother to them. The staff, along with Mr Murdoch and Mrs Appleby, would know that you have the final word in all matters of importance. I need someone I can trust so that I am confident to devote my time to the business.'

'Yes, Izzy, that would be very satisfactory. I could not have asked for more.'

~ ~ ~

Towards the end of these three years another event influenced the success of Izzy's business, an event that she could never have imagined would have such a personal effect on her. She first heard of it when she visited Charles and Harriet in their Knightsbridge residence. They had stayed on in Britain after their tour of Europe had been cut short by the revolutions of 1848, but they were due to return to Melbourne in the next few months. Harriet was breathless with excitement as she ushered Izzy into the parlour.

'What is it, Harriet? What had happened to excite you?'

'Izzy,' she said, grasping her by the shoulders, 'Charles has had wonderful news. We are to stay in London for another twelve months.'

'Really, that is wonderful news, but why? Why?'

They entered the parlour and Charles rose to greet them, folding the newspaper and smiling as he reached for Izzy's hand.

'My dear, I can see that Harriet has already told you that we are to stay.'

'Yes, but why? What has happened?'

'*The Great Exhibition of the Works of Industry of All Nations*,' he said, pronouncing each word of the extended title clearly and slowly.

'But what is that?'

'His Royal Highness Prince Albert has been negotiating for a Great Exhibition for some time, to display the advances in manufacturing and technology that are sweeping this nation. It is a chance for Britain to show her leadership of the world, the power of steam and the superiority of Britain.'

'But how does this affect you?'

'The Australian colonies are major contributors to Britain's wealth and will be well represented at the Exhibition. I have been asked to stay and represent the fine wool growers of Port Phillip and Van Diemen's Land by overseeing their exhibition.'

'And,' said Harriet, 'look at this; the Exhibition will take place in Hyde Park in this, they are calling it the Crystal Palace,' and she handed Izzy a lithograph of the most extraordinary building Izzy had ever seen, an entire building constructed of glass panels.

'It is enormous, and all of glass? How long will it take to build?'

'Work is due to commence soon, the decision to accept the proposal only recently being agreed to by Parliament. If all goes well the opening will be next year on May 1st and it will run until October.'

'Do you realise,' added Harriet, 'that this will have a profound effect on your business? There will be balls and galas and parties associated with the Exhibition and the ladies of London will need to be outfitted for every one of them. Not only that, they will want to outdo each other. I expect you are going to be very busy during 1851, Izzy.'

~ ~ ~

All of London was talking about the Great Exhibition and nowhere was the chatter more elevated and excited than in Izzy's workroom as the women arrived and were settling to their daily work. The women all knew men, brothers, husbands, fathers, sons, who had been requisitioned to work on the amazing structure that was the Crystal Palace for the nine months before the May 1st opening.

'My Johnny spends his entire day up the top of a ladder fitting those glass panes in place,' said Molly, a young apprentice from Spitalfields. 'D'yr know, there's going to be nearly three 'undred thousand of 'em by the time its finished? I can't even begin to think about that number. I told 'im, I said, "You'd better be careful, Johnny Baxter, those panes of glass could be very *painful* if you fell through 'em."' The room erupted into laughter.

Molly took a bow, and one of the embroiderers said, 'But

where do they all come from, the glass panels and the iron posts? I see them as I walk past each morning, piled high ready to be used.'

'From up Birmingham,' supplied Molly, 'all good British produce, all made right 'ere.'

'That is what it is all about,' chimed in Mrs Holland. 'It's all about showing the world what we can produce and how we are leading the world in manufacturing. We have so much we can be proud of.'

'But other countries are going to exhibit their goods too, aren't they?' asked Jeannie, one of the seamstresses.' I read that India is going to send an elephant. I would love to see that.'

'What I can't wait to see is the entrance hall,' cut in Mrs Sheedy, the workroom manager. 'Did you hear about the elm trees? There are three of them, enormous, fully grown elm trees. They were going to cut them down to make way for the building, but the builders decided to build the entrance hall around them. Those trees are going to be *inside* the Crystal Palace.'

There was silence for a minute while the women imagined that.

'That surely will be something to see,' said Mrs Holland, 'and now ladies, we should settle ourselves to our work, for this Exhibition is creating much work for Madam Chevalier, and we need to concentrate on each stitch so that the ladies of London look sublime and are the envy of the world.'

~ ~ ~

Harriet was right. The year proved to be extremely busy with Izzy's existing clients ordering not one new dress but several to see them through all the social events associated with the Exhibition. Added to that were the number of new clients that were attracted by the individuality and quality of the work of Madam Chevalier; women from as far away as

Edinburgh, Yorkshire and Cardiff visiting London in the months before the May opening so that their wardrobe contained several new additions for this, the grandest of years. The Exhibition coincided with the Season, of course, that time in London when debutants were presented at Court, when matrons were making matches, when all of the female population was on display. The balls and parties this year were peppered with an international flavour as visitors from all over the globe took up lodgings in the city. Among them, much to Izzy's delight, were Anton and Madam Foveaux. They stayed in the Mayfair Hotel and Izzy visited them there almost as soon as they arrived.

'Madam, it is wonderful that you were able to come.'

'Yes, Anton insisted that I accompany him. His wife is in confinement at the moment and he will be here several months. He is to oversee the Lyon exhibition, the textiles and printing machines that France excels in.'

'London is abuzz with excitement. They say there will be 25,000 people at the opening ceremony. The Queen herself will open the Exhibition. Prince Albert, I believe, has promoted it enthusiastically for years.'

'And you, my dear, have you been busy with so much demand?'

'Oh yes, Madam, I have had to employ double the staff to complete our orders. I am fortunate that there are many fine needleworkers in London, and that they desire to work in my establishment. They know that they will be treated fairly and that they must maintain the highest of standards but they are rising to the test and I cannot fault any so far. Mrs Holland, my assistant and Mrs Sheedy, the workroom manager, run the workroom with a quiet and firm manner.'

'I would love to visit it, to feel the atmosphere of it, your workroom, I mean. I will visit the Exhibition, several times I should think, but I am mostly looking forward to being in the atmosphere of the workroom, just as we were in Launceston.'

'Of course, Madam, you are always welcome to visit and of course to advise us. The women will be honoured to have you there as their guest. They are in awe of your reputation and the reputation of the *House of Foveaux.*'

And so, *The Great Exhibition of the Works of Industry of All Nations* began in the Crystal Palace in Hyde Park and every aspect of life in London revolved around it for the next six months.

Chapter 30

London 1851

Izzy stretched in her bed, luxuriating in her waking thought that today was Sunday, the day of rest. This week had been particularly busy, from the activity in the workroom to the genteel homes of her clients, from the bustle of the London streets to the quiet of her late-night account keeping. The Great Exhibition had spawned a rush of frenzied activity with so many commissions to complete she had had to limit her patrons to two dresses for the moment lest, in the rush, her staff were to produce less than perfect results. But tomorrow would be time enough to worry about the business.

Today was Sunday, her day with her children. She and Maria and the boys would drive to Hanover Square for the service at St Georges with Edie and Helena and the other assembled students of Mrs Appleby's Academy. After church they would drive to Green Park, Hyde Park having been taken over by the Crystal Palace, where they would walk for an hour or so before returning home for the dinner hour. The girls would stay for the long, lazy summer afternoon, playing with their little brothers and telling Izzy and Maria all the stories from school, the gossip and the scandal that their ten- and eleven-year-old minds and hearts embraced. Both girls loved school, were clever at their lessons and especially enjoyed the status that their mother's fame bought them, the surname Chevalier distinguishing them immediately.

Sometimes Madam Foveaux and Anton joined them for tea on Sunday, sometimes Charles and Harriet and their children and sometimes all of them together. Then the house echoed with happiness.

How fortunate I am, thought Izzy as she returned alone in the carriage after farewelling the girls at the school gate. London has been my saving grace; never again will I depend on a man, never again will I live in penury.

She thought about those years of uncertainty, her dark days, her dependence on the men in her life, and they seemed far away. Francis had disappeared completely; she had heard nothing of him since that terrible letter. She had no more sorrow or regret but gained some satisfaction from the fact that she was using his name; that in some way he was paying for her success. She had not heard from Bryn in nearly four years but Charles had heard through his Melbourne contacts that Dr Carrick had relocated to the newly settled area of Gawler in South Australia and that the rough living of the frontier suited him. Charles said that this year, 1851, had seen many changes in Melbourne. The Port Phillip District was officially separated from New South Wales and the new State of Victoria was proclaimed on July 1st. She had no desire to return. Her life in London was fulfilling and she had everything she wanted; security, her children, respect and most importantly, financial and personal independence.

~ ~ ~

Three days later as the June sun streamed through the

skylight onto Izzy's design desk in the airy office attached to the workroom, Mrs Holland knocked gently and entered.

'Pardon this intrusion, Madam. Could I speak with you?'

'Certainly, Mrs Holland, is there a problem?'

'No, not a problem exactly, it's more a dilemma.'

Izzy put down her pencil and twisted in her chair to face Mrs Holland, indicating the spare chair opposite her. Mrs Holland sat and Izzy saw that in her hand she carried a bundle of at least a dozen requests. These were letters from clients and potential clients inviting Madam Chevalier to attend them to discuss the design and making of new garments. 'There are fifteen, Madam, most of them new clients. I'm afraid we cannot cope with this many, the women can only do so much, but to reject them seems foolish.'

'Oh,' said Izzy as Mrs Holland handed her the bundle, 'thank you, Mrs Holland, it is indeed a sorry task to reject offers of commission.'

'Perhaps, Madam, you could select half of them and ask the other half to wait a month or two until we are able to cope better with the enormous workload.'

'Yes, I will do that. Mrs Holland, the ladies seem happy enough, are they finding the pace of work too much?'

'A little, Madam, they are keen to fill each order, but we must ensure that they maintain their standards.'

'Yes Mrs Holland. Will you do something for me? Will you go to the bakery and order a selection of tarts and cakes for tea? We will have an hour of rest and sweetness between eleven and twelve today; they deserve the rest and I'm sure their work will benefit from it.'

'Thank you, Madam. That will be just what we need.'

~ ~ ~

Izzy slowly rifled through the envelopes, noting the addresses; Grosvenor Square, Berkeley Square, Belgrave Square, all the best and most fashionable areas for the

London town mansions of the landed gentry. Lady Sarah Richmond, Baroness of Milford; Lady Anne Connolly, Countess of Kenmare; Lady Elizabeth Chelmsford, Duchess of Lancaster; Lady Jane Marchbank, Duchess of Winton. Izzy stopped and read again: Lady Jane Marchbank, Duchess of Winton. It was her. Izzy immediately recalled the tilt of her head as she withdrew from the posy, the look of disdain as she turned and moved towards the window, saying 'Who is in charge of this child?' It was her; Miss Jane Paul, her father's fiancé, now Lady Jane Marchbank, her father's wife.

Izzy opened the envelope to read the usual brief format written by a secretary or a lady-in-waiting.

Madam Chevalier,

Her Grace, the Duchess of Winton, requests your presence as soon as possible at her London residence, 3 Grosvenor Square, to discuss the completion of several garments needed for the Season. Please address your response directly to me so a suitable time can be arranged.

Margaret Kingston
Secretary to Lady Jane Marchbank, Duchess of Winton

Izzy noticed her hand was shaking as she returned the letter to its envelope. She felt hot and unsettled. Her immediate impulse was to tear the letter into tiny shreds and throw them out the window, but she resisted. She rose and made her way through the workroom taking her bonnet and a light shawl with her. 'I won't be long, Mrs Holland, I am just going out for some air.'

Izzy walked up and down the street for twenty minutes, turning this new problem over in her mind. Suddenly it ceased being a problem as she realised it was in fact, an opportunity, an opportunity to be inside the Marchbank house, to meet Lady Jane, maybe to see her father. She will depend on me, thought Izzy. She will be under a compliment to me, without knowing who I really am. I have dealt with enough society ladies to know that Lady Jane will fawn over me, compliment me, be grateful to me for making her look more beautiful than she ever has. Yes, I will take this commission and Lady Jane will never know my true identity. One day, at the right time, perhaps I will reveal it.

Izzy arrived back at the workroom just as Mrs Holland arrived with the cakes to the delighted exclamations of the women. Izzy sat with them and rejoiced silently that her life seemed to be on a very satisfactory path at the moment.

~ ~ ~

Izzy and Mrs Holland were ushered upstairs to Lady Jane's private parlour. Lizzie, their youngest apprentice, followed, carrying a large roll of fabric samples and trims. This was Lizzie's first fitting session and at fourteen Izzy guessed that she had never before been inside such a grand house. Mrs Holland had inspected her hands, shoes, dress and hair before leaving the workroom, insisting that she was neat and clean. Molly had tied a new ribbon at the back of Lizzie's hair, declaring, 'Now you looks like a lady yourself, Lizzie.'

They arranged the samples and Izzy took out her sketching pad, pencil and several magazines that Anton had given her just yesterday. The door opened and Lady Jane entered the room with her lady-in-waiting. She was shorter in stature than Izzy remembered. I guess I was just a child, she thought, everyone looked tall to me. Izzy had done a quick calculation; if Miss Paul was twenty years old when Izzy last saw her twenty-two years ago, she would now be forty-two. And as she swept into the room Izzy noted that she certainly looked like a middle-aged matron, a little stouter than she should be, she thought as she curtsied and waited for Mrs Holland and Lizzie to do the same.

'Madam Chevalier, it is good of you to come. It seems the Great Exhibition has provided us with an excess of social occasions and one must ensure that one's wardrobe is not repeated.' In twenty years she has not lost that superior air, thought Izzy.

'Thank you for your kind custom, Your Grace, I am sure you will be radiant. Shall we begin by browsing the latest magazines from Paris? And when you have selected something that you like, or a combination of features that you like, we will explore the samples of the *House of Foveaux* fabrics that we have brought with us.' Lizzie curtsied again as Lady Jane glanced towards the fabrics.

'Madam Chevalier, I see that you are well conducted and most deferential. I know that your garments are highly prized but I was not expecting a person of such breeding to be attending me in this matter.'

Izzy lowered her eyes, lest they betray her. Hah! You wouldn't! If only you knew where that 'breeding' came from! she thought, but she said nothing. Lady Jane took the magazine and began turning the pages. Izzy stood a few feet away and in the silence that followed had a chance to assess her new client in a professional manner; short legs, and at least thirty inches around the waist, but her neck is slender and her shoulders are adequate and she has good posture. We will have to accentuate the upper body, a deep vee to slim the waist and wide on the shoulders, perhaps with a bertha collar of lace.

The consultation took more than two hours with Izzy firstly measuring (thirty-one inches of the waist, but she murmured 'twenty-six' as she wrote the number in her notebook) and then listening intently as Lady Jane became expansive about the social engagements of the Season.

'This gown is for the Stuart Ball at Buckingham Palace on June 13th. It will be the event of the Season and I want the best, the most beautiful gown I can have.'

Izzy was thinking quickly. 'In that case, because it is a

costume ball, we could incorporate some of the features of the Court of Charles II, some rich brocade and some raised-point needle lace, Irish perhaps.'

Izzy began sketching quickly, calling Lizzie to show lace and trims, Mrs Holland presenting choices in fabrics that would complement the design. Finally, the combination of all these factors led to a sketch that Lady Jane was delighted with.

'It is perfect, Madam Chevalier, I will be the envy of everyone. The deep blue of this silk brocade will match my features and the family sapphires will add to the effect.'

As Izzy began to gather her sketches into her folio she said casually, 'Thank you, Your Grace, and may I presume that your secretary will have a bank note ready for me before I leave?'

'Of course, Madam Chevalier, if you wait here, she will attend you shortly.' Her voice was cold, but not as cold as Izzy expected when money was mentioned. She had obviously heard of the embarrassment of the ladies who did not pay beforehand and consequently were not accepted for commission. Like all ladies she was in love with the sketch, the vision that Izzy had given her of how beautiful she would look, and for that she would pay the world. Izzy silently thanked Madam Foveaux yet again.

~ ~ ~

The dress was dazzling. Lady Jane looked slimmer, younger and more attractive in it than she had ever looked in anything. Izzy's ability to design a garment which would accentuate the good points and lessen the faults in a client's figure was legendary and as Lady Jane Marchbank admired herself in the glass a full month before the ball, she vowed that she would have Madam Chevalier design more garments in the future, no matter the cost.

~ ~ ~

Madam Foveaux loved to visit the workroom, to sit with the ladies as they sewed, to admire their work, to advise on difficult features. They loved her immediately as she praised them for their skill and gaily joined in their chatter.

'Your workroom has made me young again, Izzy,' she exclaimed as Izzy returned from the final fitting of Lady Jane's ball gown, 'and tell me was Lady Jane pleased with her image in the glass?'

The whole workroom paused and waited for Izzy to speak. They had all worked on parts of that gown, the seams, under skirts, silk trims to lighten the heaviness of the brocade, the pleated panelling, and the intricacies of the lacework. Izzy looked at their faces, expectant and a little fearful, and held up her hands in an open gesture as her face broke into a smile. 'She was delighted,' she said, 'delighted with every aspect of it. Thank you so much for the excellent work that you did.' Izzy brought her hands together in applause for her workers and they replied with their own clapping and cheering.

~ ~ ~

The next day Madam Foveaux came to the workroom earlier than usual and came straight into Izzy's office.

'Pardon my early visit, Izzy, but I have a message from Anton.'

'Sit down, Madam. What is it? Is everything all right?'

'Yes, everything is fine. Anton told me last evening that the French Ambassador has received ten invitations to the Stuart Ball next month and has asked Anton to be part of the French party. As you have made several gowns for this occasion, he wondered if you would care to accompany him.'

'Oh, that is so kind of him.'

'It has been unfortunate that his wife was not able to be here, and I am not much company in the late evening anymore. If you are agreeable, he would be most grateful.

He has not participated much in the social aspects of the Great Exhibition and would relish the chance to attend a ball at Buckingham Palace.'

'As would I,' said Izzy.

'Shall I tell him that you agree?'

'Yes, thank you, Madam.' She paused. 'I have not told you this, Madam,' she lowered her voice to a whisper, 'but I remember Lady Jane Marchbank from my childhood. She was Miss Paul, who married my father. She was the reason I was sent away, the cause of all my grief. I knew as soon as I saw her name.'

'Does she know who you are?' There was excitement in Madam Foveaux's voice.

'No, I have not revealed my identity to her and I will not, but at the ball I will have the chance to see my father, to observe him from a distance. Is that a wrong thing to do? Should I tell Anton that beforehand?'

'My dear ...' Madam Foveaux took Izzy's hand, 'this is indeed a boon for you. To see your father while you remain anonymous is perfect. It has been so many years for you and you have come so far. As for Anton, I can inform him if you wish. I am certain that he will support you in your secret quest.'

Chapter 31

London 1851

Izzy thought back to the New Year's Ball in Melbourne ten years ago. The ball when she saw Francis across the room, when she watched the yellow cuff of his uniform moving as he conversed with Charles, when his grey eyes sought hers over the shoulder of Harriet and she felt her heart leave her body as he swirled away in the dance. She blinked and blinked again. This was no colonial outpost and no imitation of society. This was Buckingham Palace and these people around her were the leaders of society. The Queen herself was present, though the crowd was so dense one would never hope to see her.

Izzy could not believe that she was really here. Anton took her arm as they waited in line to be announced. Others in their party were ahead of them and the French Ambassador and his wife were being announced already. Izzy was strangely calm. She knew that eyes were admiring her gown, the deep green silk shimmering in the light of a hundred candelabra. The ladies of the workroom had excelled themselves, working longer hours to ensure its perfection. Suddenly they were at the door. Anton handed the card to the page.

'Monsieur Foveaux and Madam Chevalier,' he boomed and Anton strode forward confidently holding Izzy's hand high on the back of his hand, allowing the assembled guests a fine view of both of them. There was a great deal of chatter in the room, but there was a momentary lull as heads turned and eyes appraised the couple, both names drawing the attention of mainly the women. They joined the rest of the French party and moved into a side room where ices and drinks were served. The rooms were crowded and noisy as guests greeted friends and acquaintances and matrons positioned their daughters near potential suitors while the young men, some in uniform, cast their eyes over the field. Izzy noticed that the music from the main ballroom lent a magical quality to the gathering, transforming it from a noisy throng into a romantic interlude, an otherworldly atmosphere where one's heart could be captured or broken in the wink of an eye. Her mind went back again to that poor imitation of a ball in Melbourne, but she hastily dismissed it in favour of the present scene.

'Izzy, shall we join the dance?' whispered Anton. 'We will need to work hard to cover all the rooms here if we are to watch for our quarry.' He smiled and led her to the dance floor.

'I do not know what he looks like, but I will look for Lady Jane,' said Izzy.

'And I could not recognise either but I will look for the blue silk brocade; I know it well as it is one of our most expensive fabrics. Together we will succeed, Izzy, just wait and see.' He smiled again as he waltzed her onto the ballroom floor.

They seemed to have been looking without success, dancing, talking and moving from room to room when suddenly, as they entered the supper room, Izzy froze because there ahead of her was Lady Jane, her arm held by the impeccably dressed gentleman beside her. They had their backs to Izzy and Anton, but she felt Anton stop too as he saw the fabric of her dress. They retreated into the crowd by the door but kept their eyes on the couple. Izzy felt that she was spying but she could not look away. The man was taller than average, his hair dark with threads of silver woven through it, his stance strong but a little stooped as though there was pain somewhere, perhaps in his back or legs. The age would be right for her father, maybe fifty-six or fifty-seven. He was helping Lady Jane to some cakes when he turned towards the door as the orchestra in the ballroom reached a crescendo.

'Is that him?' whispered Anton.

'Yes,' breathed Izzy, 'that is my father.' Her eyes were fixed on him and Anton could see the pain that the recognition brought. 'He is older than I remember, but his face is the same.'

'Do you want to move closer to hear their conversation?' asked Anton.

'No, I think not,' said Izzy. 'Lady Jane would recognise me and I do not wish to cause her embarrassment. I am still a dressmaker and she a lady. I would not expect her to acknowledge me in society. There will be time in the future to see my father again, now that I know his looks.'

'As you wish,' agreed Anton. 'Shall we return to the dancing?' As they turned to leave there was a crash of glassware accompanied by stifled squeals and raised male voices. They looked back and saw that a waiter had upended a tray of champagne glasses. Edward was red in the face and shouting. Lady Jane was trying to brush the liquid off her dress while the waiter tried to rescue the glasses. Izzy moved straight towards Lady Jane, picking up a damask napkin from the table as she went.

'Lady Jane, allow me,' she said confidently as she dabbed at the dress.

'Oh, Madam Chevalier, thank you, I hope the dress is not ruined.'

'No, it is not ruined, if you will allow me to accompany you to the Ladies Room, we will dry it properly.' Edward was still shouting at the waiter, the poor boy scrabbling on the floor to remove pieces of broken glass.

'Sir, I will take Lady Jane to the Ladies Room,' said Izzy and their eyes met, only feet apart. His shouting stopped mid-sentence and Izzy thought she saw a flicker in his eyes. She held his gaze for second then led Lady Jane away.

Anton had moved with Izzy and now addressed Edward. 'It was an unfortunate accident, Sir, but little harm done.' The people around them returned to their supper.

'Yes, indeed,' said Edward his eyes following the retreating figures of his wife and the beautiful young woman. 'Tell me, Sir, who is that young woman?'

'That, Sir, is Madam Chevalier, of the *House of Foveaux*, the toast of London's ladies. They claim she is a magician with dress fabric and design.'

'Ah, I have heard the name. And you, Sir?'

'I am Anton Foveaux, at your service, Sir.' He made a sweeping bow.

'And I am Edward Marchbank of Winton in Yorkshire.'

They chatted about the Great Exhibition and about France. They drank several glasses of wine together and Anton had managed to restore Edward's good humour by the time the ladies returned.

As they approached Anton said, 'Madam Chevalier, may I present Lord Edward Marchbank.'

Edward bowed and Izzy curtsied.

'And, Lady Jane, may I present Monsieur Anton Foveaux,' replied Edward. The same formality was followed and Lady Jane turned to Izzy.

'Thank you, Madam Chevalier,' she said, 'your assistance was much appreciated.'

It was the cue for them to leave, so Anton and Izzy bowed and curtsied again and made their way back towards the ballroom.

~ ~ ~

It was later in the evening when Izzy and Anton were sitting chatting and watching the dancers swirling to the music that Edward came into the room alone. He saw them and made his way towards them, explaining that Lady Jane had retired for the evening. 'May I have the pleasure of this dance, Madam Chevalier?' It was obvious that he had consumed more wine and it had elevated him.

Izzy glanced at Anton and he smiled and stood to let her take Edward's outstretched hand.

They danced in silence for the first few minutes; his hand of the small of her back was firm, holding her towards himself. Then he leaned towards her and said, 'A pretty woman like you could have your pick of a room like this.'

'I am not looking for an attachment, Sir.'

'I could change that. I could offer you an entrée to the best that London has to offer.'

'And at what price would that be, Sir?' She kept her voice steady.

'It would be just a small price to you. We could have an arrangement. No-one would need to know.'

Izzy could feel her face burning as the music rose towards the end of the waltz and then fell to silence. They bowed to each other and as their fellow dancers began chattering and leaving the dance floor, she saw his expectant face. Suddenly she could not resist.

She inhaled and stood as straight as she could and, holding his gaze, raised her eyebrows and said quietly and firmly, 'I am your daughter, Sir. I am Izzy.'

Chapter 32

London 1851

Izzy awoke the next morning long before dawn, her father's face imprinted on her mind. His expression was mixed; smugness, shock, fear, relief, she couldn't tell. She had felt him tremble as she took his arm and returned to the waiting Anton.

'Good night, Sir Edward,' she had said before taking Anton's arm and leaving Edward in his speechless half bow.

Anton had been shocked when she told him of Edward's proposal and had agreed that she had done the right thing.

'But Izzy, he is a gentleman. He made a mistake and he will apologise.'

'Do you think so? I'm not sure that I want one. I feel so disappointed in him.'

'Try not to think about it too much. Just wait and see what happens.'

She stared into the darkness knowing that Anton's advice was wise. She would have much to think about in the next few weeks as the Season climaxed with the Great Exhibition closing ceremony in October. Then quiet days would return as the nobility left London for their country estates, with their focus now on hunting.

~ ~ ~

So, she was shocked when a letter was waiting at her workroom at such an early hour.

Madam Chevalier,

I know you will find this missive unusual but I beg you to consider meeting with me today so that I can apologise to you for my indiscretion. I can only say that I had imbibed too much and was not in control of myself.

There is so much I want to say to you and hear from you, so many apologies I have to make for the mistakes in my life, for my wrong choices, beginning with letting you go when you were a child, and rejecting you in Ireland when you were so in need.

If you refuse me, I will understand and will regret this lost opportunity for the rest of my life. When I first saw you last night, when you came to the aid of Lady Jane, I was struck by your resemblance to my first love, your mother, my beautiful Rosita.

Please Izzy, have pity on me and grant me this wish. Lady Jane will be calling on her friend Lady Morton this morning so if you could come to Grosvenor Square at the 11th hour we could meet before she returns. If you have a trusted friend to bring, you may feel more comfortable.

I remain in hope, Edward Marchbank

Izzy read the letter several times, stopping each time at the reference to her mother. That was it of course; she could not let the opportunity to know more about her mother pass, even though her impulse was to refuse his wish. He held the key to so many questions in her life, to the very essence of her being and her history. Although she was offended by the proposition he had put to her last night, she was not an innocent and knew that for a gentleman like him, that was common practice. No, it was not for the proposition that she wanted an apology, but for the greater sin of his abandonment of her.

She took a hansom cab to Harriet's house and after a brief summary of the evening Harriet read Edward's letter and agreed to chaperone the meeting.

~ ~ ~

They were shown into Sir Edward's private study and introductions were made. Edward looked older this morning, his face lined and colourless, his lack of sleep obvious.

'Thank you for coming,' he said and he motioned for them to sit on the chesterfield sofa, while he pulled up a single chair for himself. 'I am so ashamed, Izzy, to have treated you as I did last night. Mrs Peabody, I am presuming that Izzy has confided in you the facts of the matter?'

'Yes, Sir Edward, Izzy has suffered much in the recent past and I am privileged that she calls me her friend and confidante.' She squeezed Izzy's hand. 'But this matter is between the two of you. I am here only as a matter of protocol to protect Izzy's good name and to help you come to an amicable agreement. Izzy, what would you like to say to your father?'

Izzy knew exactly what she wanted to say and Edward was surprised by the clarity and confidence with which she spoke.

'The insult that you offered me last night gives me great pain; that you would expect a woman, any woman, to do your bidding simply because you have wealth and power.'

She paused and there was silence in the room as she inhaled deeply before continuing. 'But far greater pain is mine when I consider how you abandoned me as a child and rejected me when I was desperate in Ireland and pleaded for protection.'

'What can I say?' His words seemed to stumble. 'I can only ... only offer you my apologies and perhaps make some financial settlement on you, if that would help.'

'No, that is not what I want. I have worked hard to provide for my family and finally I am free of being indebted to anyone. No, what I want will be much harder for you. I want to be acknowledged as your daughter. I want to spend time with you learning about my mother. I want you to know and love my children, to be their grandfather. I want to be able to visit Winton, to show my children where we belong. I want to be reconciled to you.'

Edward's right hand was covering his eyes as Izzy was speaking but when she finished, he looked up and Izzy could see tears in his eyes. 'My dear child,' he croaked, 'that is no punishment.'

'But Lady Jane will not be agreeable to any of that.'

'No, you are right,' he sighed, 'but it is not for Lady Jane to say. She will get used to the idea. I will tell her this afternoon and she will fume for a day or two and then she will settle. No, my dear, this is about you and what I can do to make up for my poor behaviour, not just last night, but over the last twenty years.'

They were silent again for several minutes, Edward's face buried in his hands, his body heaving with silent sobs.

Finally, Izzy said quietly, 'Perhaps a first step would be that we agree never to mention last night again.' She waited but he said nothing, his right hand again covering his eyes, his head bent in shame. 'Papa,' she said softly as she reached out and touched his shoulder, 'you are forgiven, Papa.'

He took her hand and then embraced her and their tears

flowed freely. Harriet rose and went to the window to allow them these few minutes in private. Oh Izzy, she thought, I hope this is the right outcome for you.

~ ~ ~

The revelation that the renowned Madam Chevalier was indeed the wisp of a child who had so embarrassed her twenty years ago sent Lady Jane into a quandary. She was, of course, annoyed that Edward had made such a fool of himself, but at least he had done it in private; no-one knew of the dance floor exchange. No, the perplexing issue was the reconciliation and how it would affect her. Edward had said that Izzy wanted no financial benefit for herself or her children, so that would have to be legalised first. There could be no risk to her own dear Pamela, her only child. Then there was the social uncertainty of opening up one's home and life to a natural child. She knew the Marchbank family was quite progressive on the issue. She and Edward had argued this topic twenty years ago and thankfully her own conservative attitudes had prevailed.

Now it was a different, more liberal society with several of Edward's cousins openly admitting their natural children. There could be little harm in embracing the reunion, she supposed. After all there was no real risk to Pamela who was now married six months and living in Wales. Her lack of objection would please Edward and he would be indebted to her. And the name of Madam Chevalier was so respected as a woman of independent means and she did make the most divine dresses. Perhaps there would be a priority for family members. She knew it was vanity but it could be disguised as magnanimity and she would gain everything and lose nothing. 'So generous of Lady Jane,' she could hear them say, 'to welcome her husband's natural child back into the family.' Yes, that would be satisfactory.

~ ~ ~

The year of the Great Exhibition, 1851, the joyous year that had seen Izzy reconciled with her father, the year that had seen her business fly to unexpected heights and her reputation secured in the world of London fashion, ended with sadness when she said farewell to Harriet and Charles as they returned to Melbourne.

'Who knows when we shall meet again?' Izzy whispered through her tears. 'For I cannot see that I will ever return to Melbourne.'

'Nor I to London,' sobbed Harriet. 'We were so lucky to have an extra year here, but now we must return and I shall miss you, my friend.'

'Will you write to me, Harriet? Write often for I will miss our conversations and the love you have given me. You have been my confidante and friend and even though a letter is a poor substitute for an embrace, it is one that I will look forward to.'

'Yes, yes, of course I will write to you.' Her eyes cleared and she smiled. 'I will tell you all the gossip of Melbourne, all the scandal. You shall be better informed than the locals.'

Chapter 33

London 1858

The seven years since the reconciliation between Edward and Izzy had brought great joy to both of them with several visits to Winton and introductions to other members of the Marchbank family. Edward's pride was obvious. He watched the children's progress eagerly and although Izzy refused his financial assistance, she agreed to him using his influence to ensure that the doors of Eton College were open to her sons with an eye to Oxford to complete their schooling. The girls had just completed their education with a year in Paris, Madam Foveaux overseeing their progress there. Both girls were interested in the business and Izzy set about teaching them the basics, not only in technique but in administration. She was, of course, determined that they would retain their financial independence, no matter where their hearts led them.

~ ~ ~

The Great Exhibition of 1851 had set Izzy on the path to enduring success but several later developments affected the way she did business. Firstly, the introduction of the cage crinoline in 1856 meant that the layers of heavy petticoats were discarded and dresses became lighter and easier to wear, and for Izzy, easier to design and make. Anton had shown her Thimmonier's sewing machine at the Great Exhibition and she had marvelled at its speed and accuracy and at the consistency and strength of the stitches. But it was only experimental, a novelty. Then Anton, on a regular trip to London late in 1856, brought her the news that the machines were to be mass produced and were an affordable price.

'You need to embrace this new invention, Izzy, or you will be swamped by it.'

'But I don't want to lose my staff. I have over one hundred skilled workers. How can I keep them and use the sewing machine? What can I do?'

'There will always be a place for exquisite handwork, Izzy, but you must also retrain some of them to become expert in the use of machines,' said Anton.

'Do you think I can have both?'

'Yes, you can, but I think you should start small. Buy one or two machines and see how they assist you. You can always increase the number and it will give your staff time to get used to the idea and to see the benefits that these machines can bring.'

Then two years later Anton brought news of another change.

'I know there will always be those clients who prefer an original creation but in Paris there are two changes occurring. Firstly, the sewing machine is making the production of gowns quicker and cheaper and secondly there is a change in the way gowns are designed and sold. The new trend is for ladies to visit a salon in the city in order to view six or so specific designs shown by live mannequins. The design that they choose is then made up to their measurements in their choice of fabric. The *House of Worth* is the leader; its creator Charles Worth, although an Englishman, has revolutionised fashion in Paris. He has great fame as the Court Designer for the Empress Eugenie, the most fashionable woman in Europe, but those ladies who can afford his designs can now buy them in his salon. His name is embroidered into the inside of the waistband of each gown; it is his "label".'

Izzy and Anton talked for hours about the possibility of replicating this idea in London. The business was ideally located in Bond Street; still the most fashionable shopping street in London and the premises could be easily renovated to include a salon at the front, on street level. Izzy was reminded of Madam Foveaux's salon in Launceston and she described to Anton its soft mauve curtains, large mirrors and marble fireplace. He smiled. 'My mother was always ahead of her time,' he said.

So, in 1858, ten years after she had launched *Madam Chevalier of the House of Foveaux*, Izzy opened her salon in Bond Street. Anton agreed that it should have the French title: *Madam Chevalier de la Maison de Foveaux*. She watched as the pink and gold lettered sign was erected, the colours and style reminiscent of Madam Foveaux's sign in Launceston, and smiled at how far she had come.

~ ~ ~

Harriet was true to her promise and proved to be an entertaining and prolific correspondent and Izzy was always filled with joy when she returned home in the evening to find a letter from Harriet on the silver tray in the hallway. Harriet had a sharp eye and a sharper wit and filled her letters with news of the rapid development of Melbourne, now the capital of the newly created State of Victoria. During these eight years she described in detail the progress of the gold rush, from a trickle of people in 1852 to a torrent which had engulfed the city, as thousands upon thousands of people, mainly men, arrived in Melbourne by ship to make their way to Ballarat and Bendigo.

You will recall Nell and Jacob Reardon of course. Do you remember that Jacob was a blacksmith and tool maker by trade? Well, some years ago he went into the business of importing tools from England and now, with the rush for gold, the demand for his products has increased five hundredfold. He has become a very rich man and he deserves to be as he has worked hard and made some wise business decisions. I see Nell often at various functions. She is a gentle and lovely person and always asks after you. She has very fond memories of you and asked to be remembered to you. She has five children and the family has recently moved into a mansion in Collins Street.

It was in one of Harriet's letters that she heard news, for the first time in years, of Bryn. She read it with cool dispassion, as an interested outsider.

Bryn had come by ship from Adelaide on his way to the goldfields and Charles met him and in the spirit of old times, invited him dine with us. He entertained us with stories of his life in the small settlement of Gawler, his life on the riverboats of the Darling and the river towns of Swan Hill, Menindee and Wentworth where he is the only doctor providing any sort of comfort in that far flung region. He asked after you, of course and was pleased to hear that you had gained such success in business and that the children were progressing so well. He told us too, that he is to marry a widow, Serena Elkington, in Gawler. He voiced his distaste for Melbourne, the scene of his financial embarrassment and vowed that he would never return here as a citizen. Charles told me that Bryn's reputation as a doctor is still as honoured as ever, but he suspects that brandy is his constant companion.

It all seems so far away, I'm glad to be done with all of that, thought Izzy, with the uncertainty and the dependence, the smell of brandy and the anger and unpredictability it brings. I hope his new wife has better luck than I. My life is so full, so complete, I have no need for men. The law says that a woman's possessions become her husband's when she marries. For that reason alone, I will remain single. I might take a lover or enjoy the delights of a paid companion, but marriage, never.

Chapter 34

Cadiz 1859

The plan to visit Cadiz was Edward's idea. 'My pain is increasing slowly,' he said to Izzy, 'and I would like to know that you have seen Cadiz and met Rosita's family, if they are still there. I think it would be wise if we were to go as soon as possible; in the New Year maybe, mid-January perhaps. I'll warrant it will be warmer there than here.'

'Yes, January would be perfect,' agreed Izzy and set about making sure the business would run smoothly. January and July were the months that Anton usually came to London, so he would be on hand if necessary, though Izzy had every faith in the management skills of Mrs Holland and her workroom supervisor Mrs Sheedy, who had both remained with her.

~ ~ ~

In preparation for their visit, Edward began a correspondence with the Cardinal of Cadiz and a pleasant relationship was established which had many practical benefits.

Your Eminence,

I write to you as a visitor hoping to return to Cadiz, a place that I hold dear to my heart. I was stationed there 1812–1816, during and after the Siege of Cadiz as part of the 52nd Regiment, as we successfully defended the town from the persistent attack by the French.

If I could prevail upon your time, I would appreciate your attention in listening to my story and perhaps indulging me in my request.

During the time I was there my Commanding Officer Colonel Peabody, in an effort to lift morale, often entertained the officers in his own home. It was on one of these occasions that I met Rosita Ortega, a serving girl employed by Colonel Peabody. We became lovers and Rosita consequently died giving birth to my child. The baby, Isabel Rosita Marchbank, was Baptised in the Cathedral de Santa Cruz in April 1815. I took the child back to England and she was raised by my family until the age of twelve years. Then, with Colonel Peabody as her guardian, she travelled to New South Wales and, to my disgrace, I lost contact with her.

However, she has returned to England now as a mother of four children and we are reconciled. Her life has been difficult and I am determined to make sure that I am now a true father to her and grandfather to her children in the years that remain to me.

I want to bring Izzy and her children to Cadiz in January and I wonder if you could help me by enquiring as to the situation of Rosita's family. They lived in the poor area in the backstreets somewhere near the Cathedral. Her mother's name was Isabel and my child is named for her. I would like my child to

*meet the family of her mother and for my grand-
children to have some knowledge of their heritage.*

*I thank you for your help in this matter and I remain
your humble servant,*

*Edward Marchbank,
Duke of Winton, Yorkshire, England*

*Cathedral of Santa Crux
Cadiz, Spain
25th August 1858*

Your Grace,

*Thank you for your letter of the 12th Ultimo. I read it
with great interest and can understand that you wish
to make reparation to your child for your earlier
disregard. God is always forgiving to those who seek
His mercy and it seems that, in reconciling with your
child, you have also reconciled with God.*

*As to your request, I have made some enquiries and
it seems that the Ortega family is a very large one in
Cadiz. My secretary has been examining the Parish
Records and reports that the specific family to which
you refer still lives in the same area near the
Cathedral. He has found the record of your daughter's
Baptism and also of her mother's death and of the
more recent death of her father (your child's
grandfather). However, we believe his wife is still alive
and resides with her youngest daughter in the old
family home.*

*My secretary could make contact with the family
prior to your visit if you desire it, to ascertain their
situation and their willingness to meet with your
family. You must accept that they may choose not to
see you and you will need to respect their wishes.
Sometimes the hurt of so long ago is too deep for*

erasure, though I would counsel them, for their own peace, to accept your invitation to meet and to rejoice in this reconciliation.

I remain your humble servant,

Juan Jose Arboli Acaso
By the Grace of God, Cardinal of Cadiz

9th October 1858
Winton, Yorkshire

Your Eminence,

Your letter brought me great comfort. I do, indeed, wish to be reconciled with the family and my hope is that my daughter and her children can maintain a loving relationship with them in the future, for I know that my days in this world are limited and this will be the last time I leave my native land.

I would greatly appreciate your secretary's approach to the family on my behalf and of course, I will respect their decision as to whether or not we shall meet.

I eagerly await your response and pray that they are agreeable to my request.

I remain your humble servant,

Edward Marchbank,
Duke of Winton, Yorkshire

20th December 1858
Cathedral of Santa Crux, Cadiz

Your Grace,

May the blessing of the joyful season of the birth of our Saviour, Jesus Christ, be upon you and your family; the Lord is truly great and wonderful for his love has prevailed.

Let me take your time to recount the events as they were told to me by my secretary, Padre Rodrigo Caro, in his recent endeavours on your behalf.

Padre Caro made enquiries of Cathedral parishioners and having obtained the address, he visited the Ortega family home. He carried a letter of introduction from me so that the family was assured that he acted on my behalf.

The matron of the household, Luisa Ortega, Rosita's sister, greeted him and heard what he had to say. She asked him to wait so that she could bring her aged mother to him so that she could hear his request. The old lady (who, as you said, is also named Isabel) is in her eightieth year and is physically infirm but Padre Caro reported that she understood immediately his mission and that her face was filled with joy at the thought of meeting her granddaughter, so long ago taken from her.

She told Padre Caro that she had prayed every day for her lost granddaughter and that she always believed that our Heavenly Father would guide her steps back to Cadiz and that her only prayer now will be that she can live the next few weeks before meeting her. After that she will be happy to leave this world.

So, you see, my friend, that there is always hope in this world and just as the coming season brings the joyful news of the birth of Christ, so our actions bring joy to those around us. Your decision to reconcile with your daughter and her mother's family has brought great joy to everyone.

Let me know the date of your arrival in Cadiz and I will look forward to receiving you here at the Cathedral House so that Padre Caro can accompany you on your mission.

I remain your friend,
Juan Jose Arboli Acaso

~ ~ ~

The port of Cadiz had changed little in the forty years since they had left. Izzy, of course, remembered nothing but Edward smiled as the little ship docked. The Spanish sailors secured the ropes and the porters, seeing the assembled family on board, began shouting their service from the wharf.

'Look,' said Edward, 'there is the Fort and next to it the old army barracks. And over there, on the hill,' he pointed to a rambling, once white house, surrounded by an overgrown garden, 'that was Colonel Peabody's house.'

'Peabody?' asked fifteen-year-old Frank. 'Like Uncle Charles?'

'Yes,' said Izzy, 'Uncle Charles was not born here, but his brothers Wesley and Will and John were, and in that house I should think.'

'Yes, I recall them but not very clearly,' said Edward. 'Colonel Peabody always invited the men to celebrate special days at his home.' He smiled to himself as he saw Rosita flick her skirt and toss her head as she left the dining room. 'There were lavish dinners and it was a welcome break in our dull routine.'

They disembarked and immediately became a focal point of the townspeople; six English visitors, their wealth obvious from their clothing. Izzy and her two daughters, Edie aged nineteen and Helena aged eighteen, although dressed in practical travelling clothes, still looked fashionable, their bonnets bright in the morning sunlight, like three jewels on the drab background that was the wharf at Cadiz. Edward leaned on his cane, his pain momentarily displaced by his excitement at being here, his two upright grandsons ready to take his arm if necessary.

Edward's secretary, William Starkey, had arranged their lodgings. An entire house in a quiet street not far from the waterfront had been made ready for them for the month and they settled in quickly. The housekeeper and the butler both spoke perfect English and welcomed them enthusiastically. The boys were anxious to explore the town but Izzy insisted that they see their grandfather to his room first, then change into their day clothes and wait for their sisters to do the same. She watched as her four children made their way down the cobbled street towards Plaza San Antonio, the main square. 'How lucky they are to have each other,' she said out loud and she watched until they disappeared around the corner.

'Indeed, they are, and lucky to have you.' It was her father, emerging from his room which was situated on the ground floor, his limp betraying the strain of the journey.

'Oh Papa, you should be resting.'

'There is plenty of time for rest, my dear, and besides, my valet needs to be left in peace to arrange the wardrobe. The house is pleasant enough, don't you think?' He had joined her at the window and they both watched the expanse of sea before them, the seabirds darting and calling, the smell of the salt pervading the air.

'Yes, Papa, it is perfect. Thank you for bringing us here. I remember nothing of Cadiz, but it still feels that I am coming home.'

Edward put his arm around her and they stood at the window in silence for some time. 'Tomorrow,' he said, 'when we meet the Cardinal and Padre Caro takes us to meet the family, I think it would be better if it was just the two of us.

'The children can meet their great-grandmother at another time, but I think tomorrow should be just about you and her. Izzy and Isabel,' he said with a smile.

Epilogue

Cadiz 1859

The seabirds are laughing again in the blackness, but I realise now their laughter is not in jest, not making light of men and women. No, their laughter is their celebration of family, of forgiveness, of love that endures despite time and distance.

When I came to Cadiz four weeks ago, I hoped that my father's optimism would be fulfilled, that my mother's family would welcome us. But secretly I doubted it. I did not know how they would feel meeting these strangers who claimed their blood.

But I looked into my grandmother's eyes and saw my own and I knew that she was mine. I felt her embrace and knew that she had pined for me for forty years. I kissed her tears and knew that I was complete. Here was the mother I never had.

And when she finally met them, I saw the way she searched my children's faces and found Rosita. I saw her rejoice that here was Rosita alive again through them. I saw her despair when I told her of the fifth, of baby Isabel and how we loved her but could not save her. And both of us, having lost a daughter, salved the other's grief.

Moira McAlister

I know now that life will never be the same for me. Wherever I go in the world, wherever my children go, we will know where we came from. My children in time will know their father, will understand and forgive his faults and embrace him simply because he is their father. I too can forgive him for he has no more power over me.

If wisdom is the prize of experience, then it rightly belongs to me.

The End

Author's Note

Although based on fact, this novel is a work of fiction. The character, Izzy, is based on Inez Seville Fitzgerald, my great, great grandmother who, like most women of the 19th century, left very little evidence of her life. I first discovered parts of Inez's story when I was researching the life of her husband, my great, great grandfather, Dr Barry Cotter, who was the first doctor in Melbourne. The evidence I found pointed to an interesting woman, bound by the conservative attitudes of her time, with few rights and limited opportunities for economic independence.

I published *Dr Barry Cotter: The first doctor in Melbourne* in 2015 as a website (drbarrycotter.com) and immediately set about preparing to tell Inez's story. The known facts of her life were like lampposts on a dark road, illuminating just a small space around them. I could see the next lamppost in the distance, but needed to employ plausible and well researched, but fictitious, characters and actions to get there. This is the image that sustained me throughout the writing. If you are interested to find out which events are fact and which are fiction, you could visit drbarrycotter.com. You might be surprised.

Many characters in this story are based on fact – Izzy, Bryn, Nell, Francis and Mary Parkins to name a few. Renaming them gave me more freedom to explore their characters and motivations. Others, like Charles La Trobe, William Buckley, John Batman and Joseph Gellibrand are historical figures and their lives are well documented. Others are purely fictional like Mrs Betts, Madam Foveaux, Harriet and Sarah and their task is to give direction to the story when I did not have any facts to rely on. It was challenging to weave the facts and fiction together to create a credible sequence of events and a convincing story.

Acknowledgements

Thank you to the many people who have helped me along the way. To my writing group – Catherine Corver, Fiona Hamer, Neera Mahajan and Theresa Layton – who have critiqued, discussed and guided my work from the beginning.

To Sherryl Clark for her generosity in sharing her years of writing experience, her excellence in editing and her personal encouragement.

I would like to acknowledge Cathy Harrison, Fr Kevin Barry-Cotter and John Vignoles, whose research provided many of the facts used in this story.

Thanks to my manuscript readers Jenni Shum, Lesley King, Keith Penhallow, Clare Zacharias, Jane Allen, Rachael Hind, Claire Percival and Heather Curran, whose comments and editing were invaluable.

To the staff of IndieMosh, especially Jenny, Debbie and Ally, whose professionalism and patience made the publication process a dream come true. Also, to Adam Finlay of Writefish Professional Writing and Editing, for his amazing attention to detail.

To my family, large and small, for whom this is written and finally to Ian McAlister for believing it was possible and sustaining that belief in me through many a doubtful day.

About the Author

Moira McAlister has spent most of her life in the classroom as a teacher, teacher-librarian and student. It was while studying for her Masters in Writing and Literature that Moira first found snippets of the story of her great, great grandmother, Inez Seville Fitzgerald. Realising there were huge gaps in the information available, Moira put this story aside to concentrate on the facts concerning Inez's husband, for the narrative non-fiction work *Dr Barry Cotter: The first doctor in Melbourne* (drbarrycotter.com), which she published in 2015. Since then, Moira has used the painstaking and fascinating research for that story as the basis for her fictional reinvention of Inez in her novel, *Izzy*.

Moira also writes short stories and stories for children, some of which can be found on her website (moiramcalister.com). Moira is part of a large and busy family and she and her husband enjoy the best of all worlds, alternating between Canberra and Batemans Bay on the beautiful south coast of NSW.

CPSIA information can be obtained
at www.ICGtesting.com
Printed in the USA
LVHW012204151121
703363LV00003B/304